Praise For
MATT WALLACE
AND
SAVAGE LEGION

"Cunning plotting and brisk action elevate this impressive tale of swords and super-science. . . . [I]t's rare for anyone in this epic's expansive cast to remain as they first appear, as Wallace masterfully subverts readers' expectations. As the plot spins through convincing battlefield combat and personal confrontations, . . . readers will be left thoroughly satisfied and eager to know what's to come."

—*Publishers Weekly* (starred review)

"Smart characters and brutal action create an intriguing story about power and the decisions made to keep it. Wallace introduces a new epic fantasy trilogy filled with rich worldbuilding and people who battle bravely."

—*Library Journal* (starred review)

"The stylish first book in the Savage Rebellion series promises that Wallace will do for epic fantasy what he did for urban fantasy with the Sin du Jour series."

—*Booklist*

"Matt Wallace has written a rich multiperspective fantasy; it's not every day that a brilliant woman with paraplegia who uses a mecha-magical wheelchair offers her voice to a narrative. This is a big, fun book, and anyone seeking a dose of large-scale epic fantasy with some fresh viewpoints will be right at home."

—*BookPage*

"It will make you think. It will challenge you to analyze the world around you . . . Just read it. Five stars."

"Stunning . . . inventive . . . top notch, pulse pounding, and excellently done. . . . most definitely the best work from the pen of an author whose skills are growing by leaps and bounds."

SAVAGE REBELLION
BOOK I

SAVAGE
LEGION

Matt Wallace

SAGA PRESS

LONDON SYDNEY **NEW YORK** TORONTO NEW DELHI

SAGA PRESS
AN IMPRINT OF SIMON & SCHUSTER, INC.

1230 AVENUE OF THE AMERICAS, NEW YORK, NEW YORK 10020

For Laython Wilkerson, my original instructor in savagery.
And for Monkey Empire.

SAVAGE

LEGION

PART ONE

THREE SIDES
OF A COIN

THE MOURNING AFTER

AHEAD OF EVIE, DOORS OF ROTTING WOOD ARE FLUNG OPEN. The sun is a curse shouted into her eyes, and she is prodded by the impatient end of a club up the mucky membrane of the darkened tunnel and out into the light of day. She feels soft, mostly even terrain under her moccasin-covered feet. She holds up a dirty hand, saluting the void of sharp gold filling her vision, and blinking until the motion snaps the world around her into something akin to focus.

The space is vast and walled and forgotten. It must have been a training field for soldiers once, no doubt covered by green grass that is now just a memory made of yellow bladed husks. Broken wooden men slouch from their buried tree trunk bases, as if the hapless vague bipedal shapes are supplicating in defeat. Practice weapons dangle from rusty, loosened nails at the end of sticks mimicking an enemy's sword arm.

There are stubby little men and women armed with blunt sticks prodding them along, Evie and the rest of the drunks and dregs and bandits from the Capitol's dungeon, herding them like feed into the center of the field.

"Form a line!" a voice shouts with all the power and rage of a minor god burdened by their peers with mortal concerns. "Shoulder to shoulder and an arm's span apart! I don't care how you stand, but stand! *Stand,* I said, you miserable pickled jars of skin!"

The voice continues to boom and command. Evie steps between

two equally ragged, unwashed bodies and plants her feet in the neglected earth. She hopes the fabled "line" of which the angered god speaks will form around her so she'll be required to move no more. Her head feels like a melon pressed between two scorching boulders.

The demigod's raging commands cease, and for a moment there is only blissful silence on the field, save for the steady, gentle rasping of hurried drunks.

Then *he* steps before their assemblage.

It's him, the giant from the cells. He's the one who took them all from the dungeon, loaded them onto a wagon, bagged their heads, and rattled them what felt like halfway across the countryside. He's the tallest man she's ever seen. His torso is like a hundred-pound sack of taro, bulging rolls of flesh pushing through the impossibly small vest he's somehow managed to toggle together around them.

"I am your wrangler," he announces. "My name is Laython. You will call me 'Tasker' or you will call me 'Freemaster.' And from now till your bloody deaths on the field of battle in service of Crache . . . your name . . . is Savage."

Savage. Evie turns the word over in her mind, finding it offensive even by her standards.

"Look to the spires of this field," Laython instructs them.

Evie tilts her head and squints through the harsh sunlight at the towers crowning the walls of the training field. They are each crewed by Skrain, the elite soldiers of Crache, resplendent in breastplates embossed with the ant, the nation's symbol. Rich folds of leather extend from each shielded chest to cover their arms all the way to their wrists. They carry master-crafted Ancestor Hafts, long weapons crowned with horse-cutter blades. The faces of the Skrain aren't visible to the rabble on the field, which seems appropriate.

"What you see are soldiers. What you see is the exact opposite of what you are. There will be no shining armor, oiled leather, or fine steel for the lot of you. Oh no, my friends. You're Savages. The rags you've come here in and any rusted pieces of scrap you can scrounge from the armory wagon is all you'll need on the battlefield."

"What in the Fire Star's light are you going on about?" Evie asks him.

Laython scowls. "Calling out the name of outlawed gods is exactly what landed your raggedy ass here, girl! Now shut it!"

Evie finds it easy enough to obey that command, as speaking hurts just as much as everything else right now.

"You will not loot," Laython informs them, casually returning to his public address. "You will not pillage, you will not rape, and you will not take battlefield trophies of any kind."

He walks up and down the first row of them, and by now Evie's stomach has settled into the same perpetual numb state as her head.

"You will not desert your regiment. You will not quarrel with, nor kill your fellow Savage. These commands are sacred, and the violation of any of them will result in your immediate execution."

"You expect us to fight?" another prisoner, older and portlier, asks.

"I expect you to cause the same chaos and mayhem on the field of battle that you so dearly love to cause in city taverns. You're not soldiers," he reiterates. "You, each of you, are weapons. You'll be hurled at the front lines of Crache's enemies in waves thick enough to smash them. And in that chaos our Skrain will wipe away what remains. That is how we win. That is how Crache prevails, by the blood of Savages. Your blood."

"Why don't you just kill us now?" the same portly old man asks, more meekly than defiantly.

"Because that would waste good, solid material. And Crache does not waste any of its resources."

"We're not the condemned," Evie insists. "This isn't right."

"It's service," he says with finality. "It's a service to which you've all been called. That call cannot be refused. If you choose death then you'll choose it meeting our nation's enemies.

"Welcome to the Savage Legion."

THE KNIGHT BEFORE

"YOU'VE HAD HALF A GALLON OF WINE," THE BARTENDER warned her as gently as a man missing half his face from an apparent mauling warns anyone. "I wouldn't go mixing that with Voxic's sting. This last batch I got'll take the paint off a wagon."

Evie saluted him with her cup and a half smile while completely forgetting what he had just said. She retreated to a lone table in the middle of the dingy little establishment tucked into a secluded corner of the Bottoms. She was indeed drinking even more than usual, but that was entirely intentional.

She'd just finished burning most of her throat away with half the cup's contents when the apotheosis of all drunken, horrid bit players in sad tavern scenes straddled a chair beside her.

"Have we fucked before?" he asked her, quite sincerely.

Evie squinted, attempting to bring him into focus and immediately regretting the decision.

"I can honestly say I've never felt worse about myself over anything in my life as I feel about the fact I can't definitively answer 'no' to that question."

That was apparently far too many words for her potential suitor. "Eh?"

"Just go away," Evie said wearily.

"Look here," he began anew, "I didn't mean to give offense. I just thought if we *hadn't* had the pleasure of knowing each other—"

And Evie had already had enough of the pathetic, predictable exchange. She already knew he'd keep talking. She already knew she'd keep rebuking him. She already knew he'd get angry and belligerent. She already knew when she finally crossed some irrational verbal line he drew, somehow "offending" this clod who had invaded *her* sacred space, he'd progress to physical violence. She had no patience for such a tired back-and-forth. She chose instead to skip straight to the end of the story.

Evie moved faster than anyone that drunk is generally capable of moving. She stood up like a shot, her legs straightening so violently they knocked over her chair. One hand grabbed the man by his greasy hair and jerked his head back while the other took up the nearest bottle and smashed it against his cheek and jaw. The force and momentum were twin demons dragging him over the back of his chair to the stained floor of the bar.

Evie's mind left the flow of normal time then, although her body proceeded to kick the man on the floor as around her the rest of the drunken assemblage took their cue to descend into a full-on riotous brawl. She was only vaguely aware when other bodies assaulted her own, and even less aware when the city Aegins arrived to break things up and cart the chief offenders, mainly her, off to the dungeons.

The cell was the next thing to cling to her awareness. It stank of shit and earth and unwashed bodies, as dungeon cells are wont to do, but it also smelled strongly of anise. In fact, it smelled mostly of anise. It may very well have been the sweetest smelling dungeon in which Evie was ever flung.

"They feed it to us," one of the other drunks explained after several minutes of Evie's befuddled sniffing at the air.

"Howzzat?" she managed, such as she was.

"Anise," said the drunk. "It riots wild out the back there. They feed it to us. It's in everything, even the water. Makes your shit and piss smell like soap. Easier'n cheaper than washing us, or the damned cell. Starts to taste like poison after a few days, though."

Evie just nodded solemnly.

Everything, absolutely everything, makes sense to a drunk when they're deep down the well of their bender.

"It's not the taste that's bad for you," a much smaller voice assured them from the shadows. "Too much is bad for your insides. You can tell by how it changes the color of your water."

Evie squinted into the corner of the small cell at a slight girl propped there against the rough-hewn walls. Her legs were impossibly withered.

"Did the Aegins do that to you?" Evie asked her.

The girl shook her head. "A cart ran over them."

"How do you move yourself around?"

"I have sheet tin under me most days," the girl explained. "I grease the bottom with renderings from the bins behind the eating houses."

Evie nodded, just enough as not to upset her already throbbing skull. "Smart girl. What's your name?"

"Dyeawan."

"That's not a Crachian name."

Dyeawan shook her head, but offered no more than that on the subject.

"All right, then. I'm Evie. What did they arrest a little thing like you for?"

"Begging."

"Is that right? I thought no one begged for food here."

"Well, I didn't have the chance to do it for long, did I?"

There was no trace of bitterness in her voice. In fact, there was playfulness, the kind that only a child can keep in such a dark place.

Evie couldn't help but smile.

Dyeawan smiled back, and even through the grime streaking her face, through the shadows banished to the corner there with her, that smile shined.

"Why did they put you here?" Dyeawan asked her as they both dozed upon the bare and stained cell floor.

"I don't think it was the drinking," Evie mused. "I drink every night. It might've been the fight I maintain I did not start in the tavern, although that happens just as often. Of course, this was the first time I was still there when the Aegins arrived."

"So they arrested you for fighting?"

Evie thought about it sincerely for a moment. "No. They let most of the folk in the brawl go."

"Then what did you do?"

"I . . . vaguely recall squatting and relieving myself on the boot of one of the Aegins."

Dyeawan laughed.

"While singing," Evie added.

The girl laughed harder.

"That would do it, then," she said.

"No," Evie said seriously, and something in her tone put an end to Dyeawan's laughter. "No . . . it wasn't until they asked me if I had a home to go to and I told them I didn't. That's when they arrested me. When they found out I was a vagrant."

For the first time sadness crept into Dyeawan's small voice. "They didn't even bother to ask me."

Evie reached up and stroked the stringy tendrils of the girl's hair.

"You'll be all right, little slider," she assured the younger woman, trying to make her voice motherly without really knowing what that sounded like.

"You don't look like you belong here," the girl said, surprising Evie. "Not really. And it almost sounds like . . . like you wanted the Aegins to come."

Evie stared at Dyeawan oddly in the half dark.

"What an odd thing to say."

The younger girl shrugged. "I notice things other people don't see sometimes. That's all."

Evie nodded thoughtfully. "It appears you do."

Before the dawn, Laython came, wrapped in a heavy furred coat, and surveyed them in the cells. He barely said two words to the jailor, but they were enough. The cells were emptied, and all of them were loaded onto Laython's wagon behind the dungeon. He left Dyeawan behind; he only took the able-bodied.

Dyeawan never awoke to find Evie and the others missing from the unusually sweet-smelling cells. She did, however, awaken to a face mostly hidden beneath a black hood. A cloud of acrid dust, dancing in the light of the morning pouring through the window's bars, dredged her face and lips, filling her nostrils. Somehow she knew the unnatural sleep would overtake her before she felt it begin to spread icy numbness through her arms and torso. She also knew she would indeed wake up again, but it would be someplace else, far from here.

As she'd told Evie, Dyeawan had a way of seeing things, mostly subtle truths, that wouldn't otherwise occur to most people.

WHERE ONLY
STONE STEPS ASCEND

WE ARE NOT FLOWERS. WE DO NOT WILT.

Lexi hears her mother speak those words in her memory as she sits outside the chambers of the Gen Franchise Council. It's here her grandparents and Brio's grandparents came to petition to form Gen Stalbraid. They named their franchise after the steel woven together to push and pull the city's first sky carriage.

The bench beneath Lexi is carved from the translucent white-and-blue stone of the chamber wall itself. The entire Spectrum, including most of its fixtures and even furnishings, are carved from a single mountainous piece of stone, a marvel of engineering whose secrets are lost even to the best masonry Gens in Crache. The Spectrum is the physical, intellectual, and bureaucratic center of the Capitol, making it the center of Crache itself. No structure in all the nation's sterling ten cities rivals the scale or beauty of the Spectrum's massive domes, sky-piecing spires, and corridors so tall and expansive they feel more like mountain halls than the arteries of a city edifice. The sculpture of the national ant in the Spectrum lobby is said to be the largest ever crafted.

Oval lamps are ensconced up and down the towering walls of every one of those corridors; the same lamps that hang from stakes curved like shepherds' staffs along every city street and on every corner. The lamps were one of the first major innovations of the Post-Renewal Age. Each lantern houses two insects, a male and a female. They're nocturnal creatures, hibernating in the bottom of the lanterns during the day and rising at the edge of dusk, precisely when darkness spreads through the streets. Upon rising, the two insects couple, consummating their nightly union. As they do, their small and bulbous bodies are filled with a bright luminescence that streams through the panes of their glass cage and radiates in every direction.

They make love all night, lighting the entire city with a preternatural passion that is the sole engine of their brief existence, never with the slightest awareness of the gift they're giving to the citizenry. After a month they wither to ash, from which their offspring rise and begin the cycle anew. With very little maintaining, each lamp and its inhabitants can light the night for years.

Lexi often reflects upon how it's all quite beautiful, if one chooses not to focus on the whole "incest" aspect of it.

We are not flowers. We do not wilt.

Those are her mother's words, spoken to her from a room in Lexi's mind where she keeps the memory of the woman as she was.

It's very different from the final room in which Lexi saw her. It's a room in which the air doesn't smell like death. Her mother sits there with her head raised high and proud, not pressed into a pillow, its slip stained brown by the poison expelled from her lungs. In that room in Lexi's mind, her mother's hair shines three different fiery colors in the light of the midday sun, hues for which they made up names when Lexi was a child. The day Lexi's mother died, what remained of that hair was a few wisps gone gray that moved against her scalp like lonely spirits in bone-white graveyard.

On that day, her last words to her only daughter were the same ones she'd spoken to the girl whenever strife crashed in heavy slate waves over their lives.

The great stone doors to the Gen Franchise Council chambers open, somehow without the slightest scraping sound, and an elderly Aegin pokes his graying head through.

"Lexi Xia!" he calls out.

Lexi rises from the building's translucent appendage and smooths the colorful material of the formal wrap she wears. The Aegin steps aside, bowing mechanically and with the disinterest of many years spent opening and closing a door, as Lexi moves past him.

The Council chamber is essentially one long ascending staircase with several spacious plateaus, the first and lowest of which is assigned to petitioners. Brio always told Lexi the chambers were built this way to achieve two effects. The first, giving petitioners the illusion they are rising in status, but only so far. That illusion is central to the second effect; looking up at the next plateau, seeded high above them, they accept that the state officials are their superiors in every way.

Brio also told her the most dangerous people in Crache, according to the Spectrum, are the ones who look to that handmade horizon and see a beginning rather than an ending. Lexi once asked him if he was one of those people. Her husband had only smiled and shrugged and professed that he was a simple pleader, and for the poorest people in the Capitol.

It pains Lexi to think of him then, remembering his words and his easy, reassuring smile. She longs for both every moment of every day. It pains her to force those images and the feelings they cause into the farthest corners of her mind so that she may focus on the business at hand.

The petitioners' plateau levels off a dozen steps from the chamber entrance. Its surface shines like glass reflecting some invisible jade pool, a natural feature of the stone when it is polished deep and rigorously enough. There are no seats or other furnishings for petitioners, only perfect painted blue circles in the center of the space, perfect prompts for petitioners to stand.

Order and deliberation in all things, that is the Crachian way.

The three members of the Gen Franchise Council, on the other hand, are seated on the next plateau; a good two dozen steps up from those blue circles. The thin oval backs of their naturally carved and shaped chairs rise high above their heads. They each wear Spectrum tunics, the cuffs of their sleeves draped in crisp triangles. The runic pin representing their individual kith-kinship is worn in the corner of the right cuff, the pin representing their Gen attached to the left.

Senior Councilman Stru is a hairless, ancient thing. Every inch of his flesh seems to be straining toward the floor. He sags in the center of the trio. To his right is Councilwoman Burr, the youngest of the three by a good two decades, a sharp-eyed, ambitious upstart with close-cropped dark hair and impatient fingers that quietly punish the armrests of her seat. To Stru's left is Councilman Jochi, a short, cherubic man with a thin mustache and a perpetually welcoming expression on his impossibly round face.

The fourth occupant of the Council's plateau is a state scribe, a young scholar standing behind a lectern upon which rests a tome thicker than three battle shields. The scribe attends it dutifully and intently with quill in hand.

Gens are the foundation of Crache. They began with a simple, revolutionary idea: that any group of people, regardless of birth or social standing, could come together to serve a function for the greater good of the nation. It began with humble kith-kins joining together and pooling what resources they had to create something larger than the sum of their parts in order to produce a good or a service that would be useful to the community. In recognition and as reward for this, all of that Gen's needs, be it food or clothing or shelter, were provided for from the coffers and larders of Crache itself, coffers filled by heavily taxing non-Gen merchants and collecting from Gens who produced hard revenue, and by the spoils of war efforts that seemed to press ever forward without end.

Of course, not all Gens received the same allotment of resources or access to them. From the beginning, the amount was supposed to be determined by a Gen's size and particular requirements. However, it was well known that priority and special consideration were given to Gens whose work the state deemed the most valuable, or whose leaders were savvy enough to curry favor with the right state officials. Better and bigger food allotments, finer clothing, and larger estates were all common rewards for Gens who excelled at playing the political game.

The system grew to become what it is now: the great engine at the heart of the Crachian machine. Once the Franchise Council approved a proposed Gen to attend to one of the state's vital needs, that Gen could then form to oversee that vital need. There is a Gen behind every facet, service, and trade in Crache, from maintaining city sewers and sweeping streets to milling flour and farming rice to forging weapons and capturing stray animals. Their labors guarantee each member of a Gen a place in society and all their needs sponsored by the nation itself.

That was, as Brio used to put it, the gleaming side of the coin, anyway. Like any system composed of and controlled by people, Gens were susceptible to corruption and greed. There were always rumors of graft and favoritism, contracts being taken away or passed to Gens who showed the Council favor, larger Gens absorbing weaker or rival ones to eliminate competition, or any number of other unsavory practices no one spoke of in polite company. The ultimate irony, however, is that the Gen system was created to replace and prevent inherited wealth and power, at least by arbitrary bloodlines. Yet Gens that solidified their control over a city trust are rarely supplanted or replaced, and the formation of new Gens has become equally rare.

In many ways, Brio had often mused ruefully, Gens became the thing they sought so hard to kill.

For all those reasons, Lexi knew enough not to trust wholly to the goodness in these people or the fabled fairness of their process, however well-meaning some of them seemed.

"De-Gens," Lexi greets the male Councilmembers, and then, to Councilwoman Burr, "Te-Gen."

"It's good to see you again, Lexi," Stru says, each word seeming to be dragged over burning sand as it exits his mouth. "I do so wish the circumstances had changed."

Lexi nods, tightly. "As do I."

Stru sighs. It's an ugly, sickly wheezing that causes Lexi to feel pity for the decrepit old man even as the irritation she felt in the corridor outside refuses to fade.

"I have nothing well to deliver to you today, Lexi," he finally pronounces. "Nothing. And for that I am truly sorry."

He can't be dead, Lexi immediately and frantically assures her own mind. *They wouldn't summon you here to tell you that he's dead. You would have been notified at home. He's not dead.*

"Well has been in scarce supply for longer than I wish to detail," she says evenly, maintaining her composure.

Stru nods, the gesture jostling every sagging inch of skin protecting his skull. He seems hesitant to speak his next words. The tension between his seat and Councilwoman Burr stretches thinner and thinner with every passing moment of silence.

"We have no choice but to revoke your Gen's franchise," she finally says, bluntly, almost impatiently.

There's no remorse in her voice.

Stru's face sags impossibly, lower than she's ever seen it, as he looks to his right.

It's as if Lexi has lost any ability to discern her native tongue. She looks between the varied faces of the Council. Lexi blinks several times, the motion serving the same effect as toggling a great switch. It allows her to brush away the din of emotion and focus on the practical staked to the road before her.

"My husband has been missing for less than a month," she begins. "Surely this is . . . to say the very least, premature—"

"New evidence has come to light, I fear," Stru informs her, sounding genuinely sympathetic.

Councilwoman Burr remains unmoved. "This Council has received a dispatch from the Protectorate Ministry. They have sufficient evidence to support that Brio Alania was neither abducted nor the victim of an ill fate. This evidence suggests he has fled beyond Crachian borders with the intention of defecting to our enemies. Such is their conclusion."

"Please. Councilmembers. I should very much like to examine this 'evidence' for myself."

"That's quite impossible," Burr informs her, and Lexi is certain now there's something akin to actual pleasure behind her words. "The Protectorate Ministry will not allow such sensitive material to be examined in an open Council session. To do so would expose the agents who risked their lives in service to the nation to obtain it."

"I have the utmost respect and admiration for the agents of the Protectorate Ministry and the perilous work they do across our borders. I would never risk our nation's security for personal benefit. For the very survival of my Gen, however, I must insist I be granted the basic right to defend my husband against such charges."

Councilwoman Burr begins to respond, but Stru raises a spotted hand to silence her, drawing a look from the younger woman as sharp and ill-intentioned as a dagger striking from the shadows.

"Lexi," the old man begins, "I must speak frankly with you now, and it is my hope you'll know what I have to say is unaccompanied by malice of any kind."

She only nods.

"Lexi, you are now the senior member of Gen Stalbraid, and you are no pleader. Nor is there a suitable replacement within your Gen. Without a pleader, Gen Stalbraid cannot serve its function. Your likelihood of recruiting a competent replacement willing to plead for Division Nine is minimal, to put it mildly. Your Gen chose an inglorious role to fulfill, however necessary, and it has always relegated Stalbraid to the two small kith-kins who founded it. Even if this . . . unfortunate turn had not occurred, within a generation I can reasonably say a review of your franchise would have been mandated."

"A Gen is not about family, it is about function," Burr insists to Stru, with the earnestness of one who has been deeply and successfully indoctrinated. "Gen franchises are approved and folded based solely on the needs of Crache and the value provided by a Gen. We do not stand on sentiment here. Gens are not affectations of 'legacy' or a false sense of 'nobility.' We have risen above the notion that blood or lineage should determine some aristocratic ruling class. Function is the only determining factor. Your Gen is no longer functional, Lexi. It can no longer serve Crache."

"Thank you, Councilwoman Burr, for that rousing reaffirmation of Crachian ideology and the Gen Franchise Council's role within it," Jochi says, speaking for the first time, and making no effort to mask the sarcasm in his voice.

Stru ignores them as the old often ignore bickering children. His sunken eyes are filled with Lexi, and they hold her with regret.

"You're a strong woman, Lexi. You've shown that strength in Brio's absence. I believe you will find prosperity in life as a private citizen. To that end, and in recognition of your Gen's service to Crache, this Council will approve a generous stipend to help you transition into that new life."

"New life . . ."

Her mind reels, threatening to unspool entirely.

We are not flowers. We do not wilt.

Lexi draws in a breath that might be made of fire, it so twists the features of her face, but when she exhales her expression flattens into a hard mask.

"With respect," she addresses the entire Council, the words made hard and tight by her clenched jaw, "there is no more extreme measure than folding a Gen, however humble that Gen may be by the standards of most. In the case of Gen Stalbraid, this action would leave the people of the Bottoms with no pleaders, and I sincerely doubt any other Gen will be clamoring for the contract. I've had no preparation . . . no time to ingest what you've handed down today, or the reasons for it. I accept I cannot examine whatever evidence against Brio you've reviewed, but if for nothing else than the basic standard of courtesy, and to prevent the residents of the Bottoms to be left without basic advocacy, I ask that this session be continued that I might have time to prepare, if not a defense, then a formal response."

Councilman Stru sighs. "It is within our purview to continue this session. However, barring some truly illuminating new evidence . . . the return of Brio himself and an explanation that would exonerate him . . . I simply do not foresee an adjustment to this Council's decision, regardless of the formality of your response."

"But you *will* grant me that continuation," Lexi says, adding quickly, "As I request."

The ancient figure turns his head, stretching the flesh of his neck in such a way that makes Lexi want to avert her eyes. Stru looks to Councilman Jochi, who only shrugs. Stru looks to Councilwoman Burr, who shakes her head.

Finally, the senior councilman looks to Lexi. Those eyes hooded by the overgrown hollows of his face are unreadable in that moment, a moment in which Lexi feels an intangible part of herself leave her body. She can almost see it, corporeal and faceless, wearing the halo of some great ethereal guillotine in front of her whose blade is tethered to the next words that will be emitted from those withered lips.

"One week," Stru declares, and Lexi exhales a small piece of her soul. "We'll continue this session one week from today, out of respect for what remains of Gen Stalbraid."

"Thank you, Councilman," Lexi says, almost automatically.

"This is a final courtesy, Lexi," the senior councilman insists, his tone harsher than it has yet been. "I advise you attach no more meaning or weight to it than that, and use the time to accept what comes next."

"Thank you," Lexi repeats, just as mechanically as before.

She's already forgotten whatever words he spoke beyond granting her request.

The next few moments are the same detached haze; Stru dismissing her and the Council adjourning, Lexi shuffling from the chamber past the disinterested Aegin, moving among the sea of bodies filling the cavernous corridors of the Spectrum, and finally arriving at the great receiving hall where she began the day what seems now like a short lifetime ago.

Taru refuses to sit the way a tree refuses to bend, and they loom with the same height and unyielding poise. They await Lexi just beyond the point at which weapons are permitted to be carried inside the Spectrum. Taru refused to be parted from the short sword sheathed in a scabbard made from the same thick leather as the rest of their armor, or the unusually crooked blade hanging from their opposite hip.

It's not only their height or plain armor or the weapons that cause Taru to stand out among the soft colorful tunics and wraps of the Capitol citizenry. It's not strictly the shorn sides of Taru's head or the sun-bleached shock of hair worn in a topknot, a style not typically seen in Crachian cities that draws the wary eye of everyone who passes. Taru's features and the color of their skin are just slightly off for a Crachian, but more than enough to be noticed in the Capitol of a nation whose borders are closed to foreigners.

"You may rest yourself in my absence, you know," Lexi reminds her Gen's towering retainer.

"That is precisely what I may *not* do, Te-Gen," Taru replies, adding quickly, "With respect."

Lexi has little reason to smile these days, but Taru is her last lingering source of inspiration for the expression.

"Do you find the Spectrum to be such a threatening place?" she asks her retainer, the question meant as no more than a joke.

Taru doesn't answer at first.

"Not the Spectrum itself, Te-Gen. No."

Some subtle force seems to drag Taru's eyes away from their usual singular focus on guarding Lexi's space. It's only for a moment, but Lexi notices, looking for the source of the distraction. Upon the wall at the center of the reception hall fork is a wayfinding tablet, also carved from the Spectrum's own stone. Its purpose is to direct visitors to the various chambers and authorities and their respective corridors. One word leaps immediately at Lexi from the stone's surface.

It reads SELECTION, with an arrow indicating the corridor branching off to the right.

Lexi's brief, rare smile slowly dies. It never occurred to her that being Undeclared Taru might feel uncomfortable in close proximity to the place where children like them are often forced to choose a gender assignment.

"I'm sorry, Taru," Lexi says. "I didn't realize—"

"There is no need for *you* to apologize, Te-Gen," they assure their mistress, with the clear implication that those actually responsible for the selection process did, in fact, have much to answer for.

"Still, I should have thought. It was a careless thing to say to you. You didn't have to accompany me at all."

Taru stares down at her then, the tundra contained in their eyes as fierce and unrelenting as a real ice storm. Taru doesn't respond, but their gaze spells out well enough where the retainer feels they belong.

Lexi says no more about it, but she can't shake loose the feeling of guilt.

Thankfully, Taru asks, "What did the Council have for you, Te-Gen? News, or more platitudes?"

Lexi's sympathetic demeanor turns hard. "They're using Brio's disappearance against the entire Gen. They want to fold our franchise. They want to end us."

"On what basis?" Taru all but demands.

"They say the Protectorate Ministry has evidence Brio defected to Siccluna. They want to name him a traitor."

"It's a lie!"

"Of course it's a lie," Lexi says without hesitation, a sweeping dismissal in her tone. "It's a very pointed lie, aimed at wiping away anything and everything Brio leaves behind in his absence. He spent his life upholding the ideals of Gen Stalbraid and speaking for the citizens of the Capitol Crache refuses to claim. For decades we've been the only thing stopping the Protectorate Ministry from razing the Bottoms altogether. Discrediting him and dismantling our Gen is to their ultimate advantage."

"But why would the Council do this? Are they the Ministry's puppets, as well?"

"It's not the whole Council, at least I do not believe so. This was spearheaded by that fanatical Burr woman. She's either in league with the Protectorate Ministry or so eager to curry favor and advance her position she'll do anything they say."

"Does she know what Brio was investigating before we lost . . . before his disappearance?"

Lexi feels a swarm of sharp hooks take root in her chest and pull in what feels like a dozen different directions. She sees the same denial being plated over in Taru's expression, the same suppression of loss and longing and fear in the face of meeting the challenges facing them now. Lexi knows no one in the world can possible miss Brio and burn for the knowledge of his fate more than her. However, Taru comes the closest to matching her feelings. They may not love Brio in the same way as Lexi, but Taru is no less loyal to him, no less attached.

"Whether Burr knows or not, the Protectorate Ministry surely does," Lexi answers stiffly. "He disappeared less than a week after he told us of his suspicions. I do not believe in coincidence, not of that import."

"Nor I," Taru affirms.

"I will not allow them to tear us apart," Lexi insists. "I will not allow them to use whatever they've done to Brio as their excuse. I've done all I can to find him. If it comes to nothing, the least I can do is hold us together until he—"

Lexi breaks off in midsentence as the sudden, stony change of expression on Taru's face halts her next words. They're staring past Lexi, down the length of the berth.

Lexi follows her retainer's gaze. Two Aegins are approaching them, one of them almost as tall as Taru and the other short and squat. Both are young, male, and the faded threadbare state of their green and black tunics speaks of years wearing them. Like all Aegins they don't carry swords; the city was designed to negate the efficacy of long blades in its purposefully narrow streets. The daggers sheathed in scabbards resting against their chests on draped baldrics are long with curved handles.

"Te-Gen," the taller one greets Lexi with mock respect, although it's clear neither of them is interested in her.

"Aegins," she responds in her best hostess manner.

"Fine day."

It's further clear he's not interested in the weather.

Lexi only nods.

"Who is this here?" the Aegin asks, his eyes locking on Taru's.

Lexi answers in the same dutiful tone. "This is my personal retainer, Taru."

"You don't look Crachian," the taller of them observes. "You've got a bit of the Isle of Rok in you. Never seen one in the city proper before."

"That's because they're not allowed beyond the docks," his stubby fellow reminds the Aegin.

"Taru was born in the Capitol, I assure you," Lexi says stiffly.

The tall one grunts. "You're one of them Undeclared, too, aren't you?"

"I don't see as that is any of your business, Aegin," Lexi answers for her retainer.

"Two blades, is it?" the squat Aegins accuses more than asks Taru.

"Taru is fully bonded through my Gen," Lexi informs them evenly. "Bonded retainers are permitted to openly carry arms in the Capitol, as I'm sure you're aware, Aegin."

The tall one nods, smiling pleasantly. "Hai. And we're permitted to inspect those weapons for the proper proofs, especially here in the Spectrum."

"Let's have 'em, ya great tree," the squat one orders, gesturing with his pudgy fingers.

"I only relinquish my weapons at Te-Gen's request," Taru answers them stonily.

"Present your arms for inspection," the taller Aegin demands, his tone no longer light or playful. "Or we'll be detaining the retainer."

Taru's forearms cross in front of their abdomen, each hand closing around the hilt of a blade. They draw the weapons so fast and with such force that both Aegins involuntarily back away a step.

Lexi couldn't swear to it, but she thinks she sees Taru grin in that moment.

Taru lets the point of each weapon linger just a second longer, then sweeps the blades of each weapon back and extends their hilts to the Aegins.

Before watching Taru unsheathe them, the tall one might've taken the weapons from Taru's hands. He seems hesitant now, resigned to leaning over them to inspect the steel of each.

"The Capitol proofs look genuine enough," the taller one admits, squinting at the small impression of the Spectrum hammered into the thickest quarter of each blade.

"I don't know about that," the squat one says. "Off-side smiths are doing marvelous things with counterfeit proofs these days. And that's an interesting blade."

He extends a chubby digit at the crooked blade Taru carries in addition to their short sword.

"This looks like a fancied rendering of a hook-end. Spent some time in the Bottoms, have we?"

"My Gen has long served as pleaders for the Division you call the 'Bottoms,'" Lexi interjects quickly.

"I was born there," Taru says, their lips tight.

"I knew it! You may be the biggest port rat I've ever seen, but your kind can never get rid of the smell. How many Aegins did you bloody with your first hook-end before your mistress had her Gen's smith forge you a prettier one?"

26

Lexi steps between them before Taru can even begin to formulate a response.

"Taru is a bonded retainer of Gen Stalbraid," she says, addressing the two Aegins with an edge in her voice that causes them both to really look at her for the first time. "*My* retainer. You've exercised your authority to inspect my retainer's weapons, which, as you've seen, bear the required proofs. By my reckoning you've now exhausted your authority, and I bid you both good day."

The squat one seems ready to press the issue, but the tall one's gaze trails down to Lexi's broach, tracing the lines of the official insignia there.

"Good day to you, Te-Gen," he says, his eyes returning to hers. "And to you . . . retainer."

Taru bows their head formally.

The two of them turn and retreat through the reception hall crowd.

"I'm sorry you're forced to endure that," Lexi says when they're beyond earshot. "Perhaps if you served a more prominent Gen—"

"They're small men," Taru says with more iron than any single forge could temper in their voice. "They're so small I can't even see them."

Lexi smiles quietly to herself.

"You'd see them well enough if you had to cut them down, I imagine," she says a moment later.

Taru snorts their reply, immediately stiffening at the slip in formality. "Forgive me, Te-Gen."

Lexi dismisses that with a wave of her hand. "You really must stop apologizing for acting as a person. I'm the one who should apologize. I've never truly tried to understand how difficult it must be for you, existing in so many worlds."

"I only exist in one. I cannot speak to my ancestry. I never knew my family. As for being *Undeclared*, I make no apologies. I may have to give up my blades for the sake of the petty comfort of others, but that is all I am willing to give up. I made that decision before I came into Te-Gen's service."

Lexi finds herself at a loss. Her only clear thought is that she wishes she'd had Taru's kind of unyielding strength in the chambers of the Gen Franchise Council.

"Well said" is all she's able to offer.

"Where do we go now, Te-Gen?" Taru asks.

Lexi is silent for a moment before answering.

"Home," she says. "We *will* find a way to prevent what they are trying to do to us. I promise you. We will do that."

A THOUSAND FACES AND NONE

DYEAWAN WAKES WITH WHAT SMELLS LIKE THE ENTIRE OCEAN filling her nostrils. Her first thought is what a welcome change it is from the dungeon's cloying anise fingers constantly probing her mouth and lungs. This leads directly to her second thought, which is that she shouldn't be able to smell the ocean from the dungeons. Accepting that, she realizes she can't possibly still be in her dungeon cell. Finally, she remembers the dark figure, the dust blown into her face, and the potion sleep that followed.

That last thought causes her eyes to snap wide open. Her awareness spreads out through her arms and torso. That awareness dampens at her legs as it always does, though she has long ago stopped thinking ruefully about that.

She's lying in a bed softer than any surface upon which she's ever slept. The room surrounding it is small, the walls stone, but it's clean and even lavish in its furnishings. There's a silk dressing screen in one corner, a bamboo chest not far from it. A pillowy reading chair sits in the opposite corner.

There's one other piece of furniture in the room, and when Dyeawan's eyes settle on it the wheels in her head stop turning completely for a moment.

The contraption beside her new bed isn't quite a chair and isn't quite a wheelbarrow. A platform of polished wood rests atop two tracks of a dozen medium-size wheels. A thick rectangle of lush red and gold carpet has been laid over the platform. There are paddles attached to each side of the platform, a complicated series of strings and sticks connecting them to the tracks of wheels beneath. The tops of the paddles are like the armrests of a chair, thin and long.

Even if she can't immediately understand it, Dyeawan somehow realizes why, and for whom, the conveyance has been placed there.

Rolling to the edge of the bed beside it, she presses her hands into the soft carpeting of the contraption's platform. She crawls over it, pulling the weight of her legs behind her, and settles atop it just as she would the tin sheets she appropriates to slide herself around the city.

Settled comfortably, Dyeawan rests her arms atop the paddles, fingers curled around the end. Her natural instinct is to drag them backward. When she does, the motion of the paddles causes the contraption wheels to roll forward smoothly and easily almost a foot.

A sound somewhere between a laugh and a gasp escapes her lips.

It's like rowing a boat without having to grip the oars or bear their weight. Dyeawan simply moves her arms back and the momentum of the wheels causes the paddles to complete a full arc.

She realizes the motion to control the contraption is exactly the same as those she uses to slide herself along the city streets, only a million times cleaner and more comfortable, and requiring not even an ounce of the effort.

It's as if the conveyance beneath her was designed and built specifically for her.

Dyeawan experiments with the paddles, moving one forward and the other backward. As she suspected, it allows her to turn the contraption right or left effortlessly. By reversing her stroke on both paddles, the entire thing shoots backward at alarming speed.

After several minutes of wheeling herself around the confined space of the room, Dyeawan realizes she's giggling and crying all at once. She's seen chairs fashioned with wheels in the Capitol, usually supporting high-ranking Gen members, but she never even allowed herself to dream she'd possess one of her own.

And this is so much better and more magnificent than any chair could ever be.

She slides herself over to the room's sole window, raising herself up as high as possible to peer outside. There is a mountain capped by clouds in the far-off distance to her right. To the left she sees water. There's a beach not fifty yards from the window, although it's far, far below. From there the ocean stretches until it hits a white misty nothingness miles offshore. There are no boats, no other landmasses in view.

There's a knock at the door; Dyeawan can't yet think of it as *her* door. The knock is soft, unobtrusive.

She stops herself at the foot of the bed, unsure of what to do. It doesn't occur to her that permission to enter the room is hers to grant.

"Hello?" is the best she can come up with.

The door opens. A figure so tall it has to duck to enter the room. The man is as gaunt as he is lengthy, his nondescript brown robes hanging from him as if he were a coatrack.

"Good morning, young lady," he says with a kind smile. "My name is Quan. I am certain you have many questions about where you are and how you've come to be here. If you would kindly follow me, I will take you to someone who will explain all these things."

Dyeawan can't think of anything to say to that; he's addressed most of what's going on in her head right now.

Instead she just nods. "Okay."

The corridor outside is more spacious than the room, lit by the same lamps used in the Capitol streets, and it is all Dyeawan can do not to wheel herself in giant circles or weave fast and free just because she can. As Quan leads her, she notices the corridors wind in large circles that grow smaller the farther they move through them. The building itself must be shaped the same way, like a circle. Dyeawan has never seen a structure like that in the Capitol.

They pass a lanky man polishing one of the fixtures housing the lamps. He's missing his left leg below the knee, as well as his right arm nearly at the shoulder. The stumps of both have been expertly treated and well healed, and the man looks clean and nourished. He smiles at them as they pass.

They must have reached a center point in the winding corridors by the time Quan motions to an open door. "Through here, please," he bids her.

Dyeawan wheels herself inside, surprised when the door shuts behind her with Quan on the other side and she hears a heavy latch secure it.

She turns her head from the door and is immediately convinced they've locked her in a room with a dead man.

They've dressed the corpse in a simple gray tunic, upon the breast of which is pinned a simple steel crest of a dozen concentric circles. He's much older than her. Threads of gray are steadily overtaking his thick, dark hair. The man is seated in a large chair in the center of a featureless room. His icy blue eyes are wide and glazed, and the features of his face are completely slack.

Dyeawan squints, examining his neck, and then her eyes go as wide as they've ever been. There's some form of reptile affixed to his throat. Thin, hollow spikes, at least a dozen, protrude from the back of a body that's bulbous like a toad, but the creature's snout is long and scaled and latched firmly onto the man's neck. There's no blood that Dyeawan can see, but the complete void of expression on the man's face says death.

When his hand moves, Dyeawan almost wheels her brand-new conveyance back into the door.

Splayed atop a long tray in front of his chair is what looks like dozens and dozens of silk fans attached to sticks. As he selects one and picks it up, she realizes they aren't fans, they're silk masks. The one he holds in front of his face by its handle is painted with a perfect likeness of his face. Rather than the blank expression of his slackened face, however, the artist has rendered him with a cordial smile.

The effect is eerie, alive and lifeless at the same time.

"Good morning, young lady. My name is Edger. It's a pleasure to meet you."

His voice is even more unsettling than his inhuman smile frozen in silk and oil. The words don't come from his mouth; instead, they seem to be pumped through the spiky tubes growing from the back of the creature attached to his neck. It's like being spoken to by the wind in a deep canyon, more elemental than voice.

"I know my appearance can be jarring to the uninitiated, and for that I apologize. I was born with a condition that paralyzes my face. As for my little friend here, his name is Ku. He's a wind dragon. I assure you he is not harming me. He allows me—"

"You're talking from your throat," Dyeawan says, fascinated. "And it's . . . it's making the sounds for you, like your mouth would, through those little pipes on its back. That's so . . . amazing."

Edger lowers the stick mask with its cordial smile and replaces it among the others in front of him. He selects a new silkscreen portrait, this one with the raised brows and tight mouth of surprise.

"You obviously have a keen mind. That's just right, yes. May I ask your name?"

Dyeawan hesitates. Though she isn't sure why, something in her warns against telling this man her given name. She thinks of the time she spent in that cell with Evie, the conversations they had.

"Slider," she answers. "My name is Slider."

Edger lowers his surprised face and replaces it with the cordial smile that first greeted her.

"That's very appropriate," he says. "May I ask you a question, Slider?"

She nods.

"How did you remain on the streets of the Capitol for so many years on your own? And without being arrested by Aegins? The Capitol is more fanatical about clearing out vagrants and the homeless than any other city in Crache. And most of the ones Capitol Aegins target are able-bodied."

Dyeawan isn't sure what to say at first; she's never thought her daily life a special or unique feat.

"I . . . I learned to stay down by day. Most of us get taken during the day."

"And where would you stay?"

"A lot of places. The hulls of ships that haven't been put all the way together yet are best most of the time. The Capitol makes more ships than it can ever launch. The hulls are stacked deep at the port. They're all covered up and barely guarded or even tended to. A lot of us live in those hulls. But I've spent weeks inside an empty barrel before. Anywhere that's dark and hidden and no one bothers to look."

"And at night?"

Dyeawan shrugs. "It's easier to move around without being noticed. There are taverns and streets Aegins are afraid to go. But they can be good places to find food or beg for it. A lot of people are generous when they're drunk."

"Isn't that equally dangerous for you, though?"

"Sometimes. Mostly they ignore *cripples*." It is clear from the resentment in Dyeawan's voice that she's repeating a word hurled at her as an insult or dismissal many times throughout her short life. "I'd always make sure my face and hair were dirty, and the real trick is to never have anything worth taking. Mostly they leave you alone."

"That's very smart. Strategically speaking."

"Thank you."

"Why hide from the Aegins though, Slider? Especially when you're cold and starving. Do they harm you and your friends? Beat you, or otherwise molest you?"

"No. They're not allowed to. Most of them, anyway."

"Then what do you fear? Other than shelter and food for a few nights?"

"Where I come from, everyone knows when Aegins take you, you don't come back. We don't know why, but if it were a good thing we'd see the ones who were taken again. Somewhere."

"I see."

Dyeawan fears he'll press the subject, her blood rushing unpleasantly, but to her relief Edger moves on.

"Tell me, Slider, do you like your new tender? The conveyance we've fashioned for you?"

She looks down at the masterpiece of motion beneath her, rubbing her hands and forearms against the top of the paddles just to feel the high polish in the wood.

"It's . . . the most wonderful thing I've ever seen," she answers honestly.

"I'm very glad to hear that. I'm pleased to say I designed it myself. We have many very fine wheeled chairs, but when I was informed of how you devised to move yourself around . . . quite ingenious, by the way . . . I thought this would be better, would feel more natural to you."

"It does," she assures him, gratefully. "I'm sorry, De-Gen, but—"

"There's no need for that," he corrects her. "I'm not a member of a Gen. You may simply call me Edger."

That only confuses Dyeawan further, but her burning question takes precedent. "Did you say . . . that you made this for *me*?"

"I did, yes."

"But . . . why? Why would you do that? I'm . . . I'm not anybody. I don't understand—"

"How else can I expect you to do your job efficiently? Besides which, those raw sheets of tin would wreak havoc on our floors."

Dyeawan begins to feel as if she's falling down a long, dark, narrow hole, and just slow enough to make her believe the fall won't hurt.

"My job?"

"Yes. I'd like to offer you a job here, if you're willing."

"And where is here, Edger? If it's okay to ask."

He nods, dipping the mask in time with the gesture and making both motions seem awkward and unnatural.

"Of course. You're on a small island off the coast of the Capitol.

It's very lovely and very private. And this place is called the Planning Cadre. We help solve Crache's . . . well . . . everyday problems. The sky carriages, the streetlights, they were all invented here, by people like me. It's our job to come up with ideas that would make Crachian life better, and then devise how to make those ideas real."

When Dyeawan slid atop the tender less than an hour ago, she was certain nothing would ever be that remarkable again. But hearing such a place could exist, does exist, and more than that she's inside it, is beyond remarkable.

"But what could I do here?" she asks. "I'm not . . . like you."

"It takes all types of ingenuity to keep this place running, I assure you. You'd be a helper. And much needed, believe me. We have many, and they're still never enough. In the early mornings you'd help sweep up the floors. That tender we've given you will be ideal for ferrying equipment and deliveries from place to place quickly within the Cadre."

"I can do all that," Dyeawan says quickly. "I'd be happy to do it."

Edger replaces his cordial smile with a mask that captures his face in the midst of laughing heartily, and though it's even more disturbing than the frozen smile, Dyeawan has become determined not to let it bother her.

"I'm delighted to hear that, Slider," he says. "And I appreciate your enthusiasm."

He lowers the laughing mask and selects a new one. The expression isn't quite stern, but it's the most serious face he's yet worn in front of her.

"Now, to the matter of your compensation. We are not a wealthy arm of the nation, you understand. But we can offer you room and board. Three meals a day. And I assume your current accommodations are to your liking?"

Dyeawan quickly nods. "I've never had a room of my own before."

"I'm very sorry for that, and glad to change it. Does that mean the conditions are acceptable to you?"

She nods.

"May I ask one more question, though?"

"Of course, Slider. And for future reference, you need not request permission to ask a question. Asking questions is what we do here."

"How did I get here? And why don't I remember leaving the dungeon?"

"Ah yes. I'll ask your indulgence in that. For security reasons only a few may know our exact location here. Some of what we build is for the Skrain, and we can't have Crache's enemies gaining knowledge of such things."

Dyeawan nods genuinely, accepting that.

"I understand."

It's the third thing he's lied about since they began talking. Dyeawan always knows when someone is lying to her. It's a gift she's possessed for as long as she can remember, and though she doesn't fully understand *how* she comes by that knowledge, life in the streets of the Capitol has taught her to always trust it.

Edger was lying when we spoke of the scale of what the Planning Cadre does, especially just solving "everyday" problems. He lied when he spoke about being a poor arm of Crache able to offer her only room and board (not that it mattered; Dyeawan would agree to scrounge her meals from the garbage and sleep on the beach she saw from her window if it meant being allowed to stay here).

And he's lying about why they don't want her to know precisely where she is.

It's a troubling lie, even to her, but what he's told the truth about thus far outweighs any other concerns Dyeawan has. She knows Edger has no ulterior motives like most men in the Capitol streets who would offer her favors. He wasn't lying about the job or its parameters; she truly is being hired to clean floors and cart deliveries.

Looking at Edger, and judging from the helper she watched polishing fixtures in the corridors, it's not difficult to discern that the voiceless, expressionless man in front of her has a soft heart for cripples of all varieties. He's obviously led a sheltered life, one of privilege and comfort. He's no doubt fixated for much of that life on the unfairness of his condition.

Dyeawan has never been concerned with what is "fair" or "unfair." She concerns herself every day with what is, and what needs to be done to survive. And if today Edger's pity can secure her future then so be it.

So Dyeawan nods and makes her eyes wide and doe-soft and completely trusting. He can have his secrets if it means she can call this place of wonders home.

"Thank you so much, Edger," she says, and her gratitude is sincere. "I won't let you down."

He replaces his serious expression with the familiar cordial smile, which seems to be his default.

"I know you won't," he says. "You may return to your quarters now, Slider. There will be a bell for dinner, and I'll have Quan come to escort you to the commissary. We can talk more about your daily duties then."

Before Dyeawan can answer, the door behind her clicks open and the tall, gaunt attendant is there, waiting with his kind smile.

She drags her left paddle back and rows the opposite one forward, turning her toward the door.

Dyeawan stops.

"Edger?" she asks. "This isn't a dream, is it? I'm not . . . I'm not still in that cell? In the dungeon?"

"No, my dear," he answers without hesitation. "This place is realer than most."

Dyeawan can't be certain what he means by that, but she knows beyond any doubt that he's telling the truth.

BLOOD COINS AND
BLOOD COIN HUNTERS

THE STEADY STRIKE OF THE SMITH'S HAMMER IS MEANT TO BE a siege tactic. Evie knows this. They, the new recruits, have been gathered here beside the thatch lean-to shielding the blacksmith from the midday sun to watch the old woman work. They're left to stand without instruction for several long moments, the silence narrated solely by the brutal fall of that steel hammer. It's no different from drums beating outside a besieged fortification, only the target is the invisible parapet guarding their minds.

Evie studies the elderly woman whose flesh has been hardened to near stone by decades of intense heat and labor. She is fashioning coins. They aren't large coins, only slightly rounder and wider than the tip of a thumb, and they aren't gold or silver. They look to Evie to be cheap copper, or perhaps tin. After she cools each one, the smithy carefully brushes both sides of the small coins with a mixture from a bowl near her forge.

Evie has no idea what the substance is, but its slicks on top like oil, green and purple and black all at once, and the smell as the old woman lashes each coin with it is awful.

Laython is standing behind a waist-high object covered with an old moth-eaten blanket, watching the smithy. When he seems satisfied she's minted enough, he gathers the cover of the object in front of him with one giant hand and whips it away, revealing a chair fashioned from both wood and steel. Its back is deeply recessed and a panel has been added to cradle the legs and feet. Its most menacing feature, however, are the many buckled leather straps dangling from its joints.

"By now you've no doubt absorbed the fact there are no guards," he addresses them all in his bombastic way. "The few Skrain you'll see about are mostly here as punishment for some dereliction of their duties. They don't want to be here and they certainly don't like you. I'd keep that in mind before running afoul of any of them. No, this isn't a prison and you're not prisoners. If we had to waste walls and towers and guards on you it'd defeat the purpose. If you're of a mind late tonight after everyone's fucked off to sleep to run, you'll have an easy time of it. I promise you. In fact, there's no need to run. I'd walk. Hell, I'd *stroll*. No one will stop you."

Laython gives a nod to his tasker underlings. The pair of them stride forth and seize the first new Savage within reach, the same portly, bearded man who was the only one besides Evie to protest their conscription.

"What now?" he half whines, half demands. "I'm just a pickpocket! I don't deserve this!"

His struggling goes barely noticed by the taskers as they ferry him under the lean-to and tip him back into the chair, one of them hoisting his legs up onto the wooden rest. They each firmly secure one of his arms, waiting.

Laython steps over to the forge and picks up one of the newly minted and treated coins. He holds it up against the rays of the midday sun.

In the light it looks more copper than tin to Evie. She can also make out a design pounded into the coin, not the Crachian ant or any other national symbol. It appears to be a crude face, bearded and with wild hair. The eyes and mouth are just hollows.

The face of a Savage, she realizes.

"This is a blood coin," he informs them all. "This is Crachian ingenuity at its finest and most elegant. And this is why none of you are going anywhere except where I *tell* you to go."

Laython turns and strides to the reclining chair, leaning over its burly, terrified occupant. With his free hand, Laython reaches past the man's bushy beard and painfully grips his lower lip, yanking it until the man has no choice but to open his mouth. As soon as he does, Laython jams the coin inside it. One of his massive hands clamps down over the man's lips while the other pinches his bulbous nose closed.

The poor thief has no choice but to swallow, deeply, ingesting the coin.

Laython releases him and steps away, the smithy tossing him a soiled cloth with which he proceeds to wipe his hand.

The portly man in the chair gasps for breath, but the coin doesn't come up.

"It's very simple," Laython explains. "The blood coin sits in your gut. It doesn't pass. Drink all you want. Puke all you want . . ." He looks at Evie. "There it stays, inside you. Over time the dye the coin is treated with gets into your own blood. It raises those runes you see on your new brothers and sisters. It marks you as a Savage for all to see. The runes don't scrub out. And it should be obvious tryin' to cut 'em out produces the same effect as letting them show."

Behind Laython, the other taskers are affixing the chair's half dozen straps around the man's legs, arms, torso, and head.

"Why're you strapping him in after you've already shoved it down his throat?" Evie asks, disturbed and angry.

With an angry dog's expression, he strides over to her and puts his face directly above her, his shouts like thunder from a stormy sky.

"You're developing a distasteful habit of telling me my business, little girl! I suggest you save that sass for the Sicclunan front line where it might actually serve you well, lest you find my boot burrowing toward where I'm about to deposit a blood coin!"

Evie says nothing. She's long sober now and able to see there's no percentage in it for her to speak another word.

Her silence only serves to highlight the screams that pour forth from the chair in the next moment. The portly, bearded man begins thrashing against the tight straps, struggling more fiercely and violently than he did when the taskers seized him. They all watch as for the next thirty seconds straight all-consuming agony has its way with the man, no one lifting a finger to help or even attempt to help him.

Finally, gratefully, he falls still and silent.

Laython turns back to him, walking over to the chair and gripping the half-unconscious man by his abundance of beard. Laython tilts the portly man's head to the right for them all to see.

There, on his cheek, is a bluish green mark almost like a sickle.

"That's a good'n," Laython remarks, releasing the man's beard and making a show of wiping his hands on the cloth again. "The marks'll fade if you ever get the coin out. And the only way that happens is if we give you the right mixture to help you pass it. To earn that particular cup of wine, you only need to survive one hundred battles. It's that simple, children.

"Now then. Any man, woman, or child who returns a blood coin, either still inside a runaway Savage or a coin on its own, will be rewarded with one of these."

He reaches inside his tunic and removes a small stringed sack. Loosing its ties, he opens the sack and upends it over the smithy's anvil, raining small, intricately cut multicolored stones down atop the pounded-raw steel.

They're star rubies, so named because each color represents a god star of the old and abolished religion.

"No questions asked," Laython adds as they all stare at the priceless stones in awe. "Imagine how hard and how far you'd ride and how many of you you'd kill to claim such a reward. Then look at the mark on the fat man's cheek here, the first of many to come. Then decide if you want to run."

Even Evie has to admit to herself he makes a powerful and salient argument.

"And lest you think we rely solely on the initiative of the good citizens of Crache," Laython continues, "I'd like you to meet some close friends of mine."

Laython ducks under the lean-to awning and steps out into the harsh sunlight. He sticks two lengthy digits in his mouth and whistles shrilly.

Evie and the rest hear hooves tearing up the dry grass. A second later two riders charge around the lean-to and rear their mounts beside the group's new freemaster.

Laython gestures grandly up at the pair. "Savages, meet Tomoe and Namrok, two of the finest blood coin hunters alive."

The woman must be six feet tall, perhaps over. She appears absolutely gigantic sitting atop her mount. Her armor is composed almost entirely of bone, human and animal, from what Evie can discern. A whole rib cage is laid over Tomoe's own, tooled upon thick leather. Her helm must've been fashioned from a bear's skull, and Evie can scarcely summon in her mind the scale of that creature when it was alive. The fanged jaws that serve as the helm's face shield are pulled apart, revealing a face whose gauntness and many scars haven't dulled the shine of two perfect jade eyes.

Tomoe's primary weapon appears to be a poleax. From bottom tip to blade it must be as tall as she is and weigh more than one hundred pounds. A pair of matched daggers is sheathed in gauntlets, also shaved bone, clamped around her forearms. The handle of each is angled to allow the smoothest possible draw by the opposing hand.

Tomoe's companion, Namrok, is of average size and shape, and would be thoroughly unremarkable save for one feature. Half of his face is dark a cavity with jagged edges; he's missing an eye, cheek, and the corner of his mouth. Rather than leave the sinkhole of flesh exposed, Namrok has taken a wedge of hardwood adorned with dozens of tiny steel spikes and plugged most of the empty space with it.

"By my count, Tomoe there is well rich enough to retire in luxury and comfort," Laython tells them. "But she keeps hunting, for the love. Namrok, well, I'm not sure he knows where he is right now, but with a face like that he just needs to be pointed in the right direction."

Namrok laughs raucously at that, though Tomoe only grins thinly and much more, it seems to Evie, at something in her own head.

"Why don't you show 'em the catch of the day, my friends," Laython bids the blood coin hunters.

Tomoe reaches behind her and unties a large bundle concealed in dark cloth atop her mount. It takes some tussling with the bundle, but she quickly unfurls and muscles the bundle from its perch, spilling its contents onto the hot grass.

The eviscerated corpse once belonged to a middle-aged woman. Runes that were once bluish-green have now turned gray, but they still stained the cold flesh of her face and hands.

From her saddle, Tomoe reaches inside her armor and removes a blood coin, flicking it to Laython, who catches it expertly.

He holds this one up to the sun as he did with its newly minted fellow.

This coin, unlike that fresh-forged one, is stained brown and red with the eviscerated woman's blood.

"So you know it's not just a clever name," Laython informs them, tucking the coin inside his belt.

"Why bother digging it out of her?" Evie asks Tomoe directly, sounding very tired all of a sudden.

"I believe in being certain," the blood coin hunter answers her in a voice far softer and more feminine than Tomoe's visage.

"Was she still alive?" Evie presses.

"Not for as long as I'd hoped," Namrok answers for them, and laughs again, a disturbing cackle.

"Any more questions, my presumptuous girl?" Laython asks Evie.

She only hangs her head in silence.

Laython points directly at Evie. "You're next in the chair."

She looks inside the smithy's lean-to, where the other taskers are removing the newly anointed Savage's portly frame from the recliner.

"Well," she says, "at least you're feeding us."

FALLING STARS

THE ANCIENT COIN FLIPS END OVER END THROUGH THE AIR, its green and gray patina swallowing the rays of the afternoon sun before it can touch the metal beneath. The coin descends and its face lands atop the flat of Daian's blade. He drops his wrist just enough to cradle the coin and slow its momentum, keeping it poised on the hardened steel of his Aegin's dagger. Daian briefly examines the five stars crudely stamped on the other side of the coin, at least those visible through its aged scars. He quickly flicks his wrist, the dagger's blade propelling the coin up once more so he can repeat the process.

He says little to the other three Aegins waiting with him. Daian often finds he has little to say to most of his fellows in the Capitol. They talk about their daggers and how many arrests they've made that week and share crude, often violent jokes about the Undeclared and offer little else conversationally. Daian doesn't share their enthusiasm for any of those topics.

"They're in there," Kamala announces quietly, returning from across the narrow street and what appears to be a disused storefront. "I can hear the chanting through the boards over the windows."

"What's the point of all that, anyway?" another Aegin asks, his disgust obvious. "Why risk staring down a knife or facing the cells just to offer lip service to some made-up monster in the stars?"

"Made-up god," Daian corrects him.

"Same thing."

"If you're going to ask questions, a more fitting one would probably be why we're made to waste our time stopping them."

"We're not here to ask questions," Kamala hisses at both of them. "We're here to follow orders. It's an unlawful gathering and they're observing a forbidden ritual. That's it. Now let's go."

"I'll watch the front," Daian offers.

"You do that," Kamala says disinterestedly as she crosses the narrow street once more.

The rest of the Aegins follow her.

Daian watches them go with a sigh, flipping his coin anew. Worshipping the God Stars was outlawed long before he was born, during the Renewal; "Reason shall take the place of religion" was one of the rallying cries of the upheaval. When he was a boy, Daian's father told him that at first the God Star priests and priestesses of the time supported the Renewal. When the common people of that age overthrew the great houses and ended the rule of noble bloodlines, the temple hierarchs assumed they would be spared. Daian imagined then what it must have been like when the people finished with the nobility and came for the temples, tearing them down stone by stone and defrocking every plump, pompous old man wearing a medallion and a fancy hat.

As a boy, thinking about the looks on their faces made him giggle.

Yet hundreds of years after the Renewal, after the abolition of nobility and religion and their false authority, there are still people in Crache willing to become the Protectorate Ministry's scapegoats in order to whisper the names of the God Stars in dark rooms. To Daian's mind, rooting them out was no fit duty for an Aegin. He wished the people would either let the ancient symbols go, or the powers behind Crache would allow them their silly gatherings; Daian has no preference one way or the other.

He watches Kamala put her boot through a small door between the boarded windows of the storefront, more or less obliterating it in a hail of splinters. She's first through the doorway, the other Aegins rushing in behind her with daggers drawn. Daian waits after the last of them has disappeared inside, the predictable sounds of chaos that follow causing a hollowness to fill his gut.

A moment later a scraggly little man in a knee-length tunic and leather sandals dashes through the wreckage of the doorway and scrambles across the street, freezing in panic as he finds Daian barring his path.

Daian looks at the brief expanse of the man's chest. A medallion rests against it, hanging from a chain. Unlike Daian's coin, the stars upon the medallion's face are bright and gleaming and clear. Each one has the shape of a basic life-giving element forged into its center; a rock, a wave of water, a flame, curling lines representing wind.

The priest's terrified eyes shift from Daian's face to his dagger.

With a sigh, Daian quickly flips the coin into his free hand and sheathes the dagger in its baldric scabbard. He tucks the coin away beneath his tunic.

"Please," the priest begs. "Please, just let me pass."

Daian shrugs. "You're mistaking me standing here for me barring your path, friend."

The priest blinks at him, confused. For a moment he even relaxes his shoulders and the terror leaves his expression.

Behind him, screams issue from inside the building, followed by what sounds like the breaking of furniture and the smashing of glass.

The priest glances back over his shoulder. When his face turns back to Daian the panic and fear have not only returned, they've melded into violent desperation.

"I'm sorry," the priest offers penitently.

The small, hemp-wrapped handle of a makeshift knife appears in his hand from a hidden fold in the priest's tunic.

Neither Daian's expression nor his posture change. His eyes remain fixed on the priest's face, almost as if he doesn't notice the weapon.

The priest lunges at Daian, and though the spindly little man is fast it's almost as if he's moving through mud, such is Daian's quickness and ease in seizing the priest's wrist with his hand and stopping his attack. Daian twists the smaller man's arm, extracting a yelp of pain and causing the priest's entire body to stiffen like tumblers in a lock. Daian effortlessly plucks the knife from the man's hand.

"You need to learn to wear this on the inside," he advises the priest, tapping the tip of the man's confiscated blade against his medallion. "That's the best place to keep the things you don't want other people to see. Believe me."

The confusion returns to the priest's face, showing through the twists of pain in his slight features. Daian tosses the small knife away and releases the man's wrist, delivering a stiff kick to the priest's ass that moves him several feet up the narrow street.

"Go," Daian orders him.

The priest hesitates only a moment, rubbing his offended wrist and staring back at Daian in abject shock. In the next moment the sound of his leather sandals slapping the cobblestones is fading around the next corner.

Daian watches him go, shaking his head in a mixture of disgust and something like sadness, less to do with the little priest and more to do with the state of affairs in general.

He returns his attention to the battered doorway. Soon the other Aegins begin reappearing through it, each one restraining a fitful God Star worshipper.

"Where's the priest?" the one who kicked in the hidden church's door demands of Daian.

"He returned to the stars," Daian insists. "It was a sight to behold. I'm sorry you missed it."

"If you weren't going to help out why did you bother to come along?" the Aegin asks in obvious frustration.

Daian smiles. "I just love watching masters and mistresses of their trade at work, that's all."

CITIES BUILT IN BOXES

BY THE END OF HER FIRST WEEK IN THE PLANNING CADRE she's learned how to fly.

Dyeawan revels in the bed they've given her, practically treats the first room she's ever had to herself as a place of worship. Home, however, has quickly become a concept best associated with the corridors outside that room. Astride her "tender," the conveyance designed and constructed specifically for her, Dyeawan is quickly becoming an expert at navigating the corridors at high speed.

In the gray dawn of every morning, Dyeawan rises and washes up before attending to her duties. Edger provided her with an attachment to her tender that allows her to sweep up the corridors simply by wheeling herself up and down their length repeatedly. The only real effort is emptying the collection cans of the apparatus when she's done, but even that is hardly a chore. When she's done, Dyeawan attends breakfast in the commissary and then spends the rest of her day delivering packages.

There are twelve levels in the Planning Cadre, each one constructed with the same concentric corridors winding to a central point, and rooms and stairs branching off from doors and breaks in the circular walls. In addition to the lamps throughout the Cadre, all the corridors are fashioned with an intricate bell system whose song can be heard on every level. Dyeawan has been given her own unique signal. When she hears three bells, she's being summoned. Those are followed by a number of bells indicating the level on which she's needed, and finally a number of bells corresponding to a specific room on that level.

Acting as messenger has allowed her to meet an extraordinary amount of people in just a week, and to Dyeawan's surprise they've all been generally kind and genuinely decent.

All except the one she's come to think of as the Man in Black.

There are no Skrain stationed in the Planning Cadre, nor has she seen any on the rare occasion she'd had to venture outside. There doesn't seem to be a military presence here at all, or even anyone assigned to security, which is odd considering the speech Edger gave her about their "sensitive" projects. Yet she hasn't seen a single blade carried by a single person all week.

In fact, she's only seen one weapon here thus far, and it's sheathed on the hip of the Man in Black.

He's not a physically imposing man, but the stark way he stands out among the thoroughly unimposing people who populate the Planning Cadre gives him an aura of menace. He's the only one Dyeawan has seen clad all in black from head-to-toe, and she's yet to see him outside it. Though the garment is designed to appear ordinary, his black shoulder cape is obviously reinforced with steel thread to armor it, as if he anticipates an attack at all times.

The dagger he wears on his hip is long, curved, and bone-handled, and the way he compulsively grips it with a black-gloved hand as he walks says nothing pleasant about the man. The only other distinguishing flourish on his person is the breast pendant he wears in the shape of an eagle's eye. It's a symbol she's never seen worn officially before.

Dyeawan has yet to exchange a word with him, not the least of which is because whenever they pass he looks straight through her as if she doesn't exist. She's glad for that.

When she asked Edger about him, he told Dyeawan that the Man in Black is from something called the Protectorate Ministry. He said they're in charge of keeping Crache safe, even if it's from something invented in the Cadre.

He didn't seem to want to say more than that.

Regardless, Dyeawan has begun to associate a good day with one during which she doesn't see the Man in Black.

Her favorite level in the Cadre thus far is seven. It's the one that belongs to the builders. Consisting mostly of workrooms of varying tools and trades, it's the place where the designs and machinations of people like Edger are given birth into the world of the real. The artisans installed there are all masters and mistresses of their crafts, and it seems every discipline is brilliantly represented. There are carpenters, smithies, stonecutters, alchemists, metallurgists, and people working with equipment and on projects Dyeawan can't even identify.

Tahei isn't a master, but he may be the most talented apprentice on level seven. He's neither carpenter nor smithy, strictly speaking. He's a plump young man of perhaps nineteen years, far too young to be in charge, but he seems to be quickly moving up the Cadre ranks for one reason.

"I make things move," he'd explained to her when she asked. "It's kind of my specialty. Whatever material you use, if you need it to move around, on its own or under power, I'm your man."

She doesn't doubt his skills, and hasn't since their first meeting when she delivered new tools to his workshop.

"You must be the one they call Slider," he'd greeted her.

"Yes."

"I'm Tahei. Are you enjoying that new tender of yours?"

"I don't know the words to say just how much."

"I'm glad. I built it. I named it too."

Dyeawan's eyes lit up. "You did?"

He nodded proudly. "It reminded me of a rowboat without the water. Of course, I didn't design it, Edger did, but I *did* fix a few flaws in the turning mechanism. Don't tell him that, though."

Dyeawan shook her head. "I wouldn't. I owe you more than thanks."

Tahei waved a gloved hand dismissively. "It's always reward

enough to see it working. And that it's made such a difference to you is a special prize."

"Still," Dyeawan insisted. "If there's anything I can do to help you—"

"Do you bake?"

"I . . . no, I've never cooked anything. I mean, not in a proper kitchen. I've roasted wharf rats and even a snake once—"

Tahei laughed. "I meant more cakes and the like. We only have cakes on special occasions. The rest of the time when I ask the cook tells me I'm too fat and he can't spare the sugar, besides."

"No, I'm sorry."

He shrugged. "Hey, don't worry about it. I was mostly joking. You're working hard enough around here. We're even, okay?"

Dyeawan decided then she liked him. He was kind, and he reminded her of a boy she'd known years ago in the streets. He'd even been plump like Tahei. She and that boy, Fedo, were friends, inseparable for weeks, until Aegins took him. They didn't get her because he led them away. Fedo could barely run, but he ran his heart out that day to save her.

A day later she returned to his workshop with two sweet cakes wrapped in cheesecloth. Tahei couldn't believe his eyes, certain she must've stolen them. But it had been easy, easier than she could've imagined. Dyeawan had gone to the head commissary cook, who turned out to be a blind old man named Makai. She'd prepared an elaborate story about why she needed the ingredients to make the cakes, telling herself she'd acquire the knowledge to actually bake them on her own.

"You're the one who slides because she lost her legs?" he'd asked her.

"No," she'd answered, earnestly. "I have my legs. They're still there. They just don't listen to me anymore."

"And what do you need?"

She told him, but before Dyeawan could recite her prepared speech and accompanying story, Makai simply asked her what she wanted to bake. When she told him that, he said, even shorter, for her to come back in an hour.

Dyeawan didn't understand at first, not even when she did as she was told, returning at the appointed time to find him offering her the freshly baked treats.

"But, why——" she began to protest, mostly out of confusion.

"Our kind takes care of one another here," he said. "You need only ask. And remember."

That sat heavily with her for a long time, until she was able to gift Tahei the cakes. He was overjoyed, and told her that now it was he who owed her.

She decided to save that favor for later.

It's Friday afternoon and Dyeawan is elated when the bells summon her to Tahei's workshop on the builders level. She glides herself there in minutes, barely even slowed by the detour up the ramps between levels that adjoin every staircase. (She's far from the only one in the Cadre who has lost the use of their legs, though Dyeawan has yet to see another use a tender as intricate as hers. She's wondered whether her conveyance is simply a new design or was designed specifically for her.)

She passes several increasingly familiar faces along the way, all of them serving as helpers like her, all of them afflicted differently by life. She's learned the man she exchanged smiles with the first day while he polished lamp fixtures is named Mott. He used to be a soldier. He lost an arm and leg fighting the Sicclunans far away. He also suffered a vicious blow to his head that expresses its effects in his slowed speech and equally slowed thoughts.

Fortunately he's very kind, and Dyeawan doesn't mind waiting the excess time it takes for him to complete those thoughts.

She finds Tahei behind his workbench, examining some extremely small wheels under a special glass held by a vise.

"Slider!" he greets her enthusiastically. "Were you already up here?"

She shakes her head.

"Wow, you are really makin' that thing fly. You do me proud."

More than a little color comes to her cheeks.

"Thanks."

He picks up a medium-size rectangular bundle and hands it over to her.

"Can you speed this down to the maps level?"

Dyeawan accepts the bundle readily, but looks back at him in confusion.

"The maps level? I don't think I've been there yet."

Tahei grins. "Oh, you're going to love it. You especially. I promise. It's level six."

"Okay. What room?"

His grin seems to widen. "The maps level is built a little differently. You'll see. Trust me."

She does, and so she just nods.

"I'll see you in the commissary later, okay?" he says.

"Oh yes. I'll trade you my taro pudding for your greens."

He laughs. "You're a strange kid, you know that?"

"I don't think I've ever gotten to be a kid," she answers honestly.

"Well then . . . now's a good time," he says, more sincerely.

There are no winding corridors on the maps level, Dyeawan discovers. When she descends the ramp from the level above, she finds herself wheeling into a large antechamber that splits off from several tall, broad archways. They're all sealed off behind closed doors, save one.

It's the largest open space she's thus far seen in the Cadre, ten times the size of the most spacious workroom on the builders level.

Of course, it has to be this big, Dyeawan supposes.

The room contains the entire Capitol.

The city sprawls out before her, every building, street, and feature perfectly captured to scale in an intricate model. It's raised on a dais four feet from the floor. The Spectrum must be as tall as Dyeawan, and she can roll freely in her tender among the cooperatives of the Gen Circus. There's even real water filling a stone pool beyond the port, tiny boats skimming its surface. There must be thousands of miniature wooden people riding the sky carriages, crewing the port, and walking the streets.

It almost looks alive.

Dyeawan is so entranced by the magnificent construction before her that ten minutes pass before she remembers her package. She looks across the model to the other side of the space, then along each side, seeing no one.

"Hello?" she calls out. "Is anyone in here?"

In answer, the section of the model comprising baker's row and the fabric Division rattles and then splits apart completely, two huge panels containing a half dozen buildings apiece rising like cellar doors. The head that pops up between them belongs to a young woman with short dark hair whose every edge looks like a blade to Dyeawan. She's wearing a sleeveless tunic with leather belts strapped in an *X* across the torso, every inch covered in pouches stuffed with tools.

"Oh, do you have my people-mover model?" she asks.

"Um . . . I hope so?" Dyeawan answers, holding up the wrapped bundle she was given.

"Great! Hold on!"

The woman disappears back down her hole, the two pieces of city slamming shut atop her. Dyeawan can hear the occasional crash and scuffle as she makes her way beneath the model. Thirty seconds later she emerges from under the North Walls, closest to Dyeawan.

"You're Slider, yeah?" she asks. "I've heard about you. I'm Riko. I *love* this . . . this . . ."

"It's called a tender," Dyeawan says.

"It's *amazing*! Edger's design?"

"Yes. But Tahei built it. And fixed a few flaws. Don't tell Edger, though."

Riko laughs. "You learn quick. I've heard that too."

Dyeawan doesn't know what to say to that, so she reaches down and offers Riko her bundle.

The young woman takes it and unties it, excited. She unwraps a small, polished wooden box with a metal latch.

When Riko opens the lid, Dyeawan isn't sure what they're looking at. Riko removes a rectangular object that appears to be two strips of cloth wrapped side-by-side around a wooden block. There's a barrier composed of steel posts and string between the two strips.

"What is it?" Dyeawan asks.

Riko grins. "I'll show you!"

She disappears back under the model, object in-hand. When Riko emerges again she's opened a panel right next to the Spectrum. As Dyeawan looks on, Riko opens the entire front of the building like a cabinet. Not only is the outside of the model a perfect rendering of the Capitol, the interiors appear to be identical in every detail too. Riko removes the first level of the Spectrum as one would a drawer.

"It's an idea I had that Edger approved for a proper test," Riko explains. "You see, the corridors in the Spectrum are the longest of any structure in the Capitol. It's been reported this leads to a congestion of foot traffic and both officiates and petitioners being late to appointments."

Riko waves a hand over the corridor in question. It runs almost the entire length of the section she's removed. She takes a slim tool from one of her pouches and begins popping up small pieces of the floor in the middle of the corridor, setting them aside.

"So, my idea is to use the method of counter-tension. It came to me when I dislocated my shoulder a few months ago and the surgeon had to use a bed sheet to pop it back in."

Riko replaces the flooring she's removed with her cloth-wrapped rectangle, fitting it perfectly into the section of the model. She snatches up two of the nearest wooden people miniatures and places one each at opposite ends of the cloth strips, on opposing sides. She begins to move one miniature down the right-hand cloth strip while she moves the other one toward it down the left-hand strip.

"You see, as people walk down one length here, they move the belt underfoot. The motion pulls the *opposite* belt in the other direction. So as people on that belt walk the other way, they're feeding the momentum of each side, moving both belts faster and faster and carrying the people along at greatly increased speed."

Riko demonstrates by striking the bottoms of the people miniatures across the strips repeatedly and then taking the miniatures away. The strips continue to move on their own, revolving around the new section of floor in opposite directions.

"I estimate it'll speed up foot traffic by half its ordinary volume, at least on busy days," Riko proclaims, beaming.

Dyeawan is astonished. She looks at the older woman in genuine awe.

"That's . . . it's as amazing as my tender. You're brilliant."

Riko's face visibly flushes, and she seems to retreat inward from the enthusiasm she wore openly just a moment before.

"It's a simple design, really. Edger has designed the most spectacular inventions in the history of Crache, which means in the world."

"I won't tell him," Dyeawan assures her.

Riko grins. "I'm glad you like it. I hope everyone else agrees."

"I'm sure they will. So . . . this model . . . it's not just a model."

"Oh no. It's the city, just smaller and quieter. It's how we test all our ideas and designs before moving to the next stage, which is building them full-scale."

"How do you test those?"

Riko points to the closed-off archway behind her on the other side of the space, then to the one at her right.

"We have bigger pieces of the city built to scale on the rest of the level."

Dyeawan can scarcely believe it; even after the days she's spent flying through the corridors of this place.

"That's . . . I can't . . . will you show me? Please?"

Riko beams at her again. "I'd love to."

As she disappears beneath the Capitol once more, Dyeawan finds her gaze drawn to the forgotten corners of the city she once occupied in fear and isolation every day of her life. She can even see the finished ship hulls she spoke of to Edger. They're perfectly re-created in miniature form, stacked neatly beside one another just off the port and covered in swatches of tarp.

For the first time since waking up in the Planning Cadre, Dyeawan looks past the wonders of their inventions and imaginations. She looks past the marvels of Crachian technology and innovation those things yield. She looks past it all and asks herself a very simple question.

If they can create all this, why are there still people like her left to rot in the streets only to be swept away by Aegins to who knows where?

It's a question she'd very much like to ask Edger, but she doesn't, not out of fear, but out of certainty.

She knows whatever he tells her would be a lie, even if he believes it.

STEEL FIELDS
OF RUST AND ROT

THEY MOVE EVIE AND THE OTHERS OUT THE MORNING AFTER seeding them with blood coins. There are no chains, and no armored soldiers of the Skrain ride out with them. They merely shepherd Evie and her newly marked Savage peers onto plain wagons without cages and point the caravan north from the Capitol along a largely disused road that winds through mostly rough country.

A few days later, Evie watches the Fourth City rise far in the distance off the caravan's right. It remains far in the distance until it disappears entirely behind them before dusk. It is clear to her then that they will avoid major cities, even smaller towns, as much as possible on their journey to wherever.

That part she still hasn't been able to discern, but a week later and with no end to the road in sight, she's beginning to suspect they'll travel far beyond everything she or the others know of Crache.

The Savage Legion keeps a cold camp, serving their new brothers and sisters dried and salted fish atop rice that tastes as though it were cooked three days before. They all finish their small cups quickly and take to their bed rolls early, most of them still finding their only solace in the hours they're given to sleep, even if they do so while shivering against the biting frost.

Evie has never cared for the little death of sleep.

She finds Laython squatting in the bushes on the perimeter of their sparse camp. He's flipping through wood block tiles carved with various physically improbable images of fornication and other debauchery.

"What do you want now, Savage?" he asks her without looking up from his literary pursuit. "Complaints about the food? Questions about your sleeping conditions? Wagon too bumpy during the day?"

"When are we issued our weapons?"

"'Issued our weapons,' she says," he mocks her. "That is mighty fancy talk from vagrant scum Aegins scraped off a barroom floor."

Evie quickly bites her lower lip, feeling caught off-guard. She knows she has only a brief second to dismiss that observation before he looks up at her and really starts to think about it.

"I'm a fellow reader," she manages. "That's a classic, you've got there."

Laython grunts in mild approval. "You can draw gear and weapons whenever you want, from the armorist's wagon. Ask around for Spud-Bar."

"Thank you," Evie says quickly.

"Thank me by letting me shit in peace."

She finds the armorist's wagon on the opposite edge of camp. It looks like a conveyance adorned for some kind of demolition contest; every inch of its exterior is covered in jagged, rusty blades and spiked pieces of wood, steel, and iron. Swords and daggers dangle from hooks. Axes fill racks and spears fill baskets bolted to the wagon's hide. Shields are piled high in rows on its roof, in between bundles of longer pikes and horse-cutters, and netting filled with mixed pieces of armor bulge over the sides.

Peering within the wagon, Evie sees a rugged but obviously skilled makeshift smithy shop. There are several anvils, large vise grips, and cutting and sharpening tools.

And, of course, dozens of more bundles of secondhand weapons.

The armorist is nowhere to be found, at least that Evie can see. Standing outside the wagon, she grabs the first short sword she spies and quickly discards it like the trash it is. She rifles through several more swords, chucking them aside each time. She snaps the blade of one in half over her knee, dropping the separated pieces in sheer disgust.

Evie finally retrieves a short ax that doesn't immediately raise any warnings as she examines it. There are no chips in the blade's edge, nor any cracks in its surface.

"You know steel," a deep voice says, and it's not a question.

Evie turns, ax in hand, having to adjust her gaze upward several feet to meet the speaker's eyes. They're tall and broad with a plain stony face.

"Spud-Bar?" Evie asks. "The armorist?"

"Yes."

Evie observes two things right away, the first being there isn't a single raised rune in Spud-Bar's flesh; no one's forced a coin down that particular gullet. The second thing she observes is that Spud-Bar is an Undeclared. In addition to their size and androgynous features, they've shaved the sides of their head in popular Undeclared fashion, gathering the hair that remains into a topknot.

Evie holds up the ax. "I didn't mean to presume—"

"You know steel," Spud-Bar repeats. "That's rare in the types they send us, particularly the new ones. Most of 'em don't know a good knife even if they've used one to stab a bartender to death."

"I . . . I've never stabbed a bartender, that I can recall."

"Soldier, then?"

Evie quickly shakes her head. "I haven't had any training. But I'm not blind, either. I can see rust and rot as well as anyone."

Spud-Bar is obviously skeptical, but they don't press the issue. "That's a good piece, the ax. It's a B'ors design, B'ors-made. Which you wouldn't know, not having 'ad any training and all."

Evie can't help but grin. "Right. It's got a good balance."

"Also rare among this lot, I'm afraid. But I take what I'm given and do m'best with it. That's all any of us here can do. The good news is, odds are fair you'll only need it for one battle."

"Is that the average life around here? One battle?"

"That's slightly above the average."

That news settles like a great granite slab on Evie's chest. She does her best not to let it show.

"A lot of these people don't look like they belong here, even for one battle," Evie observes.

Spud-Bar shrugs. "There are many reasons to 'belong' here."

"I had a friend," Evie ventures, carefully. "We were . . . separated. Is it possible you've seen him? A handsome man, my age, dark hair, dark eyes."

"This is someone you know or someone you dream about knowing?"

Evie curses herself silently. "It's a poor description, I know. But—"

"I don't look too hard at the new ones, you know? No offense, but you may be dead tomorrow. It doesn't pay to make lasting friends."

"Right. Of course. Can I use your tools to work on this?" she asks, holding up the ax again.

"Is bladesmithing something else you've had no training in?"

Evie shrugs. "I tinker."

Now it's Spud-Bar's turn to grin. "You tinker."

Evie nods.

"What's mine is at your disposal, Savage," Spud-Bar says.

Her expression darkens. "My name is Evie."

Spud-Bar doesn't respond to that at first. They're staring down at Evie quizzically, as if genuinely not quite sure what to make of her.

"Of course it is," they finally say, bowing in a formal greeting. "Evie."

Evie returns the bow. "Spud-Bar."

The armorist laughs. "It's a nickname. I've learned to like it."

"May I ask you a question that's not about steel?"

Spud-Bar's laughter fades, and they look down at Evie with renewed skepticism in their eyes.

"You may, though I won't guarantee any good answer. I stick to my trade, mostly."

"Fair. What happens when this wagon train stops?"

Spud-Bar begins picking up the blades discarded by Evie, dumping them in a basket containing similarly distressed and broken weapons. The task seems almost like a brief escape from answering Evie's question.

When they finally do, there's nothing cordial in Spud-Bar's voice as there was a moment before.

"We'll have reached the Sicclunan front line. You and the rest of this raw meat, none of whom I imagine are lucky enough to *not* have the training you say you *don't*, will join up with the surviving Savages from other companies."

"And then what?"

Spud-Bar reaches between them and gently flicks the edge of the ax in Evie's hand with their fingertips.

"You'll need that ax to be in as fit shape as possible."

RESOLVE IS THE FORGED BLADE
THAT CANNOT BE QUENCHED

"IF THAT TALKING SADDLEBAG THINKS HE CAN CALL MY husband a traitor, fold my Gen, and pay me off like a whore, his mind is as molten as his face!"

Lexi has been raging for three blocks, since they left the Spectrum. Her every step seems to pump pure fire through the rest of her body, leading to reoccurring eruptions between her ears.

Taru hasn't said a word. They've rarely seen Lexi so fiercely dispossessed of composure.

"And that self-righteous ideologue using her backside's spout as her mouth," she thunders on. "If she weren't wearing those robes she'd be scrubbing the Spectrum's stone hide every morning."

Taru frowns, offering comment for the first time. "From what you've described, Te-Gen, Councilwoman Burr *was* thoroughly unsympathetic and even unnecessarily aggressive when addressing the issue, and you in particular."

"She's an Ignoble," Lexi says, as if that one word is explanation enough.

"I'm afraid I . . . am unfamiliar with that term, Te-Gen. I was taught all forms of 'nobility' in Crache were overturned long ago. We have no nobles, of any kind."

"And so they were, and so we do not. Ignobles are the descendants of those ancient houses whose powers were revoked and wealth reallocated during the Renewal, when smarter folk than Burr finally realized how destructive it was, allowing themselves to be ruled by men based solely on whose crotch they were pulled from at birth. Burr's family was one of the richest and most powerful in Crache before that time. They commanded their own armies. For all I know the Spectrum is built on land where their great castle once stood."

"But that was . . . hundreds of years ago. How could she possibly know, yet prove—"

Lexi laughs wryly. "Ignobles became even *more* fanatical about preserving and cataloguing their bloodlines *after* the Renewal. They were all certain it wouldn't last; that the great houses would rise up and take back the realms that became Crache. They all wanted their claims to what their ancestors' lost clear as a morning stream."

"Councilwoman Burr seems to have adapted well enough," Taru observes. "She speaks the words of the state with vigor."

"Her family has learned to play a new game. If they couldn't make themselves useful, they could decide the usefulness of others. I believe she's the third Burr to serve on the Gen Franchise Council."

Taru is genuinely taken aback. "But inheriting title or position is forbidden—"

"The Renewal did many fine things," Lexi says impatiently. "It allowed common families to come together to form Gens. It replaced houses of overfed, underqualified nobles with those Gens. It did not, however, eradicate hypocrisy."

The thoroughfares of the Capitol are narrow, clean, and almost completely free of foot traffic, even at the height of the afternoon in the center of the largest city in the nation. Their streets are the same smooth, waning-moon-colored stone of the Capitol buildings. The sun's rays find not a single chip or scratch in the pavement, and it's said the Capitol streets can never be stained, not even by blood.

A towering column rises at the center of a four-way intersection ahead of them. A caged-in staircase coils around its body, leading to the top of a broad platform encircling the summit. The bottom of the steps opens onto the street below. There's also a freestanding cage resting on the ground, this one with artfully curved bars that have been gilded with gold. The top of the cage is attached to a cable running all the way up above the tower's platform. An Aegin guards its golden door.

"Use the ascendancy, Te-Gen," Taru bids her.

The Aegin spots the Gen broach pinned to the neck of Lexi's wrap. The Gen Franchise Council symbol at the broach's center permits the wearer free access to all city services, and special conveniences for Gen members, such as the ascendancy. The symbol formed along the rim of the broach, surrounded by several other small characters, identifies Lexi as a member of Gen Stalbraid, and notifies merchants of Stalbraid's allotment from the state, which determines how much credit they are to be extended at any one time.

Lexi only shakes her head, striding past him as he prepares to open the gilded door of the private lift for her.

"I like walking," Lexi insists. "I particularly like walking stairs. It forces the blood to pump, which helps me to think. If it weren't unbefitting of my station and too much to ask of my current attire I'd prefer to run the stairs, in fact."

"I understand you're upset, but I've been entrusted with your safety."

"Regardless, it doesn't exactly engender the good will of the citizenry to watch Gen members squeeze our fat asses into a gilded box to be hoisted to the platform whilst they're forced to trudge up endless flights of stairs."

"It is not my place to give words to the character or condition of Te-Gen's ass, but were such words solicited they would give contrary argument."

Lexi laughs, not because Taru is joking, but because every word is meant earnestly.

She gathers the hem of her wrap and begins jogging up the steps,

Taru hoofing it close behind her like a soldier on the march. They encounter only a few pedestrians in the confines of the staircase, and if any of them would've otherwise been possessed of ill intentions, seeing both of Taru's fists white-knuckling the grips of two blades sheathed in well-worn leather is a deterrent pointing truer north than any individual's moral compass.

Unlike the streets below, the circular platform is densely packed. The waiting passengers crowd around the four separate carriage berths. Yellow lines of warning are painted on the platform a foot from each edge, reminding the passengers that the berths are essentially large holes in the platform with five-story falls waiting on the other side.

Thick tracks extend from the center of each berth. Each hundred-foot length is carved from a single gargantuan forest star tree and reinforced with steel. They cast their shadow down on the center of virtually every street in the Capitol. Thick, coiled steel is pulled taut above each line of track, running past the open space of the berth and inside the column of the tower where it spools in massive wheels.

Pullers crew the god's-arm levers attached to those wheels. If a passenger squints along the cable into the darkness of the tower interior they can see sweat pooled on muscled arms carved like granite. Their Gens marry hearty spouses to produce children with the size to become pullers. They spend the early years of those children's lives training their arms and backs to be as solid as the sky carriage cables themselves.

Lexi is content to wait her turn at the edge of the crowd, but urged by Taru and through a combination of almost gentle nudging and even more almost-polite stares, they find themselves standing in front of the yellow line beside the nearest berth.

"You have many talents, my friend," Lexi says to her retainer.

Taru doesn't smile, but for a moment they don't smile with less vehemence.

"My mother often said you are never truly defeated until you give up laughter," Lexi adds.

Speaking the words summons another flood of memories, and her expression becomes somber.

"I regret not making her acquaintance," Taru says.

"She would have adored you. Absolutely adored you. She had a sense of people."

The great cable stretched above the berth in front of them begins grinding and snaking its way back inside the tower. Several minutes later the sky carriage begins to dock, the large rectangular enclosure rolling into the berth on its greased track (watching this, Lexi recalls idly that one of the last conversations she had with Brio was about Gen Adlonn successfully lobbying to receive the sky carriage grease concession, replacing Gen T'han after calling into question the efficacy of the grease they manufactured).

Taru raises one arm behind Lexi, and it might as well be a tree felled across the road to everyone standing behind it. Taru waits until Lexi has boarded the carriage, and then drops their arm and ducks under the short roof of the conveyance.

"Toward the back, Te-Gen, please," Taru bids her.

They guide Lexi to a seat in one of the rear corners of the carriage, where Taru can stand above her and survey the rest of the space and everyone else occupying it.

The rest of the passengers shuffle aboard, filling the pewlike seats lining the carriage rail and filling the middle of its narrow space. Stragglers stand in the aisles, reaching up and gripping loops of strong silk hung from the ceiling for that purpose.

When it is filled to capacity, the cable attached to the street-facing end of the carriage begins reeling it back out of the berth.

Lexi stares over the rail, looking down at the top of the Capitol buildings.

"That business about your knife . . . what did he call it, a hook-end?"

Taru draws in a deep breath, exhaling with their next words.

"By the ports they secure the hulls of newly crafted boats with metal hooks. They are easy to pry loose and sharpen to an edge."

The many implications of that swirl in Lexi's mind, and she turns away from the rail to look up at her retainer.

"When did you fashion your first hook-end?" Lexi asks.

"I was seven years old, Te-Gen."

"And did you ever bloody an Aegin?"

"Aegins are not all bad people. But they are in the Bottoms."

Lexi reaches up and takes Taru's free hand, the one not perpetually grasping the hilt of a blade, in both of hers. Lexi doesn't say anything, and neither does Taru, although they don't attempt to withdraw their hand. Lexi feels the many hardened calluses of swinging a blade every day, even if only in practice. She feels scars, dozens of splits in Taru's knuckles scabbed over with time, the raised remnants of cuts that now feel like thread woven through their skin.

Lexi becomes aware of a connection, and it both breaks her heart and opens her mind's eye. She realizes she can read the entire story of Taru's life with her eyes closed, just by holding their hand, by letting herself feel the tiny monuments erected there, tombstones and effigies carved in Taru's flesh.

It makes Lexi want to weep.

Instead she smiles up at the retainer warmly, squeezing Taru's hand between hers before letting it go and turning back to the rail.

The sky carriage is pulled down one of the Capitol's long main arteries, stopping alongside single platforms perched atop thinner columns at the corner of every third or fourth block. Passengers exit, permitting new ones on.

Lexi turns from the rail to watch a young couple board the carriage arm in arm. They don't belong to a Gen, but judging by the pressed appearance of their clothes they're not meager workers. One thing Lexi can observe for certain is that they are very much in love. Rather than sit, the young man reaches for a silk loop while the girl clings to his body for support during the uneven ride.

Even Taru can read the pain in Lexi's expression and identify its source.

"He did not abandon you, Te-Gen," Taru assures her, resolute. "He would never do that."

Lexi turns her head and stares out the window of the carriage, watching the rooftops roll by like parchment slowly unfurled by weak and withered hands.

"I know that," she says a moment later. "But I almost want to believe he did. None of the alternatives find him in any kind of state I want to imagine."

"I do not like imagining." Taru's distaste is obvious. "I prefer what I know is real, and what lies in front of me."

"Taru, if no one ever imagined anything, none of this would be here. All people would still live in trees."

"Perhaps all people would be better off."

Lexi laughs, shaking her head. "You should've been the pleader and Brio should have been *your* man-at-arms, guarding you with a hook-end."

Outside she watches the center of the Capitol recede and yield to smaller structures, most of them in good repair. There are other houses, however, whose clay walls rot in the afternoon sun that is also slowly searing away their thatched rooftops. They're ruins, the last remnants of a civilization in which hovels backed up against the most opulent of palaces, no middle ground between the nobility and the penniless peasants they used as they used firewood, and treated with less reverence than their horse stock.

Eventually the old houses will be demolished and swept away, replaced like the rest of Crache by unyielding modernity and expansion.

Here there's no trace of the single-block-of-stone construction that makes the Spectrum and its surrounding structures unmatched marvels. Modern builders have tried to replicate the look with paint and deftly concealed seams, but neither the translucent stone nor the methods that built the Spectrum have been seen in more than a thousand years. No one knows when or how they passed into legend, and not even meticulous post-Renewal recordkeeping has ever shed any light on the lost craft.

They say when the Capitol was first constructed horses and horse-drawn carriages filled every street. Now a horse is only seen clopping up or down the narrow pavement when there's an emergency. Sky carriages ferry people and freight goods, leaving the streets uncluttered and clean. Lexi often imagines what those days must've smelled like, before the construction of the aqueduct and sewers, when animals overran the streets.

Like shit, her own voice always answers her.

"Taru," Lexi addresses the retainer, forcing herself to break from her reveries.

"Yes, Te-Gen?"

"Those awful Aegins back at the Spectrum . . . they spoke of the Bottoms and . . . what did you call it? A 'hook-end'?"

"Yes," Taru answers, obviously uncertain where the question is leading.

"Why did you need to arm yourself so? As a child?"

Lexi can't be sure, but she thinks she catches the barest hint of a wry grin tugging at the corner of Taru's mouth.

"Forgive me, Te-Gen, but you have never been to the Bottoms yourself, have you?"

"No. Brio never wanted me to accompany the two of you."

Taru nods without further comment.

"I take it had I visited the Bottoms I wouldn't asks such questions?" Lexi presses.

"It might have . . . clarified things," Taru admits.

"I know you accompanied him for a reason," Lexi says, almost defensively. "I know it's not like the rest of the city. I've met people from there. You're from there. I don't fear you."

"I've been cultured and educated since," Taru reminds her.

"Of course. I suppose I never wanted to believe being poor makes one dangerous."

"It doesn't. Being a person does. People are just animals like any other, Te-Gen. In the Bottoms they simply do not hide their teeth like in the rest of the Capitol."

Lexi has no answer for that. She falls silent, and that seems to satisfy Taru, who clearly considers the issue settled.

"Taru?" Lexi says a moment later.

"Yes, Te-Gen?"

"Take me there."

Taru looks down at her in surprise. "Where, Te-Gen?"

"The Bottoms."

Taru obviously wasn't expecting that. "What in the Bottoms do you wish to see, Te-Gen?"

"I simply . . . I want to see how people there live. People like the child you were when you grew up there."

Taru's surprised expression is replaced by alarm. "Te-Gen, Brio would not—"

"Brio isn't here," Lexi reminds them gently. "I am. Take me to the Bottoms. I do not need a full tour. I only wish to meet some of the people Brio tries to help. I want to see them."

Taru's lips tighten until they all but disappear into their mouth.

"I'll be perfectly safe," Lexi says. "I have you. And your hook-end."

The retainer exhales through their nostrils. It's an exasperated sound.

Lexi stares up at them expectantly.

Finally, Taru says, "Very well, Te-Gen. I will take you."

THE DEAD WHO REVEL IN LIFE

IT'S NOT A FEAST; IT'S THE LAST PARTY BEFORE THE END OF the world.

Oh, there's plenty of food, more of it and better than anyone conscripted to the Savages has seen in weeks. The buttery scent of fresh rice is steaming into the canvas walls of the tent from giant bamboo bowls. Bitter melon and winegrass are both in season, and have been prepared in everything from luscious soups to cabbage cups, and mixed with cooked meat and roots. Spits with three hearty pigs skewered abreast are roasting over open flames in the kitchen. A new one makes its way to the feasting tables every few minutes, garnished with slices of fried taro.

It's the best meal most of them will ever eat, because it's the last meal most of them will ever eat.

That's why this is no feast. To feast is to celebrate, and the Savages have nothing to celebrate. They have only a moment, one in which to revel in the comforts of the flesh and the illusory freedom those comforts deliver unto the mind. As far as any of them can know, this is the only moment they'll ever have, and given a trough by the keepers of their pen they'll choose to wallow until they wear themselves into oblivion.

Evie enters the makeshift tent hall on Spud-Bar's flank. Their caravan arrived in camp only a few hours before, at which point Laython relayed the bad news: The Sicclunan army was massing less than three miles away, and in the morning when the Skrain arrived they'd all meet in battle.

Three seconds after walking in Evie ducks to avoid the arc of a knife spinning through the air. She hears the dull protest of wood stuck by steel and looks to see the blade of the knife buried in a crudely fashioned target nailed to an equally crude stake. There's half a piece of taro clinging to the exposed edge of the blade, and Evie realizes she isn't the only one who was forced to dodge the knife; an emaciated young man with a stringy beard stands up in front of the target, wiping remnants of taro from his forehead where the intact root was perched before the knife struck it.

The scraggly kid laughs, as does the woman who threw the knife. Evie looks over to see her standing with a group of blade-wielding Savages waiting their turn to throw.

Evie scowls, but before she can say anything Spud-Bar grips her lightly by the forearm and drags her along, leading her toward the center of the tent where rows of feasting tables have been arranged.

"Point your toes down," Spud-Bar advises her. "The Revel don't kill near as many as the battle, but it takes its share."

Evie nods, though in truth she's barely listening. Her senses are overwhelmed in that moment.

It's an impossible sight to take in all at once. Savages fill their mouths with fermented alcohol and spit at torches to create balls of flame. A frantic chorus of flutes and strings fill one corner of the tent hall like drunken banshees. There are the small groups engaged in games with high maiming potential, like the knife-throwing contingent. Blades seem to be a primary source of entertainment for Savages, in fact. Not three feet from where Evie stands, two surly women are stabbing the tip of daggers between their splayed-atop-the-table fingers, attempting to complete the sequence faster than the other while half a dozen men and women goad them on, betting on the outcome.

On the other side of the tent, thick curtains hide a quarter of the

Revel's space. From the other side Evie can hear moans and even jubilant screams. Solving their mystery is far from complicated, even for a new arrival like her. Young, supple men and women saunter among the tables full of Savages. They wear delicate chiffon, what little of it there is, and serve neither food nor drink. Some proposition, others merely wait and present and smile. Some Savages claim them for company at the feasting table while others haul them, sometimes over their shoulders, past the pleasure curtain.

Amidst the fire and music and flashes of steel and flesh on display, one sight does cut through the chaos. Evie first takes notice of the serving girl as she ferries flagons of rice wine and small cups between tables. She's one of several dozen, clad in peasant's wool and utterly unremarkable in every way, save one: Her eyes flash a deep purple in the light of the Revel torches, a color like that of dying violets.

Neither violets nor eyes of their color are often found in Crachian cities.

More than any of that, however, Evie sees something reflective in the girl, who can be only a year or two younger than her. The other servers have their eyes and their heads firmly mired in their task. You can see them anchored by it, keeping them grounded in a menial existence. The serving girl with the eyes like dying violets, however, is constantly looking beyond the simple actions of her hands and arms.

She's more than she appears, or at least something different than she appears.

While it may go unnoticed by every other Savage, it's an easy thing for Evie to recognize.

"Stake yourself a spot," Spud-Bar bids her, straddling the end of one of the benches lining a feasting table.

Evie slides onto the bench on the other side of the table, reaching for two empty cups and a wine flagon.

"They do this before every battle?" she asks Spud-Bar, filling a cup for both of them.

"Every one. It's what passes for mercy in the Savage Legion. It's just about the only mercy."

"Our taskers aren't worried all this wine and humping like rabbits will dull their 'Savages' on the field?"

"As long as they can stand they'll serve their purpose. And if they can't you'll watch 'em hurled at the Sicclunan front line like rocks. The taskers and whoever thought this whole machine up, they know their business."

Evie accepts this, and though questions still form in her mind she leaves them unspoken for now.

"I can't believe any of us will live past tomorrow, not from what I've seen. What I see."

Spud-Bar throws back the entire cup of wine, ending it with a single gulp.

"It's the rare blade that goes unchipped round here, to be sure," they admit. "But many will live. Many have lived far past one battle."

"Oh? Like who?"

Spud-Bar waves their cup above their heads, motioning behind Evie, who turns to look.

They sit apart from the others, around a table on a raised platform almost like a small stage. The loudest one is a stout man who must remember his fiftieth year with an increasing haze, with a great barrel of a torso and the legs required to prop it up. His mouth is more mustache than lips, and he both laughs and speaks with just the right corner of his mouth, as if the other side is paralyzed. He's bouncing one of the chiffon-draped young men on his knee, urging him to drink from the mustached one's cup.

Seated beside him is a squat, ugly woman with tawny hair cut into the shape of a bowl. She's laughing like an ass brays while cradling another one of the sculpted young men in her lap. The first thing Evie notices about her is that she's missing her left hand. The stump has been fastened off with leather straps. Four slim dagger blades and one the size of a stiletto simulate the five fingers she's lost. It's obviously meant to be a joke, though Evie has no doubt it's one that's turned lethal more than once, especially judging from the dried, crusty dark flecks still clinging to the edges of most of the blades.

The only one of them seemingly uninterested in the provided companionship is hunched over the end of the table, cradling a pint cup made of bone. He's almost the size of the mustached one. The large, scarred arms that stretch from the sleeveless holes of the cloak he wears speak of time spent pulling sky carriages or loading ships at the port. Long tendrils of string curls fall from beneath the cloak's hood. The only other feature Evie can discern is a bulbous nose and chin, as if they were features glued onto a comical puppet fashioned from sack.

"Who are they?" Evie asks.

"The closest thing the Savage Legion has to generals, I suppose," Spud-Bar informs her. "We call them the Elder Company. That's three of 'em sittin' there, anyway. There are others scattered along the front with other Skrain companies and their Legionnaires. Every one of the Elders has seen twenty battles or more."

At first Evie isn't convinced she heard the number spoken by Spud-Bar, but she also has no reason to doubt the armorist.

"And they survived? Twenty battles under these conditions?"

"Some more than others, and by their own means. The woman, Mother Manai, celebrated her twentieth by having that hand chopped off. Though you might argue it's just made her nastier and more dangerous. The quiet one is called Bam. He may seem like a little child could shove 'im from his stool, but on the field he's like a one-warrior battery.

"Now, the one with the mustache you could sweep out temple steps with . . . that is Lariat. He's not much with a sword, but his fists can break down bamboo walls. He was a skin-on-skin fighter before he came to us, brawling in alleys for prize and the like. Tomorrow'll be his thirty-second battle as a Savage."

Evie's stare sharpens on him as she tries to imagine such a feat.

"So then, just sixty-eight more battles and Lariat can go home to his family, yes?"

Spud-Bar's lips tighten against the rim of the wine cup, but the reaction is brief and quickly suppressed.

"That's the decree" is all they say.

"And what about you, Spud-Bar? When do you get to go home?"

"My sentence was commuted from one hundred battles to serving as the Savages' armorist for ten years."

"And how many years have you been here?"

"Fifteen," Spud-Bar says without the slightest hesitation or trace of rancor.

Evie nearly chokes on her wine.

"Don't you think you should inform someone about the oversight?"

Spud-Bar shakes their head. "It's no oversight."

"Then . . . no one leaves. Not really."

"We all leave. Eventually. Just not the way we'd hope."

Evie suddenly doesn't feel like drinking, let alone partaking in the mirthful madness exploding all around her.

She's not the only Savage attending the Revel who isn't here to party. Evie spots several of the older people alongside whom she was indoctrinated. They've joined a larger group of the elderly and infirm at one of the other feasting tables. They all sit in silence, morose, eating little of what's in front of them. Several look like they've been weeping.

Evie stops drinking, trying to imagine that group with melee weapons in their hands, screaming war cries filled with rage and blood as they charge the shields and spears and axes of the Sicclunan front line. It's the most absurd picture in her head, one that would inspire laughter were it not for the picture that follows, the one of piled-up wrinkled limbs and severed heads with shocked, twisted expressions on their withered faces.

Spud-Bar not only takes note of Evie watching them, they can obviously read her thoughts.

"Don't look at 'em in pity," Spud-Bar instructs Evie. "Doesn't do no good, for you or them. Instead you gotta take 'em for what they are."

"And what's that?"

"A warning."

Evie finally looks away from the doomed gathering around that table, searching Spud-Bar's face for some kind of deeper meaning. "What're they warning me about?"

"Getting old. Don't do it. It never ends well, no matter what happens."

Evie doesn't believe that, chooses not to believe it, but she also can't fault someone like Spud-Bar for arriving at such a conclusion. Evie can't know how many such groups of helpless, frail, and doomed individuals they've watched suffer through the Revel, but she doesn't imagine the number is small.

"Shut the fuck up!" Laython barks over a score of conversation that have congealed into one unintelligible organism.

The Savage assemblage quiets.

All save the old-timers.

Laython ignores their continued chatter.

"The life of a Savage is eating, fucking, and fighting. Fighting is for tomorrow. Tonight you live the first two to their fullest. Because for most of you, all that's left is the fight. There's no coming out the other side. Not as the breathing, bleeding, shitting sacks of meat you are now, anyway. Whatever afterlife does or doesn't await you, let's make a pact here and now: There will never be a night to rival this one. This is when you revel. Tomorrow is when you die!"

Most of them cheer, because it's clear from the timbre of Laython's voice that this is the moment for cheering.

Evie just stares up at him, then at the faces of the men and women around her, certain she must've heard different words than all of them did over the last few moments.

"Believe it or not," Spud-Bar remarks, "he's sharpened that speech to a razor's edge from what it was years past."

Evie can only shake her head.

As Spud-Bar pours them both another round, Evie continues to take in the sights and sounds of the Revel. A few tables down she spots another figure who stands apart from the crowd, this one a Savage, though he looks more like a valet for some highly regarded Gen. His shoulder-length hair, dark with just a few threads of gray, is meticulously kempt and combed back. He's tall and willowy and fragile-looking, as if she could knock him over with the rough jab of a single fingertip. Unlike the older ones, however, he doesn't appear to be afraid, or even maudlin.

If anything, he looks full of disdain.

"Excuse me for a moment, would you?" she says to Spud-Bar.

"I'll save you some food."

Evie snatches up the nearest unattended cup still cradling wine and rises from the bench. She walks over to the willowy one's table.

"Not into celebrating our inevitable deaths?" she asks.

His expression remains unchanged. "They aren't celebrating death here, they're celebrating life, in their own crude way."

"Then why aren't you partaking?"

"This is not life."

Evie nods, offering him the cup. "That's a notion I'd drink to."

He looks down at the wine. "I . . . appreciate the gesture. I do. But I don't drink."

"Fair enough."

One of the Elder Company, Mother Manai, shouts across the hall at them: "Is school in session, then, Professor?"

The rest of the old-timers and their coterie share a round of laughter.

Evie watches them, and then looks back at the willowy man speculatively.

"Professor?" she asks.

"Their invention," he explains. "My war name, I suppose. I *was* a teacher, once."

"Where?"

"At the University in the Third City. I belonged to a Gen of respected educators that stretches back all the way to the Renewal."

"What did you do to be sent here?"

"I asked my students questions."

"Isn't that a teacher's job?"

"I asked them the *wrong* questions," the Professor says. "According to our illustrious Nation State, at least."

A golden-skinned boy of perhaps eighteen approaches them both then, amber chiffon wrapped around his waist and barely touching the middle of his thighs. He tilts his head, smiling silently, eyes drifting between the two of them.

Evie can't help but grin back, although she's far more interested in the Professor in that moment. He seems deeply uncomfortable, averting his eyes from them both. She can see his face flush.

"I think we'll finish our conversation," Evie informs the boy, who takes the hint and saunters away.

"You really don't partake, do you?" she asks the Professor.

"I prefer an unclouded head," he answers stiffly.

"So tell me, what questions did you ask them? Your students?"

"What do you know of Crachian history?"

Evie shrugs. "I wasn't the best student of the subject, I admit. I know about the Renewal, the chaos of blood feuds and nobility that came before. The serenity and efficiency that replaced it."

"Do you? Can you recite names? Dates? Specific incidents that marked the downfall of the noble houses?"

Evie shakes her head. "Like I said, I wasn't the best student."

"You're as informed as any, I assure you. No such history is taught, at any level, in any Crachian house of supposed learning. You're taught only what the Nation State wishes you to know, and what it wishes you to know is its way is right and just and the only way."

"And you're telling me for asking questions about ancient history, you were sent here?"

The Professor nods. "History, and the war we'll be fighting tomorrow that's scarcely mentioned within two hundred miles of the Capitol."

"Crache has enemies, like any great nation."

"Does it? Or does it make enemies? Is it protecting its borders, or expanding them?"

Evie is no longer grinning, no longer playful in her questioning. She's as intrigued as she's been since waking up on a wagon with the Capitol at her back.

"Imagine if you can," the Professor continues, "that Crache and all its wonders, all its egalitarianism, is built on what it's taken from others, what it has weaponized its least desirable citizens to help take from others."

"You asked your students these questions?"

"I did."

"And for that and that alone you're here now."

"I am."

"In a place the taskers swear is reserved for killers, rapists, and the condemned alone."

"Does any of that describe you?"

"No. But mistakes are made. Acts taken out of desperation."

"That's true. And yet here we both are."

Evie nods. "Here we both are."

Over the shoulder of the Professor, Evie spies the serving girl with the dying violet eyes leaving the tent hall, not through the main entrance, not through the slit for the servers, and not even through the pleasure curtain, but through a smaller opening far removed from the others and the crowd.

It should be a wholly innocuous sight, just like that of the girl as Evie first saw her.

Yet Evie feels a spike in her blood, a wave of warning that spreads to every part of her.

She looks back at the Professor. "Thank you for talking with me. It's been . . . enlightening."

"You're a better student than you credit yourself," he tells her.

That restores the grin to Evie's face, even if only for a moment.

She leaves the Professor and walks away from the feasting tables, finding the same parting in the tent through which the serving girl disappeared.

A moment later Evie emerges outside. It's quiet, dark, and deserted, save for the noise from inside the tent and the exaggerated shadows dancing on its walls. Evie casts her gaze about, searching for the girl, but she's gone.

Several yards away from the tent hall a pile of stones forms a small dome atop the earth. Evie jogs over to it. Steps descend below the surface of the grassy terrain, leading to a single wooden door that's open, just a crack. She slips down the short steps without a sound, peering through the opening in the doorway.

A single amber candle flame lights the room inside, as well as pale moon rays allowed entrance by a tiny window in the stones just above the surface of the ground. It's a wine cellar, barrels and casks stacked atop one another in tight quarters.

Evie watches the serving girl dip a hand down the front of her dress and close her fist around the handle of a punch dagger she's concealed there. The blade is no bigger than a badger's tongue, but a razor edge catches the candlelight. The serving girl jabs down into the top of one of the barrels, twisting the tip of the blade to create a tiny hole in the wood.

It is then that Evie sees the object held in the serving girl's opposite hand; a small uncorked vial filled with a liquid as dark as pure anise extract.

Treating the vial as if she's pinched the neck of a poisonous snake just below its head, the purple-eyed girl carefully tilts it above the almost imperceptible hole she's made in the top of the barrel. She allows just one drop to escape. It falls through the pinhole at a perfect angle, not even so much as staining its edges.

Evie widens the crack in the doorway just enough to allow her slender frame to slip through.

Then she slams the door shut behind her.

Those dying violet eyes find her like the lash of a whip. The girl's body tenses, her fist raising the punch dagger while her other hand corks the vial and places it carefully atop the barrel.

"I don't think you'll be able to roll that entire barrel back to the Revel alone," Evie says.

"I'm stronger than I look," the girl assures her in an even tone.

Evie grins. "I certainly hope so."

The girl quickly turns away from the barrel so that she's facing Evie. Her dagger-wielding fist flies, attempting to drive the blade through Evie's throat.

Evie ducks easily under the girl's arm and steps closer against her. Their bodies are now less than a few inches from each other. To any casual, untrained observer what follows would look like nothing more than playful struggling between them. It would take an expert in hand-to-hand combat to recognize the skilled feints, blocks, and strikes being traded and countered by both women.

Evie is no longer fighting like a drunken vagrant lashing out in a brawl.

And her opponent definitely does not fight like a peasant serving girl.

Dodging an attempt to pierce her liver, Evie coils her arm around the girl's, trapping it. Evie twists at the waist with surprising power, extending her right leg and pulling the serving girl over it, throwing her off-balance. Evie seizes the opportunity to drive her shoulder into the woman's chest and force her into the wall of the cellar.

Evie presses her there, shoving the wrist of her opponent's knife hand against the serving girl's chest. The weight of Evie's forearm traps it there, the tip of the punch dagger's blade now angled directly beneath its owner's chin. The serving girl tilts her head back against the wall to prevent her flesh being punctured.

The fight is over, for the moment at least.

"Who are you?" the serving girl asks Evie, breathless. "*What* are you?"

Evie grins, exhilarated despite the brief life-or-death struggle. "Someone and something very much like you, looks like."

The woman's eyes darken. "You're an agent of the Protectorate Ministry, aren't you?"

Her body tenses as if she's preparing to renew the struggle, until Evie shakes her head emphatically.

"No," Evie assures her. "No, I don't work for the state. I'm just here to find a friend, one I believe people like those in the Protectorate Ministry put here very much against his will, and very much against Crachian law."

The girl practically spits. "Laws in Crache bend like cheap blades. They're meaningless."

Evie can hear the raw emotion in her voice.

"You're Sicclunan," she says.

It's not a question.

The woman nods.

"A soldier?" Evie asks, and then shakes her head. "No, you're too good. And you're too self-righteous to be a hired assassin. Siccluna has its own Protectorate Ministry, I imagine."

"We are *nothing* like you."

"Close enough, by my reckoning."

Evie falls silent, thinking.

"I understand your mission here," she says. "I really do. I can even appreciate it. But I can't let you kill all these people—"

"They're not people, they're Savages! They're the weapons you've used and will use to destroy my people!"

"They may be used as weapons against your country tomorrow, but tonight they're just people. None of them chose this, and many of them don't even deserve to be here, it seems. So I repeat, I will not let you kill these people."

"You know what they'll do to me if you alert them. You know what they'll *allow* your new brothers and sisters to do to me."

Evie nods.

The Sicclunan agent drops her chin, pressing the flesh of her neck into the tip of the punch dagger until a droplet of blood forms, becoming a thin trail that runs down the center of the blade.

"Then your choices are considerably narrowed," she says to Evie.

"I don't want your life, either."

Evie curls her fingers around the woman's fist and deftly pries the punch dagger's handle loose. She grips the weapon between her own knuckles, holding it half an inch from the gently throbbing vein in the woman's neck.

Evie juts her head in the direction of the cellar window. "You go out through there. Now. This mission you've failed. There'll be others."

She sees the resistance in the Sicclunan's otherworldly eyes. Evie can almost hear the other woman's blood rising in violent waves, calling to her to act, to kill this interloper and complete her mission.

Evie's fist tightens around the handle of the punch dagger.

"Tell me your name," she commands.

The woman hesitates, but something in Evie's eyes persuades her.

"Sirach."

Evie nods. "Sirach. You can die trying in vain to complete your mission today, or you can live to kill Savages and Skrain tomorrow. Choose."

In the end, even Sirach must see it's no choice at all. Her body relaxes and her fingers splay in supplication.

She nods, stiffly.

Evie slowly and cautiously backs away from her.

Sirach reaches up and thumbs the blood from her small neck wound. She rubs it with her forefinger while regarding Evie.

"You should come fight for us," she says.

Evie stops just short of laughing out loud. "I'll take that as high praise, but unfortunately I've made other commitments. Lifelong commitments. You'll understand."

"Not really" are the last words Sirach says to her.

Evie watches her disappear through the window without a sound, just another shadow living in seconds and small expanses out there in the night. When she's gone, Evie kneels and carefully tucks her newly acquired punch dagger inside the top of her boot, draping the hem of her stained, threadbare trousers around it.

Rising, she walks over to the poisoned barrel, picking up the vial where Sirach laid it down. Evie doesn't make the mistake or sniffing at or otherwise trying to identify the poison inside; it doesn't matter what it is. She drops the vial and crushes it with the toe of her boot, grinding glass and viscous liquid into the wooden boards of the cellar floor.

Evie reaches up and dabs a finger at the almost imperceptible hole in the top of the barrel. She runs her hand around its hammer-forged iron rim for a moment and then grips an edge. She brings her right foot back several feet and kicks clean through two boards at the base of the barrel. She quickly retracts her foot to avoid the tidal rush of wine.

Evie watches the barrel bleed its fermented blood across the cellar floor, draining to almost the final drop. She feels a brief stab of sympathy for the rats that will no doubt venture out from the walls and be found dead on the cellar floor in the morning.

She only hopes a few rodent corpses aren't enough to raise suspicion. Evie slips out of the wine cellar with the same stealth she used to survey its interior. In less than a minute she's rejoined the Revel without turning a single head her way.

She finds her seat across from Spud-Bar awaiting her, along with a bowl of rice and a small plate with several cabbage cups on it.

"Thank you," Evie says.

Spud-Bar, halfway through a bowl of sweet-smelling broth, nods.

"Saw you chattin' with the Professor before. I'd counsel you against that."

"Why's that? Too much truth there?"

Spud-Bar looks up from their bowl, genuinely baffled.

"Truth?"

"I just mean—"

"You do as you like. But of all the types here, that's the one I'd tell you to ride clear of."

Evie doesn't know what to say to that, and so she doesn't.

They eat.

A high, agonized scream cuts through the idle chatter and off-key music a moment later.

It belongs to a voice on the other side of the pleasure curtain, and there's no mistaking the bloodcurdling pain in it.

Evie springs from her seat, largely on instinct, and she's one of the first to reach the curtain, tearing it back and stepping inside, bodies quickly crowding around hers as they flock to do the same.

There's a small common area on the other side composed of a plush rug, mounds of pillows, and a few wine-stained tables. The rest of the space is smaller, private curtained-off stalls.

They're standing in the middle of the common area. The Professor, his back half turned to them, is embracing the young man who flirted with him and Evie earlier in the evening. She thinks they're dancing drunkenly at first, and then the Professor turns their bodies toward her and she sees the blade of the carving knife he's half buried in the boy's throat.

The shock is enough to momentarily paralyze even Evie. She simply can't process what she's seeing, not after the moment she shared with this same man not an hour ago.

"Lecherous *whore!*" the Professor growls through a clenched jaw, and opens the boy's throat half a foot across.

In the next moment the boy's slight, bare chest is awash in his own blood. The Professor lets his victim's body slump to the floor at his feet.

"There!" he yells at the boy's motionless form, waving the carving knife with abandon. "Is that what you want? Did you get what you wanted?"

Laython nearly bowls Evie over as he crashes through the crowd. The towering taskmaster of the Savages barrels down on the Professor without hesitation, easily avoiding the wild swipes of the man's knife hand. Laython ducks behind the Professor and clamps him in a vise-like grip, restraining the Professor's arms and controlling him by the back of his head and neck.

Laython flings the man to the ground with his full weight atop the Professor, immobilizing him, though he continues to struggle in vain.

Behind them, half naked and totally naked Savages and sex workers have abandoned their coupling and private stalls to investigate the commotion.

"Why must they come to me?" the Professor demands in a voice Evie doesn't recognize, the hysterical shrieking voice of a madman. "Why must they *always* come to me for it? I did not ask for this! I *never* asked for any of it! I only give them what they want! I only ever gave them what they begged me for, I tell you!"

He ceases struggling then and begins sobbing, like a child. He does his best under Laython's mass to pull his knees into his abdomen, attempting to curl up as he continues to wail.

Laython doesn't even loosen his grip.

Two of the Skrain soldiers push their way through the gathered crowd a moment later. Only then does Laython relinquish his hold on the now broken man contorted into a damp ball on the floor. The Skrain lift him easily with one hand apiece and carry him back through the curtains.

Hands resting against his torso high above his waist, Laython looks down with stormy, disturbed eyes on the bled boy.

It's the first wholly human emotion Evie has seen express itself on the man's face.

Evie turns, finding Spud-Bar standing a shoulder's length away.

"What . . ." Evie's mind is still reeling. She has to shut her eyes tight to focus through it. "What just happened?"

"Why do you think he's here?" Spud-Bar asks her. "The Professor?"

"He said . . . he told me the state accused him of subverting his students."

Spud-Bar snorts. "More like eviscerating his students. Five of 'em, that's how many he killed, mostly young fawns with schoolgirl crushes on 'im. Seems any time a pretty young thing turned that kind of eye on 'im something inside that man broke apart and couldn't come back together as long as the beholder in question was alive."

"But that's . . . how is that possible? I mean, I never heard anything about any murders at a Crachian university—"

Spud-Bar laughs, but there's no levity to it, nothing mirthful or genuine.

"My dove, if we don't exist anymore, you and I and the rest of this bunch, why do you imagine there's anything Crache can't hide from its people? Especially when whatever or whoever it is goes against the idea that we're living in a peaceful paradise?"

"I just thought . . . I thought I was getting a handle on all this," she says. "The Professor . . . whatever or whoever he is . . . he was making sense."

"I'm sure he was," Spud-Bar says gently, as if speaking to a small child. "Now, come on. Your food is gettin' cold, if someone hasn't already swiped it."

Again, Spud-Bar carefully takes Evie's arm and urges her away from the curtain, back to their seats at the end of the feasting table. Evie settles there, staring at a half-eaten cabbage cup with absolutely no appetite.

"What will they do with him?" Evie asks. "The Professor, I mean?"

Spud-Bar shrugs, slurping the rest of their soup without complaint. "They'll let him fight tomorrow. Probably load 'im into a suicide tumbler. If he doesn't die, then they'll execute him tomorrow night. Rules is rules. Savages can't be killin' folks off the field."

"Right," Evie says, thinking about the lives she's saved this evening, including and especially the Professor's. "Where would we be without rules, after all?"

SHAHEEN

LEXI HAS NEVER TRULY EXPERIENCED HUNGER, NOR SEEN ITS effects up close. She doesn't understand why the little girl's belly is so bloated if it's empty.

"This is what happens when one is starved, Te Gen," Taru explains gently, and only for Lexi's ear. "I imagine it is much like feeling warm though one is freezing to death."

Lexi is speechless.

The child can be no more than four or five years old. Her name is Char and her mother tells them she hasn't been able to feed the girl in four days. Char's mother cradles her under the hole-pocked eave of a disused building in the Bottoms. Like many of the abandoned buildings here, the wall of this one is marked by red paint with a symbol that designates that the Capitol is going to repair and reuse the structure for a new purpose. Taru has already explained to Lexi that this rarely occurs, and many of these old buildings have stood empty for years. Despite that fact, Aegins who patrol the Bottoms are instructed to keep the insides of every marked structure clear of vagrants. They perform regular sweeps, and anyone found squatting is often violently beaten from the buildings, while others are even arrested, and some never seen again.

Taru escorted Lexi from the gleaming, bustling veneer of the Capitol into the portside shadows of the Bottoms. It didn't take long for the pair to come upon the young woman and her daughter, both wrapped in filthy rags. The girl's mother looked up at them briefly with unafraid yet defeated eyes before returning her gaze and attention to her daughter. She was attempting to soothe the barely conscious girl, who awoke to convulse painfully every few moments.

Lexi managed to ask the girl's name before the full import of the scene truly struck her. Char's mother had told them in a whisper without looking up from the girl.

The color has been drained from Lexi's face. She removes the Gen Stalbraid pin from the breast of her wrap and practically shoves it into Taru's gloved hand.

"Go to the nearest steamer's and bring back as much rice as they will give you," she instructs her retainer.

"Te-Gen, I cannot leave you unattended—"

"Go!" Lexi orders them. "Now! I will be fine."

Taru hesitates for a moment longer, but the steel and fury in Lexi's gaze is undeniable, even to the hardened retainer.

"There is a shop just past the edge of the Bottoms," Taru informs Lexi. "I will only be a few moments."

Lexi watches them turn and quickly tromp away with the determination of a soldier double-timing it on a march. She gathers the flowing portion of her wrap and slowly crouches until her eyes meet the level of the woman's.

"What is your name?" Lexi asks the young mother.

"Does it matter?" she whispers back, raggedly, still ignoring Lexi with her gaze.

"It does to me," Lexi assures her.

"Shaheen."

"My name is Lexi, Shaheen. May I ask, do you have any family?"

Shaheen's voice becomes hoarse. "Just her," she says of the girl in her arms.

"Were you born here, in the Bottoms?"

Shaheen shakes her head. "I was a scullery maid for Gen Vang.

They put me out after . . . after she was born. No other Gen would take me in to serve them. I had no way to leave the Capitol."

Lexi suspects the child's origins are an entirely other and more disturbing tale, but she doesn't press the young woman.

Taru returns in impressive time with a small bamboo bowl, the rice piled within it releasing tantalizing steam into the alley.

Taru kneels and offers the bowl to Shaheen. "Feed her very small bits at first," the retainer instructs her. "You will make her worse otherwise."

Shaheen accepts the rice with a surprised expression on her face. She seems to really look at the pair of them for the first time.

"Thank you," she says quietly.

Lexi looks down at the small bowl, then moves her gaze to Taru.

"The steamer said if I wanted more than a single meal you will need to submit an official request for catering," the retainer informs her.

Lexi frowns heavily.

To Shaheen, she says, "I will return tomorrow with more food for you and your daughter. All right?"

She can see clearly from the noncommittal way Shaheen nods that the young woman doesn't believe her, and somehow that only heightens every ill emotion Lexi is feeling.

Taru stands and waits. A moment later Lexi slowly rises and turns away from Shaheen and Char.

"Te-Gen," the retainer begins carefully, "I appreciate how you feel, but this is a dangerous proposition. There are countless families here like this woman and her child, and Gen Stalbraid does not possess the food allotment to feed even a small number of them."

"Then we will do what we can for as many as we can," Lexi proclaims resolutely.

Taru frowns. "It could cause a riot if we try to disperse small amounts of food—"

"Being unable to solve a problem in its totality is not a reason to do nothing."

"Very well, Te-Gen."

They walk away slowly, and in silence. The mixture of confusion, anger, and sorrow is practically radiating from Lexi's every pore. She stares straight ahead, seeing nothing, lost in her own dark thoughts.

Taru waits as long as they can contain themselves.

"Forgive me, Te-Gen, but are you truly so surprised? Did Brio never share with you the condition of the people here?"

"He told me they were forgotten by the Capitol and Crache, but I never . . . I simply didn't understand what that means, I suppose. Perhaps I would not allow myself to understand."

Taru only nods.

"I should have insisted on coming with Brio," Lexi says, obviously speaking more to herself than anyone else. "I should have done . . . *something* to help—"

"Te-Gen, you helped Brio. You served as you were trained to serve. Like any of us."

Lexi is shaking her head before Taru has even finished speaking. "It's no excuse. No excuse at all."

Taru frowns, deepening the perpetual lines in their face cultivated by their usually stern expression. "I should not have brought you here—"

"Yes, you should!" Lexi snaps at them, looking up at the towering retainer, her brow even more troubled. "You most certainly should have."

Lexi returns briefly to her silent, contemplative staring.

Then, "How does this happen, Taru? How can this place exist? How can these people be allowed to live like this? Here, in the Capitol of all places? How can the rest of the city and its people thrive while these people have nothing? At every state function we praise our glorious nation and how we live free of things like hunger and poverty and violence. How can such a lie live?"

"Brio knows more about the history of the Bottoms than me, and I was born here," Taru informs her wryly. "Apparently at the tail end of the Renewal, the newly formed Protectorate Ministry oversaw all the . . .

unwanted residents of the Capitol herded like pack animals into this area of the city. Brio imagined it was to be a temporary measure, simply to allow the state to clean up the Capitol. Yet here they remained, and their children's children and so forth inherited their burdens. As long as they remain out of sight and do not stain the rest of the city or its citizens, there is no reason for Crache to deal with them."

"I understand Brio's frustration now," Lexi says thoughtfully. "His restlessness and what became his crusade. When he complained that no one in the Spectrum listened to him, or wanted to help him, or grant him the requests made for aid for the Bottoms."

"He has always done what he could as their pleader," Taru insists. "As did his father. He argued for what little he could to help the people here."

"I simply cannot accept that with all we have, Crache cannot cure this ill."

"Brio began to suspect this place was actually being used as a resource by the state, like everything else in Crache. Raids and arrests by Aegins increased. Many people spoke of their friends and loved ones disappearing in the night. That was what sparked his . . . investigation."

Lexi's aspect is imbued with a new darkness. "Of course. People no one in a position of power cares about, or even acknowledges, can be used by the corrupt in all manner of despicable ways, I suppose."

"Yes, Te-Gen, they can."

Lexi stops walking. She inhales deeply and exhales a long, trembling breath. Her gaze turns upward, to the sky beyond the tops of the buildings.

Taru watches her, unsure. "What is it, Te-Gen?"

When Lexi turns her eyes to the retainer, those eyes are filled with a new resolve.

"I told myself my job was only to preserve our Gen until Brio returned. All that mattered was finding him and bringing him home. Gen Stalbraid was an afterthought held against that."

"He's your husband, Te-Gen. Of course you—"

"We will find him. I refuse to believe otherwise. However, I will not simply preserve Gen Stalbraid's existence. These people . . . this place . . . they need us *now*. No one else will even try to help them."

Taru doesn't respond at first. They are looking down at Lexi with a thoroughly uncustomary expression of surprise.

"That is true," the retainer says.

"The Franchise Council will not stop us from pleading for the Bottoms, and we *will* return tomorrow, as I told that girl," Lexi insists.

Taru nods. "Yes, Te-Gen. As you wish."

"Good. Now follow me."

Lexi begins walking again, striding forward with new purpose.

Taru rushes to catch up. "Where do you wish to go now, Te-Gen?"

"To the steamer's," Lexi says. "To formally request catering."

THE FIRST WEAPON WAS
A STORY TOLD BY LIARS

"I'M DONE WITH THIS, TAKE IT BACK TO THE ARCHIVES."

Dyeawan thinks the man's name is Yilik, though she's not certain. She's delivered to him only once or twice, but it was enough for her to understand there's no malice in his curtness. He just seems perpetually preoccupied and oblivious to anything that isn't vibrantly colored oil with which he can paint parchment or canvas.

From what she's seen, he must be one of the finest artists on the drafting level, where the ideas, designs, and inventions of Edger and his kind are given their first real form. It's also where the Planning Cadre's architects create plans for new buildings and edifices to be erected in the Capitol. Yilik's drafting room is covered in hand-painted images representing all these things, and each one, to Dyeawan's eyes, is a masterpiece of color and form.

As he hands her what looks and feels like a tablet wrapped in oiled cloth, Dyeawan spies the painting on which Yilik (if that is indeed his name) is currently working.

It appears to be a new gated archway intended for the port. The ships and ocean have been intricately painted in behind it. The archway itself is composed of colorful koi fish of different patterns, all swimming upstream against an overwhelming current. It's a very Crachian symbol and message, matching that of the hardworking, supremely efficient national ant.

"That's beautiful," Dyeawan remarks.

Yilik only grunts, filling in the scales of one of the fish to be rendered in stone.

A new thought distracts her from the painting, recognition of a word she's yet to hear in the Cadre.

"The archives?"

Yilik grunts his assent.

It's not hard to narrow down where that must be located. There's only one level Dyeawan has yet to have occasion to visit.

"Is that at the very top of the Cadre?" she asks.

Yilik's hands stop their intricate motions for the first time, and he looks up at her as if she's dimmer than a lamp whose luminescent insects are nearing the end of their life cycles.

"Yes, the archives are still located on level twelve," he says, drawing his words out slowly.

"The painting really is beautiful," Dyeawan repeats, and proceeds to turn her wheels toward the door.

It's a hard slog up several levels' worth of ramps, even in her tender. Dyeawan realizes her arms have actually weakened a great deal since she began working in the Cadre. The ease of the tender's paddles is nothing to dragging herself around by rocks on the bare street.

As she wheels herself toward the final staircase leading up to level twelve, a harsh voice calls to her from behind.

"You there, girl! Stop right now!"

Dyeawan's first and most powerful instinct is to set her arms to moving the rest of her as fast as they possibly can, as if that voice belonged to an Aegin. Then she remembers there are no Aegins here, and even if there were, she has nowhere to run. So instead she forces calm over the hornet's nest in her veins, and stays her hands and arms atop the paddles before they run away on their own.

Taking a deep breath, Dyeawan halts the tender and spins it around.

It's the Man in Black, striding toward her with his black-gloved hand clutching the bone handle of his dagger.

"Do you have permission to visit the archives?" he more demands than asks.

"Not in particular," she answers honestly, "but Edger told me to carry deliveries wherever I'm instructed to."

He glowers down at her, his yellow eyes and close-cropped white hair seeming starker and almost otherworldly as they completely fill her gaze. She's never been this close to him before, and Dyeawan doesn't care for it one bit. He smells like oiled leather and death, and every line in his face seems to frown at her.

"Oisin."

There's no mistaking Edger's voice-that's-not-a-voice. The Man in Black (who must be Oisin) turns from Dyeawan, and they both watch Edger approach them calmly. He's wearing a simple crimson tunic with a wide belt. The sticks of several of his most common silk expression masks are sheathed through that belt.

The one Edger is holding to his face at the moment is harsher than even the stern face he showed Dyeawan during their first meeting.

This expression is blatant disapproval.

"Does this one have permission to enter the archives?" Oisin asks him.

"*This one's* name is Slider, and she's one of my finest helpers. There is no part of the Cadre forbidden to her."

This is all, of course, news to Dyeawan, though she says nothing. She imagines Edger is overstating the case simply to rebuke the Man in Black.

Oisin looks down at her, not even attempting to mask his displeasure. He looks back at Edger with the same expression.

"And I would remind you, Oisin," Edger continues, "that it is not your place to soldier the halls of this edifice interrogating my staff. Frankly, I'd expect a high-ranking member of the Protectorate Ministry to have larger concerns."

Oisin draws in a deep, steadying breath.

"I do," he says through clenched teeth, then stomps away.

He strides past Edger without a further look.

Once he's passed, Edger sheathes his disapproving mask and replaces it over his slackened face with his laughing mask.

Despite the tension and her slowly dissipating fear, Dyeawan finds herself stifling a giggle.

Edger walks over to her. "I'm sorry about him. I'm afraid even here we have to live with our version of Aegins now and then."

"I was just told to take this back to archives by Yilik the drafter," she explains, holding up the wrapped tablet.

"Ah yes, Yilik. He's an immensely talented artist, but he doesn't think much beyond his canvas."

Rather than taking the tablet away from her, Edger reaches out and pulls back a corner of the cloth covering it.

Dyeawan can't help but look. It is indeed a stone tablet, carved and still retaining the aspect of long-faded paint. The corner he reveals exposes the eye and gills of a fish, much like the koi Yilik was incorporating into his port archway. He must've been using the tablet for reference.

"Well then," Edger says, tucking the corner of the cloth back in place. "We'd better return it as ordered."

"Are you sure?" Dyeawan asks, returning the bundle to her tender.

"You heard me tell Oisin there's not a corner of this place forbidden to you. I meant that."

Dyeawan smiles, choosing to hear the truth in his words and ignoring whatever he's obviously leaving out.

Spinning her tender around, she waits for Edger to take the lead, and together they climb the stairs and ascend the last ramp in the Planning Cadre.

There are no corridors on the twelfth level. Neither are there the archways of the maps level. The highest plateau of the structure is one gargantuan warehouse, its ceiling stretching higher than any other in the

Cadre. Panes of glass fill rectangular windows high up in that vaulted stratum, allowing sunlight to pour in over every inch of the vast space and its contents.

Dyeawan smells age and dust as the sight of enough ancient artifacts to fill ten Capitol museums immediately overwhelms her. Although one thing is apparent right away: None of these artifacts are from Crache. Nothing about her surroundings speaks of the Capitol or Crachians as a people.

She sees triptychs of mighty battles featuring dozens upon dozens of soldiers on each panel, fighting with sword and bow and arrow. There are oil paintings that tower over even Edger at full height, renderings of kings and queens resplendent in silken finery and jeweled crowns. There are stone sculptures of powerful generals in military uniforms and even full battle armor. There are rows upon rows of books, ancient volumes and tomes that could break rocks with their spines.

Dyeawan rolls past monoliths of stone and tablets ten times the size of the one on her lap. They're all carved with characters from a language she doesn't recognize. Though she never learned to read beyond simple wayfinding signs in the city, it's definitely not Crachian writing. It must've been important to someone, however, to be immortalized in such grandeur and in such a lasting way.

It finally occurs to her that's what she's looking at; it's history, the history of an entire people she's never seen or even heard of before.

"What is all this?" she asks Edger.

"Relics from another world, that also happens to be our world."

Dyeawan doesn't understand, but there's more than enough to distract her from that answer.

Two truly giant stone statues tower over the endless stacks and piles. They were obviously carved to oppose each other. The first is an armored warrior grasping a curved sword. It's facing off against a monstrous creature with the head of a dragon, the body of a man, and the claws of an eagle. Dyeawan has never seen anything like it in the Capitol, nor artifacts as bold and full of life and death and human interaction as the rest of these.

Crachian art and architecture are touted as second-to-none, and they are undoubtedly beautiful, but they lack a quality she's seeing here for the first time in her life. Dyeawan can't define it for herself at first, but as she absorbs more and more of the artifacts filling the space around her she begins to realize what that quality is.

Crache never honors or immortalizes people or events, not in stone or in word or on canvas. They produce monuments only to the nation itself, never individuals, not even the Skrain, whose name is whispered in the streets among even people like Dyeawan.

She studies the images of the people in the artifacts. While the style and material changes their proportions and exaggerates their features, they're all of one discernable race. When painted in color, they have golden skin and eyes of sharp oval. Their hair, worn long most often, is either rendered black or white with age.

"These people," she says, pointing at a triptych of a grand feast. "They all look the same. I mean, not the same, not exactly the same, but all look . . . they're the same color, their faces are the same shape."

"Yes."

"Who are they?"

"I like to think of them as the first architects. They designed and built an earlier, obsolete version of our society. But we owe much to them. And they had their time of innovation, some of them worth preserving. We still eat the food they taught us to cook. We've adopted many of their weapons of wars. And many of their names and aspects live on in our people."

"Then . . . this was *here*? This was all from here?"

"Once, and no more. It does seem like an ancient, distant land from what we've built, doesn't it? Time truly is the grandmaster of artisans in that way. It can change and create things our hands will never be capable of creating."

"But why is this all here, locked up this way? Why did you put it here?"

"Not me, Slider," Edger corrects her. "My predecessors, the ones who formed the first Planning Cadre, they undertook this, thousands of years ago."

"Then why did they do this? If this is all part of us, of Crache's history?"

"Do you know what the most dangerous thing in the world is, Slider?"

"The alley between Wan's butcher shop and the gambling parlor in the Bottoms?"

Ku the wind dragon begins puffing air in short bursts through the spiky tubes on his back.

From the way Edger's shoulders rise and fall, she realizes this is the way he laughs out loud.

"That may very well be the most dangerous place you know," he says, "but what, in your unusually vast observation, is the most dangerous *thing*?"

"I don't know. A really, really big sword?"

Again, that reedy puffing "laughter."

"You are as funny as you are wise beyond your years, but no. The most dangerous thing in the world is a story."

Dyeawan is immediately intrigued.

"Which story?" she asks right away.

"The kind of story in which people believe utterly. The kind of story they believe in so fiercely they'll leave their lives in the mud to protect it. You see, Slider, people do *not* fight for nations or rulers or causes or even land they believe to be theirs by some imagined right, not really. They fight for stories, about heroes and gods and long-past ancestors who were one or the other or both. So, you have to be very careful which stories are told to the people."

Dyeawan moves her eyes over the triptychs and statues and tableaus threatening to burst forth from their canvas and stone prisons, so vibrant and striking and alive are their images.

"And these were all stories?"

"Yes."

"Whose stories were they?"

"People who left their lives in the mud. Far too many people. So, some very wise men and women a long, long time ago realized they had to take these stories away and put them somewhere they'd be forgotten. They knew the people needed a new story, one story in which they could all believe, a story that would end the wars being fought and bring them together, make them into a single people, a single nation. That's what Crache is. A better story. The best story ever told, in my humble opinion."

Something occurs to Dyeawan then. She throws her gaze all over the space, examining each piece more closely, trying to disprove the thought.

"What about the God Stars?" she asks. "Why isn't there anything in here about them?"

Edger doesn't answer right away, and he doesn't have to hold up a mask with the expression painted upon it for Dyeawan to know he's surprised.

"We have many relics of the God Star faith," he says, almost hesitantly. "They're not kept here. It was not the belief of these people."

"Where are they kept, then?"

"They're stored with the rest of the disused creations of our drafters."

Dyeawan looks up at him, first in confusion, then in shock.

"Religion, Slider," he continues, carefully, "is quite possibly the most dangerous of stories. A man or woman will put faith before their own families if it's hammered into them at an early enough age. It was one of the most difficult stories to overcome for those who founded Crache."

"How did they do it?" Dyeawan asks, though she's already gleaned the answer.

"They created a new religion, one they could control."

"The God Stars."

"Yes. As I said, they were very wise men and women. The stars are the first gods of all people, you see. When our ancestors, far back, first crawled out from some dank cave and looked to the sky for the first time, they immediately adopted that magnificence as their higher power. How could you not? There's something . . . visceral in us all that reaches back to that first sense of wonder and awe and is humbled by it. So . . . my predecessors created a new religion around it, one . . . flashy enough, shall we say, to supplant the religions that came before. They used the God Stars to wean the people off their old deities and faiths."

"But worshipping the God Stars is abolished in the Capitol."

"In all Crache," he corrects her. "Well, it wasn't needed anymore. It did its job. And as I said . . . religion is the most dangerous of stories. It's a wondrous method of control, to be sure, but who possesses the reins of that control? A priest? A church? What happens when people believe in that more than the state? What happens to the mind of the priest who realizes they're seen as a living god? No, religion . . . it just breeds monsters, as do monarchies. We're far better off without them."

"I think I understand," Dyeawan says, and she does.

She decides to keep her further thoughts on what he's just told her to herself.

Edger seems satisfied, even pleased with her reaction.

"I'd like to show you something, Slider. Would you follow me, please?"

Dyeawan nods, pressing her arms over the tender's paddles at the ready.

He leads her past scores of other relics, more books and art and statues. It's impossible to commit it all to memory, or even take it all in, but Dyeawan is determined she'll return here and study it all, every piece, up close and at length.

Eventually a clearing opens up amidst the claustrophobia of the tightly packed artifacts, and Dyeawan finds she can still be surprised, even in a cavern full of forgotten wonders.

It's a living map much like the one of the Capitol on level six, only smaller and not built to the same meticulous scale. There are a dozen of them spread out on raised platforms throughout the space, each one with a different city built upon it. Inspecting the nearest, Dyeawan begins to see that it *is* the Capitol, or at least a version of it. There's no mistaking the Spectrum, but there's little else she recognizes. Several buildings resembling the Spectrum that don't exist in the Capitol are erected in the model.

Stone plaques identify each city, but not by their Crachian designations, which are all numerical except for the Capitol. Each city modeled here has a name, and though Dyeawan isn't far along enough in her studies of language to read them all, she can make out the words on the plaque in front of the Capitol.

It reads: GOD STONE.

"Do you know what mythology is, Slider?" Edger asks her.

"I . . . think so. It's stories, like you said, only . . . stories that were supposed to have happened a long time ago. They're about us, or about a people, only they're not really true. They were made up by grandfathers and grandmothers to tell about the world around them."

"That's very good, yes. Myth can be very powerful. It can inspire people, and mislead them. Next to religion, mythology is *the* most dangerous kind of story. Once people mythologize a place or a person or an event, they become attached to it in a way that can be impossible to break them of. The ones who came before me, who built the first Planning Cadre, they knew this."

"This is Crache, isn't it?" she asks him, eyes frantically moving from model to model. "These are all the cities of Crache, but . . . different."

"This is *before* Crache," he explains. "This is the land as it was. Every city as we know it now was its own kingdom, its own realm in that time. They were disjointed, fragmented, constantly warring with one another. And do you know why?"

"Mythology?"

"Yes. Its people mythologized everything. Their cities, their rivers and lakes, even this little island on which we chose to build our Planning Cadre. They gave them fantastical names and legends. And people? Oh, they mythologized people to near-god heights. Their rulers were eight-feet-tall magicians who could split rocks with a hard stare, if you believed their stories. They mythologized entire families and called it 'nobility.' And it made the mythologized drunk with power and imagined legacy. They unleashed their false superiority on one another and the so-called lower class at every turn, and the people who believed in the myth of them followed and fought and submitted and suffered the worst."

"That sounds . . . awful," Dyeawan admits.

"It was a backward and bloody time, and it lasted far longer than it should've. And it's the duty of the Planning Cadre to ensure that those days and that way of thinking and living never return. That is why Crache has no rulers, at least not in name. That is why, as far as the people know, all decisions are made by faceless councils and committees. No one has ever gathered torches and pitchforks and set themselves upon a committee."

"But I thought . . . you said you solve everyday problems."

"We do. Some are more . . . pressing than others, that's all."

Dyeawan feels a deep sense of dread encroaching upon her guts, worming its way up through her body.

"People . . . people *now* . . . they're not supposed to know these things, are they? Any of this that you're showing me and telling me?"

"Oh no. The knowledge in this room would unravel the very fabric of Crache. That's why our friend from the Protectorate Ministry was so up in arms before. They believe this should all be burned to ash."

"Why am I allowed to know it, then, Edger?"

"Because you belong here. And because the only people you'd tell are our people."

That's the truth, Dyeawan knows, but it's not the whole truth.

She decides to simply say the rest for him: "I'm never allowed to leave here, am I, Edger?"

"My dear, where would you go if you could?" he asks, which is just another way of saying 'yes' to her.

Dyeawan is surprised to find in that moment her reaction is mixed. The dread is still there, heavy in the pit of her stomach. There was panic, too, but that's fading. In its place she recognizes an eerie calmness, an acceptance. She knows she should be angry, even furious, at the suggestion of such captivity.

The emotions simply aren't there.

It's because he's right and she knows it. Dyeawan has long understood a fundamental and gnawing fact of her existence: She shouldn't be alive. Cast out alone and small and frail, and then losing the use of her legs, she never should've survived in the streets of the Capitol. She should've been scooped up by Aegins or murdered by other dregs like her.

She was smart enough. That's all. When those times came, the ones that would've and should've ended her, she always thought of a way out. And every time, she knew the chances of her succeeding the next time grew slimmer and slimmer.

Her life is an accident with a date of expiration, and it wouldn't be long before she woke up to find that day had come, at least out in the streets.

"Thank you for telling me the truth" is all she says to him in the end.

Edger is silent. It only lasts a few moments, but it feels much longer to Dyeawan in her excited state.

Eventually, he holds up a new mask to his dead face. It's a smile, but not the cordial one with which he first greeted her. This smile is deeper, more joyous and profound.

"You . . . are a very fine pupil, Slider. Thank you for listening."

"You'll teach me more, then?"

Edger nods. "It would be my pleasure."

Dyeawan smiles, doing everything she can to make it match the one painted on silk in front of his face.

She's made a decision there in what she now understands is a tomb: Beginning today, her life is no longer an accident.

And whether or not it expires will be up to her.

HOME STUDIES

ENTERING THE GEN CIRCUS BY SKY CARRIAGE IS ONE OF THE most magnificent sights in Crache, second only to surveying the Spectrum itself from the air. The Circus is an awesome circle whose structures are unlike anywhere else in the city. It is also the grandest collection of architecture to be found this far from the center of the Capitol.

The members of every Gen reside in colossal cooperatives within the Circus. Each cooperative is like a castle-size tree carved from stone, utilized as a communal keep, with each branch serving a different Gen as their home. Some branches rise high above the others with various steps, columns, holdfasts, and towers added onto them by the more successful Gens. Most consist of more than a dozen kith-kins, families dedicated to a single purpose, function, or enterprise that furthers the interests of Crache.

Gen Stalbraid keeps the most modest home in the Circus, but to Lexi it's the whole world. Their two families have shared the two spindly towers connected by several catwalks for four generations. Brio and Lexi first chased each other across those catwalks when they were children, and it was there she first realized she wanted to marry Brio and dedicate herself to furthering Gen Stalbraid. At that time and for long after, Lexi's devotion was based on her love for Brio, her kith-kin, and their Gen. She was proud of the work Brio did, work she helped enable in her role, but that pride was always focused around Brio, his efforts and his passion.

In truth, as shameful as it felt now, Lexi had rarely considered the people in the Bottoms. She had thought of them as a cause, something abstract and singular to be saved, like a crumbling ruin or a poisoned forest. She had never conjured their faces to mind, or considered their lives or their feelings.

Now, Lexi can think of nothing else except the few faces she's seen. Rather than being repulsed or disturbed by them, she only wants to see more, to know them and their stories and bring them hope if she can.

The sky carriage is drawn into the berth of its final destination. By now the only passengers left are those wearing Gen broaches or attending to individuals who do, most of them dressed like Lexi. The carriage tower is only a brief walk from the cooperative that hosts Gen Stalbraid. Outside the cooperatives, the Circus resembles a serene park, pockmarked by the odd shop or supper stand. Lush green grass surrounds paths laid with glassy pebbles, a subtle memorial to the Circus beginning its life as a pre-Renewal stone quarry. At night, stone sconces planted close to the ground light the surface of each path.

Lexi doesn't bother acknowledging the men and women of the Gen they pass in the Circus. Stalbraid was too small for most of them to pay attention to before Brio's disappearance, and with this new revelation (the news of which Lexi would be thoroughly unsurprised to learn beat her and Taru back to the Circus) she and her Gen might as well not even exist to them. Besides, her mind is still with Shaheen and Char back in the Bottoms.

They pass the Aegins stationed outside Gen Stalbraid's keep and enter the cooperative itself. The fragrance of the hanging garden greets them. Constructed as a reception area for visitors to the Circus, it is without question Lexi's favorite place that is not part of her own home. Each Gen adds a plant to the garden when taking up residence, and is responsible for maintaining and refreshing it. Lexi still tends to the lilies floating atop bowls of water that were her kith-kin's contribution. Beyond that, the cooperative market is bustling before the onset of evening, the cooks of a dozen Gens picking up ingredients for dinner, all of it provided by the state the Gens serve and paid for by the citizens who purchase the goods and use the services the Gens oversee.

Lexi and Taru skirt the market altogether. A collection of ascendancies awaits them on the far side of the keep, each one tethered to a golden cable rising through the height of the cooperative itself. Taru pulls open the gate and follows Lexi inside the cage. Lexi reaches up and rings the hanging bell four times, its reverberations signifying to the pullers high above the number of levels Lexi and Taru wish to ascend. Several moments later the cage shifts and begins to rise through the air.

When they reach the fourth level, attendants stabilize the cage in its berth and open the gate. The sun is beginning to set as Lexi and Taru exit the keep through a tall arch leading to a parapet walk. The Stalbraid towers await them on the other side.

No other attendants or servants greet Lexi as she enters her kithkin's familial tower. She regretfully dismissed the last of the full-time staff two weeks ago, and a week after that hiring temporary help became unfeasible. Gen Stalbraid's allotment from the state has been reduced several times as pleading for the Bottoms seemed to become less and less a priority in their eyes. Since Brio's disappearance, Lexi has become increasingly convinced that the reduction in their access to resources was less about their importance and more about intentionally harming their ability to represent the residents of the Bottoms.

Lexi, hands filled with the material of her wrap, ascends the winding stairs of the tower, passing doors opening into well-appointed rooms: the salon in which her mother instructed Lexi in the ways of state functions and formal events, the balcony kitchen where most of the meals she's eaten in her life were prepared in the open air to save the cooks from the ovenlike heat within.

The Gen's library resides halfway up the tower, a small horseshoe-shaped space with two stories into which hundreds of volumes have somehow been crammed.

Lexi stands at the threshold, staring at the large wooden lectern and adjoining table in the center of the library.

"You know, I don't think I've ever stepped foot in this room before. No. I never made it past the threshold. I'd stand outside and tell Brio to come to bed, or to dinner, or to pelt him with pillows or bread or whatever I could find when I was bored or lonely or—"

Taru doesn't speak, seeming at a loss as to how to provide their mistress comfort.

Lexi breathes deeply, tamping down her emotions.

"Brio knew these stacks like he knew his own mind. He was raised to be a pleader. I was raised to be a pleader's wife. I know how to host formal events. I know all the rules of Gen etiquette. I can greet you in every recognized language in the nation. But none of that ever involved a law library. I suppose I should consider myself grateful they deemed it fit to teach me to read at all."

She looks up at Taru. "Meaning no offense, but you *can* read, yes?"

"Yes, Te-Gen. Brio's father insisted."

"Good. Because if we've any chance at all, I can't possibly read through enough of these volumes in time to make a difference."

Even Taru can't suppress their shock. "Te-Gen, surely retaining the temporary services of a pleader would be the most effective—"

Lexi actually laughs, the outburst enough to silence Taru.

"At this moment we can't afford an hour's time of the lowliest apprentice pleader, Taru. Besides, Brio always said Crachian law is far less a code of conduct and far more the most variable language in the nation. It's designed to be manipulated to create an argument for anything, and to drown novices in words and subsections and sub-subsections. But the answer is there, like a magic spell. You just have to find the right phrase."

"What phrase are we seeking in the pages of these books?"

Lexi's expression hardens.

We are not flowers. We do not wilt.

"I'm not letting those crusted, condescending cock-splats revoke the Gen that my family and Brio's family raised from dust on their bare backs. There's something in here that will at the very least buy us time. We're going to find it. And I'm going to thrust it down their throats like one of your blades."

She looks up, and is shocked at what she sees.

Taru is smiling.

In that moment, Lexi truly believes anything is possible.

REQUITAL IS THE REVENGE
OF THE WELL-READ

"IN ACCORDANCE WITH THE THREE HUNDRED AND TWENTY-first subset of the Articles of Addendum of the Adjunct Gen Franchise Protectorate Decree, I, Lexi Xia, acting on behalf of Gen Stalbraid as de facto kith-kin elder, formally protest the ruling of this Council."

It's like watching three people who are already awake somehow wake up. The spines of the three Councilmembers separate from their stone seatbacks like withered membranes pulling apart under protest, each of them pitching forward, drawn by the words of the petitioner they all thought they'd dealt with definitively and to whom this final session in the Council chambers was to be but a simple courtesy.

Taru by her side, Lexi stands precisely where she stood one week before, steeling herself under the silent thunder and civilized brutality of the Gen Franchise Council's proclamations. This time, however, she's come armed with her own bureaucratic barbs, and enough to shred the cloth from the stale robes of her enemies.

Senior Councilman Stru's expression pulls twenty year's worth of sag from his perpetually slumping facial features. He's known Lexi since she was a young woman, but in that moment he looks down on her as a stranger, his eyes shocked and almost distrustful.

Councilman Jochi, the imp of the trio, comes alight at the unexpected authority in Lexi's voice and the knowledge in her words. He looks positively delighted by the showing, in fact.

Councilwoman Burr's suspicion is as thick in her eyes as her contempt. Nevertheless, she remains silent, watchful, waiting for Lexi's next words.

She continues, drawing in as much breath as her lungs will hold. "Citing the eight hundred and ninety-seventh subset of the Gen Imperative Decree, no Gen's franchise may be revoked by the state amid unsubstantiated charges of crimes against Crache, or unsubstantiated charges of treason made against one or more of its members. Further citing the two thousand, four hundred and seventy-second subset of the Crachian Articles of Citizenry, no member of a Gen operating under sanctioned franchise of Crache may be convicted of a charge of treason *in absentia*."

Lexi watches their faces at the end of her address, and she is certain she couldn't have produced more stunned expressions if she had ascended those fabled steps separating petitioners from the Councilmembers, squatted, and proceeded to urinate at their feet.

"Stated simply, Councilmen, and Councilwoman, you cannot convict my husband of treason without him present to first face those charges, and you cannot revoke my Gen's franchise without first convicting my husband of treason."

There is silence in the Council chambers for what threatens to drag on into agony.

Stru, the oldest of them by a quarter century, is the first to stir.

"I . . . I can find no fault in your argument, or your citations—" Senior Councilman Stru begins, only to have Councilwoman Burr trample his next words as if a herd of water buffalo collapsed a fence in her mouth.

"There remains the singular core issue at hand in this case," she insists. "That issue is the most important criteria for revoking a Gen's franchise: obsolescence. You are the last kith-kin member of your Gen, Lexi. Gen Stalbraid's function is to provide the Crachian political arena with its statesmen and leaders. You are not a politician. You'll bear no children to become politicians. Does Gen Stalbraid plan to absorb a new kith-kin?"

Lexi is unshaken. "We have no immediate plans to do so, no, Councilwoman."

"Then the issue of obsolescence remains, and must be answered."

Lexi ascends a single step, breaching Council session protocol just enough to throw even Burr off-guard.

"A crime has been committed against my Gen," Lexi says, a dark fire staining the edge of her voice. "My husband has been abducted, possibly . . . murdered. I cannot know. Neither can you. And until *definitive* evidence is offered *in open council*, Brio is still kith-kin elder of an active Gen franchise, and both he and it *will* be afforded all protections, courtesies, and resources promised in your own franchise codes."

Councilwoman Burr's gaze may be composed of daggers, but none of them are lethal, nor can she seem to locate the words to weaponize her stare.

Senior Councilman Stru takes advantage of her abnormal silence. "Respectfully, can any member of this Council cite a legal precedent or subset in which a set amount of time to declare a Gen elder dead in absentia is outlined?"

Neither Jochi nor Burr offers any citation.

"Can you, Lexi?" Stru asks, and if she didn't know better she'd think he was as amused as Jochi by this turn of events.

"No, I cannot. And trust me, Senior Councilman . . ." Lexi glances at Taru, the two of them sharing the weights of five sleepless nights beneath their eyes. ". . . we looked."

Councilman Jochi actually laughs. It's brief and restrained, but it's enough to draw daggers from Councilwoman Burr's gaze.

Stru, meanwhile, is nodding thoughtfully and enough to jostle every inch of loose flesh hanging from his skull.

"Very well," he proclaims, finally. "By the laws of Crache and the subsets of our own Gen Franchising doctrine, many of them laid forth by this very Council, I must overturn our previous decree. Gen Stalbraid's franchise will remain in good standing until such time as the fate of Brio Alania can be invariably determined."

Lexi bows at the waist, a most ancient custom rarely observed anymore save for the most formal of state functions, but one that feels right to her in that moment.

"My Gen thanks you, Councilmembers."

Councilwoman Burr is already standing from her seat to adjourn. Steam is practically rising from her skin, and Jochi watches his fellow councilmember fume as she stomps off with unmasked pleasure.

Senior Councilman Stru remains focused on Lexi. "You should bear in mind, the Protectorate Ministry may see fit to resolve this matter by presenting new facts."

"If they do so, it will have to be in open session, and in that case I look forward to sharing whatever information they feel is pertinent. And answering any charges to the best of my ability."

Stru smiles, and in that moment Lexi regrets the harsh words she spoke of the man.

"I imagine you do," he says, kindly. "I imagine you would."

He rises with concerted effort, although he does so unaided.

"Good day, Te-Gen. This session stands closed."

"Good day, Councilman."

Lexi bows once more to Stru, and then to Jochi, who dips his round chin in return with a cattish grin.

"And please give Councilwoman Burr my deepest respects. She departed so abruptly."

She turns and begins descending the steps that end just before the chamber doors, Taru taking smaller strides than they need in order to keep pace with their much slighter charge. The Aegins guarding those doors pull the heavy stone slabs open upon their approach.

"Congratulations, Te-Gen," Taru says quietly, and only for Lexi's ear as they exit into the Spectrum corridor.

She shakes her head. "It's a minor victory, if at all. And temporary. We found holes in their laws. They'll find or make new ones to circumvent those holes. That's the point of the whole damn thing."

Taru frowns. "I do not like words as weapons. They're devious."

"Yet you helped me wield them well in those Council chambers, my friend. Thank you."

"It is all in service, Te-Gen."

"Brio's father had a keen eye for loyalty. He chose well in you. I am only sorry it's taken having Brio pulled from us for me to see it."

Taru has no answer for that, or perhaps the feelings Lexi's words stir make it too much to speak.

Taru swallows hard, changing the subject. "What will Te-Gen do next?"

Lexi draws in a deep, thoughtful breath. "I'm not sure what else *can* be done by us here. We have to trust our friend will send word somehow and soon, and that her word will carry news of progress."

"I am not one for waiting," Taru says.

"I used to be quite good at it. It was expected of me. I find my taste for it souring now, however."

"That was before, Te-Gen."

Lexi halts briefly, looking up at her retainer. "Before what?"

There's no hint of irony when Taru explains, "Before you became the pleader of Gen Stalbraid."

Lexi says nothing to that, slowly taking back up her stride. A moment later as they near the Spectrum lobby, she looks back at Taru with a strange smile on her face.

Pleader.

Her mother would approve.

Lexi allows herself the briefest moment to enjoy the thought before she returns her gaze to what lies ahead.

"Come along," she bids Taru. "We have food to pick up, and people waiting for us in the Bottoms."

"Yes, Te-Gen," her retainer affirms without even attempting to hide their enthusiasm.

BURIED ON THE BATTLEFIELD

FOR THE FIRST AND ONLY TIME AS A SAVAGE, EVIE FEELS herself pulled from a deep, restful sleep by the blaring of half a dozen rousing horns.

It's before dawn, and the cold of the morning is the kind that bites through flesh until it finds the bone beneath. Evie has never been the kind who wakes easily, and the earlier the worse. This morning, however, she finds the world comes into focus quickly and sharply. The reality of what's to come in the next few hours is palpable, like blood on the tongue.

She may be more than the drunken bar brawler she presented to the Aegins who arrested her, to Laython and the taskers and the rest of the Savages, but Evie has never fought in a war before.

War. She turns the word over and over in her newly conscious mind. Back in the Capitol, in any of Crache's shining cities, none of the people with their well-fed lives would even be able to reconcile what is going on here, what the Savages are being prepared to do. Evie has never been as naive as the oblivious, content masses, but even she couldn't have conceived of how vast the machinery of this silent conflict seems to be.

The knowledge that she is now part of that machinery settles like a dull blade in her gut. The idea that her first battle in that supposedly nonexistent yet very real war may very well be her last is more sobering than the coldest water.

She rubs the crusted sleep from her eyes, a sickly bluish-green color filling her vision for a moment until she pulls her hands away. Evie blinks in sudden horror and slides back against the rough ground, splaying her fingers in front of her. Her hands are pocked with strange discolored shapes, and for one wild, forgetful moment Evie rubs them together in a frantic effort to remove the stains.

Then it comes spilling through the cobwebs of half sleep, the memories of being force-fed the blood coin and the sight of the resulting runes on the other Savages.

The other Savages, like me, she tells herself, and the thought almost brings on a new panic.

In that moment it's all too real, and Evie has to arrange her body in a cross-legged position and assume a meditative state over her mind to help calm it.

You're here with a purpose, she reminds herself. *Stick to that purpose. Remember your training. Remember you're not one of them, not really.*

Calm slowly cascades down through her torso and limbs, filling her body and reining in her sleep-addled emotions. Evie quickly dresses and outfits herself with the gear she's scrounged for the fight. Upon exiting the tent she finds her fellow Savages in ruins, most of them either running around lost and frantic or deathly ill from the Revel. Evie walks past a young woman vomiting wine into the mud, feeling for her, but in no fit state to play nursemaid to anyone, least of all herself.

She spies the older people gathered around a burning fire, awake, yet quiet and sullen. The rest of the camp ignores them.

Laython walks among the tents, throwing back flaps and shouting within.

"We muster in five minutes! Any one of you still sleeping I'll butcher in their bedroll like a diseased piglet!"

The Elder Company is in no particular hurry. Lariat leads Bam and Mother Manai through the center of camp like a slow ceremonial procession, a junkyard triumph of the vagrant elite. They may be ragged and armed with weapons a B'ors tribesman would shun, but to watch them strut through the mud you would think they were Skrain field generals on the crest of a final, war-winning victory.

Evie is surprised to see that Lariat's torso is bare, except for a series of leather straps and buckles. Together they form a harness that extends over his shoulders and down both his arms to his fists. Embedded in the leather at every joint are short curved blades surrounded by jagged barbs. His elbows, his shoulders, every knuckle of his fists, even his hips have been adorned with weapons to make a strike from them lethal.

As if that weren't enough, he's fisting the horizontal grips of two katars, their triangular blades extended down a foot-and-a-half from his fists.

Go with what works, I suppose, Evie thinks to herself.

She finds Spud-Bar at their tinker's wagon from hell, frantic Savages besieging Spud-Bar in these final moments for a weapon, any weapon to see them through the morning. Evie is already outfitted for battle, or at least as outfitted as anyone can be in this makeshift legion, but she asks the armorist if they can spare a dagger.

"Why do you need two daggers?" Spud-Bar asks her, nodding at Evie's long knife.

"In case I want to stab them more than once," Evie answers without missing a beat.

Her flat, humorless tone more than anything else makes Spud-Bar laugh.

"Take mine." Spud-Bar unsheathes a beautifully flared blade from their belt, extending its bone handle to Evie. "The rest of this trash is . . . well . . . you know. Trash."

Evie accepts it gratefully. "You're sure?"

Spud-Bar nods, their voice darkening. "Just bring it back to me and I'll consider it well spared. You understand?"

Evie nods, sheathing the blade securely through her belt.

A group of new faces makes their way past the armory wagon.

There are almost a dozen of them, young men and one woman. The woman looks just old enough to be Evie's mother's age, and she walks at the head of the group as if she's their leader. They all have blankets or pelts draped over their shoulders to ward off the cold, but the bodies Evie glimpses beneath are all well shaped and heavily tattooed, the many unfamiliar symbols and animal tableaus obscured by the webs of blood coin runes staining their flesh. Most of them have shaved their scalps except for long, dark topknots of hair, or a single strip down the middle of their heads. Beneath the blankets and pelts they're clad in little more than loincloths and boots with fur tied around the calves.

They look and carry themselves like seasoned warriors, a rare sight among Savages, from what Evie has thus far seen.

"Who are they?" Evie asks Spud-Bar.

"They're B'ors."

"I can see that. I meant I haven't seen them in camp, or at the Revel."

Spud-Bar shrugs. "They keep to themselves. Live apart. Eat apart. Never seen 'em step foot in the Revel."

"My whole life I've heard about what fierce fighters they are."

"Oh, they are that. I promise you. You'll be glad of 'em on the field."

"But if they're that good, why waste them in the Savage Legion?"

Spud-Bar shrugs. "Never could tame 'em, I suppose. Oh, we conquered 'em right good. Took their land, what little they had that wasn't land. Killed 'em by the thousands. But the B'ors wouldn't be slaves or conscripts. They'd rather die, to a man, given the choice. So they send a few of 'em here now and again. Though they're always careful not to give any one fighting force too many from a B'ors tribe."

"Afraid they'd try to take over?" Evie asks.

"Oh, deathly certain of it," Spud-Bar answers, definitively.

Laython's voice cuts through. "You all have one minute . . . exactly *one mother-lovin' minute* . . . to muster at the ready, or I'll leave you where you stand, only in more pieces than I find you!"

Evie takes a deep breath, exhaling what feels like ice. She realizes she doesn't want to leave Spud-Bar. She feels the safest she's felt since being carted from the Capitol when she's near the armorist. Spud-Bar is like a tether in a snowstorm.

"I got no advice worth givin' ya," Spud-Bar says, seeing the hesitation in Evie. "Alls I can say is, whether you live or die is up to you. If you want it bad enough out there on the field, you'll live. If you give up, even for a second, well, I'll have to forge myself a new dagger."

Evie smiles, just a little. "That sounds like worthwhile advice to me."

Spud-Bar shifts uncomfortably. "Yeah, well . . ."

"Thank you," Evie says quickly. "For the dagger."

"No worries. Any soul who appreciates good steel, y'know?"

Evie nods, and they leave it at that, no further good-byes or well-wishes.

She musters with the rest at the edge of camp, Laython riding large circles around them astride a giant beast of a horse, corralling them.

"Dyin' time, children!" he calls to them when he's certain their full force is massed. "Let's go meet your executioners!"

The Savages don't march, but rather shuffle in a loose formation. Surrounded by taskers and with Laython leading them, they slouch off to meet their fate.

Evie sees them arriving just as the Savages are funneled out of camp: the Skrain, resplendent in their iron scales of armor, the Crachian ant painted on the breast. Their mounted riders carry poleaxes with sweeping three-foot blades. Their foot soldiers march in perfect formation, gauntleted fists toting horse-cutter spears. All of them carry curved swords of the finest steel sheathed from their hips.

Before she turns away, looking to the field ahead, Evie's final thought is how she'd give her left hand for just one of the Skrain's weapons.

The Savages mass atop a hill several miles from their camp's perimeter. Laython and his taskers herd them like cattle from astride their hulking horses, constant jets of steam pouring from their nostrils.

"Spread out!" Laython barks at them, revving his mount and

knocking several Savages over as he rides straight through their tightly bundled ranks. "Form a skirmish line! It don't have to be pretty, just spread the fuck out!"

Laython's armor is black leather and obviously custom-made for his massive, near-seven-foot frame. It appears to be dozens upon dozens of pieces, like scales, tightly laced together from neck to toe. The clublike mace he wields has been fashioned from black wood to match his armor.

Evie plants herself at the crest of the hilltop and lets the others fan out around her. As the Savages form their jumbled skirmish line, Evie watches several small groups carrying what look like giant octagonal wheels. They load them onto the twenty-foot trebuchets spaced far apart on the line. Each section of the octagons are hollow, with a door just large enough to stuff a full-grown man or woman inside if they were to curl into a ball. Evie watches as their bearers open each of the small doors and leave them that way.

Many of the Savages who are then forced into the human cubby-holes and shut inside belong to the group of elderly and infirm whom Evie identified at the Revel.

Among them, Evie spots the Professor, lazily grasping a short sword with more patina on its blade than steel. No doubt it'll shatter upon first impact. The entire left side of the Professor's face is swollen and purple with bright veins of red. She wonders briefly and idly if they beat him out of spite or necessity.

As he tucks himself without complaint into one of the octagon compartments, Evie feels a hollow pang of regret deep in her gut. She'd wanted and hoped for the chance to ask him if anything he'd said to her the night before was the truth.

Not that she could've trusted the answer, of course.

Evie has chosen a short single-bladed ax whose haft is crowned with a wickedly edged, rust-covered spike. The underside of the ax head is sharply curved to a deep hook at the end; it's designed to grip the top of shields and tear them down, exposing the shield bearer to a lethal blow.

Evie meticulously sharpened every edge, wrapping the rough wood of the haft in cattle cord to help secure her battlefield grip on the weapon.

Most of the armor gifted to the Savage Legion is fit only for scrap. Piecing together an entire suit, or even half of one, proved to be an impossible task. The best Evie can do is triple layer her torso with heavy wool undergarments and wear two pairs of thick leather trousers (she bartered the former articles, won the latter in a game of "de-fanging the snake" by disarming her opponent of their knife twice in a row). She scrounged a broken helm from Spud-Bar's armory, well constructed but for a shattered right faceplate. With Spud-Bar's help, Evie chipped off the remaining pieces and replaced them with a solid square of steel from a breastplate with enough holes in it to have ended half a dozen of its owners.

After thoroughly inspecting the entire pile, not a single Savage shield proved to be anything but a storm of splinters and a piercing wound waiting to happen. Evie hadn't the time or the materials along the march to fashion a proper one. She was able to salvage a leather gauntlet that almost completely covers her forearm, along with enough pieces of slim scrap steel bars to line it like a skeleton. Evie has also chosen a long knife to carry in that hand; she'll use them to deflect the strikes of spear and sword.

Evie looks around her. No, they're not an army, but she sees more fighters than victims. She'd expected to look on faces of fear and panic and even dread, and yes, she sees those expressions, although far, far fewer than she would've ever imagined. Most of the faces are twisted into masks of war, teeth bared and eyes slit and breath coming in heated gasps.

Perhaps they've convinced themselves that if they can survive the next few minutes then they can survive. Perhaps it's as simple as wanting to make it to one more Revel.

Evie doesn't know, can't know, and the time for existential questions is over before she even realizes it.

It's like watching the sun come out. The Sicclunan army appears on the horizon across the valley all at once, a wave of crimson shields and metal helms. Evie begins counting from the far left, makes it to almost two hundred, when Laython's voice calls down the line.

"Make yourselves ready!" he instructs them all. "And be light on your feet, Savages!"

Evie realizes she's almost panting. The fire in her blood is speeding up everything, her breath, her heart, the thoughts and images in her head.

She never hears Laython give the order to charge. One moment there's silence, and in the next the bloody screams of the Savages around her fill her ears and she sees dozens of them streaming down the hill.

Evie allows herself one deep, steadying breath, and then she joins them.

She can scarcely feel her legs sprinting beneath her, but she knows that's just the fear and anticipation coursing trough her body. Twenty yards from the Sicclunan line, Evie feels a shadow overtake her and hears a fierce rattling above her head. She looks up, midrun, just as one of the suicide tumblers careens overhead, rotating in a slow arc. The Savages on foot are ten yards away when the first tumbler crashes behind the Sicclunan front line.

It's impossible to see beyond the wall of shield and spear and ax and armor, but Evie watches large pieces of the wooden octagon fly into the air after impact. It must be designed to break apart behind the enemy's front line, releasing its human cargo into their ranks, or at least the ones who survive both the impact and avoid being pinned to the ground or hacked apart by Sicclunan blades, anyway.

The name "suicide tumbler" suddenly makes all the sense in the world to Evie.

There are three men directly in front of her when the first of the Savages crash upon the Sicclunan shields. Evie turns to her side and lets her lead foot skid through the muddy grass, stopping her momentum and halting her before she becomes part of the pileup. She bends her knees and raises both ax and long knife, staring through her reforged helm at a rioting curtain of shoulders and necks.

A sharp scream and a spray of blood across her faceplates cause Evie to back up a step in alarm. One of the bodies massed in front of her turns around and slumps forward, cradling a hole in his guts spilling gore down his legs and onto the grass. Evie looks down, knowing it's a mistake to do so, but unable to take her eyes off the twitching body of the impaled man until he stops moving and his eyes go glassy and vacant.

The spell broken, Evie faces forward to see that the bodies directly in front of her have been cleared. There's a hole just big enough to frame a single Sicclunan shield. It looks like a closed door marked with sacrificial blood as some type of warding ritual. It hovers there, perfectly still, the soldier holding it completely obscured from view. It's an almost hypnotic sight, even in the chaos and carnage of the moment exploding all around her.

Evie steps over the corpse at her feet, keeping herself crouched low. Her gauntleted grip on the long knife is reversed, its blade running the length of her forearm. When she steps within three feet of the shield, the largest spearhead she's ever seen emerges from behind the wall of wood and steel. Evie swings blade and gauntlet, batting away the thrust aimed at one of her main arteries.

Rather than hack at the shield with her ax, Evie leaps up and hooks the top of it with the underside of the blade. Feeling it snag, she hurls her body full force into the shield, hoping to throw the bearer off-balance. With surprising strength for her size, she grips the haft of the ax with both hands and pulls down, letting the entire weight of her body add to the power of the motion.

The shield dips forward from the top. Evie manages to yank it down to just above her waist. She doesn't wait for the armored figure on the other side to react. She hasn't even fully taken them in when she reverses the momentum of her ax and thrusts its spiked crown up into the shield bearer. Evie feels metal strike metal, and then penetrate it. The spike stops when it hits something solid, as if she's pierced the hide of a tree in winter.

Evie looks up to see that spike buried in the shoulder of the Sicclunan solider, just above his heart. She sees his other arm rise, spear shaft still held by his gauntleted hand. Frantic, Evie attempts to retrieve her ax only to find it firmly anchored in the soldier's armor. Evie reverses her grip on her long knife and drives the blade up into his abdomen, under the plates of his armor. The blow freezes his spear arm and the soldier spits blood onto the top of her helm.

She feels his body begin to topple over her. Rather than allow herself to be trapped in the Sicclunan front line under a man twice her size clad in full armor, Evie steps back, and with a determined shriek pulls the soldier's body with her, ripping him from the line. She feels them falling against and then through the bodies of the Savages gathered around her, and then there's only the wet ground welcoming her spine.

There's a brief panicked second in which Evie considers remaining like that, hiding beneath the Sicclunan soldier like a crustacean claiming the armored shell of its dead brethren. Then she hears a wet growl directly in her right ear and he begins wriggling atop her anew, still very much alive.

"Are you *serious*?" Evie spits in frustration.

Before she can react further, he's somehow managed to free his arm from his shield and grab her by the hair, thrashing her head about in the mud. Evie growls right back at him, twisting the long knife in his guts until the soldier shrieks and his body seizes in agony. Even with the leverage of her weapons buried in his armor and flesh, it takes every ounce of strength she has to move him from atop her, turning him over onto his back with her astride his breastplate.

Evie releases her grip on her embedded ax and reaches for the chinstrap of his helm, using it to force his head back into the mud. She pulls her long knife free of his guts and presses the edge of its blade against the soldier's exposed neck. Pulling his chin in the opposite direction, Evie presses down hard on the blade and drags it across his throat, a guttural sound that might belong to someone else escaping her mouth as she opens the Sicclunan's veins.

More blood splashes the faceplate of her helm and Evie leans away from the soldier in disgust. She can no longer see through the slits in the steel over her eyes. Evie reaches up with her free hand shoves the helm up over her face. She shakes her head loose of it entirely, breathing like a drowning woman who has just broken from the surface of the water.

Evie's gaze shoots from side to side, disoriented, trying to assess her bearings and any incoming threats. The Sicclunans are holding the front line just a few yards from where she's straddling one of their fallen comrades. Years of resisting volleys of Savages has obviously taught them discipline. Yet no shield has replaced the one borne by the soldier beneath her, and she can spot several other holes in the line where identical shields should be. Evie can't be certain, but through the continuing assault she thinks she sees fighting well behind the line, as well.

The bodies of fallen Savages are laid out three abreast in the mud up and down the line, and in many places they've begun to pile up. Evie turns her head and her gaze away from them, and from the broken wall of shields. She looks ahead to see dozens of other skirmishes taking place between her fellow Savages and the Sicclunans they've drawn from the line.

Through them all her eyes fix on Lariat, the old man with his walrus mustache. He's kneeling over a prone soldier after removing the man's helm. He rains left and right fists down on a thing that's barely a human skull anymore in alternating, unbroken succession.

His breathing isn't even elevated.

A furious howling shocks Evie's attention back to the line. A Sicclunan footman is charging out from the hole she's created among the shield wall. The sweeping, flared blade of his poleax is held high above his head, the entirety of the dawn seeming to be caught within the highly polished steel.

Evie has no time to extricate herself or her ax from the soldier beneath her. All she can do is reverse her grip on her long knife and hold it and her gauntleted forearm above her head, her other hand bracing it for support. She's gritting her teeth hard enough to sting her jaw, and her eyes shut of their own accord, refusing to obey her commands to remain open. Behind her eyelids, Evie watches herself being split down the middle several dozen times in bloody succession.

She doesn't see Bam's giant scythe cut the footman in half just above the waist, but she hears the sound the Sicclunan makes when the news of what's happened to his body is reported to his brain. It's that inhuman sound of shock and agony beyond belief that snaps Evie's eyes open once again. She's still holding her knife and gauntlet aloft protectively as she looks down to see the soldier lying in the mud in two separate parts.

Bam, the Elder Company's silent battery, is standing between his victim's legs and torso. His sleeveless cloak is a tableau painted in blood and entrails. He pushes back his hood, stringy curls sweat-pasted to the bulbous features of his sad puppet face, and Evie sees his eyes for the first time. She's surprised to find no malice there, nothing steeped in blood-lust or rage or even the violence he's performing.

If anything, he just looks tired.

Evie lowers her knife. "Thanks."

Bam nods once, then points at his large brown eyes with his middle and forefinger. He then stabs those digits in the direction of the Sicclunan front line.

Evie nods, the implication clear to her: Never take your eyes off the line during a battle.

The sound of Crachian horns fills the valley behind them. The next sound Evie hears is one like a single clash of thunder. It's the entire Sicclunan army standing at attention, midbattle. As she watches, their front line begins to recede, every remaining shield bearer and supporting soldier backpedaling in unison.

They're retreating.

Evie looks up at Bam in confusion. He calmly motions behind her with the dripping blades of his scythes.

She looks over her shoulder to see the Skrain pouring into the valley, charging headlong toward them.

Before she can turn around, Evie feels Bam's huge hand grab her by several layers of shirt and haul her to her feet. He begins pulling her along, walking quickly and in broad strides toward the full charge of the Skrain.

"What're you doing?" she demands, running to keep up with him.

He doesn't answer, but a moment later the shadows begin to streak across her face and Evie looks up at hundreds of arrows flying through the air. When they begin their descent she looks back, watching several pierce the body of the soldier whose throat she slit.

"Oh" is all she can think to say.

Evie can't imagine a scenario in which they aren't trampled over by the Skrain, but every soldier in their charge simply sweeps around them harmlessly as if Evie and the rest of the surviving Savages aren't even there. For a moment she's almost convinced she isn't anymore, in fact. Perhaps she didn't survive the battle, or perhaps the anonymity of her new station in life has spread that idea to every corner of her flesh, rendering her detached from the earthly plane.

Those lofty thoughts abandon her with the passing of Crache's elite soldiers, the last of the Skrain running around them as if they were obstacles on a training field.

The last riders into the valley are Laython and his taskers. The black-clad freemaster of the Savages holds his mace high like some deathly victory scepter.

"Survivors, form on me!" he thunders across the valley. "Form on me if you've still got two legs!"

Evie peers around Bam's hulking form. She counts perhaps two or three dozen Savages still upright, including Lariat and Mother Manai, and most of the B'ors tribe.

Though she never took a proper count, three or four *hundred* Savages must have charged the valley.

"So the sparrow survived her first battle!" Lariat calls to them in a voice like a gravel quarry at midday. "I should've 'ad my money on you, girl."

He's retrieved both of his katars, and there isn't a single blade on his body harness that isn't darkened with Sicclunan blood.

"Why didn't you?" Evie asks.

"Not enough hips," he answers without hesitation. "I never bet on a woman who hasn't passed at least a few pups."

"And I keep tellin' him he's a moron," Mother Manai says, joining them.

"I've never once disagreed," Lariat points out, laughing.

Evie's almost inclined to join in, but something distracts her.

"Hey," she says, pointing across the field. "What are they doing?"

Several of the B'ors warriors are carrying dead Sicclunan soldiers across the mud.

"I thought we weren't allowed to take trophies."

"That's not what they're doing, Sparrow," Lariat assures her.

"Then what?"

"The B'ors look at their enemies a lot different from Crachians," Mother Manai explains. "They honor the strongest of their opponents defeated in battle by giving them a proper burial."

"Makin' 'em part of the earth where they fought or some such thing," Lariat adds.

"If I can persuade you children to end your prayer meeting early," Laython cuts in from atop his perpetually snarling beast, "It's time to collect the maimed and deal mercy to the mortally wounded."

"I'm not a doctor," Evie objects. "How do I know the difference?"

Laython talks patiently down to her. "If they can get up, they're wounded. If they can't, they stay here. Is that simple enough for you? And d'you think you can manage it without puking your guts out?"

He rides off without waiting for an answer, although Evie had only a scowl to offer him, anyway.

When she looks back at Lariat, he's in the middle of drawing a small cut in his forearm with the edge of a katar.

It's one of many small cuts, the rest fully healed.

"Sixty-eight more to go, then," he mutters beneath his mustache.

Evie can't be sure whether the old man truly believes it, but lie or not, the cuts are very real.

ON AND OFF

THE OCEAN SINGS TO HER EVERY NIGHT, AND IT'S BECOME ONE of Dyeawan's favorite things about life in the Planning Cadre.

It's after dinner, and she's retired to her room for the evening. She's folded her legs beneath her on the floor beside the reading chair in the corner, and though there are books piled beneath her bed, it's not reading with which she's occupied tonight.

There's a knock at the door, stronger than Quan's and less timid than Tahei's when he dares to visit. Dyeawan guesses it must be Edger.

"Come in," she calls.

It's him, that cordial smile frozen in oil and silk held over his face.

"Good evening, Slider. May I come in?"

"Of course."

Edger steps inside and quickly stops short. The mask lowers from his face, and Dyeawan knows he's taken aback. It's not difficult to understand why. Tools and tubing and spools of twine have overtaken Dyeawan's small room. There are raw building materials of wood and steel and iron, and she's even procured a hand torch, the flame of which is lit and wafting in the ocean breeze from the window.

"What's happened in here?" Edger asks.

"Oh. I've been . . . it's just . . . a project. I've been working on something. An invention. On my own. In my own time, I mean. It hasn't interfered with my duties."

He sees that she's constructed some type of apparatus by joining two lamps together, removing the glass panes from one side of each and melting their metal frames together with hot flame. There are luminescent insects coupling inside one of the lamps, lighting it brightly. The other lamp appears empty. A blacksmith's bellow is held between the grips of a vise beside the lamp housing the insects. The bellow's mouth is protruding through a delicate hole cut into the glass.

Several thick cables running to an iron box tether the entire contraption. There are two short levers attached to the box itself, which rests on the floor beside Dyeawan.

"Where did you obtain the materials and tools?" Edger asks.

"From Tahei, the builder. They're all extra tools and spare parts, he said."

"I see."

Dyeawan's features darken. She begins to suspect she's done something wrong.

"Are you upset?" she asks. "Is this against the rules?"

"Not . . . strictly speaking, no," Edger answers, then seems to remember himself and replaces the mask over his face. "I'm not upset with you, not at all. I'm intrigued."

That brings a grin to Dyeawan's face.

"May I show you how it works?" she asks.

"Please do."

Excited, Dyeawan snatches up the box tethered to the conjoined lamps by those cables.

"There's a small portcullis separating the two compartments, you see."

"I do."

She pulls one of the levers connected to the box and a small wooden panel is drawn up from between the two lamps.

When Dyeawan pulls the box's second lever, the vise grip bracing both sides of that blacksmith's bellow tightens, compressing the accordion folds of the bellow and spitting a puff of white dusty power into the lamp.

Whatever the compound is, the moment it hits the insects they uncouple, their light dying as they flit as far and as fast apart from each other as possible. This sends one of them careening into the glass and the other through the open slot between the two lamps.

When that happens, Dyeawan reverses the first lever on the iron box and the portcullis lowers, trapping the bug inside and separating it from its mate.

"That is . . . quite remarkable," Edger observes.

"But wait!" Dyeawan pleads. "That's only half of it. You see how the little ones can't bear to be separated?"

Indeed, the insects are both digging at the portcullis sectioning off the two lamps, desperate to return to each other.

Dyeawan again pulls the first lever. As soon as the portcullis opens the two insects return to their primal instincts and couple, lighting the lamp anew.

She closes the portcullis and beams up at Edger. "You see? You can turn the lamp on and off with the flick of a switch! It saves energy and prolongs the lifespan of the creatures, and allows you to control the light in a room or corridor much easier than separating or replacing them by hand."

Edger lowers his mask, sheathing its handle through his belt and drawing another.

It's his surprised expression.

"That is utterly ingenious, my dear."

"It's crude and unwieldy right now, I know," Dyeawan insists. "But the principle is sound. I know I can make the whole thing lighter, smaller, and easier to implement. And I know the proper way to do it would've been to design it and have it drafted, but I didn't want to waste the drafters' time—"

"Slider . . . the words you're using . . ."

"You mean my vocabulary?" she asks without a trace of irony in her voice.

"Yes . . . including the word 'vocabulary' . . ."

"I suppose I've picked them up from the reading I've been doing."

"In our library?"

Dyeawan nods.

"And that's how you acquired the knowledge to do all this?"

"Well, Tahei helped me understand a lot of it. But I didn't want him solving any of the problems for me, so the rest came from books."

"Could you read before you came here?"

"No. Not really. Except for some signs in the Capitol."

"May I sit?" Edger asks.

"Of course."

He settles himself gently on the foot of her bed, the hollow bones in the back of the wind dragon with its jaw perpetually clamped on his throat exhaling slowly.

"I came here tonight because today marks three months since you've been with us," he says. "I wanted to see how you felt, how you'd adjusted. Are you telling me in one month you taught yourself to read, learned advanced principles of alchemy, engineering, and metallurgy, and adapted them all to build this wondrous device?"

"I just . . . I have a head for it, I suppose."

"You do indeed, my dear. In fact, I have drastically underestimated you. I owe you an apology."

Dyeawan frowns. "No, you don't. You've given me everything. Every morning I wake up breathless because I'm afraid I dreamed all this, and I'm back inside a stinking empty wine barrel in some alley. I owe *you*, not the other way around."

Edger nods, replacing his surprised face with his cordial smile.

"Still and all," he says, "the fact remains that I have woefully underestimated your potential. And I do not do that. Not ever. It's quite shocking, really. I simply didn't see it."

He rises from the bed, turning and walking toward the door.

"Is that a good thing or a bad thing?" Dyeawan calls after him, the concern in her voice unmasked. "That you underestimated me, I mean."

"I don't know yet," Edger says without turning around. "But I promise you, we shall see, one way or the other. Your new invention is marvelous, Slider. Reward yourself with sleep, and see what else you can dream up."

He leaves her with that, closing her door behind him.

Dyeawan stares at the door for a long time after he's gone, her heart beating faster than normal. To calm herself, she pulls the levers on her invention several times, running through the sequence or extinguishing the light and then reigniting it.

It works precisely as she intended.

She never allowed herself to acknowledge it while she was designing and building the device, but it wasn't and isn't simple curiosity or inspiration. She *wanted* to impress Edger with it. She wanted to feel pride.

Now that she has, Dyeawan finds there is no pride within her, only a quiet sense of fear.

SAVAGERY PAYS A CALL

LEXI SITS BESIDE THE WINDOW IN THE HIGHEST ROOM OF HER kith-kin's tower, sheer silken drapes the color of pomelo meat dancing around her in the high winds of the elevation. They call this room the surveyor's quarters. A massive bamboo table upon which reams of colorful maps are splayed and piled dominates the space, some of them drawn by Lexi as a girl and detailing the city and the surrounding country that can be viewed from her window.

There's a medium-size instrument resting on the sill in front of her, its slender, three-stringed neck curving into a heavy wooden potbelly. Crachians call it the reed-of-the-stone-lake, and it's a general and agonized portion of formal Gen education to learn the instrument as a child. When they were young and betrothed, she and Brio would sit at their windows in their opposite towers and play matching reeds. The more poorly they each played, the more they made each other laugh with every sour, thronging note.

She hasn't played or even picked up the reed in the three months since Brio disappeared; even the sight of it is enough to cause tears to threaten the corners of her eyes, but she can't bring herself to displace anything in the towers, or in any way change the configuration of their home from how it was before Brio disappeared. In an absurd and almost masochistic way, Lexi is grateful to have this mess with the Franchise Council to give her thoughts a different dire focus. Having the very existence of her Gen threatened is the only thing that could possibly distract Lexi from how much she misses Brio and how terrified she is of receiving indisputable confirmation that she'll never see him again.

When she isn't distracted, Lexi desperately wants to be angry with him. Anger is so much easier and brings so much more solace than fear and loss. She knows, however, that whatever befell Brio was in the course of serving the post and the people he cared for so deeply. Lexi can't force herself to feel anything other than a deep and gnawing emptiness when she thinks of Brio now. It's better, even necessary, not to think of him at all.

Far below her, the Circus is quiet and appears very serene. The wraps and tunics of the men and women of the Gens are small splashes of color on the pebbled pathways and green grass. Lexi can see steam rising from her favorite soup stand in the Circus, though at this height she can't smell the heavy ginger and onion essence of the delicious broths. Sometimes, if she's out early enough, she'll stop and watch the owners stretching and shaping noodles for the day in the open-air kitchen.

Beyond the Gen Circus, the Capitol rooftops are a perfect grid separated by the amber light of the streetlamps.

"'S like a poem, it is," a voice that does not belong to Taru, and therefore does not belong in this tower, says from the door of the surveyor's quarters. "A pretty lady by a window in a tower."

Lexi rises and turns from the window, the drapes still blowing around her bare shoulders.

They're men, though they scarcely appear human to Lexi's eyes. They wear rags covered in thick hide cloaks and hoods. One of them, bald and half his face having long been chewed up by what must've been a wild animal, clutches a short double-bladed ax. The other one, lankier and malnourished-looking, is leaning on a tall spear with a length of bright horsehair streaming from the base of its barbed tip.

It's the physical detail they share that initially distracts Lexi from her shock and panic. Her first impression is that they're diseased, covered in some kind of sickly blue and green welts. Then she realizes the patterns look too much like writing, like some arcane runes, and aren't raised enough on the skin. They must be tattoos. They seem to cover every inch of flesh on the bald one that isn't scarred. The lanky spear-toting one has far fewer of them pockmarking his face and hands.

Lexi blinks rapidly, her mind racing to accept the scene and process the reality of these intruders.

She asks the inevitable question, trying to make it the demand of one who is in authority: "Who are you?"

"Death," the bald, chewed-up one happily answers. "My companion is also so called."

"Taru!" Lexi calls out, still and perhaps absurdly trying to keep her voice deep and authoritative and free of cracks.

The two of them share a brief, frightening bout of the giggles.

Lexi feels the trembling begin in her every muscle. She reaches up and grips her own biceps, squeezing hard to quell the physical panic before it spreads to her mind, overtaking her reason. She lets her nails dig painfully into the flesh of her arms to keep that bubbling rush of inner mayhem at bay.

"Your big retainer is in the other tower," the lanky one informs Lexi. "It'll be a long while checking every room and cranny for our type. Very diligent guard dog, they are."

Lexi turns back to the window, staring out at the opposing tower of Gen Stalbraid. She searches the windows frantically for some sign of Taru, the light of a torch or the flash of her retainer's leather armor.

There's nothing. Alania Tower appears as cold and deserted as it has stood since the last of Brio's family passed away.

She hears footsteps approaching behind her, light and hobbled, aided by the tapping of a spear's shaft.

"You can jump if ya want," the lanky one assures her. "It all ends the same, but I think I should like to see such a fall. It'll certainly make things less of a mess for us."

"Speak for yerself," his companion says.

Lexi looks down at the Circus spread far below her, still the picture of serenity, still the steam of dozens of boiling pots pouring from her favorite soup stand.

She has no intention of jumping.

Lexi lets her arms fall and her hands deftly slip over the neck of the reed on the windowsill. She waits until the lanky one's footsteps place him and his spear directly behind her and then stop.

"Shall I give you a nudge?" he asks, taunting her.

"Allow me," Lexi whispers, an incantation of strength and will more for her than for him.

She grips the reed's curved neck with both hands. When Lexi turns, her entire body becomes a fulcrum, beginning at her feet and rotating up through her hips, chest, and shoulders. When she swings the instrument's wooden belly into the side of the lanky one's head, it's with the full force of her weight and power behind it.

His neck crooks awkwardly and his body collapses under it. Even so, Lexi raises the reed above her head and brings it down on him again, smashing him in the shoulder as he falls to the thick rug beneath their feet.

Lexi can't hear herself screaming. If she could, her own ferocity would shock her.

The half-face is much quicker than he appears. No sooner has Lexi dropped his companion than that heavily inked, disfigured head is looming above her. Lexi cries out and takes another swing with the reed. The half-face doesn't react with the lanky one's frozen surprise. Instead he takes an easy, measured swing with his squat ax, its double blade shattering the instrument into several pieces.

Lexi drops the bit of splintered wood she's now holding and begins to back frantically away.

"Come 'ere," he bids her, the bald, scarred thing that Lexi is forced to accept is a man. "I won't kill you right off. I won't violate you, neither.

Nothing like that. That's not part of it. I just . . . I just want to smell you a bit first. Smell a proper lady. It's been so long, it has. So very, very long. Give us that and you can have a bit more time. I do have to kill you, though. No way round that."

"Why?" Lexi asks. "Why do you have to kill me? What are you doing here?"

"Following orders, miss."

Lexi stops near the edge of the map-laden table, staring at him, suspicion overriding her fear for the moment.

"Orders? Whose orders? Were you sent here? By who? Are they paying you to do this?"

The half-face shakes his head. "Savages don't draw pay. But we did get this lovely furlough. I hadn't seen the Capitol in a year. Never thought I would again. A bit o' murder is a small thing to ask against getting to come home, even for a bit."

"Who sent you?" Lexi asks again.

Again, he shakes his bald head.

"No more questions."

He begins stalking around the bamboo table in the middle of the room. Every microscopic, ethereal element that makes up her being is screaming primordially at Lexi to run, but she can scarcely force one foot forward.

"Stop!" he commands her, spittle flying as he growls the word.

She does, half leaning over the tabletop with her hands pressed flat against it.

"Don't make me angry," he almost pleads with her. "I don't want to do this angry. I just . . . allow me my moment, and I'll make yours quick. Those are my terms. I advise you to accept them."

Lexi says nothing, merely waits, standing there against the table.

The half-face moves around the mound of maps and closes the gap between them, standing behind Lexi.

"Turn around," he instructs her.

At first she can't move. Lexi has to close her eyes and practically push herself off the table to force her feet into action, turning her body into his.

The half-face smells of the earth, dirt and grass and chalky granite. It's far more pleasant than the unwashed odor of his body beneath.

Her would-be killer leans over her shoulder, wide nostrils pressing into her neck. Lexi can feel her hair touching the waxy, twisted lines of the scars dominating his face. He inhales deeply, and it makes her shiver, desperate to recoil, but she doesn't.

"The smell of a lady is a fine thing indeed," he says, sounding almost drunk.

"I'm sorry you've been so deprived," Lexi laments, and it almost seems sincere.

Her scent is followed by two of Lexi's fingers, which she spears inside the man's nostrils as deeply as she can plunge them, his head tossing back and his spine arching at an awkward angle as her nails dig painfully into his membranes.

The bald man shrieks and swipes wildly with his double-sided ax. Lexi presses her body deeply into his, giving the blind, panicked swings as little distance as possible. She reaches up with her other hand and grabs as she digs her fingernails into his hairless skull. The two of them dance around the surveyor's room, the half-face trying to pull away from her, and Lexi intent on riding him through it, curling her fingers in his nostrils and securing her grip. She feels warm, sticky blood oozing over her knuckles.

When the gyration of his body and flailing of his arms stops, Lexi thinks they've crashed into one of the room's walls. Her ankles cross and she almost loses her footing as both of their bodies halt in midstruggle. Then his growling ceases and his body stiffens.

Lexi looks up, squinting through their tangled limbs. The expression is frozen on his face as if his head were a bust of human rage itself. Taru stands behind him. They jerk his body away and disengage the attacker from Lexi. She rolls away and finds herself falling onto the floor.

She looks up and watches as Taru thrusts the tip of their blade out through the man's chest, lifting him a foot from the floor. With great strength, Taru steps forward and shoves the man free of their blade. His body is hurled over the top of the table, landing with enough force to crack the top of it down the center.

Taru is holding their blooded short sword in one hand and their hook-end in the other. It's the first time Lexi has seen her Gen's retainer out of armor. Taru is wearing only a long nightshirt and boots. Their chest rises and falls with every shallow breath brought on by the exertion and rush of battle.

"Te-Gen, are you—" Taru begins to say before all their senses come to bear on a stirring by the window.

The second assassin, the one Lexi brained with her reed, has regained consciousness, albeit a diminished form. A shocking amount of blood has drained from his left temple and pooled around his neck. He uses the shaft of his spear to pull him to his feet.

"Sneaky bitch," he curses groggily.

"Stand and face me!" Taru commands him in a voice whose power makes even Lexi shudder.

The lanky one looks up, blinking against the harshness of the lamp-lights until he finally sees Taru.

"Oh, fuck me."

He raises his spear and immediately thrusts it into Taru's face, only to watch Taru effortlessly move their head from the weapon's path. He takes several more quick jabs, and each time Taru either feints or knocks the head of the spear away with their sword.

With a cry of frustration, the lanky one rears back several steps and springs forward with twice the force behind his thrust, attempting to skewer Taru through their middle. Instead Taru envelops the shaft of the weapon with their hook-end, trapping it between the opposite planes of the blade. The lanky man, teeth clenched and grinding in frustration, pull and jerks at the spear. It's as if he's buried the tip in solid stone.

Taru draws their short-sword-wielding arm across their chest.

"Taru, wait!" Lexi calls to them. "We need to question him—"

With one backhanded swing of the blade, Taru opens the lanky one's throat. The force of the blow alone jars his hands free of the spear and he staggers back several feet. Then, as the blood begins to escape, his trembling hands clutch at a throat that's no longer there. Taru has practically cleaved his neck in half. He's still searching the now empty space with bloody hands when he falls to the floor.

A moment later, in the lingering silence, Lexi finds she's clamped both hands over her mouth. She's staring at the body almost completely separated from its blood, which is seeping through the rug beneath and spread almost to its very edges.

Taru looks from their felled opponent to their mistress, realization dawning on their face. Taru strides over to Lexi and kneels before her, laying weapons down at Lexi's feet, head bowed in abject supplication.

"I am sorry, Te-Gen. I did not mean to disobey your orders—"

Lexi is already shaking her head. "Rise, rise!" she insists. "Stop all that. You saved my life. He was trying to take yours. You couldn't know."

Taru stands and looks down at both bodies.

"Thieves?" they ask, genuinely confused.

Lexi shakes her head, unable to vocalize an answer at first.

"No," she finally says. "No. They . . . they came here to k . . . kill me. That one told me as much."

She points at the half-face sprawled on his stomach atop her kithkin's map table.

"They're assassins? Sent here to kill you?" Taru can scarcely believe their own words. "No Gen member has ever been assassinated. Such arcane practices have not been seen in Crache since . . ."

Lexi nods, fully aware of the implications. "Have you ever seen tattoos like these?" she asks. "In the Bottoms, or . . . ?"

Taru shakes their head.

"Summon the Aegins," Lexi instructs. "We must report this, have an official record of it set down immediately. Wait!"

Taru, who was ready to sprint from the room and down the length of the tower, stops. They look to Lexi expectantly, blood-spattered hands clenched around their blades.

Lexi's eyes are lost in thought. She's no longer seeing the bodies or the blood or the chaos of the room.

"Te-Gen?" Taru prompts her, gently.

"They could not have gained access to us without help," she whispers, talking to herself. "It's impossible. There are not . . . they weren't stealthy operatives. They were . . . brutes. They were allowed entrance into the Circus, into our towers."

"By Aegins?" Taru asks, a hateful edge in their voice.

Lexi thinks in silence again before answering. "At the very least there must be Aegins in the Circus who are complicit in this. We can't know who or how many."

"Then what is your command, Te-Gen?"

"Go to the cooperative keep and raise the Circus alarm, on my authority."

"That alarm is reserved for disasters that threaten the entire Circus, Te-Gen—"

"When you are being attacked in an alley, you don't call for help, not if you want people to answer that call. You yell 'fire!' Everyone comes when they hear that."

Taru nods, understanding. "Very wise, Te-Gen."

"When everyone arrives I will demand an Aegin from outside the Circus to oversee this, one who could not possibly have been involved."

"Also wise, Te-Gen."

"Go," Lexi bids. "Quickly."

Taru bows their head and strides to the surveyor's room doors, turning back to Lexi before closing them.

"Please, Te-Gen, lock the doors upon my exit until I return."

Lexi nods quickly and assuredly, her thoughts still firmly mired in the events of the last few moments. Nevertheless, after Taru is gone she moves over to the closed doors and sets their heavy latch.

Lexi moves slowly and purposefully about the room, collecting the shattered remnants of her reed-of-the-stone-lake. She does her level best to ignore the bodies, their worsening stench, the rug near the window almost completely soaked through with blood. Picking up the pieces of the demolished instrument gives her just a small sense of focus, enough to carry her through what's to come.

When she's certain she's located the last splinter, Lexi carries them over to the windowsill and carefully lays them out, arranging them as best she can to reform the instrument. It's like putting together a puzzle made from her own memories, and when she realizes her hand is trembling around a length of the reed's neck, tears beginning to prick her eyes, Lexi stops.

Thankfully she hears the first of the horns bellow a few moments later. It's the gargantuan bone siren that arches out from the top of her cooperative keep's parapets. Its call is deep and rippling, like the call of some great sea beast singing underwater. It's soon answered by the horns erected in their neighboring cooperatives, and then the cooperatives beyond that, until the entire Gen Circus is a warning choir.

When Taru returns, knocking at the surveyor's room doors and calling to her from the other side, Lexi's eyes are dry and her hands as still as the corpses at her feet. She moves across the room and unseats the latch on the doors, opening them to find her retainer filling the passage beyond, once again clad in their leather armor, blades sheathed at the hips.

Behind Taru, it seems as though half the cooperative is gathered in the tower stairwell. Gen members, workers from the bazaar, and cooperative attendants all stand shoulder to shoulder in collective shock. There's confusion on some of their faces, but word of what awaits them behind Lexi has obviously already started to spread.

At the head of the crowd are half a dozen Aegins. She recognizes several of them from inside the cooperative and the Circus paths outside. Lexi tries to read their expressions as well, but it's more difficult. While one or two of them share the assemblage's disturbed concern, most of their faces are stony, their eyes dark and guarded.

Most of the Aegins have their gaze locked on Taru's back. They're not even looking at Lexi or the scene behind her.

Taru speaks quietly and only for Lexi's ears. "Te-Gen, I've explained the situation and your command to them. They are . . . not pleased. But I made it clear the only way anyone would enter this room is through me."

"I imagine they were even less pleased with that," Lexi remarks.

Taru nods. "And yet there they stand. Behind me."

Lexi wants to grin, but she can't locate the expression in that moment.

"They've sent word," Taru says. "A third-class Aegin or above from outside the Gen Circus will be here soon."

"And until then?"

"I will wait with you."

Lexi nods and steps aside, allowing Taru to enter the surveyor's room. She's allowed one last look at the resentment and bitterness on several of the Aegins' faces before Taru pulls the door closed once more. Lexi wonders if those looks were for her, or her retainer.

The thoughts are banished as she turns back to the carnage overtaking the small space, no longer able to ignore the gruesome scene or block the fresh memories of how it came to be so.

Lexi draws a deep, troubled breath. "I truly do not wish to spend any more time in this room. In fact, I may never be able to sit in here again."

"I am sorry, Te-Gen. You could wait in another room, but I will be unable to guard both you and these bodies."

Lexi shakes her head. "We must preserve what happened here and not allow anyone to tamper with the bodies until an official record is made by someone beyond reproach."

Taru doesn't even attempt to mask their disdain. "You ask a lot of Aegins."

They seem to immediately regret speaking out of turn, but before they can apologize Lexi dismisses the incident with a wave of her hand.

"Perhaps I am. But it's the best a Gen of two can do under the circumstance, unfortunately."

They wait while the horns continue their bellowing, then one by one cease until only the call of Gen Stalbraid's own cooperative remains. That horn discontinues its steady blowing in favor of short, signaling bursts every few moments, to mark the cooperative as the source of the emergent disturbance.

The next knock at their door is lighter and less insistent than that of Taru's hammerlike fist. They cross the room to unlatch and open the doors. Taru's towering height and wide frame obscure Lexi's view of the petitioner, but she hears them exchanging words before Taru permits him admittance.

The Aegin is tall, though not quite as tall as Taru, and perhaps a few years Lexi's senior. Short, dark curls crown his head. His face is clean-shaven and hard-lined with several thin scars permanently slashed across his right cheek, but something in his expression softens what would otherwise be a severe visage. There's an openness about him, an approachability that all Aegins should practice, yet very few manage.

He does in fact appear to be, at least on the surface, the exact opposite of the two Aegins she and Taru encountered beside the sky carriage berth.

"Te-Gen," he greets her formally. "My name is Daian. Aegin, third-class."

"Lexi. My name is Lexi. I get enough of that from this one, thank you."

She flicks her chin in Taru's direction.

The Aegin grins, though it's fleeting. His eyes have moved from Lexi to the stiffening corpse on the table behind her, then to the one steeped in its own blood on the rug by the window.

"I hope these weren't . . . servants of yours, Te-Gen."

"No, they were not," Lexi firmly states.

Daian looks back at her. His expression is genuinely disturbed. There's remorse in his eyes, for her and for the dead.

"I'm sorry. Are you all right? Did they harm you?"

Lexi shakes her head.

"I'm assigned to Old City. I'm told you requested an Aegin not assigned to the Gen Circus."

Lexi nods.

"May I ask why?"

"Those men . . . they were sent here to kill me. One of them told me so. He did not say who sent them or why, but that much he made clear."

Daian looks over his shoulders at the Aegins assigned to patrol the Gen Circus and guard the cooperative housing Gen Stalbraid. It's a brief glance, and he drops it quickly.

What he says next he says quietly. "Your request was not . . . unwise . . . under the circumstances."

She can see it's difficult for him to admit, but the admission is enough to convince Lexi he's both trustworthy and at least of above average intelligence.

"Te-Gen," Daian begins, then corrects himself. "Lexi . . . if what you're saying is true, we have to contact the Gen Franchise Council and the Protectorate Ministry. An assassination attempt on a Gen member is . . . beyond my grasp of words to describe. It's also beyond my authority to investigate or even . . . confirm."

"I understand that."

"Then you understand that even a random attack in the Gen Circus by simple vagrants is an event that has never and will never happen, as far as the citizens of the Capitol have been led to believe. Such news is shattering enough. This city . . . this entire nation is built atop the notion Gens are untouchable, and the protection of Crache is absolute. The idea that the head of a Gen was hunted by assassins, successful or not, will crack the entire Capitol."

"I understand that, as well. I simply want a record of what happened here, as you see it, set down before anyone else becomes involved. I want those details preserved and protected against corruption."

Daian nods. "That I can do. I promise you."

"I thank you."

"It's my duty."

"I am sorry to say not all your colleagues I've encountered are so . . . forthright in that arena."

Rather than taking umbrage, Daian actually smiles. "A person in an Aegin tunic is still a person, Lexi. Some are good, some are pig shit on two legs."

Taru visibly tenses, and even more visibly scowls.

Daian holds up a hand. "Excuse my language, Te-Gen."

Lexi, however, has to stifle her laughter, not the least of which the chaos of the last hour would no doubt turn the brief bout of levity into hysteria.

"I appreciate your honesty," she says, composed.

Daian bows his head. "May I involve my colleagues now?"

"Of course."

"Thank you, Lexi."

"Let us take you to another room in the tower while they work," Taru bids her after Daian has taken his leave. "You don't need to be here any longer, Te-Gen."

Lexi permits herself one last view of the carnage she helped create.

"Very well."

As she allows Taru to escort her from the room, past the baleful eyes of the other Aegins and the concerned well wishes and queries of the Circus residents, their assurance that Lexi need not be here any longer lingers in Lexi's head.

She will never tell Taru, or anyone else, but Lexi already knows a part of her will never leave that room and the violence that will forever stain it.

WHEN GHOSTS SPEAK
YOUR REAL NAME

THEY NEVER RETURN TO THE CAMP THAT HOSTED THE REVEL. Instead, the wounded and the surviving Savages are herded onto wagons and carted thirty miles along the Sicclunan front—at least, what used to be the Sicclunan front. At dusk Evie hears a thunderclap directly behind the Legion caravan that turns out to be riders from the victorious Skrain, specifically the battalions who moved in to sweep away what was left after the Sicclunan retreated from the Savages.

From what Evie gathers listening to the chatter among the taskers and the soldiers, they're now at the absolute vanguard of the conflict. The Skrain have pushed the Sicclunan armies farther back into their own lands than they have in decades, and they intend to press the effort until they reach the closest Sicclunan city.

"If they . . . we . . . *win* this war, what do you think will happen to the Savages?" Evie asks Mother Manai, who's in the middle of sharpening the blades that have replaced half her fingers.

The older woman laughs. "Girlie, the reason you never hear about this 'war' in the Capitol is there ain't no war. That's not what this is."

Evie has only just begun to grasp the idea that such consuming violence and all-out conflict can exist just beyond the borders of Crache. What she has witnessed and taken part in is bigger and bloodier than anything she had envisioned, even during the process of becoming a Savage. What's coming can be nothing other than open warfare.

"If it's not a war . . . what is it?"

"Something . . . *vastly* more dangerous. Expansion. Crache isn't a country, it's a great scythe cuttin' down everything around it. That's how it feeds its cities and keeps 'em so clean and free of woe. And it'll never stop. It don't know how. When it eats Siccluna it'll move on to the next people, the next realm, the next meal."

Evie falls silent after that, thinking again of the Professor, remembering what he said about Crache and history.

It's south of a freezing midnight when Evie spots firelight from the back of their wagon. They're spread out for half a mile, and unlike the journey to the front, this is no cold camp. They're greeted with small bowls of hot broth with noodles and sprigs of winegrass and even a few slices of dried pork. There's rice wine, too, though they're each given scarcely a sip apiece.

Evie can see the smoke and flame rising from a giant bonfire at the center of the camp, but the Savages never get near it. Most of the encampment is reserved for the Skrain's revelry and comfort. Evie can smell the meat and wine. She can hear the music and the celebratory laughter. The Savages, meanwhile, are herded into one small corner with much smaller fires.

Apparently, their celebration is over.

Rather than stake out a spot around one of the emaciated fires, Evie chooses to keep warm by searching the Savage quarter of the camp, careful to make it look like aimless wandering. She uses the barest corner of her eyes to examine every face she passes, never looking at anyone directly. None of those faces register even the slightest spark of recognition from her.

She ends up standing at the edge of the firelight, past the last of the raggedy tents. Evie stares into the darkness of Siccluna, a land she seems to know even less about than she did when she killed one of their soldiers for defending it.

Back near the largest gathering of fires, the Elder Company are enacting their own small Revel with what little resources they have, refusing to let the Skrain be the only ones to enjoy the day's victory. Evie watches from a distance, admiring them, their resolve and their ability to laugh like the masters of all creation even in the deepest of bondage.

It's not an ability Evie possesses. She walks away from the merriment, intent on finding the warmest place possible to sleep.

She sees the man hunched over the dying embers of several burned logs. Evie stops dead. He's grown a beard that, while unkempt, is thick enough to obscure half his face. The other half is covered in a dozen tiny blue runes brought about by the blood coins, but there's no doubting it's him, not to Evie. His dark hair is longer, but he's obviously done his best to smooth it behind his ears and into some passable shape with his fingers.

Evie can't believe it at first, let alone accept it. Part of her wants to look away and then back to see if he remains sitting there, as if he might be a specter or her mind's own creation.

But he's real, and he's sitting no more than six feet away from her.

"Brio," she says, almost tentative.

He looks up immediately, a new light coming to his eyes.

When he sees her, really *sees* her, that light gives birth to tears that shine.

Brio rises, slowly and with an obvious pain shooting through one of his legs.

"Ashana?" he asks in utter disbelief, using the name she left behind when she became Evie, when she volunteered to infiltrate the Savage Legion in order to find him, if he was still alive.

And he is.

Unbelievably, impossibly, he is.

Evie nods. "It's me."

Brio can scarcely force the words out. "How . . . how can you be here? What are you doing here?"

"It doesn't matter how I got here," she insists, and then, with the resolve of a blade forged in the hottest of fires: "All that matters is that I'm taking you home."

PART TWO

UNRAVELING
THE EDGES

THE BLACK EAGLE

IT'S SAID NO ONE IS EVER BROUGHT BEFORE THE PROTECTOR-
ate Ministry; they always come to you.

More to the point, they always come *for* you.

It's said there isn't a soul in Crache outside their ranks who knows
where the Protectorate Ministry is located. They have no chambers or
quarters in the Spectrum, at least none above ground. There are rumors
they live and work in secret far below the Spectrum floor, in subterranean
caverns that date back before the Renewal and the very founding of Crache
itself. That's why they clad themselves all in black, so they may wear the
cloak of darkness to which they're accustomed out into the light of day.

Lexi knows very well those rumors and all others are worth about as
much as a handful of mule dung.

It's not difficult to hide a building, even a large one, when you control
virtually every piece of information released to the public. She imagines
it's even easier when your entire existence is structured around secrecy
and subterfuge. It's the Protectorate Ministry's job to keep Crache's
confidence while learning everything about its enemies they don't want
Crache to know. Concealing an address is child's play to such people.

Yet they do intentionally cultivate themselves with an air of the
removed, even the otherworldly. The one standing in the Gen Stalbraid
reception parlor, who introduced herself to Lexi and Taru simply as
Ginnix, looks like a ghost attending her own funeral. Her stark white

hair is cut close enough to the scalp to look like the top of a skull, and the strange pink of her eyes is light enough to be almost imperceptible from just a few feet away.

She's covered in leather and silk as black as pitch from top to bottom. The darkness of her tunic even swallows her entire neck. Her only truly resonant features are the eagle's eye pendant adorning her chest and the bone-handled dagger politely concealed behind a length of her shoulder cape.

"You say you're alone in these towers?" Ginnix asks Lexi as the Ministry agent paces around the parlor.

Lexi is seated formally on one of the lounges, Taru standing sentinel beside her.

"Brio's father occupied the other tower in his retirement until he passed away several years ago," Lexi explains. "We shuttered most of it after the funeral to conserve. There was a small staff tending to this tower up till a month ago. I was forced to let them go. Now poor Taru is all that's left to oversee everything."

"Forced, you say?"

"I reallocated all Gen Stalbraid's available assets to finding my husband. There simply wasn't enough left to sustain a full-time staff."

Ginnix ceases her pacing, turning to face Lexi across the spacious, well-appointed room.

"I'm confused, Te-Gen. The search for your husband has been fully funded and undertaken by Crache on your behalf and on behalf of your Gen."

"I felt additional resources were required."

"And have those resources yielded results?"

"They have not."

"Then to say you were 'forced—'"

"Perhaps the word was poorly chosen. May we not allow ourselves to be bound up in semantics, please?"

"Especially since you've yet to explain why you're here," Taru adds, a rare unsolicited statement.

Lexi looks up at them, the shock quickly giving way to visible approval.

"Your retainer?" Ginnix asks her.

Lexi looks back at the Ministry agent and nods, quite proudly.

"I cannot say I've ever approved of private retainers."

"And yet I do approve quite strongly of the point Taru has made," Lexi fires back. "Why are you here? What is it that *we* can do for you?"

Ginnix doesn't answer at first. She's still staring at Taru with open contempt. The gaze Taru offers her in return echoes the message in their hand wrapped around the hilt of their sheathed hook blade.

Lexi doesn't need to see the animosity between them; she can practically feel it, heating the very air.

"What is your official title?" she asks Ginnix.

"I don't have one. I serve. That is who and what I am."

Though her answer is frustrating, Lexi's question accomplishes her goal of drawing Ginnix's attention away from Taru.

"While that may be admirable on a philosophical level," Lexi says, "I find it a wholly impractical way of organizing."

"I introduced myself as Ginnix because that is how you may address me as needed."

"Very well, Ginnix. Why are you here?"

"We at the Protectorate Ministry place the highest possibly priority on this unprecedented attempt on your life and display of violence here in the heart of our nation."

Her mechanical tone only serves to raise the temperature of Lexi's blood.

"And what, may I inquire, has come from placing the highest priority on the targeted destruction of everything I know and love?"

"Our initial findings point toward Sicclunan provocateurs."

Lexi has to be careful to measure her words, not letting her temper run away with them.

"How could Sicclunans reach us in the Capitol? We have been told our entire lives that Crache's enemies are few and scattered and a thousand miles away. That they are merely jealous dissidents envious of our way of life who seek to undermine it, and that we have long been on the verge of eradicating them. What you are saying speaks of a much broader conflict. Is this fight larger and closer to our doors than we have been led to believe?"

Ginnix looks upon her wearily. "Of course not. The assassins themselves were no doubt hirelings, local dregs employed by a lone Sicclunan agent. They are a devious lot. We have shaken most of them out. However, a few obviously remain hidden here and there."

"What of the marks all over their flesh? These 'hirelings' that tried to kill me."

"A new gang organizing itself in our streets, possibly a fanatical faction worshipping the Five. We are investigating that, as well."

Taru, born and bred in the Bottoms where gangs are little more than temporary bands of rabble scrounging for food, stops just short of laughing.

"But why?" Lexi demands. "Why would the Sicclunan government want to assassinate me, the wife of a middling statesman, let alone risk so much to do it? It doesn't make any sense."

Ginnix ignores the breadth of her reactions, remaining neutral.

"What I tell you now was until very recently a closely held state secret, and may come as quite a shock to you. Your husband, Brio, was in fact an agent of the Protectorate Ministry. He worked clandestinely for the Ministry in an effort to secure the trust of Crache's enemies working within the Capitol to undermine our nation."

Neither Lexi nor Taru know how to react to that. Taru looks down at their mistress, searching for some cue, but Lexi is silent and still.

"As I said," Ginnix repeats, "I know this will come as a shock to you—"

Lexi bursts out laughing.

It's loud and unrefined and wholly inappropriate, and Taru stares down at her as if Lexi has launched into convulsions.

Even Ginnix, the ghost attending her own funeral, appears taken aback.

"I'm . . . I'm sorry," Lexi manages through the fit, wresting it slowly under control. "Please, excuse me. It's just . . . I feel as though it was yesterday the Gen Franchise Council, citing conclusive findings by your Ministry, attempted to declare my husband a traitor to Crache. Now, suddenly, he's a hero of the nation working in the shadows to protect us from our enemies."

"Collaborating with those enemies was part of Brio's assignment," Ginnix says.

That stamps out what's left of Lexi's laughing fit, leaving her pensive and more than a little uncertain.

"You're telling me . . . Brio . . ."

"He was straddling both sides of the fence, as it were. It became necessary to paint him as a traitor for him to solidify the trust of the Sicclunans, who were beginning to grow suspicious of his motives. Making his treason a matter of public record was an extreme measure, but an undeniable one from their point of view."

"Then where is he now?" Lexi asks, very near hysterics. "Where is Brio now? Is he here, in Crache? Is he in Siccluna? Will he be there for weeks or months or years? *Where is he?*"

Her voice is steadily rising, higher than Taru has ever heard it in such formal company.

Taru leans down, placing a gauntleted hand on Lexi's shoulder. "Te-Gen—" they begin quietly.

"No!"

Lexi shakes free of Taru's hand, violently, rising to her feet.

"I want to see my husband!" she all but screams at the Protectorate Ministry wraith.

"Brio is dead," Ginnix states flatly with all the warmth of a tombstone in winter.

Those three words succeed where Taru failed, breaking Lexi free from her outburst.

There's even less emotion in Lexi's voice when she says, "What happened?"

"Sicclunan agents discovered his true allegiance. They murdered him for it."

"I want to see his body."

"Of course. We're working even now to recover it . . . that is to say, him. Brio was killed near the Sicclunan front. It will take some time—"

"I *will* see his body," Lexi vows darkly. "None of this means *anything* until I do. Do you understand? Nothing you've said is worth a *damn* until I see my husband with my own eyes."

It's unclear whether Ginnix is offended or disturbed, but Lexi's words obviously resonate.

"As I said, we will do all we can," she reiterates carefully. "In the meantime, Ministry guards will be stationed in your cooperative for your assured safety."

"Te-Gen's safety is already quite assured," Taru informs her.

Ginnix actually smiles. It's a thin, joyless expression on her.

"I should also inform you, Te-Gen," she says, looking again at Taru while speaking to Lexi. "The Gen Franchise Council will be summoning you once more in a week's time. You will receive official notice soon. You see, if the case is left open and you and your Gen are left free of consequence, Brio's true loyalties will always be in doubt."

Lexi returns the smile, grimly. "So truth and law no longer have any place in this matter."

"Both are being temporarily subverted for the greater good. But I assure you, once Brio's mission is complete, everything you will appear to have lost will be restored."

"Of course they will."

"I'll take my leave of you, then, if you have no more questions."

"I have many questions," Lexi says, "but I've gathered all the information from you I expect to."

"Very well, then."

The Ministry's agent bows formally.

"It's funny, isn't it?" Lexi asks before Ginnix turns away from her. "How quickly one can go from servant of the state to enemy of the state to national hero?"

"We are all what Crache needs us to be, Te-Gen," Ginnix says. "Function is purpose, after all."

Lexi swallows whatever else she might have said, silently watching the woman's black shoulder cape flutter away.

"Believe none of it, Te-Gen," Taru urges her after Ginnix is gone from the tower. "Not a single word."

"I don't."

"Then why, if I may ask, do you appear to be in such conflict?"

"I cannot decide if that bitch and the rest of those black-clad spawn are responsible for everything that's happened to my Gen, or if they are merely attempting to clean up the aftermath for someone else."

"How can we know?" Taru asks.

Lexi realizes she's been clenching her fist for the past several minutes, digging her nails painfully into the meat of her palms. She forces her knuckles to unlock and gently rubs her trembling hands over the front of her wrap, smoothing them until both the sting and the tremors subside.

"We need help," she says, finally. "Thankfully, our choices are very few. That will make it easier."

THE MESSENGER

"ASHANA——"

"My name is *Evie*," she corrects Brio, urgently. "You have to call me that while we're here."

"What? Why?"

"The Aegins arrested a drunken vagrant bar brawler named Evie. Laython crammed a blood coin down Evie the vagrant's gullet."

She watches him slowly process this, no doubt hindered by the other major revelations that have very recently blindsided him.

"We've all had our true selves stripped from us here," he says. "That's what they do. They don't care who we really are. What difference does it make what you call yourself?"

"You are proof that isn't entirely true," she reminds him. "They may try to take your identity from you here, but they abducted you precisely *because* of who you are, Brio. Treating us as Savages and appointing callous brutes to whip us into submission is a tactic. That doesn't mean people smarter and more important than those brutes aren't paying attention. They care who is here and for what reason. I'm choosing caution for now."

Brio opens his mouth to reply, but in the end, perhaps due to exhaustion more than anything else, he only nods silently. His eyes are wet and bloodshot. They flicker red in the light of the fire she's fashioned from his pitiful burned log.

Brio never was much use sleeping rough.

She watches the ragged man she remembers as so crushingly hand-some. Once, she lost everything she had because of him. Now she's chosen to leave everything she knows behind for him. Evie is forced to consider the notion she's either a hopeless glutton for punishment, or just an incredible devotee of symmetry.

"Do you understand now?" she asks Brio.

"I don't understand any of this," he says. "I mean . . . I understand where we are and what you're saying, but . . . how are you here?"

"I'll explain, but first I need to have a look at this leg."

She kneels in front of him. The right leg of the filthy hemp pants he wears are already ripped and crusted with dried blood. She tears the rest of the stained material over his knee, exposing a deep gash that must stretch six inches down his calf. The wound is mostly black, and much of it is scabbed over. Evie knows the scabbing is only superficial, nothing but more dried blood. There's no healing going on underneath.

"Is it numb?" she asks, trying to keep her voice even.

"I can feel my toes, but not much between my knee and my foot."

Evie says nothing else. She stares at the wound with eyes full of storm clouds.

"Judging purely from your expression I take it my prognosis is not good," Brio says, trying to sound playful, but the wavering in his voice betrays that utterly.

"It's already festering." She frowns up at him, her eyes flashing harshly. "Did you even clean it out?"

Brio actually laughs. It's a hollow, mirthless sound.

"With what?" he asks. "Clean wraps and fresh water are difficult to come by in this camp. They don't even have a surgeon for Savages."

Evie's eyes soften, just a little. "Have you had anything to eat?"

"Barely since the Revel. It appears to be the one time we're treated like something resembling human beings. That courtesy does not extend to the cold camp. Food and water are doled out scarcely, and it seems to be first come, first served. We were watered and fed jerked duck on the road."

Evie nods. "Us too. Wait here. I'll be back, okay?"

His eyes widen, a desperate expression overtaking his face. "Where are you going?"

She raises a hand. "Relax, Brio. All right? I'm used to being served last. I know how to make do."

Evie rests that placating hand on the knee of his injured leg. The desperation leaves his haggard features and his eyes soften on her. Brio covers her hand with both of his. Evie looks down at the tangle of their fingers, both relishing and resenting the falling sensation in her stomach the sight of it causes. She feels too much like the little girl who would've followed him anywhere, and Evie has no time for such saccharine flights. This isn't a place for sentiment.

She slips her hand from beneath his.

"Just wait here," Evie repeats. "I won't be gone long."

Brio nods, twining his fingers atop his knee tightly to steady his hands.

Evie holds his eyes reassuringly for a moment longer before rising from her knees and walking away, almost sprinting. She returns no more than ten minutes later, a cracked horn goblet in one hand and a bundle of drab but unstained rags in the other. A crooked and broken stick is balanced atop the goblet. Steam rises from the hunk of cooked meat skewered around the end of the stick. She kneels once more at his feet, placing the goblet on the ground.

Brio leans forward, picking up the skewer and peering down at what looks like clean water filling the horn from which the goblet is fashioned. He examines the meat, the smell of it causing his mouth to water painfully.

"What is this?" he asks, swallowing hard.

"Just eat it," Evie instructs him.

She begins laying out the strips of cloth she's collected on the boulder beside him.

Brio bites gratefully into the scorched skin of the mystery meat.

"How did you get all this?" he asks as he chews.

Evie shrugs. "The Savage who had them was otherwise occupied."

"With what?"

"His arm. It broke."

Brio looks away from her, grinning ruefully. "I see."

"I need to clean this out and burn it," Evie tells him, sounding dubious. "Even then, it'll be by the grace of the outlawed gods that we *don't* have to take your leg off."

Evie bunches a length of cloth in her hand and dips the end of it into the water, soaking it through.

Brio watches her, his shoulders stiffening. "I should be frightened, I suppose, but I'm mostly amused you're *still* invoking the God Stars at your age."

"I like the stars. I can see them. They're always up there."

"The trouble you got us into as children, refusing to let go of those old symbols even when my father—"

"Let's not visit the past right now," she says.

Brio's face drops. "All right."

"Everything I'm about to do is going to hurt," she warns him.

"I'm becoming used to it."

Evie begins cleaning his wound, wetting the dried flecks covering the gash with her cloth and wiping them away as gently as possible.

Brio tenses, sucking air through his lips sharply, but he neither protests nor shrinks away.

"How have you survived?" she asks, both to distract him and because every bit of information is useful to her in their current state. "How many other battles have you seen?"

"Two. Both were further north from here. The first was little more than a skirmish, an outpost, a few dozen soldiers at most. We barely lost a Savage to the battle. The Skrain just watched. The second was a siege, what I take was the last Sicclunan stronghold halting our advancement. They sent the Savages over the wall first."

Evie is already on her second strip of doused cloth and there's still muck to dig from his wound. She pauses and looks up at him, genuinely taken aback.

"You? Scaled a castle wall?"

Brio tries to laugh, but what he comes out with is more like a sigh. "I tried. I made it about halfway up when I felt something slash through my leg. It was an ax blade. I don't know if it was Sicclunan or Savage, but someone dropped it. I lost my grip on the rungs and fell. Fortunately the ground was mostly mud. I decided I much preferred wallowing there. Again, I got lucky. We took the castle in the first attack."

"I doubt very much it was fully reinforced. The Sicclunans had to have known that their line was folding. They probably left a skeleton battalion in the keep to buy time for them to fall back and establish a new one. The force the Savages put me with faced south of here seemed like a half-hearted effort as well."

Brio braces himself as Evie digs particularly deep into his wound with the wetted cloth, closing his eyes.

"I imagine the Sicclunans have become expert at falling back," he says, shaken.

"We give them little choice in the matter."

Evie finishes cleaning out the gash and tosses the stained-black rag aside.

"Who took you?" she asks. "And how?"

"I was in the Bottoms. I turned down an alley, a shortcut to the sky carriage. I'd used it a hundred times before—"

Evie grunts. "That's why they were waiting for you there. They were, weren't they?"

"Yes. A bag was thrown over my head, and the next thing I remember is standing in a field shoulder to shoulder with the people I used to plead for. My clothes had been stripped from me. I was wearing rags. When I tried to explain what had happened I took the butt of a mace in my gut."

"Do you remember anything before the training field?"

"I caught a . . . a flash . . . of a black cape. Black boots."

Evie's brow hangs heavily. "The Protectorate Ministry."

"Most likely. The only good thing is they took me leaving and not going. If they'd caught me while I was headed the other way they would've had what they were no doubt looking for."

"What's that?"

"Proof, of what's really going on here, what the other purpose of the Savage Legion is."

"What proof?"

"Dispatches, between the Protectorate Ministry and the Capitol's Aegin commanders, instructing them to increase arrests in aid of filling the Savage ranks, focusing on vagrants. They stated explicitly they were expanding their recruiting beyond the condemned, against Crachian law. There were also decrees sent out to all the councils that any petitioners speaking against the state be reported to the Ministry. I found dozens of them, copies made of the originals, stored away in the Spectrum archives. Can you imagine? This wonderful, oppressive bureaucracy of ours, every document required to be penned three times for the sake of posterity or records or whatever."

"They didn't think anyone would ever bother to look."

"Of course not. No one else cares."

"Why did you?"

"I began to hear disturbing things. People were disappearing, from the Bottoms. They were being arrested and never returned. Husbands, wives, parents, brothers, and sisters, they came to me in secret, terrified of even talking about it, afraid they'd be next. I begin to hear muddled whispers about this . . . the Legion. People used as flesh weapons, hurled at the front line of our enemies like artillery."

"And when you inquired at the Spectrum you were reported."

"No doubt."

"I'm sorry for what you've been through, Brio."

"I'm fine," he insists. "Now will you tell me how you came to be here?"

"Lexi," Evie explains. "She came to me. I was working as a retainer for Gen Ultimo. The kith-kins wanted an unassuming woman to escort their children to and from lessons in the city rather than a pack of hulking armored guards. It's very in fashion just now, apparently. Lexi told me what happened, or what she suspected had happened, and your theory about conscripted vagrants and this place. She had a plan. I became Evie. I changed my clothes, stopping bathing with any regularity, and started frequenting every tavern in the Bottoms, picking fights. It seemed like such a far-fetched scheme . . . but it worked. The Savage Legion is real, and we're both here."

"How did you convince Gen Ultimo you were unassuming?"

"I see you haven't lost your sense of humor."

"Oh no," Brio assures her, sounding magnanimous and for the first time like the man she remembers. "I've lost my freedom, my wardrobe, a fair amount of blood, and all memory of personal hygiene . . . but never my sense of humor."

Evie unsheathes the flared blade of a dagger from her belt and holds the tip to the fire she built.

"Well, hold on to it now," she advises him. "Because this next part is going to hurt far worse than the last part did."

Brio draws in a deep breath and exhales serenely. "All right, then."

While the tip of her blade continues to heat up, Evie offers Brio one of the remaining strips of clean cloth.

"Ball that up and bite down on it," she instructs him.

He nods, taking the rag and rolling it up like a handkerchief. Brio holds it up and clamps his jaw around the thickly scrolled fabric.

When the dark steel of the dagger has turned bright orange with a smoldering red heart, Evie removes it from the flames. She reaches down with her free hand and grips the ankle of Brio's injured leg firmly, looking up at him with sympathetic yet resolved eyes.

"Ready?"

He leans back and grips the stone on which he sits as best he can, nodding.

Evie presses the red-hot tip of the blade into the bottom of the gash, scorching the lower half of the wound. His throat fills with a horrific gargling noise, but Brio manages to neither scream nor jerk beneath her.

"One more time," she tells him gently.

Again, Brio nods. Sweat is beginning to drip from both of his temples.

Evie burns the second half of the wound, and this time Brio tosses his head back so fiercely he almost flings himself over the stone. She tightens her grip on his ankle to steady him, and a few moments after she removes the still-burning blade he begins to relax, though his rune-covered face is now pouring with sweat.

"It's all over," she practically coos to him. "You did well."

"You lived on the streets?" Brio asks, breathless, as Evie begins wrapping his calf with the remaining rags. "As Evie, I mean."

She shrugs. "It's no worse than how I began life."

"A life I promised you'd never return to."

"If you had that kind of power *neither* of us would be here in this place now. I was playing a role, that's all. And it worked."

Brio nods, accepting that as best he can. "Why did Lexi seek you out for this mission she concocted?"

"She remembered me from when we were children, and she remembered how devoted I was to you after your parents took me in. She said I was the only other woman you've ever loved. I was surprised that it didn't sound at all like an accusation."

"If Lexi even possesses lesser qualities, jealousy isn't one of them, especially in the face of a task to which she's appointed herself."

"She's a very determined woman."

"Apparently it's a virtue I seek out in the women I love."

Evie ignores his implication, finishing a perfect field dressing on his leg.

"I understand why Lexi did this," Brio says carefully, "but why did you agree to it?"

Evie shrugs. "Maybe I feel like I still owe your kith-kin."

"They put you out," Brio reminds her.

"And before that they saved my life."

"Ashana, why—"

"Where's all the proof you uncovered?" Evie cuts him off. "What did you do with it before they took you?"

"I left it with a friend, someone I trust. She'll still have it, believe me."

"We have to get word to Lexi, now," Evie insists.

"Why can't we tell her ourselves, after we've escaped?"

"Because it may take some time for that second part to happen. But we may be able to have a message delivered to her."

"How?"

"A new friend of mine. If you lean on me, can you walk?"

"If you tell me I need to, then I can."

Evie takes his hands in hers once more, this time using them to pull Brio to his feet. He winces and grinds his jaw to muffle whatever agonized sound is ruminating in his throat. He secures one arm around Evie's shoulders and with her supporting half his weight is able to limp with relative ease and pain.

They find Spud-Bar sitting against one of the armory wagon's rear wheels, sharpening the blade of an ax with a whetstone the size of a brick.

"Make a new friend, Sparrow?" Spud-Bar asks, using the name under which the Elder Company has adopted Evie. "I've warned you about taking in strays."

"He's an old friend," Evie assures the armorist.

Spud-Bar grunts. "This ain't much of a place for reunions, sorry to say."

"In this one case it's the best of places."

Evie bends at the knees, sinking down to help Brio in lowering himself to the mostly dead grass.

"That don't look good," Spud-Bar remarks, eyes drifting to Brio's leg wound.

"It's not," Evie says bluntly. "But I've tended to it the best I know how."

"You really do have a deep bag of skills fer a vagrant, don't ya?"

"When do you return to the Capitol?" Evie asks.

"I leave in the morning," Spud-Bar answers. "It's been a busy few days fer the Savages on the front. Need to replenish the ranks. We'll barely have time to break 'em in and get 'em coined, from the look."

"I need you to take something back to the Capitol for me."

The armorist shakes their head. "Against the rules."

"This is important, Spud-Bar. This may be the most important thing you ever do."

The spit-dampened surface of the whetstone pauses halfway over the crescent of the shoddy ax's poorly smithed blade.

The armorist looks up at Evie, heavy, thick brows hung low over dark eyes. "I suppose you'd be askin' me to take him? Is that it? Get him to a surgeon?"

Evie shakes her head. "He's my responsibility. I only need you to carry a message to a Gen in the Capitol. It's a short message, one you can carry in your head. It needn't even be put to parchment."

Spud-Bar frowns. "Why would you wanna make my life difficult? Haven't I been good to you since we met?"

"You have," Evie assures the armorist, sincerely. "Because you're a good person, too fine a person to be responsible for the monstrosity that's been created here with this Legion. That's why I'm asking you."

"I'm a simple sort, Sparrow, and you're losin' me in a fog here."

Evie looks at Brio. "Tell my friend who you are."

"My name is Brio Alania, leader of Gen Stalbraid," he says. "I'm the pleader for the Bottoms in the Capitol."

"Now tell Spud-Bar what you did," she urges him.

"If you mean what law I broke, then nothing. I did nothing."

Spud-Bar snorts, staring down at the darkened surface of the whet-stone.

"Nothing," he repeats. "I obtained evidence I meant to present to the Arbitration Council that the Savage Legion was filling its ranks, not just with the condemned, but with minor offenders, and with people they simply snatched from the streets in the Bottoms. I also suspected the Legion was being used to dispose of those the state views as enemies, the dissident, anyone who speaks out openly against them. My being here proves that."

"It's exactly like the Professor said," Evie implores the armorist. "He may have been mad, but he wasn't lying about Crache."

Spud-Bar is still staring into the microscopic crags and crannies of the whetstone, silently.

"Spud-Bar," Evie pleads, "you *know* what's going on here. You've always known. You think you're beyond it because they allow you to travel to the cities and back, but you're not. You will die serving this Legion. We all will, unless something is done, unless the truth is made known."

"Crache don't run on truth," Spud-Bar says quietly.

Evie reaches out and cups her hand around the hand holding that whetstone.

Spud-Bar doesn't look up.

"I know it's easier to believe we all belong here, but I tell you, *this* man does not. He's spent his life pleading for the people in the Bottoms, never asking nor taking from them. He's here because he doesn't want anyone else to suffer his fate. You must believe me, Spud-Bar."

"And if I do?" Spud-Bar asks, still not meeting her eyes.

"Then I simply ask you to deliver a short message to the Gen Circus. That's all."

The armorist finally looks directly at her. Evie sees a deeper torment she never would've expected of the perpetually passive and dismissive Undeclared.

"Who are you? Really?"

"I'm a warrior, like you," Evie answers. "And I fight for the people I love when they're threatened, whatever the odds and however certain defeat. Because that's what I was taught warriors do."

Spud-Bar grins ruefully. "You 'ad better teachers than me."

"Will you carry the message?" Evie presses, her desperation threatening to rip through the veil of the person she's created to walk among the Savages.

Spud-Bar shakes their head darkly, but says, "All right, then. What's the message?"

Evie looks at Brio once more, eyes urging him to seize the moment quickly.

"It's for Lexi Xia," he says, "also of Gen Stalbraid. It's from Brio. I've been conscripted into the Savage Legion and Evie has found me. I'm alive and well and I need her to know there's a merchant ship that docks in the Capitol for two days every fortnight. It's a Rok vessel named *The Black Turtle*. The captain is a very old friend of my father's. Her name is Staz. There are few people I trust more. She's carrying the decrees and dispatches I found that prove everything about the Savage Legion."

"And that's all I need to tell this fine Te-Gen of the Capitol?"

Brio nods. "She'll know what to do from there."

Evie gently squeezes Spud-Bar's hand. "Can I ask you to leave tonight, right away?"

Spud-Bar nods. "Hai. Probably best I do, before the crazy wears off."

The armorist stands and chucks the whetstone into a bucket hung from a nail in the wagon. Spud-Bar returns the ax to one of the over-encumbered racks of rusted, secondhand weapons.

"Why can't we go with your new friend here?" Brio asks Evie, quietly.

"Because we will *all* be executed if Spud-Bar is caught with us. You can deny carrying a message. Two people in your wagon is much more difficult."

"You're right, of course," he says. "Spud-Bar is risking more than enough already."

"We'll find our own way," Evie promises him. "When you're healed."

"I believe you."

Evie walks over to where Spud-Bar is quickly hitching their small team of mounts to the wagon.

"Thank you for this," she says.

"Don't expect I'll see you again, at least not like this" is all Spud-Bar offers.

"Do you feel like I lied to you?" Evie asks.

"Nah. I knew you weren't what you seemed the second I spied you goin' through my blades."

"My name and my clothes may be false, but the rest is me. And I do consider you a friend. I wouldn't ask such an important thing of you if I didn't."

Spud-Bar remains noncommittal, lashing the final bridle to their horse. "That's good to know, I suppose."

"Would you like to know my real name?"

Spud-Bar appears to think about it for a moment.

"No," the armorist says, and walks away.

A PEBBLE IN A MAZE

THREE MORNINGS AFTER PRESENTING EDGER WITH HER invention, Dyeawan awoke to the first task.

It was sitting atop the blanket as if someone had brought her breakfast in bed while she slept. The sack was small, but bulging, made of silk cloth the color of dead violets and tied off with a midnight ribbon that shined in the morning sunlight. When her rapidly blinking eyes first took it in there was panic, the errant thought that it must be something bad, like a message, perhaps the Planning Cadre's way of telling her she had to leave.

When Dyeawan realized such an idea was absurd, it occurred to her that it might actually be a gift, from Edger or perhaps Tahei. It never occurred to her, however, to find the notion of somebody, or some-bodies, sneaking into her room while she sleeps disquieting; she's spent most of her short life on the streets of the Capitol. The idea of privacy or sacred space is unknown to her.

Pulling the loose end of the ribbon, the cloth fell away to spill dozens upon dozens of small, intricately carved wooden pieces over her blan-ket. They appeared identical, rectangles with forked ends, but Dyeawan quickly noticed tiny differences in their cut. She picked up one of the pieces and examined it closer, then another. When she fit them together it was like a lightning crack between her temples. Dyeawan looked down at the pile of wood and saw with her mind's eye what they could be, and what they should be.

She began picking up piece after piece and slotting them together. It took her less than a minute to assemble all the pieces into one object, a full-bodied wooden star that could stand on its own when she placed it back down atop the blanket.

Dyeawan stared at that star for a long time in silence, marveling at how so many seemingly complete parts could compose such a whole when properly joined together. She supposed it was meant to represent some aspect of the Planning Cadre itself, and wondered if that was the lesson to take away from it.

She'd climbed out of bed and onto her tender to begin her day. She delivered messages and parcels and materials between the concentric floors of the Cadre. She took her meals in the great hall, eating with Riko and Tahei, never mentioning the strange puzzle.

On the few occasions she'd crossed paths with Edger, not a word was exchanged about it.

When Dyeawan returned to her room in the evening, the wooden cipher was gone. That night she dreamed of a sky whose stars she could reach up and rearrange with her bare hands, forming magnificent shapes and patterns that she made swirl and shine by touching each star with her fingertip. The dream lasted all night, and by morning she'd created a vast heaven of wheels and mandalas and triangles that somehow all fit and moved together like a great, brilliant machine of pure light.

When she awoke, large sheets of parchment covered the blanket over her legs. She sat up and reached for them. One of them was colored from corner to corner with a beautiful drawing of a building much like the Capitol Spectrum, surrounded by city streets and foliage, none of which Dyeawan recognized. It must've been a scene from another Crachian city, or perhaps even something new for a city yet to be built.

The other sheet of parchment was blank, and resting on top of it was a leather case containing coal sticks of many colors.

That's when she understood there was a test being administered to her, and it had begun the morning before. Dyeawan picked up the pouch and sorted through the sticks of colored coal, her eyes flitting between them and the colors used to create the rendering of the building on the first sheet of parchment. She'd never drawn much before, let alone painted. She would often trace shapes in the dirt or the dust on alley walls, but that was the extent of Dyeawan's artistic endeavors to date.

Still, she'd observed the finest architects and artists in the Planning Cadre at work dozens upon dozens of times by then. More than that, as with the wooden pieces, she could look at the drawing and simply *see* how it was supposed to be done.

Dyeawan removed a red stick of coal from the pouch and touched it to the blank sheet of paper.

Less than an hour later all the sticks were nubs and she'd not only perfectly replicated the drawing, she'd made several improvements to both its composition and the design of the building. Her use of shadows and the illusion of light made the scene look far more vivid and more real than the original. The windows of the building appeared to be less cluttered together, and Dyeawan moved the main entrance to what seemed to her to be a more logical place to avoid bottling up the people seeking audience inside with those simply moving through the streets.

Dyeawan left the drawing behind as she'd left the star model and went about her day. At breakfast and lunch she was aching to tell Tahei and Riko about the tests, but something held her back. She couldn't be certain what it was, perhaps her long learned instincts to make herself as small and unobserved as possible. It might've been as simple as the fact she hadn't had friends in a very long time, and she was afraid they might become suspicious or, even worse, jealous.

She continued to wake up to tests for the next four days. The morning after the drawing she found a miniature maze constructed out of sandstone walls set in a box the size of her room's sea-facing window. The top of the box was covered by glass. A smoothed, rounded pebble had been placed beneath the glass on the outside of the maze. She couldn't touch it, but she found she could maneuver the pebble by holding and moving the box.

It took Dyeawan precisely eight movements to guide the pebble to the center of the maze.

The morning after that she found a small table that was new to her room, upon which an array of potions and elixirs had been arranged in mostly small vials. A large, bulbous beaker stood at the center of it all. Its viscous contents were a barrage of colors, red stacked upon orange stacked upon green stacked upon lavender. Dyeawan marveled at how, despite being liquid, none of the colored layers ran together.

She'd been provided with an empty beaker the size and shape of the rainbow one, and it wasn't difficult, even for a mind not belonging to Dyeawan, to discern what she was supposed to do. Never studying or working with potions before, it was the first task to take up an hour of her everyday rounds. She also accidentally dyed half her room a patchwork of colors from the various vials in the process.

Her attempts to mimic the rainbow beaker resulted in a mess of every color bleeding into every other color, no matter how carefully she poured each one, until Dyeawan noticed the weight and thickness of each elixir varied from vial to vial. The heaviest of them was the lavender.

Instead of pouring the lavender first, she tried reversing the process. She poured the red, the top color from the rainbow beaker, into the bottom of her empty beaker. Dyeawan could scarcely believe it as she poured the orange and watched it not only soak completely through the red, but also force every drop of it to the top, the two elixirs remaining completely separate.

The fifth task was a stack of ancient volumes accompanied by a scroll and quill. Questions about the contents of the tomes and their subject matter, largely concerning the laws and doctrine of Crachian society, were penned on the scroll parchment awaiting her answers. Though Dyeawan had only just read her first real book days after arriving at the

Planning Cadre, she found she could now absorb every word of a three-hundred-page volume in a matter of an hour or less. She needed only to glance at an entire page to commit its contents to memory, and the meaning of most words she'd never heard before she could intuit from their relationship to the words she did know.

It took her all of a morning and an afternoon to become an expert on Crachian law. The only aspect of it which confused her were why it was written in such an unnecessarily convoluted way with so much excess verbiage, and why every process seemed to include a dozen more steps than were necessary to arrive at the same conclusion.

Most of the questions in the scroll simply required her to remember facts and quotations, but the final one asked her to interpret the overall purpose of the Crachian doctrine.

After a few minutes of thought, Dyeawan wrote down: *To confuse people like me.*

The sixth task was a small, jade-feathered duck in a straw bottom cage. It was the first one to truly baffle Dyeawan until she saw that the creature was in distress. It was lying on its side, its breathing labored and belly distended. She opened the cage to examine it, out of concern more than anything else. She could feel a small, hard object pressing against the duck's belly from inside. She could only guess whatever it was would not pass on its own.

Dyeawan had watched more than one person die in that way on the streets.

She rowed herself to the Cadre commissary to see Makai. Despite Tahei's wonderfully constructed, silent running wheels, the blind cook heard her coming and was smiling before she even entered the kitchen. She asked to see a duck that was being dressed for cooking. As before, Makai asked her no questions, simply gave her what she needed. She scrutinized a freshly slaughtered duck, inside and out, for the better part of a half hour.

When she was done, Dyeawan requested a finger of Makai's

strongest spirit, one of his sharpest boning knives, twine, needle, and a handful of clothespins. She was relieved to find the duck still breathing when she returned to him with the kit she'd assembled. Dyeawan fed him wine from a thimble until the lids of his tiny eyes began to droop heavily. She cut low and shallow just below his belly, careful to avoid the area where she'd seen so many small organs.

Prying what turned out to be a bound stack of coins loose of the duck's gizzard was a simpler process than she'd thought. There was less blood than she expected, and he barely moved during the impromptu surgery. Stitching the incision closed proved to be the difficult part. Dyeawan realized the twine from the commissary was far too thick; she had to carefully strip single threads from it one at a time. Fortunately she had the clothespins to use as makeshift tourniquets.

She returned to her room after lunch to check on the duck, who Dyeawan had secretly and unbeknownst to him named Greenfire. Not only was he still breathing, he actually quacked as she rolled into the room.

It was after that test that Dyeawan finally opened up to Tahei and Riko. They were all eating dinner, Tahei loudly slurping his noodles as she'd become accustomed to both watching and hearing him do, when she told them both she'd been waking up to find a new task in her room every day for the past week.

"Building the wooden star and the pebble in the maze were two of the tests they gave me when I first came to the Cadre!" Riko informed her brightly.

Though Dyeawan had formed her suspicions, much of her still refused to believe them. "Really?"

Riko nodded excitedly.

"You too, Tahei?"

The eldest of the trio shook his head. "No. I'm a builder, remember? All my tests were smithing metals."

That gave Dyeawan pause. "So . . . neither of you had to save the duck?"

Riko laughed. "No! My hands stayed one color too."

She reached across the table and pinched Dyeawan's forefinger, shaking it. There were still faint traces of the colored potions seeped into her skin.

Dyeawan smiled, but she couldn't help puzzling over what appeared to be an oddity among Planning Cadre recruits. "Then . . . why me? Why so many different tests?"

Tahei shrugged. "Maybe they don't really know what you're good at and they're trying to find out. They did bring you to clean and make deliveries, after all."

"Anybody can see you're capable of more than that, Slider," Riko assured her with a reprimanding look at Tahei.

His eyes widened. "That isn't what I meant! I know how smart you are, Slider."

"It's okay," she said. "I don't . . . I didn't expect any of this. I'm happy just to be here. I'm more than happy. I'm . . . lucky. *Fortunate.*"

She annunciated the word carefully. It was obviously the first time she'd said it aloud.

"Well, all that reading is certainly showing," Riko said, sounding genuinely proud of her.

On the seventh morning the tasks stop appearing at her bedside. Dyeawan wakes to an otherwise empty bed and an equally empty room. By her reckoning she has been tested in almost every basic skill used by members of the Planning Cadre, and on virtually every floor, save the builders. She expected a building test today, something they would've given Tahei. Dyeawan wonders briefly and with a sinking in her chest if she hasn't done as well on the previous tasks as she thought.

Then she remembers the lamp she built, the one she presented to Edger that made him act so oddly with her.

THIRTY TONGUES AND
NOT A WORD SPOKEN

LEXI AND TARU DISEMBARK THE SKY CARRIAGE THREE BLOCKS from the Capitol's Aegin Kodo. The only even slightly satisfying aspect of the events of the past week, at least for Taru, is that they've provided proof of an existing imminent threat to Lexi; as such, she's finally agreed to use the ascendancy reserved for Gen members rather than the public staircase.

"Accepting that it's not my place to question Te-Gen's stratagems or decisions—"

"I really do wish you'd stop that," Lexi urges them, exasperated, as the two take to the narrow streets together. "Gen Stalbraid currently consists of just the two of us. I can scarcely afford to feed or shelter you. It's almost laughable to keep referring to you as my 'retainer' when I'm offering nothing in retention."

"Then what are you saying, Te-Gen?"

"At this point you're either my partner or my former employee. Choose."

"I serve Gen Stalbraid," Taru says without hesitation and with the firmest of resolve. "I always will."

"Good, then that's settled. If you feel seeking this man out and taking him into our confidence is a mistake, tell me and I won't do it."

"I am . . . uncertain, Te-Gen."

"Well, when you *are* certain, let me know so I can either stop walking or hasten my speed."

Taru frowns. "I do not understand why you are so quick to trust him. I . . . find it highly convenient he was the Aegin to respond to our request after you were attacked. That we should meet the one honest man to wear that tunic."

"You are right to be suspicious, Taru. Of course you are. Perhaps I want to trust him. Perhaps it is because he reminds me very much of Brio."

"He is *not* Brio, Te-Gen," Taru insists with a resentful edge.

"Of course he isn't. No one else is. However, Brio was the one honest man in a sea of predators and cheap opportunists. He chose scarcity and the scorn of lesser pleaders over playing their game and using the people of the Bottoms as pawns for his own personal gain. Such men do exist, though they be few and far between. If you had met Brio now, not known him for so much of your life, you might think him too good to be true, as well."

Taru seems to unwillingly consider that scenario. "It is . . . possible I would think that, yes."

"I want to believe this Daian is a man like my husband. Yes, we met at an opportune time. Yet so much has gone so disastrously wrong as of late I choose to believe we were owed a small victory, if even by accident or pure chance."

Taru almost laughs at that. "I suppose we were due."

Lexi's expression, however, turns very serious. "I may be wrong, Taru. I may be fatally mistaken, in fact. But here and now I choose to hope. Am I mad?"

"No, Te-Gen."

"Then you are with me still?"

Taru can't help but grin. "I follow your lead, Te-Gen. You've seemed to know precisely what you're doing thus far."

Lexi laughs hollowly. "I only wish."

The Kodo is where the Capitol's guardians of day and night go to receive training in the application of Crachian law and learn Aegin methods and procedures. The building itself is a three-tiered structure of bamboo and ceramic filling a corner only a few blocks from the Spectrum itself. A bright red awning falls over each tier, and upon each of those roofing layers is painted the Aegin symbol of the owl's claw.

"Perhaps you should wait out here while I inquire," Lexi suggests to Taru.

Taru frowns. "I have no fear of Aegins in any number, Te-Gen."

"I'm aware of that, and though they no doubt should, they don't seem to have a fear of you, either. Combined with the irrational animosity so many of them seem to feel toward you I'd rather not needlessly provoke any altercation, especially now. I need you too much, Taru."

It's that last admission that seems to quell Taru more than anything.

"Very well. I will remain right outside the doors."

"Thank you, my friend."

Lexi briefly clasps a hand around Taru's gauntleted wrist before drawing up the hem of her wrap to ascend the front steps of the Kodo.

She returns a few minutes later, much to Taru's relief.

"Thankfully," she says, "our man is training in the dojo today."

She is thankful for the sole reason they won't be required to spend any length of time inside the Kodo. Its dojo is housed on a patio detached from the corner of the building at the end of the block. Slender columns and a sturdy roof are all that obscure the dojo from the outside; Crache likes the citizens of its cities to watch their Aegins in training, feeling it inspires potential recruits and instills reverence in everyone else.

Lexi and Taru walk the length of the building's exterior until they reach the edge of the open-air dojo. A small crowd, mostly children, has gathered on the sidewalk, looking in on the class with interest. The duo can hear the collective kiai of dozens of young voices before they look upon its source.

A group of thirty acolytes are spaced an arm's length apart in rows of six atop a straw practice mat. The edges of their daggers are all blunted for training purposes. Over their keikogi they wear a series of straps connected to strategically placed leather pads protecting their most sensitive and commonly struck areas: the heart, collar, crotch, thighs, and the middle of the abdomen.

Beyond the mat, at the head of the class, Daian leads the trainees with a practice dagger of his own.

"One, five, three!" he calls out, then performs a series of slashes and thrusts with his dagger at different angles and different levels.

The acolytes filling the mat mimic Daian's expert movements to the best of their abilities. Two other Aegin instructors, meanwhile, pace up and down their ranks, barking corrections at anyone failing to match the form to their satisfaction.

Daian calls out a different series of numbers in no order Lexi can follow and performs another sequence of strikes with the training blade.

"Are you familiar with this form of knife play?" Lexi asks her retainer, quietly.

"The dagger was the first weapon Brio's father taught me, because I was so small."

Lexi grins. "When were you ever small?"

Taru stiffens self-consciously. "Comparatively, I mean."

"What do the numbers mean, then?" Lexi asks.

In answer, Taru points inside the dojo, high above the heads of the instructor and his trainees. There's a large canvas hanging from the ceiling. The outline of a human body is sketched upon it, and over that a series of straight lines has been drawn, four of them, all intersecting in the center of the illustration. Large numbers are painted beside and correspond to each line. The same is true of the fields created between the lines. The former obviously relates to slashing, while the open areas relate to thrusting.

"I see," Lexi says, watching Daian intently.

He guides the class through several more sequences before a downward slash pulls his body in Lexi's direction. He spots her and Taru standing at the edge of the crowd gathered beyond the dojo floor. There's surprise, then an undeniable pleasure in his eyes as he looks upon them.

"Class, return!" he calls out, lowering his dagger to his side and standing straight.

All thirty acolytes adopt a neutral stance reflecting his.

"Form for sparring!"

The mat empties, each trainee sprinting and kneeling along its edge until they surround the entire square of straw and canvas.

Daian takes the opportunity to walk to the dojo floor's edge in front of Lexi and Taru. He kneels there, bowing his head with a smile.

"Te-Gen," he greets her. "Or Lexi. I remember your instructions."

Lexi bows. "Daian. It is not our intention to interrupt your class."

He waves his training blade in dismissal. "That's all right. It's rare we receive such esteemed patronage. What can I do for you?"

"A word in private," Lexi says, her tone turning more serious.

Daian hears the urgency barely contained there, and his expression darkens for it.

"Of course," he says, motioning them both to a staircase leading up onto the platform.

Lexi gathers the hem of her formal wrap and Taru follows her down the sidewalk and up the half dozen steps.

Daian meets them there, sheathing his practice dagger. "If you'll follow me," he bids them. Then, to the other instructors, "Grath, Kamala, take over. I need to step out for a moment."

"What are *they* doing in an Aegin dojo?"

The question is asked by one of Daian's fellow instructors, a handsome chestnut-haired man who is obviously aware of just how handsome he is. He must be Grath.

The question is directed at Taru.

Lexi sighs. She's felt tired since meeting Daian over two corpses she helped along their way to the other side of the veil, and this conversation is only wearying her further.

"Taru is my retainer," Lexi says. "And that is the last time I will explain myself to Aegins whose brains are as obviously small as their knives."

The third instructor, a woman with her dark scalp practically shaved smooth and a scar over one milky eye, joins them.

"Never understood the need for private retainers," the woman named Kamala says. "You're an antiquated notion at best. At worst you interfere with Crache's chosen peacekeepers."

Daian is obviously battling with himself to remain composed. "That's enough out of you, I think."

"Speaking of blades, small or otherwise, those look well-used," Kamala says, ignoring him.

She's pointing at Taru's short sword and hook-end.

Taru says nothing.

"The retainer here's the one who bled those two in the Circus, no?" Grath asks Daian.

"What did I just say, Aegin?" Daian asks, his voice on a rise.

"It's quite all right," Lexi says, stepping directly in front of the smug Aegin. "Actually that would be me who drew blood first."

"Forgive me, Te-Gen," Grath says immediately, and with the appropriate bow of contrition, though the unhidden smile on his handsome face belies it all. "We Aegins are always . . . intrigued . . . by the decision of our city's highest servants to supplement their personal safety with such people."

Kamala adds, "And yours is a choice even more . . ."

"Intriguing?" Lexi asks, and she seems all at once more composed than she did a moment ago.

The Aegins say no more.

"Perhaps we can sate your curiosity, Aegins," Taru offers, surprising everyone, including Lexi. "This is a place of learning, is it not?"

"What are you proposing?" Daian asks.

"Yes, what are you proposing, Taru?" Lexi seconds, though she seems less concerned and more amused than Daian.

"A simple exhibition of knife skills," Taru explains.

Clearly Daian doesn't know what to say to that. Grath and Kamala, meanwhile, both stare up at Taru uneasily, the sudden reality of actually meeting the retainer on their own training mat changing their attitudes.

"Our business will keep a moment," Lexi says to Daian brightly, though she's looking at the other two Aegins. "And I don't believe this matter will require much longer than that to resolve. "

The retainer looks from Lexi to Grath and Kamala, then back at their mistress. Taru unfastens the heavy belt securing short sword and hook-end to their owner's waist. Lexi accepts her retainer's weapons and holds them close as Taru extends a hand toward Daian.

Though he slaps the handle of his training dagger into Taru's palm, it's Lexi he's watching.

She looks back at him with hard eyes.

He seems to take something from that, and nods, relenting. "Very well, then. Class!"

The Aegins-in-training kneeling dutifully around the perimeter of the mat all shout "Hai!" in unison.

"We have a special guest in our dojo today," he informs them. "A retainer serving Gen Stalbraid. This retainer has volunteered to pit their skills against those of your Aegin instructor so that we may study the contrast in styles and training, and learn how to overcome that clash of aesthetics in combat."

Daian nods to Taru, who steps onto the straw-stuffed training mat. Three strides carry them to its center, where Taru looms impossibly tall over the supplicating class of novices.

Daian leans close to Kamala and Grath, speaking for their ears only. "You two can decide among yourselves which of you gets the honor of following through on your words."

With that, he walks away from them, leaving his fellow instructors huddled at the edge of the mat. Daian moves to stand beside Lexi, though he doesn't acknowledge her, keeping his attention focused on the situation developing before them.

Grath and Kamala, both watching Taru, appear to be conferring in hushed tones among themselves. Presumably they're deciding who will cross training blades with the retainer.

Then, in the middle of his next sentence, Grath breaks away from Kamala and rushes across the mat, headlong at Taru, slashing vertically and diagonally with his dagger. Taru simply backs away, careful never to cross ankles, keeping out of range of the strikes. Taru waits, watching the rise and fall of their opponent's arms. When he follows through on a wide slash, Taru steps in and presses a large hand against the center of his chest, shoving him back with their full weight behind it.

Grath is caught totally off-guard, and the surprise combined with Taru's shocking strength knocks him totally off-balance, as well. He loses his footing and falls backward onto the mat. Recovering quickly, and with an angry growl, he lunges at them from his knees, attempting to slash and thrust at Taru's legs. The retainer avoids the strikes deftly and with a grace and speed even more surprising than their brute strength, twisting and turning and leaping until finally bringing a knee up and driving it into Grath's jaw.

It stuns the Aegin, who drops forward onto his hands and knees. Taru quickly places a boot between his shoulder blades and drives his body flat against the mat, leaning enough weight on that foot to hold him there. Taru stares at Lexi over the heads of the stunned Aegin acolytes, not quite grinning yet not entirely concealing a grin, either.

Taru is blindsided by what feels like a falling maple tree. The retainer is knocked forward onto their hands and knees. Taru spins around just in time to register Kamala falling on top of them, training dagger clutched between her joined fists with its blade angled down. Taru raises a forearm, knife hand reinforcing it, and jams it against Kamala's wrists, under her blade, blocking her from driving that blunted point into Taru's chest.

The Aegin, snarling so fiercely she dribbles on Taru's armor, uses the whole of her body to press down on her white-knuckled knife hands, trying to weaken Taru's arms. The retainer's face is the antithesis of their opponent's; those watching can scarcely tell Taru is even straining with effort.

Taru twists their hip atop the mat and drives a shin into Kamala's kidney. Though her protective padding largely absorbs the sting, the force of the blow is enough to knock her clear of Taru and send her rolling across the mat. Both retainer and Aegin recover quickly, leaping to their feet and rushing at each other. Kamala thrusts with her knife, aiming for the center of her opponent's abdomen. Taru spins with a speed and grace that belies the retainer's size, grasping Kamala's extended wrist with their free hand as the Aegin charges past.

Taru yanks on Kamala's arm with the authority of a metal vise, turning the Aegin's body and throwing her off-balance even as Taru reels her back in toward their body. Taru hooks their knife hand under Kamala's arm and lifts her off her feet, slamming her down to the welcoming embrace of the mat's feather arms. Despite the softened landing, the impact is enough to force most of the air from the Aegin's lungs and cause white lightning to strike her field of vision.

When the effects of the split-second stunning have worn off, Kamala finds Taru pressing the blunted blade of the training dagger into the flesh of her throat.

"This is the part where your blood would spray across my breastplate," Taru informs the Aegin.

Behind Taru, a kneeling Grath claws at the hem of his training pants leg, drawing the material away from the top of his boot to reveal the hilt of a push dagger concealed there. He closes his fist around the weapon's handle and draws a blade of sharpened steel, rising as he does.

Lexi, watching, widens her eyes and looks to her left for Daian, only to find he's already stepped away. When she returns her gaze to the training mat she finds Grath advancing on Taru's back.

Before Lexi can shout a warning, Daian appears at Grath's side and clamps a hand around his fellow Aegin's wrist. He twists it, Grath crying out more in pain than surprise as Daian's other hand pries the push dagger from his fingers.

Taru rises and turns at the sound, allowing Kamala to roll away and get back to her feet.

"This lesson is over," Daian says, no doubt he's speaking directly to Grath and not the class.

Grath jerks his wrist away from Daian's grip, something dark and malevolent moving across his face.

He quickly dismisses it with the practice of a man who has trained himself to hide the darkness inside him, replacing it with his easy, handsome smile.

"And an exhilarating lesson it was too," Grath says. "Don't you agree, class?"

The Aegin acolytes, in unison: "Hai!"

Grath turns to regard Kamala, who is still breathing shallowly and staring a promise of pain at Taru.

"Don't you agree, Kam?" he asks, and when she doesn't answer him immediately, "Kamala! Don't you agree Te-Gen Lexi's retainer has provided us with a very informative experience?"

"They move well for a Gen fighter" is all Kamala will concede, and that through clenched teeth.

Taru nods stoically. "And you move every bit as I expect Aegins to."

Kamala takes a step forward at that, but Daian is ready for her reaction.

"Class, on your feet!" he instructs the group, who leap to attention in one mechanical wave.

Kamala suddenly seems aware of all their eyes on her.

That first step toward Taru is the only one she ends up taking.

"Take over for me," Daian says to Grath. "While I attend to Te-Gen and our new guest instructor."

Grath bows. "Of course."

Daian waits while Taru exits the mat, returning to him and Lexi. Taru flips the training dagger, catching it by the blade and offering its grip to Daian.

"Thank you for the loan."

Daian accepts the practice weapon and holds it up in salute.

"You made good use of it. Now might we adjourn somewhere more private so that I might assist you two however I can?"

"Thank you, Aegin Daian," Lexi says pleasantly.

The trio exits the Dojo through the Kodo entrance, Lexi and Taru following closely behind their guide. They wait while Daian changes back into his uniform, and then he escorts them out of the Kodo and back onto the street.

"I apologize if our presence caused friction between you and your fellow Aegins," Lexi begins.

"What, Grath and Kamala?" Daian asks, sounding almost offended. "I can't stand either of them." He spits upon the sidewalk. "Excuse my vulgar gesture, Te-Gen."

Lexi shakes her head. "I've heard it's good for the constitution."

Daian smiles. "Yeah. Well, the only reason I teach alongside those two is that they're among our best with the dagger."

Taru cuts in. "Says who?"

Daian grins up at them. "Present company excluded, of course. Now, how can I help the two of you?"

"We've sought you out today because I believe you're a person who can be trusted."

Daian doesn't seem to know what to say to that, so he settles on: "Thank you."

"I say person, not Aegin, because I cannot trust Aegins as an institution right now. I can't afford to. But I have to believe the man beneath tops the uniform, if he's a good man."

"I believe in what I do, Lexi. But I've also seen enough to know not to let it be all that I am."

"I find myself in desperate and dire straits. Gen Stalbraid is out of time, out of money, and most importantly out of allies. Agents from the Protectorate Ministry are probably already watching our home day and night. I don't know how much more progress, if any, Taru and I can make on our own."

"Progress with what?"

"Finding my husband, Brio, dead or alive, and exposing the ones who took him from us. The same ones who tried to kill me, I'm sure."

"And who do you imagine did all this? Do you have any clue? Any leads?"

Lexi draws in a deep, labored breath. "My husband began to notice what he suspected were disappearances. People disappearing from the Bottoms. People no one else would ever notice or report missing. The poor, the homeless. Some were arrested for petty crimes and once they were taken to the dungeons . . . they never returned. Others simply seemed to vanish off the streets without any record or trace of arrest. He began investigating. He discovered what he believed was evidence that these people were being conscripted . . . forced . . . into some clandestine military legion. I urged him to present what he found to the Council, but he wanted to gather more proof. Before that happened, he . . . disappeared too."

Daian registers what appears to be genuine surprise, although it is perhaps less directed at the existence of the Savages and more at the fact that Brio and Lexi were able to pierce the bureaucratic shield that protects Crache's secrets.

"Where is your husband's evidence now, Te-Gen?" he asks her.

"Either that evidence was taken away when he was, or he hid it somewhere beyond my reach," Lexi concludes.

"My policy is always to assume the worst."

"Then we have to start from here and now," Lexi insists.

Daian is quiet.

"Will you help us?"

He looks up in even starker surprise.

It's not Lexi asking the question, but Taru.

"Would you trust me to?" he asks the retainer. "Truly? Your eyes are cold when you look at Aegins, but I know you're burning deep inside. You hate us."

"I distrust your uniform, especially when it is worn by ones like those others in your Dojo," Taru corrects him. "You're different. You stayed their hand. You have no malice in you."

Daian is obviously moved by Taru's words, even if he works not to show it.

"So you'd trust me, then? Because of that?"

Taru draws in a deep breath, raising the thick leather breastplate protecting the retainer's heart.

"Te-Gen is willing to trust you. I trust Te-Gen. Implicitly."

Daian nods, looking from Taru to Lexi. "Can I share with you a secret, one difficult for me to part with, although one I'm sure is no secret to you?"

Lexi looks confused, but she nods all the same.

"There are vastly more men and women like Grath and Kamala wearing this uniform than people like me."

Lexi nods with more clarity. "And this naturally creates dangerous waters for you to tread, should you agree to aid us."

"I'm more concerned about you, Te-Gen," he says, and it sounds sincere.

"I believe we've proven we can handle Aegins," Lexi reminds him.

"Quite," Taru adds.

Daian can't help but grin at the pair of them.

"All right," he pronounces. "I'll do what I can. I make no promises, save I'll seek and report the truth."

Lexi accepts that. "And what should we do?"

"You two return to the Gen Circus, to your towers," he instructs them. "If the Protectorate Ministry has it in mind to watch you, then you will be watched, no matter what you do or where you go. It's best you put them to sleep. Give them nothing of interest to observe or report."

Taru is dubious. "Then how will you contact us?"

"I'll figure that part out later," Daian assures them. "Let's just hope I can uncover something worth reporting."

"Where will you start?" Lexi asks.

"With what we have," he says. "Two dead bodies, marked with blue tattoos."

TEARS MADE OF FIRE

"HOW ARE WE GOING TO MAKE IT BACK?" BRIO ASKS HER IN the dark. "We're in the vanguard of the Sicclunan front. There's a hundred miles of Skrain, Savages, and blood coin hunters behind us. It will be nearly impossible to make it to the border of the Tenth City, let alone all the way back to the Capitol."

"We'll have to wait for that leg to heal. You're useless on the run with it. But we're not going anywhere tonight. Go to sleep."

The tent is scarcely big enough to sleep both of them on the cold, hard ground, but Brio is grateful for even the thinnest barrier between them and the cold. One of the many fervent whispers around the camp is that the Sicclunan nights are getting unseasonably colder every year, and the days unseasonably hot. No explanation has been offered for either that Brio has gleaned, but he's felt the truth of it in his time among the Savages on the front.

He lies facing Evie, only the scarcest contours of her face visible to him in the dark, but it's enough. He remembers her face as well as his own mother's. Ashana was one of many children his and Lexi's parents took in from the Bottoms, like Taru, out of sympathy or necessity or because they saw something unique in a particular person. Ashana was the only one, however, their parents ever sent away. They had plans for Brio and Lexi, and those plans involved marriage and continuing Gen Stalbraid.

Of course, bloodlines weren't supposed to matter; many Gens, and the most successful, were composed of dozens of unrelated kith-kins who often married to expand their ranks or skills or capabilities. Brio and Lexi's two families, however, had formed their small Gen together. Their fathers were aspiring pleaders with a shared interest in helping revitalize and help the people of the Bottoms. They had grown Stalbraid together, their kith-kins forming a fierce bond in the process, and however Crache attempted to stamp it out of them, people remain creatures of habit and tradition. There was no law or rule, even in the extreme and unending minutiae of Crachian doctrine, that demanded Brio and Lexi marry in order to continue their Gen. But bloodlines mattered to his father, and so they mattered to Brio. He knew what the man expected of him, and that was to carry their Gen forward in what his father deemed the "right way," though he and Lexi had yet to get around to that part of it. He had always imagined there would be more time for things like children.

All those things are why Brio didn't question their decision to turn Ashana away, deeply though it panged him as a child.

Now, after everything he's been through in the past few months and seeing her willingness to go to such lengths on his behalf, Brio wishes he'd protested when it mattered. He will never stop revering his father, but he's past viewing the long-deceased man as infallible. Brio knows now that his father was wrong about her.

"I shouldn't have let them turn you away," he whispers suddenly in the dark. "It was wrong. I knew that."

"You were just a boy," Evie reminds him dispassionately.

The lack of emotion in her voice surprises him. "How can you say that so easily? How is it you don't hate all of us? How can you not hate me for what happened? Why would you even agree to risk your life like this for me?"

At first Evie is silent.

Brio can scarcely make out the lines of her face, let alone read her expression.

"I was angry at the time," she finally says, her tone more thoughtful than anything else. "And for a long time after. I was furious."

"What changed?" Brio presses her.

"Your Gen plucked me off the streets, Brio. They fed me, clothed me, educated me. They gave me a way into a world I never would have found on my own. They didn't owe me anything. None of you owed me. If anything, I owed all of you for what you did for me. Your father had every right to put me out. His reasons were his own, whatever I think about them. I made my way, didn't I? What do I have to be angry about now?"

"That's very enlightened of you," Brio says with irony.

"It's the truth. Besides, holding on to that little girl's anger would only hurt me now, wouldn't it? Your father is beyond feeling remorse."

"I'm not," he reminds her.

"I can see that. This isn't a place or the time for those feelings, Brio. We're in the middle of a war. We're trying to escape captors who look at us as little more than animals fit for slaughter. The past is the least of our problems. If we survive, then we can talk more about feelings."

Brio is unconvinced. "I still want to know why you agreed to do this. If you've let go of the past, why are you willing to die to save it?"

"I have no plans to die," Evie assures him. "And I said I've let go of my anger. I didn't say I've let go of the past altogether."

Brio wants to ask what that implies, particularly about her feelings for him now.

The desire to ask that brings thoughts of Lexi, and with those comes guilt.

"Go to sleep, Brio," Evie urges him.

Exhaustion more than anything else puts an end to Brio's questioning. Without the hungry quaking in his gut and the constant gnawing of his leg wound, not to mention feeling almost safe for the first time in three months, Brio soon drifts off to as peaceful a rest as he's known outside the Capitol.

LATE-NIGHT CALLERS

EVIE REMAINS AWAKE UNTIL SHE'S SURE HER FIRST LOVE AND current charge is out. She studies the lines of his face, or at least what she can discern of them in the darkness. He hasn't changed all that much, at least to her mind. He still looks youthful, handsome, and kind, despite what he's been put through recently.

She spent so much of her childhood thinking about how the two of them were different, and how it kept them apart. Their differences weren't relegated to where each of them were born in the Capitol, and the social status attained (or, in Evie's case, not attained) by their respective families. The two of them looked different, clearly descending from different ancestries. Brio and Lexi matched. Brio and Evie did not. Evie didn't share the fine, sharp features of their families' faces. Her features were far wider and more rounded. Neither did she share their straight, silken hair, though hers was just as black. Evie's locks were far coarser and grew in springy curls.

Brown skin and coarse curls were not why Evie was ostracized from Gen Stalbraid, but she always knew they further set her apart.

Brio always seemed blissfully ignorant of those physical differences and their impact, but those not treated as the other in the room had that luxury.

When Brio's breathing becomes deep and even, Evie allows her eyes to close and her body to go slack. She soon finds that restful, sunken place in her sleep.

Evie told Brio she's let go of her anger, if not the past. That much is true. Her thoughts of the past are no longer angry ones, but she does still dwell there in her mind, particularly in her dreams. When Evie dreams of Brio, as she does now, she sees him as the boy he was. She sees them playing as children in those small towers that seemed at the time like the whole world to her. She feels the way she did as a girl, and the piece of that girl which remains with her even now wants back what she lost, and what she never allowed herself to feel again after she was put out of Gen Stalbraid.

Perhaps it was that more than anything that moved Evie to answer Lexi's call and accept her current mission. Perhaps it had something to do with how bored and restless Evie was with guarding well-to-do children who didn't need guarding.

However, she did truly sympathize with Lexi. Evie could plainly see the genuine love and concern Lexi had for Brio, and it stirred all the feelings she *hadn't* let go. She never asked why Lexi chose her, or what made the woman think of Evie for this task. Evie supposed it was because Lexi wanted to appeal to someone she knew loved Brio as much as she did, even if it had been long ago.

The hollering of the Savages wakes her. They sound like angry dogs being taunted through a fence, barking somewhere very far away. Evie crawls over Brio's snoring, motionless body and a moment later her head is birthed through the flaps of their tent. The first things she sees are the backs of several dozen Savages running toward dots of light in the distance. Evie has to squint to see clearly through the dark of night between her and those lights. It takes her only a moment to realize they are small fires on top of tent roofs, where small fires very definitely do not belong.

Then Evie hears the first screams, not of warning or panic or orders being called out, but the wholly unique and singular screams of pain and death-fear.

Her mouth opens to yell for Brio to wake when a warning issued from the corner of her eye causes Evie to drop low defensively. The arrow has struck the ground half a dozen feet in front of her, its tip aflame and scorching the already-dead grass trampled sparsely there. Several other fiery arrows follow, falling closer and closer to where she crouches. She sees others piercing the tops of tents in the distant, the flames they ferry spreading quickly.

Evie retreats within the tent and grabs Brio by his shoulders, shaking him none-too-gently.

"Wake up!"

"What?" he croaks before his eyes have even opened. "What is it?"

"The camp is under attack!"

She's still staring into Brio's confused and sleep-addled eyes when she hears the blade cutting through the fabric of the tent. By the time Evie looks up, the black-clad figure is already slipping deftly through the tall slit they've made. Their face and head are hidden beneath a pitch hood, the barest sliver cut away to reveal only hints of dark eyes. The grip of their gloved hand is reversed on the tsuka of a short sword, the tip of its curved blade pointed at the ground.

Evie quickly stands, stepping over Brio to shield his body. Her stance widens and she rubs her palms and fingertips against the thighs of her trousers, wiping away the dirt smudges and drying the natural oils there to keep as much purchase in her grip as possible. The black-clad figure takes one step forward and swipes at her with their upended blade. The strike is fast and powerful and skilled enough to separate her neck, but Evie bends her knees and ducks. The razor edge of the blade slices away several dozen tiny threads of her hair, each wisp still hanging there in the air as the black-clad figure brings their arm back for a stabbing thrust.

Evie sidesteps the blade and traps their arm, twisting her body into them and flipping her attacker onto their back. The point of the blade is now angled above its owner's chest. She quickly leans all her weight against the bottom of the sword's tsuka, driving the blade down deep into the black-clad figure's heart.

Evie turns her head away from the sight of the dying enemy beneath her. She feels heat on her face. Opening her eyes, she sees that the roof of their tent is now ablaze.

"Shit" is her only comment on the current situation.

There's no time for further contemplation. No sooner has the body gone limp than a second attacker slips inside the tent, also draped head-to-toe in black, also wielding a short sword in one gloved hand. Rather than invest precious moments into wresting the blade buried in the first attacker's chest from their death-locked hands, Evie abandons the body and draws the push dagger from her boot, the one she took from the Sicclunan agent at the Revel. Behind her, Brio does his best to roll out of the way, dragging his injured leg with him against the wall of the tent.

The second attacker is on her, slashing with their short sword, almost before Evie can square her posture. She reacts without thinking, feinting and ducking the first volley of strikes and using the push dagger's blade to deflect the blows she can't outmaneuver. Her heart is racing and that curved short sword seems to find less and less air between them with each stroke, yet she trusts to her training, the years of endless repetition until her body responded to assault from any angle without the need of conscious thought to guide it.

Evie awaits an opening. She ducks under a slightly too wide, slightly too frustrated swipe of her enemy's blade and launches a shin up into their groin. The momentary recoiling of their body is all the time she needs to grab the wrist supporting their short sword. Evie thrusts the point of her dagger into their forearm, twice, then aims it at their neck. By the time the black-clad figure's other hand moves to stop her, the push dagger's blade is already deep in their throat.

Evie watches the cloth of the mask over their mouth soak through with blood as they sink to their knees. She moves with the body all the way to the ground before extracting her blade. A single hot spurt of the darkest red streaks across her neck and chest. The black-clad figure collapses onto their right side, leaving Evie kneeling above them, her breathing shallow and ragged. She remembers Brio and looks for him in the light of the burning tent above them.

He's staring at her with wide eyes and a half-gaping mouth.

Evie looks down at herself, the enemy blood decorating her dirty, tattered clothes.

She nods. "That's right. I'm not that little girl any longer. Now, get on your feet. We have to move."

Evie pries the short sword from the death-clawed hand of the body at her feet. She turns and rips the other sword free of its victim and former owner's chest. Kneeling beside Brio, she leans down to allow him to slip an arm around her shoulders, at the same time shoving the tsuka of the sword against his stomach.

"Take this," she instructs him. "Slash at anything in black that comes near you."

Brio obeys, holding the sword away from his body as if it were a lit torch.

Evie shakes her head, but there's no time for further instruction, let alone reprimand.

"We'll have to run," she warns him.

"I'll do my level best," Brio says, a distinct mock-optimism in his voice.

Despite the last few moments and the dread of what's to come, Evie finds herself laughing.

They exit the tent seconds before the blazing curtain overhead collapses it behind them. She sees the rest of the camp is also on fire now. She sees Savages fleeing the interior of burning tents on their hands and knees only to have their throats cut or heads lopped off by the blades of pursuing shadow warriors. She sees a stray Skrain soldier in blood-splattered armor, weaponless, running for his life through a camp upon the ground of which his kind ordinarily wouldn't deign to piss.

They must've hit the Skrain encampment first, quietly slitting sleeping throats, before the flaming arrow volleys began.

Evie breaks into a run, pulling Brio along as needed. He half hobbles, half skips to keep up, grunting through ground teeth without complaint. She deflects the blade of a black-clad warrior who rushes them, and opens his flesh from neck to shoulder with a swipe of her own. Her plan is to flee back through the Skrain encampment. Her hope is that the night force deployed by the Sicclunans has moved on, and she and Brio will be able to escape if they can just make it past the slaughter and razing of the Savage tents.

Both her hope and her brief plan are dashed upon the rocks as Evie halts Brio in midhobble.

If it weren't for the firelights they might have continued melting in to the shadows, but the rippling amber reveals an entire battalion of the black-clad warriors marching toward them in formation from the remnants of the Skrain encampment. Unlike their stealthy vanguard, each of these soldiers has long swords sheathed at their hips in addition to a short sword. Held aloft and at the ready are wicked-looking double bladed battle-axes and horse-cutter spears. Whether the Savages before them attempt to flee or are foolish enough to attack head-on, the masked battalion never breaks rank as they cut down the enemy.

If she weren't cradling Brio directly in their path, Evie would have to admire the tactical precision of it all. The Sicclunans are not only tearing a page from the Crachian war manual, they've improved upon it. The fiery arrows and two-warrior tent incursions created the same chaos caused by the Savages, yet with far more bloody and lethal effect. Now their main force is sweeping through the camp to clean up anything and everything that's left.

Evie turns just in time to glimpse Lariat, several yards ahead of them, uncross his arms and decapitate a black-hooded head between the triangular blades of his matched katars. She briefly and frantically looks around, searching for other members of the Elder Company, but there's no time even to call to the old man standing over the newly headless corpse. Evie can only hope Spud-Bar's wagon made it clear of the camp without encountering the night force.

She grabs Brio by the arm and forces him into a half-burned tent that's been extinguished with water from one of the horse troughs.

"What're we doing?" he whispers breathlessly at her as she practically stuffs him inside the foul-smelling wreckage and crushes her body atop his on the ground.

"The only thing I can think of that might not end with us watching our own bodies fall from a distance," she hisses at him. "Now shut up and stay still!"

Evie kicks out with one foot and shatters the burned husk of the nearest tent post. The other posts and what little charred cloth still flaps in the wind collapses atop them. Evie presses herself flat beside Brio, digging into the cold, hard ground beneath them as best she's able. If the remnants of the tent appear flat enough, they might just get away with it.

She only hopes that, at a glance, they won't be visible through the wreckage.

"You shouldn't have come after me," Brio whispers to her, the guilt beneath his words totally unmasked. "My life isn't worth yours."

"That depends on whom you ask," she assures him. "Now, I told you, be quiet and stay still."

"For how long?" he asks.

Evie closes her eyes and tries to block out the sounds of clashing steel and bloody screams rising just above their heads.

"As long as it takes," she says.

THE MATING CALL OF
THE CRACHIAN WIND DRAGON

THE BELLS RING THREE TIMES, SUMMONING DYEAWAN AND
her tender to Edger's office.

It's the middle of the day, and the hard, wiry muscles of her arms,
as strong as many a grown man's from years of pulling the rest of her
along, are feeling unusually strained from cleaning and her deliveries.
She wonders if the miraculous ease of the paddles that turn her wheels
is actually a double-edged sword; perhaps using less effort has weakened
the upper part of her body.

Or perhaps she's recently become bored and restless with sweeping
floors and ferrying hastily inked message scrolls.

She's never been summoned to Edger's private office before. As she
thinks about it, Dyeawan realizes she's never before been summoned to
his public office, either. She had thought the room in which she first met
him was his private space, but it turned out to be just a reception area.
Whatever Edger actually does and wherever he actually does it, he has
yet to make use of Dyeawan's spirited heralding services.

It's a door like any other in the Cadre, left open as Dyeawan wheels
in front of it. A chorus of reeds whistling a soothing melody in perfect
harmony greets Dyeawan. It's dark inside. A long, thick tapestry has
been hung over the window. Edger is reclining in a luxurious lounging
chair in the middle of the room. His head is tilted back, and he turns his

expressionless face toward her. He raises one of his masks, its features molded into a broad welcoming smile of greeting.

Quan, the gaunt, impossibly tall brown-robed attendant, is practically doubled over Edger. Permanent bite and claw marks are deep, red grooves in the flesh of Edger's throat. Quan is gently applying a salve to each of those deep grooves with a square of silk. The creature that made them, Ku, is conspicuously absent from the man's neck; it's the first time Dyeawan has seen him without the wind dragon that allows him to speak affixed there.

"Good day, little Slider," Quan warmly greets Dyeawan.

"Hello. Did I hear the bells wrong?"

"No, no, you were summoned. I apologize. I should have had him cleaned up by now."

"Where is Ku?" Dyeawan asks.

Quan, continuing to treat Edger's scars, points with his free hand at the far corner of the room.

Dyeawan leans over the side of her tender and peers around them both. Behind thick glass erected on a stone dais, Ku's scaly green body is wrapped around the pale pink form of another wind dragon. Their hollow, bony protrusions are all vibrating in unison, the source of the soft music Dyeawan first heard upon entering the room.

"Is he all right?"

"Oh yes. You see, we inject Ku with an elixir to keep him docile while he is joined with Edger, but once every month he undergoes the mating cycle of the wind dragon. His nature becomes violent, and more importantly, strong enough to overpower the elixir. In such a state he'd surely tear out Edger's throat. He must be removed and his mating instinct sated before they can be safely coupled again."

"I see. I'm sorry, Edger."

He doesn't change his mask of expression, but he does wave a hand dismissively.

"It's quite all right, little Slider. In fact, I relish the break from this one's endless prattle."

Quan laughs at his own jest, and Dyeawan thinks she sees Edger's shoulders rise and fall silently as if he's attempting to do the same.

Quan finishes treating Edger's neck. He slips both the silk cloth and the salve inside his robes and strides over to Ku's home away from home. Dyeawan watches with interest as the tall attendant reaches down inside the glass and gently unfolds Ku from his companion. The wind dragon seems half asleep and offers no resistant. Quan reaches inside his robe and removes a horsehide bellows small enough to fit in the palm of his hand. A long, thick needle is attached to the mouth of the bellows.

The attendant lovingly cradles the green wind dragon in one hand. The other deftly slips the tip of the needle between two of his scales. Quan gently squeezes the bellows, the elixir of which he spoke traveling through the needle and filling the wind dragon's small body.

Quan returns the bellows to his robes and carries Ku over to Edger's chair. Cupping both hands around the creature, he very delicately presses its body against Edger's exposed throat. The attendant's hands are obscuring Dyeawan's view, but she watches as Edger's body stiffens, just for a moment, and then relaxes. The rushing of air is audible, and when Quan removes his hands the wind dragon has its spread jaws clamped onto Edger's neck anew.

"Thank you, Quan," the voice made of wind and piped through Ku says to the attendant. "You may leave us now."

"Of course."

Quan bows and strides away from the lounger, past Dyeawan, whispering to her, "Used and discarded daily, that's me."

He punctuates his words with a wink, and she can't help giggling.

If Edger heard the statement, he must be accustomed to such things.

"Good day, my dear," he says to Dyeawan. "Thank you for your patience."

"Oh no, it's very interesting to me."

"I've always believed we need only use the resources we've been given."

Edger holds the mask to his face he wears for conversation, a passive, friendly visage that doesn't express any particular emotion.

"Now, how did you find your week of tests?" Edger asks her.

Dyeawan's breath catches briefly. She was both hopeful and fearful this would be the topic he wanted to discuss.

"Challenging," she answers carefully.

Edger's empty, haunting form of laughter is expelled from Ku's spine hollows.

"I doubt that very much," he says. "In fact, I have come to believe nothing is challenging for the likes of you."

Dyeawan's brows furrow. "I don't understand."

"Slider, my dear, simply said, yours is easily the most naturally keen mind I have ever known."

She is no less confused. "I don't know what to say to that."

"There is nothing to be said. It is not praise. It is the truth."

Whether it is true or not, Dyeawan can't deny that Edger believes it. Still, there's always more with him, something he's not saying. It's a thing Dyeawan has come to know about Edger, even if she doesn't fully understand it.

Even when he tells the truth, he's always lying.

She just doesn't know *what* he's lying about.

"I see that great machinery between your ears working even now," Edger remarks. "What are you thinking, Slider?"

"I want to know what you want from me."

"I only want to help you reach your full potential so that you may help Crache."

Again, he believes what he's saying, but Dyeawan knows the key to fully understanding his intentions and motivation lies in what the word "help" means to him.

"Usually when we bring a recruit to the Planning Cadre, we have a sense of their talents, what they are naturally gifted to do. You were a blank slate in the best of ways. I only expected basic functions of you.

You would think I, of all people, would have learned by now not to judge someone based on where they come from and especially what maladies they may suffer. I'm sorry."

"You give a new life and a purpose to people everyone else wants to forget ever lived," Dyeawan says, and this she truly means. "You don't have to say sorry to me, or to anyone."

"Still and all," Edger insists, "I was wrong about you. As wrong as I've ever been about anything, and I do not boast when I tell you I am rarely wrong."

"I believe you. Thank you, Edger."

"You're most welcome, my dear. Now, I'm sure by this time you have deduced that the tests you've been given throughout the past week are the same tests we administer to Cadre members across all our varied pursuits."

Dyeawan nods. "I named the duck Greenfire. He's my friend now."

Edger briefly replaces his conversation mask with one frozen in gaping laughter.

"That is delightful!" he proclaims. "And well done. Well done to you."

"I always wanted a pet. I tried to tame a rat once, but . . . never mind. You were saying, about the tests."

Edger exchanges masks before returning to the topic at hand. "Yes, of course. By presenting you with this unusually varied array of tests, my colleagues were hoping to discern what part of the Cadre you'd be best suited to join. I had . . . larger aspirations. And I am pleased to say mine were met. You simply crushed every task we gave you. It has been precisely forty-three years since we have witnessed results such as yours."

"What does that mean? What would you have me do?"

"I would have you do what I do. I would have you be a planner, the highest order in the Cadre. I would have you join us in overseeing all that the Cadre does, originating the ideas that drive it."

Of all Dyeawan's expectations after the testing, none reached the heights expressed in Edger's words.

"I would . . . yes, I would like that, Edger. Very much."

"Wonderful! That is simply wonderful. I am very pleased to hear you say that, my dear. With that settled, you must realize while the results were indeed impressive, the tests we placed before you were meant for novices. And planners are not novices."

"You mean . . . there are more tests? Harder tests?"

"In your very special case, just one, but yes, it will be significantly more difficult. My . . . colleagues . . . have insisted."

"Do they not want me?"

"No, no, nothing like that. They simply haven't been privy to our conversations. They don't know you yet. And admitting new recruits into planning is a very rare thing indeed."

"All right. What is this final test? And when is it?"

"I am afraid I cannot tell you either of those things, my dear."

Dyeawan only nods, unsurprised and undisturbed. "That's part of it, right?"

"That is correct. For now, you will return to your regular duties. What comes will come, and my faith in you remains absolute."

Dyeawan knows what faith is, but she's never experienced it, and in that moment she can't decide if she's sorry or grateful for that.

"Thank you again, Edger. Thank you for everything. I don't want to let you down."

"That is impossible, little Slider."

Dyeawan smiles for him. It's clear to her that he doesn't think he's lying. However, she has learned that people lying to themselves about a thing doesn't make that thing true.

ONLY FIRE AND ICE GROW
IN CHARNEL HOUSE GARDENS

IT'S THE SMELL OF WINTER ROTTING.

The benefit of visiting The Dry House is that the small domed structure has been set far apart from the rest of the Spectrum. The robed Councilmembers, their clerics, and the many daily Capitol petitioners also avoid The Dry House like a plague, making it the most peacefully serene and vacant spot in the city's bustling epicenter. It's a perfect escape from the constant bureaucratic chaos and its million tiny agonies.

The downside of visiting The Dry House, obviously, is that it is filled with the dead and rapidly decaying.

Crachian burial rites revolve around one's station and importance within their Gen. Agricultural workers are returned to the earth as compost to aid the next harvest while their departed overseers are planted with a tree sapling that will sprout into a mighty monument. Sailors are given to the sea in quiet ceremonies while the bones of shipbuilders are fashioned into polished masthead sculptures adorning the finest seafaring Crachian vessels. Those not belonging to a Gen are slotted into space efficient stone mausoleums where the summer will bake them to ash, freeing their tier for the next body.

Whether they are to become dust or pillar, however, the dead's first stop is The Dry House, where they are laid upon blocks of imported ice to preserve them until family can be contacted and burial or ceremony can be arranged.

Daian doesn't mind being among the dead, or their scent, like animal carcasses half buried in snow. He enters the spare stony confines of The Dry House without hesitation, unmoved by the sight of row upon row of bodies resting on their ice-block cairn. Of course, it helps that the dead are draped in woven hemp shrouds (for preservation's sake more than modesty, which most Crachians consider a wasted quality).

He finds only one living soul occupying the space. Keepers of Dry Houses are known as "huskers." The husker on duty is an unusually young man with his long, hay-colored hair tied back and an even lighter, almost invisible scruff smattering his cheeks and jaw.

It's uncommon for the Capitol, where dark hair like Daian's is overwhelmingly handed down between generations. The boy's ancestors must have come from across the sea some time after the Renewal, before Crache placed a ban upon such visitors settling within the nation's borders.

"Can I help you, Aegin?" the husker asks around a mouthful of rice.

Whenever he's had cause to deal with a husker, they always seem to be in the middle of a meal.

"I'm looking for two men," Daian informs him.

The husker swallows, staring at him in confusion.

"All right, but unless I'm one of 'em I can promise you there's no one here in a state to be arrested."

"That's funny," Daian says in a tone that clarifies it was not funny at all.

Daian begins pacing between the rows of giant ice blocks propped on their wooden frames, copper drip pans carefully arranged beneath them. He peels back the shroud covering each unnaturally still face. Most of them are puckered with the wrinkles of old age. The few younger faces he uncovers are composed of smooth, well-fed features unmarred by the abrasions of a life spent in physical toil, let alone touched by any violence. None of them are tattooed, and all of them appear to Daian to be high-ranking Gen members.

"They're not here," Daian pronounces, equal parts confused and irritated.

"If you'd tell me who you're looking for, Aegin, I can have a look at my tally here."

The husker holds up an unfurled scroll lined with columns and hastily scribbled lists of names and other related information.

"Is this all the recently departed in the Capitol?" Daian asks, ignoring the offer.

The husker hesitates.

". . . no, 'course not."

"Why not? Where are the rest?"

The husker sighs, relenting. "D'you know what Gen All's-Breath is charging the Capitol for ice these days? I don't have a block for every pauper who keels over in the Bottoms."

"I'm not here about paupers, I'm here about two assassins."

The word "assassins" quickly sobers the young man. "Oh. Them. Yeah, I heard about them."

"Good, you know who I'm talking about. Now, where are they?"

"Follow me," the husker bids him tentatively.

Abandoning his rice bowl and chopsticks, the husker leads Daian away from the rows of the dead. He escorts the Aegin through an archway on the opposite end of the room from the entrance. What lies beyond is an antechamber where they clean and prepare the bodies before committing them to the surface of the ice for preservation. The slab upon which the newly dead are laid out is currently empty. The water bucket beside it is dry and the tools occupying a table adjacent to the slab are clean.

There's a small door on the other side of the room. The husker opens it, daylight illuminating the dust-speckled air of the confined space. The younger man motions Daian through.

The small stone courtyard behind The Dry House smells far worse than any part of its interior. The garbage and other refuse piled there has yet to be claimed by Gen Tallman's waste collectors.

"Don't tell me they're in there?" Daian asks in shock, pointing at the garbage bins.

"Of course not," the husker assures him, trying and failing to sound genuinely offended.

"What're you gonna learn from 'em anyway?" he asks. "They're dead."

"What do you learn from a trail after your quarry has already come and gone from it?"

The husker only stares back at him, his face a blank canvas that will never see an artist's brush.

"Just show me the remains," Daian orders him wearily.

The young man nods, walking past the bins. In the far corner of the courtyard rests a stone box almost but not quite big enough to allow a full-grown adult entry. It has a door but no roof, only an iron grate with slender, charred-black bars.

The husker opens the door, stepping aside to allow the Aegin full view and access.

Daian immediately covers his mouth and nose with his right hand, eyes narrowing in disgust. The stone surfaces inside the box may have once been gray and white, but now every inch is black and thick with layers of soot and waxy, molten splotches that aren't soot.

The bottom of the box's interior is piled high with scorched bones, mostly large femurs, skulls, and portions of rib cage; the rest has been burned to black ash.

Daian turns to the young man, demanding, "What is this?"

The husker meets his judging eyes with a hard, resolved expression.

"Ice for those can afford it, fire for the rest," he says.

Daian has no answer for that. It's simple enough to him. Instead of replying he puts his hand to his chest and unsheathes his dagger.

The husker shuffles backward, eyes widening as if the blade is meant for him.

Daian turns back to the box and crouches low before its open door. He extends his arm inside and begins prodding among the bones with his dagger. He hooks ribs and the inside of skulls with the tip of the blade and holds them up to examine them before slinging each burned-black remnant aside.

Eventually there are only ashes left to explore. The edge of Daian's blade scraping against stone sets the husker's teeth on edge behind him, but Daian is determined to sift every inch of the space. In truth he expects to find nothing, especially since he has no idea what he's even looking for to begin with. He's mostly going through the motions to punish the husker.

Then his blade touches metal, and Daian's entire mood shifts.

He taps the blade against the sudden obstruction, the report confirming there's something metallic buried there. Scraping it free of the ashes and remains, Daian discovers a small circular object that looks to be a coin of some kind. He picks it up and smooths both blackened sides with his thumb, cleaning them the best he can. The coin is copper, but it's no currency he's ever seen, from Crache or beyond.

There's a face hammered into one side. Not the visage of a historical figure or even any distinct person. It's a vague face crudely rendered with a wild beard, shaggy hair, and hollows for eyes.

It's the face of a Savage.

Daian finds another, identical coin while sifting among the rest of the black ash. He sheathes his dagger and stands, holding up both coins for the husker's inspection.

"What are these?"

The young man shrugs. "One of 'em must have swallowed some coins. I dunno."

Daian nods. "Or they each had one of the same coin in their bellies. Just like they had the same marks on their skin."

"I suppose. What does it mean?"

"Nothing for you to concern yourself about."

The husker is obviously baffled by the whole thing. "If you say so, Aegin."

Daian places the coins in his pocket and fixes the younger man with a hard stare. "Who told you to burn these bodies?"

"Who says anyone told me—"

"These men violated a private home in the Gen Circus and attempted to kill the mistress of that house and Gen!" Daian thunders at him in the voice he uses to interrogate witnesses and suspects. "It wasn't your place to do anything but preserve them as needed for identification!"

The husker doesn't say anything, but he's clearly holding whatever he's not saying just below the surface now.

Daian lowers his voice, his tone taking on a gentler mantle. "Listen here. Either this was your fault, or you were ordered to do it by the proper authorities and you are at no fault. Choose."

Those words seem to register with the husker. He nods, albeit reluctantly.

"One of them Protectorate Ministry ghouls," he confesses. "He came here. I'd never even seen one with my own eyes before. I'd only heard about 'em. He told me to burn the bodies right away. He said they were a . . . a 'blight' on the Capitol. On Crache itself."

Daian knows the Ministry too well to be surprised by such a revelation.

"Thank you for your help," he says to the husker. "You did nothing wrong, under the circumstances. You can forget all about this."

That last Daian says pointedly, emphasizing the "forget" element.

Even the dim-witted young man is able to recognize the implications in the Aegin's words.

Daian leaves The Dry House, waiting until there are closed doors between him and the husker to once again examine his discovery. He holds the coins up to the light of the afternoon sun and squints, eyeing every detail.

Eventually he gives up. Daian has to accept the coins themselves have told him all they will.

Fortunately, he knows someone who speaks far louder than burned copper, and that individual owes Daian several favors.

SCATTERING THE ASHES

SHE'S FELT THE WARMTH OF DAWN SEEPING THROUGH THE charred holes in their prolapsed tent for nearly an hour, but Evie insists they remain in hiding. The abject silence has lasted even longer. Not even the chirping of birds or the scuttling of insects underscores the morning outside. They never heard the Sicclunan night force march out of the camp; the chorus of clashing steel simply stopped, followed by the slow waning of tortured moans and agonized screams. They heard the final death throes, no mistaking the sound or what it heralds, several hours ago.

"Ashana, they're gone," Brio insists. "We should be using this time to our advantage. Let's go now! Please!"

"Evie," she reminds him, ignoring both his pleas and the logic of them.

Brio's voice rises in frustration. "What difference does that make now? Everyone out there is dead!"

"Be quiet!" she hisses in his ear.

With a growl that's far more Savage than a Gen-raised pleader, Brio wrests himself free of the hold she's had on him all night and begins clawing through the remnants of the tent cloth camouflaging them from sight. Evie tries in vain to pull him back down to the ground, but Brio persists. She has no choice but to follow him out, if only to protect him, and then only so she can knock some sense into him herself. The sudden light slices into their night-laden eyes, stinging them. Brio and Evie both raise their hands to shield their gaze from the blinding sun.

The atrocity of what they see can't be blunted by such temporary shadows.

The entire camp has been razed. Every tent is a flattened pile of what look like burned-black leaves fallen from some gargantuan dead tree. The only noticeable movement comes from the wisps of white smoke rising like escaping spirits from the ashes. The bodies of Savages are strewn everywhere, open throats and severed necks feeding scores of carrion flies. There are more heads decorating the field than boulders. The blood fouling what's left of the grass is already turning yellow, but far worse than the smell of decay is that of bowel and bladder spilled in death.

"We shouldn't have survived this," Brio says, the horror overwhelming most of his senses clearly etched on his face. "We shouldn't have—"

"But we did," Evie reminds him. "And we'll keep surviving. Keep all this outside you where it belongs. Don't take it in. You don't have room for it. Trust me."

Evie tries not to see the faces of the dead. She tries not to remember the old, the infirm, and the simple folk of the Bottoms who never belonged on a battlefield and committed no crime meriting this kind of execution. Still pictures of their faces, sullen and accepting of their fate around a table at the Revel, flicker and are banished from her mind. She tries to dismiss these butchered bodies as the condemned, as strangers unremarkable and unrelated to her. Above all, she refuses to remember that most of the night's victims were just people, like her, with others waiting and weeping and praying silently to the forgotten God Stars for a return that will never come.

"All these people—" Brio begins, only to have Evie shut him down immediately.

"We're pushing the Sicclunans to the edge of annihilation. They're desperate, dying. They can't be blamed for this. Conscripted or not, the Savages are one of the fiercest weapons being used against their people."

"Such a waste . . ."

Evie only nods, saying no more.

She wanders through the burned camp, forcing the grief and revulsion gnawing at her guts to subside, at least for now. Evie's eyes, adjusting to the light of day, search through the human and material wreckage for anything usable the Sicclunan night force might not have scavenged after their assault. She and Brio need food and water if they have any hope of surviving an extended journey on foot, not to mention weapons other than the pair of short swords Evie appropriated during the attack.

She sees nothing but burned wood and bloody, torn rags clinging to the dead, all of them in even worse condition than the filthy garb in which she and Brio are clad. Evie wonders if they'll fare any better in whatever's left of the Skrain camp, although the thought of running across any surviving Crachian soldiers gives her pause.

"Evie!" Brio hisses at her back. "People!"

She turns, fist already closed around the tsuka of the short sword tucked under her tunic belt.

"Little Sparrow!"

A jubilant voice among such carnage sounds as out of place as laughter in a charnel house. That voice issues from beneath the broom-like mustache of Lariat. The barrel of a man is trampling the husks of tent poles and bones alike as he ambles toward them. The series of leather straps that fasten hooked blades to his every joint creak loudly with every step; both steel and leather have been soaked through with blood. The matched katars that transform his fists into short swords are sheathed awkwardly and dangerously through his belt.

Mother Manai and Bam, the rest of the Elder Company, follow closely behind him. Several of the steel "fingers" protruding from the leather-wrapped stump of Manai's right hand have been bent in battle, and all five blades are crusted with Sicclunan blood. In her remaining hand she holds the wooden handle of what looks far more like a large kitchen cleaver than any kind of ax belonging on a battlefield. Bam looks no different from the first time Evie laid eyes on him, with the hood of his sleeveless cloak pulled low over the bulbous features of his face. The haft of a giant mallet is slung over his shoulder; what's happened to his equally giant scythe or where he's acquired his new weapon she can only guess. Both heads of the mallet's wooden hammer have what must be brains clinging to their worn surfaces, drying in the sun.

"You're a wily one, Evie," Mother Manai compliments her. "A woman after my own heart."

"It's good to see you, too," Evie says, and it is, though it's difficult to feel it, or anything else, at that moment.

Lariat laughs, heartily, obviously suffering none of her qualms. "Yer just fulla surprises, ain't ya? Here I wouldn't have thought you'd live to see your second battle, and you go and survive a dust-'em-up like this'n without a scratch! Though it looks like they tested ya, eh?"

Evie looks down at her hands, unable to distinguish dirt from dried blood. She stares at the streaks of both across her chest, rubs at the same grit suddenly itching her neck.

"Life is a test," she says quietly.

Mother Manai laughs. "And death's the only real answer."

"Made a new friend there, have ya?" Lariat asks, sizing Brio up with a hard gaze.

Evie glances back at him. "This is . . . we knew each other in the Bottoms, back in the Capitol."

"Ah. Capitol boy. We won't hold that against ya none."

"Did anyone else survive?" Evie asks.

"The dozen'er so B'ors that were in camp, they all came through," Lariat informs her. "They're havin' a rest in back the weeds, where we were hidin' out, but I wouldn't count on 'em stayin' long. They'll take their chances runnin'. Hardheaded bastards, the lot of 'em are. They'd rather deal with coin hunters on one side and Sicclunan soldiers on the other, and the Sicclunans don't like B'ors any more than Crachians do."

"Other Savages? Skrain soldiers?"

"A few stragglers who took to the brush with us when the Sicclunans marched on the camp in force," Mother Manai says. "No Skrain that we've seen."

Lariat snorts through his mustache. "They picked the Skrain camp clean of armor, weapons, supplies, anythin' worth taking. We looked."

"Of course," Evie says ruefully.

"If you wanna keep surprisin' me by livin', little Sparrow, you'll come east with us and hope we find the Skrain before the Skrain or the blood coin hunters find us."

"I suppose it won't matter to them that our only crime was surviving an ambush in the night."

Lariat shakes his head. "A Savage outta camp is fair game, reason don't matter. They ain't so good at listenin' to us."

"That's assuming the Sicclunans haven't pushed the line back and are holding it," Manai offers helpfully.

"Right," Lariat says. "In that case we're behind enemy lines and they'll be happy to kill us themselves. Won't care about the reward."

"There's something to be said for denying the coin hunters their due," Mother Manai remarks, actually sounding delighted.

"I can't let my friend be returned to the Legion," Evie insists.

"Why, 'cuzza his leg?" Lariat asks. "It'll probably haveta come off anyway, from the look. Might as well let a surgeon—"

"It's not that."

Evie again looks to Brio, this time holding his eyes with hers, a silent question passing between them.

He only shrugs, looking as weary as she's ever seen him.

Evie turns back to the Elder Company. "I did not come here by accident. I'm a retainer serving Gen Ultimo in the Capitol. This man's name is Brio Alania. He's the head of Gen Stalbraid and pleader for the Bottoms. He spoke out openly against the Legion. Then he found evidence of the crimes they've committed. He was illegally detained and sent here among you. I wasn't sentenced to the Savage Legion, I came here to find him and bring him back to the Capitol to put an end to this, for all of us."

They're silent at first, then, as Evie might've expected, both Lariat and Mother Manai begin laughing uproariously.

"What was your crime, Mother?" Evie asks Manai, speaking over their reverie.

More than anything else, it's the weight in her voice that silences Mother Manai's laughter. She stares oddly at the younger woman.

"My eldest took ill. I stole a pork shoulder to feed the grandkids."

"*Only* the condemned are supposed to serve in the Legion. The councils and the Gens don't know what's happening here. The Protectorate Ministry is conspiring with our taskers to conscript not just petty criminals, but all those without homes in the Bottoms and every place like it in every city in Crache. They're doing the same to anyone who speaks out or looks into what's really going on here, including Gen members. Brio has proof back in the Capitol. If he presents it in open session in front of the Arbitration Council he can put an end to this. You can all go home to your families."

She can feel Brio's eyes on her in that moment, concerned she's overpromising, but there's nothing to be done as she sees it. If the Elders and other Savages aren't with them, they will never make it.

More silence, yet this time it isn't followed by laughter.

"We don't know where any of the Skrain or Savage encampments are," Mother Manai points out. "They don't exactly share strategy and troop movements with us. Whatever we do we're like to end up stumbling on one."

"We'll stay away from the main roads and hike over country," Evie says. "I can't believe this camp was the only one hit in the night. That wouldn't be a strong enough move for the Sicclunans. I'd lay odds their night soldiers struck every Crachian post, all the ground they gained in these last battles. They'll all be scrambling to recover. We can use that."

"Little Sparrow, I promise ya, we've all 'eard these notions before," Lariat says, sounding like a gruff father placating a child. "I tell ya they're just daydreams. Only they're daydreams that'll see your head on a spike if you take up chasin' 'em."

"What about the blood coin hunters?" Mother Manai asks Evie, ignoring Lariat.

Evie briefly studies the older woman. She sees an earnestness in Mother Manai's expression, in the way she's regarding Evie. It occurs to her in that moment that Manai is the only one taking her seriously, willing to see what Evie sees in their current circumstance.

"That's why I'm telling you all this," Evie says, holding Manai's gaze. "We have a better chance together, small enough to slip through the line but with enough force to defend ourselves if need be. It's *not* a daydream or a fantasy. It's an opportunity, perhaps the only one you'll ever have."

"You tell a fine story, little Sparrow," Lariat commends her. "Yer a finer speaker than any Savage I've yet known. So I'm sure yer smart enough to know we can't put any stock in it."

"I can only offer you the truth. It's your choice to believe it. Brio and I are headed east, but we're not giving ourselves over to the Skrain. I will see this man returned to the Capitol or I'll die in the attempt. It's that simple for me. Whatever you have to do for yourselves, I understand, but will you answer me one question, and answer it with absolute truth?"

"I always tell the truth," Lariat mockingly protests. "Except when I lie."

"Ask your question," Mother Manai bids her, far more serious.

"Do any of you truly believe you will ever see your families again?" Evie asks them all. "Do you truly believe you will survive long enough to earn your reprieve, and that it will be granted if you do? Do you really believe you will ever be allowed to leave the Savage Legion?"

Silence answers her.

Even Lariat doesn't quite seem to know what to say to that.

Evie waits, somehow knowing not to press them in that moment, to let them sit with the weight of her questions, with the answers the Savages don't wish to speak aloud, and the futures those answers conjure whether they want to see them or not.

"No," Mother Manai says at last, quietly. "No, of course we don't."

"Then I will ask you one final question," Evie says. "What difference does it make? You can die in your thirtieth or even fortieth battle, and it will be no different than if you died in your first. What do you have to fear by escaping? By trying? At least you'll have a chance, a hope. And even if you're right and it's futile and we're captured, you'll have died trying to get back to your people instead of fighting for the ones who forced coins down our gullets and hurled us at enemy shields with rusted weapons. You'll have died fighting, truly fighting, instead of submitting."

Unnoticed by the others, Bam slips a hemp-wrapped hand beneath his hood and it pushes it back over his long, stringy hair.

Evie stares past Lariat and Mother Manai at the silent juggernaut of a man. Bam has the face of a sad hound, but his eyes are suddenly boring into her with a fiery light that she's neither seen nor would expect from him. After a moment the other members of the Elder Company look back at Bam as well, and the surprise is evident on both of their faces. Evie opens her mouth to speak, but she's unsure of what to say, or what his gaze is saying to her.

Fortunately, when the silence threatens to become unbearable, Bam raises his hood and lowers his face into its recesses once again. He strides forward, past his compatriots, and joins Evie and Brio. He stands beside her, hugging his huge arms around the haft of his mallet, seeming to wait.

"Well, that's a new thing," Lariat grumbles.

Mother Manai grins. "Fair enough, Sparrow, or whatever your name is. If Bam's convinced, I won't be the one to disband our company. And in truth, you've almost convinced me, as well."

She looks up at Lariat, who sighs deep enough to bristle his mustache.

"We'd do better with the B'ors on our side" is all he says in the end. "Can you convince 'em the way you convinced Bam here, Little Sparrow?"

Brio leans in over Evie's left shoulder. "You're a better pleader than I've ever been, it seems," he tells her quietly.

Evie drops her head, the grin that comes to her lips devoid of anything resembling joy.

"All right," she says, lifting her chin to regard Lariat with a hard stare. "Take me to them."

THE JEOPARDY ROOM

THE BELLS SUMMON DYEAWAN TO SANITATION ON THE THIRD level. She's been there dozens of times before, and aside from the smells she always finds it as fascinating as any level in the keep. It's there that the Cadre tests different means of disposing and even utilizing waste, from rotting food to fallen leaves to filthy water to every resident's supper from the night before. The last time she carried a message there they were working on a new kind of cistern that used a combination of potions to turn solid refuse into liquid waste so it could be more easily drained.

The assemblers hadn't quite perfected the balance of potions yet, but just the *idea* of such a thing lit a fire inside Dyeawan's head.

She rows her tender through the circles of stone that have become so familiar to her in such a short time. She's not certain when these corridors began to feel like home, or even when "home" became an idea she both accepted and even craved, but she's never felt more safe or welcomed or content in her entire life. The door to Sanitation is open, as most of the doors in the Planning Cadre are. Dyeawan begins to purposefully breathe through her mouth rather than her nose, and wonders what sort of invention she'll witness today.

The part of her mind that seems to know things before she does recognizes what's happening as soon as she rolls through the door. It takes the rest of Dyeawan only a moment to catch up.

Sanitation is gone. There should be a wide-open workspace filled with dozens of assemblers performing at least half that many tasks. Instead Dyeawan finds herself in a cramped antechamber no larger than a closet, staring at the entrance to a narrow corridor so long she can't truly distinguish where or how it ends. A single torch in a single stone sconce lights the space. That becomes even more important in the next moment when the door behind Dyeawan slams shut.

She peers over her shoulder, staring at the heavy slab of wood and metal. She hears a heavy metal "snap" followed by a brief grinding of steel against steel. It doesn't take a mind as keen as hers to know the door has just been locked from the outside. Dyeawan's heart begins beating faster and she realizes she's stopped breathing for several moments. She inhales sharply and grips the edges of her tender's paddles.

"All right," she whispers to herself in the darkened space lit only by a few gentle flames. "All right."

Dyeawan turns from the door and rows her tender forward, halting at the threshold of the corridor. Instead of staring down its pitch length, she examines the entrance and what she can see of its structure.

The corridor is far too narrow to permit her tender. It looks barely wide enough to allow both her shoulders movement through its confines, and that's if she were to drag herself over the ground as she used to in the streets and alleys of the Capitol. She finds the very thought of doing so here, now, fills her with dread and something deeper, a sense of intense loathing, frustration, and even anger.

Dyeawan pushes herself up on her tender's platform, straining to reach the torch on the wall above her. Grunting from the effort, she manages to snatch the torch from its sconce without losing her grip and dropping its flaming head. Leaning over the front of her tender, Dyeawan extends the torch to the bottom of the corridor. What she sees first causes her to squint, then makes her eyes widen in disbelief.

Most of either wall is smooth. However, beginning perhaps a foot from the floor, sharp, jagged spikes begin protruding from both sides of the corridor. Some are set lower and some higher, but a spike on the opposite wall matches each one, so closely no human body could fit between them. What's more, the floor between the corridor walls is also covered in spikes, much shorter than the ones above, but so many of them that a person with full use of their legs couldn't take a step without piercing their foot.

She couldn't even crawl under the wall spikes.

This seems impossibly cruel. It seems to go against everything she's heard and experienced in her time with the Planning Cadre. This is the Crache Dyeawan glimpsed so often in the streets, from her many hiding places and while sliding away from Aegins and drunkards and sneak thieves.

It's a test, she reminds herself. *This is the test Edger talked about. This is the test they give planners.*

The knowledge, the certainty of it, brings her little comfort. Clever puzzles in the comfort of a soft bed that belongs to her seem like a very distant memory, something that happened in another place, or perhaps another life.

Either you want this or you don't, another voice that sounds much like Edger's goads her. *You can pound on the door and beg to be let out of this place. They will open it. You know they will. You can go right back to sweeping the floor and delivering parchment scribbles and the inventions of others. You can spend the rest of your life here in comfort, like blind old Makai toiling every day in his kitchen, or the one-armed mute who tends the sconces, never having to face another test again. You can still be Edger's favorite pet cripple. You don't have to do this.*

She doesn't have to, but she *wants* to. For the first time, Dyeawan admits to herself that she wants what Edger has dangled in front of her. In truth, she wants even more than that. She doesn't just want to be part of the Cadre, and she doesn't just want to be a planner; Dyeawan wants to be Edger. She wants to be the one who can reach into the gutters of the Capitol and scoop out the unwanted at will. She could do so much more with that power than he has.

Her mind begins to unfurl such pictures, such fantasies of the knowledge she could attain, the wonders she could create, and the souls she could save. Dyeawan forces that mental scroll to wind back up so she can stuff it away in a corner of her head somewhere. Desire is dangerous, especially for someone like her. It can drive you insane, or worse, it can drive you to act foolishly, even lethally against your own survival.

Is that what I'm doing now, she wonders.

Dyeawan drops the torch to the floor. She slinks from the tender's platform and lowers herself onto the antechamber ground outside the corridor. Situating herself in front of her tender, she reaches up and strokes a hand against the steel frame of its front wheels, against the fine polished grain of the wood. She's come to love the contraption as much as she loves Riko or Tahei. It's allowed her to be more than she ever thought she could.

It has allowed her to fly.

As gently as possible, Dyeawan reaches up and rips loose one of the cords that connects the left paddle to the wheel track. Her body jumps, just so, as she feels it tear away, almost as if she's dealt her body a physical blow. The next piece she removes from the tender is easier, and by the time she's disassembled the left paddle her mind is focused only on the mechanical task she's given herself. It takes her more than an hour to carefully demolish the tender and lay out each individual part before her meticulously.

She's left both wheel tracks and their axles mostly intact, only removing the large front and back wheels. Between the remaining axles of the smaller wheels, Dyeawan lays a single plank from the tender's wide platform, just wide enough to accommodate both her knees if they're pressed tightly together. She snaps off several thin metal wires from the frame of a large wheel and bends them into "U" shapes with her hands. Dyeawan uses one of the disjointed paddles as a hammer to pound them through the plank and secure the axles to its bottom. The points that poke through the top she bends against the wood's surface covers with strips she tears from her tunic so they won't cut into her legs.

When the base is ready, Dyeawan hoists herself up onto the plank between the wheels. It's snug and she barely fits, but the wheels will still turn. She uses several lengths of the extra cord to lash her folded legs to the wood securely. Leaning forward, she touches her hands to the ground and pushes and pulls the wheels back and forth experimentally. They roll evenly enough, and the entire sled contraption seems to hold together.

It's better than sliding, anyway.

Dyeawan takes up the torch from where she dropped it on the floor and casts it down the length of the corridor. It lands on the ground beneath the spikes halfway down the corridor's length, spreading enough light in the narrow space to brighten her way.

Dyeawan wheels herself to lip of the corridor. The first pair of wall spikes rises just above her knees. She inhales deeply and exhales with purpose. It takes all her strength and several attempts, but Dyeawan lifts her body and the front of her wheels onto those two slender steel spikes. Leaning into the corridor, she presses her hands against either wall and, gritting her teeth, pulls the rest of the wheels up and over.

She'd hoped to wedge them between the next set of spikes and then repeat the strenuous action, however difficult it would be on her arms and on her makeshift miniature tender. Dyeawan should've known Edger and his planners weren't testing her mastery of brute force, however. As soon as her back wheels clear the first set of spikes she dips dangerously forward. Dyeawan closes her eyes and throws her arms in front of her face, expecting to be spilled onto the razor-sharp floor below.

Instead her makeshift tender glides down and then back up effortlessly, with only a few gentle bumps, clicking to a stop and remaining there, suspended.

Dyeawan lowers her arms and opens her eyes, her breathing still elevated. She looks down. The next pair of elevated spikes is holding her front wheels. Looking behind her, she realizes that what seemed like a random pattern of spikes is actually a track built specifically for exactly the wheeled contraption she's constructed from her tender. The spikes continuously dip and rise like the curls of waves in perfectly symmetrical sequence.

All Dyeawan has to do is grip the walls and urge her wheels over the highest peaks in the pattern of spikes. Once they're tipped past the peak, she rolls easily down the next sets of spikes and that brief but powerful momentum is enough to carry her back up to the next peak. The strain on her arms is minimal, and after she adjusts to the ebb and flow of the track, Dyeawan even begins to enjoy the short rides. The sudden dips create a wonderful dropping sensation in the pit of her stomach, and the upturns cause the space between her ears to fizzle delightedly.

Halfway through the corridor she finds herself laughing and envisioning a much larger version of the tracks, perhaps as tall as the Spectrum itself. People in wheeled carts could be propelled across them purely for fun. Even imagining these sensations on such a massive scale makes her dizzy with pleasure. As she reaches the end of the corridor, however, Dyeawan forces herself to put away such flights of fancy, reminding herself she's in the middle of a test that will see her become a planner like Edger or return to battling dust and footprints on a daily basis.

The final dip in the spike track has no upturn; it merely ends, sending Dyeawan careening out the other end of the corridor. Her front wheels hit the floor and she leans far back to compensate and prevent herself from tipping dangerously forward. Fortunately her back wheels touch down evenly enough that she stays righted, even if it is a hard landing that jars her from her gut to her jaw.

The chamber beyond the corridor isn't like any she's seen in the Planning Cadre, other than its circular shape. It's almost completely empty and there are no windows. The floor is smoothly cobbled, like rolling over the scaly back of some great unimagined beast. It's an impossible room; Dyeawan *knows* that the door through which she entered belonged to Sanitation. Unless the spiked corridor wound so deftly, it seemed to be a straight path while leading her into a completely different part of the keep.

Resting in the center of the chamber, slightly tilted to one side, is a rowboat barely large enough to fit one fully grown person. There are no oars, only large and empty rusted rings. It sits there, looking particularly lonely in these contrary surroundings.

The chamber's only other distinguishing features are torches lit in sconces and half a dozen or so wrought-iron grates bolted along the walls. The grates are set much higher than the sconces, several dozen feet above the cobbles. Their bars are thick and the grates themselves are large enough to herd hogs through.

"Hello?" Dyeawan calls out, mostly to break the oppressive silence of the space.

It's no surprise when only her echo answers.

She urges her wheels forward, staring at the shoddy little rowboat that looks as though it's been left behind in the wake of some hasty rush to clear out the chamber. Dyeawan knows it must mean something; every choice Edger and the planners have made thus far has been deliberate, precise, and connected somehow to another piece of a puzzle.

Her mind is racing to discover that missing piece when a very distinct scent hits her and Dyeawan sniffs at the air.

She smells the sea.

That might only have puzzled her further, except for one alarming and undeniable fact; she did *not* smell the sea just a moment ago.

She hears the first dribbling of water before she sees it, a stream of unending tears pouring onto the shiny cobbles beneath her. Dyeawan looks up and sees the bay water beginning to spill through all the grates in the walls. At first it merely drips through the bottoms of the heavy iron bars, but a deep and distant rumbling informs her ears of what her eyes will confirm moments later, that more water is coming, and it sounds as if it might be the whole of the bay.

Dyeawan, panicked, grabs for her wheels and begins whirling

herself back toward the corridor. She stops midturn, remembering the locked door beyond the rough ride over those spikes. Surely they can't really mean to drown her here in this dark place. It's still a test. Perhaps she can retreat and use the remnants of her tender to force the door open or otherwise disable the lock.

No, that can't be the test. They wouldn't have created such an elaborate chamber just to have her unlock a door. Tahei could unlock a hundred doors, and no one was leaving puzzles at his bedside.

The rowboat.

By the time seawater is blasting through the grates full-force and from every direction, Dyeawan has wheeled herself beside the tilted ramshackle-looking vessel in the middle of the chamber. She's reaching down to untie the cords encircling her folded legs when a new thought halts her anxious hands.

She looks up at the chamber ceiling. There are no openings there, not even more grates. Inside the rowboat she'd rise to meet solid stone, and if the water didn't cease filling the chamber, the small wooden vessel and she would be crushed against the ceiling with no other way out. And even if she managed to steer the boat to one of the grates set in the walls before the water rose above them, she has no way of opening the grates.

It didn't make any sense.

Unless.

Dyeawan forgets about untying herself from her wheels. Instead, with the water already swirling around her waist, she angles herself up against the small vessel's port. She leans over the tilted side of the rowboat and takes hold of the large, rusted ring on the opposite side. She's thankful the deceptive strength in her arms hasn't abandoned her totally. Dyeawan is able to capsize the rowboat and pull the inside of its hull over her. She takes hold of both its rusted oar rings for support, gripping them tightly and pulling the rowboat as deeply around her as possible.

The weight of her wheels and axles helps keep them both anchored to the cobbled floor. Inside the rowboat, the water is up to her chest, but there it stops, even as the chamber continues to fill and the upended bottom of the rowboat slowly becomes completely submerged. Dyeawan can breathe, for now, but she knows every hole in a boat fills eventually.

Dyeawan *knows* there is a way out of all this. She knows that's the entire point of this room, to find that way out. That's the test.

The water around her is dancing in the faint amber light cast by the torches on the walls. Dyeawan stares at that light, thinking, recalling every detail of the chamber, the corridor, the antechamber, even the locked door. None of those perfectly rendered pictures in her mind yield a solution, or even another piece of the puzzle.

Eventually, inevitably, the water overcomes the torches on the walls, extinguishing each flame. The water below Dyeawan goes dark. That water is now threatening her neck, filling the inside of the upended rowboat as it has filled the chamber around it. Dyeawan's breathing becomes as shallow as the depths in which she's anchored. Until now she wasn't truly afraid of dying or failing, and now both feel like the tips of very sharp swords pressed to her temples.

She closes her eyes, preferring the darkness behind her eyelids to that of the drowned chamber. When she opens them again, Dyeawan discovers a new light spreading through the water surrounding her. It's not the fiery reflection of torchlight, or any kind of flame Dyeawan has seen. Glimpses of bright and unnatural blue begin blinking in and out all around her. Curious, Dyeawan stretches her arms and dips her head below the surface of the water, eyes open and ignoring the salty sting.

It's fish. They're swimming into the chamber through the grates. That isn't particularly odd or alarming, but Dyeawan quickly notices they are all the same kind of fish, dozens and dozens of them, and no other type of sea life is finding its way in.

She's also never seen fish like these before. They're almost more like sea snakes with fins as thin and willowy as wisps of smoke stretching their length. They appear almost black, but every few seconds their bodies come alight, crackling blue like tiny lightning strikes underwater.

Their luminous forms flicker and pop with some palpable energy, then the light once again goes dark.

One of the creatures swims across the sole of her foot, close enough to brush the unnaturally soft skin there. The first sensation experienced by Dyeawan is surprise, followed by two bouts of brief yet intense pain. The first bout surges through her entire body. The second bout is focused solely on her hands grasping the rowboat's oar rings, both of which let off a volley of sparks even beneath the water and cause her hands to lose their grip.

Dyeawan's head is thrust beneath the surface. Her stung hands scramble to regain their grip on the rings. She grasps their rough edges, ignoring the pain, and pulls her head above the water, although now her chin is barely able to clear the surface that's almost reached the bottom of the rowboat's hull. Almost as dire, whatever coursed through her and touched off the oar rings has left them loose and threatening to pull free of their wood and steel moorings.

Dyeawan blinks, her focus recovering from the painful contact with that fish. Her body is quaking and she can feel the residual touch of the creature in the ends of her hair. She struggles to both push the oar rings back in place while also holding the rowboat over her, a task that seems completely contrary and is starting to feel impossible to enact as her stinging hands begin to numb.

However, it's the loosening of those rusted rings that plants an idea in the back of her mind. If everything in this chamber has been erected deliberately, then all these fish are no different, and Dyeawan is quickly becoming convinced their purpose is *not* to provide her with sporadic light. That grain of an idea becomes a fully formed plan, but it's one that calls for a possibly lethal amount of conjecture.

In that moment Dyeawan has to decide exactly how much she believes in her own mind. If she has as much faith in herself as Edger claims to, then there should be no doubt she'll choose the right course of action.

Dyeawan hooks one arm around the large plank at the rowboat's bottom to steady the vessel while her other arm delves deep beneath the water. It's difficult untying the cords around her legs with one hand, but it gives her time to take deep, measured breaths and steel herself for what's to come.

Dyeawan spent most of her life in the Bottoms, next to the ocean, and much of that while blessed with motion solely from the waist up. Every brief friend she made in the streets, every drunken sailor who took pity on her, they all warned her never to fall into the water. *A cripple without the use of their legs would surely drown,* they said. She never believed it. She's seen a dog with no back legs paddle to safety. She's seen motionless hunks of wood float perfectly well, not to mention more than a few still bodies.

She's also learned never to trust others' opinion of what she can and cannot do.

Dyeawan, free of her makeshift tender, draws in as much air as she can hold and seals her lips shut. She abandons the oar rings and drops below the surface of the water, letting the rowboat float away. She strokes her arms against the depths, letting her legs float weightless behind her as she moves her body easily through the water. After a lifetime of pulling herself across the earth, swimming underwater is like a dream.

She reaches the nearest grate in little more than a minute. Her hands are scarcely large enough to encompass one wrought iron bar, and the spaces between the bars aren't wide enough to fit her body through. She expected that. Dyeawan examines the spots where the grate meets the stone, discovering hinges on one side and a large square pad of steel protruding from the other. That pad seems to be the only piece of metal truly tethering the grate to the wall.

Dyeawan extends an arm out into the submerged chamber and tries in vain to usher one of the crackling blue fish toward the lock without touching their body. Herding them quickly proves to be futile. She knows what she has to do, and probably has known since the first acorn of this idea fell from the evergreen tree that is her mind.

Dyeawan lets go of the iron bar and places her hand over the grate's lock pad, gripping it tightly. She lets the rest of her body float as far out into the chamber as possible while keeping a hold on the lock. Her other arm stretches deeper still, poised and waiting. She begins to feel a silent protest rising from her lungs to her throat, both seeming to painfully constrict, but she ignores it, concentrating solely on the task ahead of her.

Several of the luminous serpentlike fish glide by, just out of reach. With each missed opportunity Dyeawan feels the pressure within her body mounting even more desperately and painfully, and each time it becomes more difficult to ignore. Finally one of the creatures swims close enough to her hand to be seized, but Dyeawan forces herself to wait. She keeps the splayed fingers and thumb of her hand perfectly still, letting the creature become comfortable resting in that spot.

When she's sure it is relaxed and unaware, or possibly when her aching lungs finally demand it, Dyeawan moves her hand through the water as quickly as she can and seizes the crackling blue/black fish.

The hand around the creature's snakelike body is immediately punished, but Dyeawan holds tight and tenses the muscles of her face to keep her lips sealed. The rest of her body is treated to waves of sharp pain. She feels sparks scorch her palm, and it's all Dyeawan can do not to let her mouth fly open to swallow a gallon of seawater, but she also feels the pad under her hand give way, separating from the wall.

The entire grate swings open, dragging her body with it. Dyeawan releases the luminescent sea serpent and takes hold of the grate with both hands to prevent her from being flung across the chamber. Her palms and fingers are stinging and numb at the same time, but she manages to right herself. She quickly wriggles her body through the space no longer barred by the grate.

Dyeawan doesn't swim as much as she pull herself along through the water-filled shaft beyond, her lungs on fire and her entire skull feeling as if it's expanding from within, threatening to burst. Her eyes register light ahead, and not the ghastly blue luminescence of those damned charged serpent fish. It's sunlight, rays filtered through the water of the island's bay. She digs harder and faster against the narrow walls, pulling herself along at a desperate pace. Every piece of her is screaming until she clears the end of the shaft and enters the open depths of the bay, bathed in a sun that seems so near and guides her like a beacon to the bay's surface.

Her first breath is agony and ecstasy wrestling for control. Several times she drops back below the water and has to flail her exhausted arms to regain her posture above the surface. As the precious air fills her, Dyeawan is able to force a renewed calm over her body that enables her to float atop the water without constantly working her arms. The fire in her muscles and her lungs finally begins to subside and her gasping returns to shallow breathing.

It feels almost better than being back in her bed.

She hears wooden oars lapping gently and rhythmically against the calm surface of the bay. Dyeawan, her arms protesting as vehemently as her lungs did beneath the water just moments ago, turns herself around to watch a rowboat far larger and more pristine than the one she abandoned in the chamber approaching her. She sees Quan's lanky torso rising high above the boat. He's happily crewing the oars all by himself, enjoying the afternoon sun. Quan pilots the vessel alongside where Dyeawan is bobbing above the water.

Before she can manage a word aloud, Edger leans over the boat's stern. He's shielding himself and Ku from the sun with a silk parasol the rich red of heart's blood. Small circles of glass that appear to have been painted black are held over his eyes by thin, intricately woven leather straps. Despite everything Dyeawan has just endured, she consciously notices for the first time just how pale the man is; he must not venture outside the Cadre often.

"You are a strong swimmer, little Slider," he says brightly. "And it surely is a fine day for it, I must say."

Dyeawan stares up at him, a rage she can't remember feeling before welling in her guts. It's surprising, both in its intensity and how *good* it threatens to make her feel. She's never truly understood just how integral to her survival it has been, suppressing her darker feelings, never letting the putrid circumstances of her existence overwhelm her, either with sadness or fury.

In this moment, she knows how empowering that fury would be, but another thought stems it, the question of where it will lead her if she allows that tidal wave of emotion to crash freely.

"Would you really have let me die in there?" she asks evenly.

Edger leans even farther over the side of the rowboat. The glazed eyes of his expressionless face stare at nothing somewhere past her right shoulder, yet somehow Dyeawan imagines him smiling. The body of Ku the wind dragon convulses gently against the man's throat like a small, beating heart, and through the bone flutes perforating the creature's hide the voice made of wind that belongs to Edger whistles to her.

"What do *you* think?" he asks.

HEAVEN'S HOSTESS
IS HELL'S HANDMAIDEN

LEXI CAN ONLY IMAGINE THAT THE AGENTS WERE PAIRED BY the Protectorate Ministry for their shocking contrast, which is either uproariously humorous or deeply disturbing, depending on the beholder.

She spotted the first one from the cooperative's bazaar right away; it was impossible not to, as the man towers a full two heads above even Taru, is slender as a willow, and draped head to toe in midnight as all Ministry agents are. As if his height and frame weren't striking enough, the man's head is shaved completely bald and shines like a beacon. A storm-tossed ship could follow it all the way to shore.

It isn't until she and Taru approach the archway to the bridge leading to Gen Stalbraid's towers that they notice his companion. The second agent is a head shorter than Lexi, as round as a wheel of cheese and four times as pale. His ghostly complexion is made even more off-putting by the slick of hair atop his head that is even darker than his uniform and the equally black and oily beard that covers most of his bulbous face.

Lexi greets them each with a deep bow. "Agents."

"Te-Gen," the towering skeletal one says in a surprising baritone.

"Te-Gen," his squat companion echoes, his voice alarmingly high-pitched.

Taru says nothing, and the Ministry men seem happy enough to ignore the Undeclared.

"The Ministry honors Gen Stalbraid with its protection," Lexi assures them, her tone, expression, and posture all affecting the practiced benevolence of her hostess training.

The agents trade a silent glance, both of them unsure how to respond to that. They are not known for their imagination, thus neither of them can imagine a scenario under which they have been dispatched, not to spy on Lexi, but to "protect" her.

"It is the charter of the Ministry," the tall one begins, staggering each word as if he has to think about the next one to follow, "to protect the machinery of the state. It is thus our mandate to preserve and monitor each part of that machine in equal measure."

"It is always beneficial to understand one's place in the whole," Lexi replies without missing a beat or even the slightest crack in her welcoming smile.

"Or one's place outside it," Taru adds quietly but with what might as well be the conversational force of breaking explosive wind.

The Ministry agents shift their feet uncomfortably, their black gauntleted hands tightening around the handles of their daggers.

Lexi's smile remains unshakeable. "Well said, Taru," she commends her retainer.

Then, with another pair of deep bows: "Again, I extend the most heartful appreciation of my Gen, agents. Good evening."

They both return the bow without comment, visibly relieved as Lexi and Taru take their leave and make the long trek over the arched bridge to Lexi's kith-kin tower.

"They are not even assassins," Taru remarks in disgust halfway across the bridge.

Lexi isn't precisely certain what Taru means by that, but it is clearly the retainer's lowest form of classification.

Later, sitting at the drafting table in Brio's law library, Lexi labors over a sheet of parchment with a heron quill.

Taru sits on the expansive rug in the middle of the room. The retainer has stripped off their armor pieces and arranged them with militant symmetry in front of them. Clad in a simple tunic and leggings, Taru is currently oiling and massaging the leather of a pauldron.

"Begging Te-Gen's pardon," Taru begins tentatively.

Frustration that is rapidly approaching irritation's national border causes Lexi's lips to purse. "I thought we'd dispensed with all that cloying formality and preamble, Taru."

"Very well," Taru says, although her retainer's discomfort is obvious. That long-learned formality has become a second set of armor for Taru. "Seeking the aid of that Aegin, however necessary from your point of view—"

"Daian," Lexi says patiently, still writing.

Taru grunts, dubious. "Even if he is trustworthy, how much can you truly expect of him? We are dealing with such large forces aligned against us."

"I expect nothing from him," Lexi says, her focus never leaving the parchment. "But I believe he will try. And any information benefits our cause greatly at this point."

"But one Aegin alone—"

"He is not alone. We haven't given up our own search, and we won't."

Taru slaps a gauntlet down upon the rug in frustration. "But how can we continue with those . . . oddities . . . from the Ministry ghosting our every step? And you know they will, the second we leave the cooperative. Where they have stationed themselves they can see everyone coming or going from the towers."

Lexi waves her unburdened hand dismissively while her other hand continues to write. "Let them watch, let them follow."

Taru stares up at her from the rug, trusting in Lexi's confidence while questioning her logic.

"Then how—"

"They are watching us to see if we continue pursuing the truth behind Brio's disappearance and the attack on this house," Lexi explains. "That's what they expect. What they *want*, no doubt, is for me to continue fighting futilely with the bureaucracy to preserve our Gen's franchise. Seeing that won't alarm them, or cause them to act."

"Then which shall you choose to do?"

"Oh, we are going to do both," Lexi proclaims. "What the Ministry agents won't recognize is that we are doing both at the same time. They will only see me making a last desperate attempt to preserve these crumbling little towers of ours. And, hopefully, that is exactly what they will report to their superiors."

Lexi signs her name at the bottom of the document she's just drafted. She underlines the signature with a flourish of her heron quill before sheathing the quill in a small glass inkwell.

Taru is left puzzling over the plan behind Lexi's brash words. What that plan could possibly be eludes the retainer.

"How will we accomplish this, Te-Gen?" Taru asks, watching Lexi emboss the document with her Gen's state-issued seal.

"I am going to do what I should have done months ago."

"What is that?"

"Ascend," Lexi says.

The pleading floor of the Spectrum is much different from the private chambers of ruling bodies like the Gen Franchise Council. Here there are no ascending steps engineered to make petitioners feel like supplicants, no plateaus like false horizons giving them heights to which they might delude themselves into aspiring. The pleading floor is smooth and level, just two stone altars separating pleaders from the half dozen Capitol Arbiters that preside over all matters involving and facing the various small hamlets and economies and communities that make up Crache's Capitol city.

The true difference is the galleries. Any resident of or visitor to the Capitol may attend the open sessions, and they do, every day, dozens and dozens of them filling the ingrained stone benches surrounding the pleading floor. Many come to attend matters relating to their particular section of the city, but many more come simply to have a place to go during the day or to have someone representing the Spectrum at whom to yell at about any number of issues afflicting them or their homes.

Crache knows what its long-ago predecessors forgot, and to their total erasure from known history; the angry people in the galleries far outnumber those who rule, therefore it behooves those who rule to see them appeased. Making those perpetually discontent people believe they're allowed to argue on a level field, both figuratively and literally, is perhaps the subtlest and most effective form of control.

Lexi and Taru sit among them in the gallery beside the aisle that ends behind the pleaders' altar. Thus far they've sat through a petition to have new sky carriage tracks diverted through Division Seven, whose pleader claimed its residents are suffering from a lack of conveyance and jobs, and a border dispute between Divisions Five and Six over a supposed "conspiracy" by the former to funnel its waste into the latter's streets and alleys.

For the last ten minutes, the Waterfront Division's pleader has been arguing against the proposed replacement of the arch that's served as the gateway to the docks for centuries. Though the commerce of the docks fuels the Bottoms, the docks themselves are considered a separate entity entirely, because those who secretly control the docks don't want their concerns attached to those of the poor who dwell there. Thus they have their own pleader from a much larger and more influential Gen than Lexi's humble joining of two kith-kins.

Finally, the floor's page announces Gen Stalbraid, representing the Ninth Division of the Capitol. There's a brief murmuring from the galleries at that, and not just from residents of the Bottoms who've been without their pleader for four months. News of Brio's disappearance has become citywide gossip, particularly after the attack on his house and wife by unknown assassins.

That murmuring becomes a resounding wave of shock and confusion as Lexi stands and approaches the pleading altar. The surprise of the

271

denizens from the Bottoms quickly turns to applause as they recognize the woman who has begun bringing them food and offering them aid and comfort almost every day.

Though Taru is unarmed, forced to relinquish their weapons to Spectrum Aegins, the retainer tenses against the stone bench as they watch Lexi walk alone. The approbation of the crowd seems to do nothing to outwardly soothe their nerves. Taru's every impulse is no doubt to stay by Lexi's side, especially in the midst of all these unknown people.

Lexi carries a bundle of scrolls with her as she takes her place on the pleading floor. As she does, she notices Councilwoman Burr, the fiery Ignoble from the Gen Franchise Council, seated among the galleries, watching the proceedings with a stony and unreadable expression mortared on her face.

Lexi finds her presence curious, but quickly forces the questions surrounding it from her head. The matter at hand is dire, and the stand Lexi is about to take will either be her first or her last. She must put all of herself into it.

The Senior Arbiter's name is Tang, and Lexi has hosted him half a dozen times at official functions. Lexi knows him to be an intelligent, fairly boring man who abhors pointless small talk and who only smiles with a touch of resentment.

"Forgive me, Arbiters," Lexi begins. "I know you may view this as highly unusual, but I must be allowed to speak before you today."

"Te-Gen," Tang begins, the pace of his words careful, "this body is, of course, aware of the loss you and your Gen have suffered with the disappearance of your husband. Brio Alania was . . . excuse me, *is* . . . a highly respected officer of this floor. However, he is the recognized pleader of record for the Ninth Division of the Capitol, not you. To this body's knowledge, you are not even a recognized pleader."

"Gen Stalbraid is the recognized pleader of record for the Bottoms,"

Lexi corrects him. "Brio was the current pleader for our Gen, as was his father before him."

The Senior Arbiter looks to his colleagues, either for support or to convey his frustrations. In either case, ten vacant eyes stare back at him.

Tang regards her with hesitance. "Your interpretation of the law is not . . . incorrect."

Lexi smiles pleasantly. "Thank you, Senior Arbiter. I have recently received what one might consider advanced training in Crachian law and procedure."

Even Taru, still seated in the gallery, is forced to stifle a laugh at the truth behind that statement.

"Be that as it may," Tang says, "Gen Stalbraid has no other pleader to stand for Brio in his absence. Unless you've absorbed a new kith-kin or have taken a new husband, and I am unaware."

"No, Senior Arbiter, we remain as we have, and I am still married to Brio. However, I would like to submit myself to stand, in what I hope will be the short remainder of his absence, as pleader for the Bottoms."

The galleries stir, excited chatter spreading like a sickness through the crowd.

"Silence from the galleries, if you please," Senior Arbiter Tang calmly requests.

To Lexi, he says, "Te-Gen, we are all certain you mean only the best in appearing before us here. I also sympathize with your Gen in its time of strife. However, you are simply not qualified to plead on behalf of a Capitol Division, not in an official forum."

"You are correct, Senior Arbiter," Lexi agrees. "I am not yet qualified. I do, however, plan to be as soon as is possible."

She unfurls one of the scrolls in front of her and holds it up. "This is an official request to undertake training at the Academy. A copy has been dispatched to the Tenth City."

Lexi drapes the scroll over the front of the pleading altar and the floor page quickly scurries across the gap between it and the Arbiters to collect the document.

"That is admirable, Te-Gen, but until you've completed that lengthy training—"

"As I said, Senior Arbiter, I have recently immersed myself in Crachian law and procedure. The Doctrine of Arbitration clearly states that a novice *may* substitute for a standing pleader in the event that pleader is unexpectedly detained or incapacitated, providing that novice has begun the *process* of training and has observed a standing pleader for at least twenty sessions. By submitting my request I have clearly begun the process, and I have observed Brio in countless sessions on this very floor."

"That is a *very* loose interpretation of that particular provision, Te-Gen. It is meant as a temporary relief measure, for a single session at most, not to appoint a permanent replacement for a Division's pleader of record."

"You will forgive me, Senior Arbiter, but I don't believe that is left to you alone to decide."

"Of course not," Tang admits readily and without any sign of ire. "This matter will be put to a vote by the Arbitration Council."

"May I address the Council before that vote takes place?"

Tang pauses before answering, his expression changing just slightly as he looks across the well at Lexi. She can't be sure how his perception of her is changed in that moment.

"Please, proceed," he bids her.

Lexi is careful to meet the eyes of each member of the Council individually as she speaks.

"Te-Gens, De-Gens, I know you may view my request as some kind of stratagem born of a desperation, a gambit to keep my Gen thriving in dire times. I will not tell you that very thing does not at least in part motivate my every action. But I would also tell you that for generations Gen Stalbraid has been devoted to defending and giving voice to those who are born, live, and often die outside the grace and favor of the Capitol, even as they subsist in the shadow of this very Spectrum. Stalbraid took up the cause of the people in the Bottoms when no other pleading Gen would choose to represent them.

"I have spent my entire life serving that cause in whatever capacity I could. Today, this is what that cause demands of me, and I want only to meet that demand. Yes, I wish to hold my Gen together. However, there is a much larger concern involving a great many others who do not live in the high towers of well-kept cooperatives. A number of those people are in this room today because they have nowhere else to go. I would ask you to allow me to do this, not for the sake of Gen Stalbraid, but for the simple reason that it needs to be done."

Almost half the galleries erupt in applause on the heels of Lexi's final word. There are indeed many residents of the Bottoms in attendance, and their voices quickly overtake the entire floor. Taru looks around, seeing at least a dozen men and women rise to their feet in support of Lexi. Seizing the opportunity, Taru bolts up from the bench and begins thunderously applauding Lexi's speech. The retainer seeks the gaze of every ragged body still seated and gestures for them to do the same.

Soon it seems more people in the galleries are standing than sitting. Their cheers reach a deafening crescendo.

Senior Arbiter Tang is waving his arms. "Silence from the gallery, please, people! Please, we must have silence!"

It's another full minute before the commotion begins to die down, longer still until those on their feet sit down once more. Taru is the final one to return to the bench.

Lexi realizes she's never been so acutely aware of her own heart beating, but her composure, long practiced even if it has never been such a focal point for so many, remains intact.

"The Arbiters appreciate those words, Te-Gen," Tang assures her. "We recognize both the need for attentive pleading on behalf of Division Nine and Gen Stalbraid's long commitment to that cause."

"Thank you, Senior Arbiter."

"Are my colleagues ready to vote on Te-Gen Xia's petition?"

There are no dissenting voices from the other five members of the Council.

"Very well," Tang proceeds. "We will vote on this matter now. Those who would oppose Te-Gen Xia's petition to be recognized as pleader for Division Nine of the Capitol, make yourselves heard."

"No."

"No."

"No."

The three votes come so quickly that Lexi barely has time to register their implication. It takes her another moment to accept that a fourth dissenting vote isn't forthcoming, meaning the matter is not yet settled. Sudden panic giving way so quickly to relief sends a rush of cold running through her.

Senior Arbiter Tang allows several silent ticks before calling for the other half of the vote. "Those who would favor Te-Gen Xia's petition to be recognized as pleader for Division Nine of the Capitol, make yourselves heard."

"Hai."

"Hai."

"Hai."

The final assent belongs to Tang. His eyes meet Lexi's as he casts his vote, and she finally realizes he's studying her and has been since she first stepped up to the altar. If he has yet to form a conclusion, he must at least be swayed.

"Stalemate," Tang announces. "As Senior Arbiter, it is left to me to decide. And it is my decision to allow Te-Gen Xia to represent the Ninth Division, as I feel it is in the best interest of its people."

The reaction from the galleries may be mixed, but the jubilant are far more vocal in their celebration than the disapproving are in their doubt. Taru's smile is thin and subtle, but present.

Lexi finds she's almost numb. As often as she watched Brio plead before the Council, she never truly understood the pressure, like canyon walls pushing in on you. She also never understood the power that fills ones veins, like lightning striking the ground beside a tree. It is all at once frightening and uplifting.

She also finds she already craves more of it.

"I would add," Tang continues, raising his voice to be heard above the lingering applause, "that this is provisional. Te-Gen, this Council will not treat you lightly because of your inexperience. In point of fact, we will hold you to the highest of standards when pleading before us. Should you prove unequal to those standards, I will revoke my decision. Is that understood?"

"Of course, Senior Arbiter," Lexi assures him with a deep bow.

"We will consider this matter closed for the time being, then. You may step down, Te-Gen."

Lexi offers the entire Council another deep bow as she backs away from the altar. She spies Councilwoman Burr from the corner of her eye, rising and exiting the galleries, her face's reaction to the events of the last few moments hidden behind those granite features.

When she finally turns, Taru is waiting for her in the aisle, still smiling.

Lexi offers them a sly smile in return, deftly motioning for Taru to return back up the aisle with her.

"That went well," Taru remarks as they walk side by side.

Lexi's expression quickly turns serious. "If killing me was meant to silence me, then I want to see to it that I have the loudest voice possible when the time comes."

"When the time comes to do what, Te-Gen?" Taru asks.

Lexi lowers her voice. Somehow it makes her words sound more powerful.

"Swing the truth at the entire Capitol like a fucking sword," she says.

THE BONES OF THE WORLD

BELOW THE CREST OF THE HILL IS WHERE THE WORLD ENDS and nothing begins.

It's a pitch-black pit that seems to stretch all the way to the horizon, as if a patch of night sky fell to Earth and sank into the ground. The pit possesses the depths of a shadow; there's no way to discern how deep its belly truly descends. What's more, the surface appears as tentative and fragile as turtle jelly. It's utterly impassable and spans miles in either direction.

The Savages line the hillcrest, staring down into the unknown depths. Evie, Brio, and the Elder Company are joined by a scraggly collection of almost twenty others who survived the late-night ambush by the Sicclunan masks. All of them seem content to follow the commands of the Elder Company, who are, at least for now, following Evie's lead. Unfortunately, most of them are spindly sneak thieves and sickly old or infirm Bottoms residents who fled the moment they saw the first flaming arrow. Evie estimates there's scarcely a fighter among them, perhaps a handful of battle-hardened Savages. She cursed herself for measuring their worth by that yard, but she also knows their journey will be a bloody one.

Fortunately, half a dozen members of B'ors tribes join them. They all agreed to make the trek with Evie's band in force, at least for the time being.

Bam dips the end of his mallet's haft into what is immediately revealed as mud-soft ground. The end of the haft quickly becomes its middle as the wooden pole arm slides easily into whatever substance the soil has become. Bam halts, despite the obvious fact the unnatural depression could swallow his weapon whole. When he extracts the haft of the mallet it clings to the pit with tendrils of black tar.

"What in the light of the Fire Star is it?" Evie asks no one in particular.

"What's left," Mother Manai answers her simply, offering no more.

"What was it before?" Evie presses. "And how did it become . . . *this*?"

"The machine," a withered voice offers from somewhere down the line.

Evie leans forward and peers across the dirty, rune-stained faces of the surviving Savages.

The speaker is a scrawny man of middle age, his long hair and beard overtaken by more gray than brown. He has a hawkish-pointed nose and deep-set eyes that seem to be ever staring at something Evie and the rest of them can't see. Evie quickly realizes he's not looking into the pit, he's watching something illusory far beyond it, perhaps the past.

"What machine?" Evie asks him.

"*The* machine. The Crachian machine. I was a worker for Gen Terran before . . . well, just *before*, is all. They had one of the mining concessions along the front. This is what we left behind when we'd stripped the land to its guts. This is how the cities get fed, how life is so good for so many folk. It's why we keep pushing and pushing and pushing the front, eating every patch of ground and always needing more. Crache feeds on the bones of the rest of the world."

The ghost of the man's words seems to linger in the air between them all like the echo of distant thunder.

"What's your name?" Evie asks him.

"Doesn't matter anymore."

There's nothing rueful or sour in his words. It's as if he's stating that the sky above is blue.

Evie looks from the nameless Savage to Brio, questioning him with her eyes.

He shrugs, looking older and wearier than she's ever imagined him. "If you'd asked me a year ago I might've offered an alternate explanation. Now . . ."

"It was the same before these wars," another voice, as cold and hard as a gravestone, adds from farther down the line.

It belongs to a B'ors woman Evie has come to know as the de facto leader of the small contingent composed of several different tribes. From what Spud-Bar and the others had told her of the B'ors and their fiercely individual and independent nature, Evie expected to have to convince each of them individually to join their fleeing Savage band. She'd been surprised to find not only had they all come together as a unit, but they'd also elected their own captain and followed her unquestioningly.

She is called Yacatek. The others, all men, seem to readily defer to her despite the fact she's neither the largest nor the strongest warrior among the small band (it occurs to Evie that's another perception she created in her own mind about them). In fact, the only weapon she carries is a decorative stone dagger hung in a leather sheath around her neck. The B'ors refuse to wield the shoddy secondhand steel supplied to the Savage Legion. Valuing their fighting ability if nothing else, the Legion has allowed them to retain whatever weapons were in their possession upon capture, clubs crowned with knotted wooden fists hard enough to split skulls and short axes with heads of carved stone or the jawbones of stallions.

Evie's conversation with Yacatek before they departed the razed Savage camp had been brief. Evie told Yacatek that they were stronger together than separated. She told Yacatek that they were the same, all condemned as Savages.

"We are *not* the same," Yacatek had immediately corrected her in a voice that commanded Evie's attention, "and I am not here to teach you the difference. You only need know we will band with you for *our* reasons, not yours. Those reasons may change as the wind does. You must be prepared."

That sounded more than fair to Evie, not to mention that having been raised in the Crachian Capitol she'd learned to appreciate honesty as blunt as the head of a mace.

It wasn't the only thing about the B'ors to surprise Evie, especially once their trek began. They started out with little food and virtually no drinking water. The state of the surrounding countryside provided no relief; Evie had yet to hear so much as a single bird chirping in the distance. Her only secret, desperate hope was that they'd come upon some small oasis, or even a small Sicclunan or Skrain force they could overpower and whose supplies they'd then raid.

Several miles before they reached the foothills, Evie realized she and the other Savages had left the B'ors behind. They'd all fallen out of the march silently, deftly, as they'd no doubt learned to exist in a world that treated them like wild animals fit only for the hunt. When Evie walked back to investigate, she found them standing in a circle around an unpleasant and wholly remarkable patch of land.

Though she was never a farmer, the surface of the ground there looked as sallow as scorched earth to Evie. She watched as one of the B'ors, an old man with a shock of hair as white as sea-foam but whose skin was still as tight and hard as someone twenty years younger, twisted a slender stick from one of the few fossilized trees standing dead amidst the landscape deep into the dirt. They'd passed a dry, cracked riverbed not far from camp. The old man must've plucked from it several husks that were once reeds. He removed the stick and threaded one of the hollow stalks through the hole he made, puckering his cracked lips around the end and sucking until it concaved the stony flesh of his cheeks.

It took several moments, but then Evie saw the liquid rise up and darken the inside of the reed.

It was water, fresh and nourishing from a place below the salt, where the earth was still alive.

Evie had called the Savages back with a joy she thought lost after taking in the sight of the camp slaughter. They all drank, not nearly their fill, but enough to keep going, and with a renewed hope that their B'ors companions possessed the knowledge necessary to survive this wasteland.

Now, standing atop a hill overlooking this sunken abyss created by her people, Evie stares down the line at Yacatek and the other B'ors with fear-swollen confusion clouding her eyes.

"What do you mean?" she asks the B'ors leader. "What happened before the war?"

"This is what you did to our land, long before you began claiming your empire of cities," Yacatek says. "This 'machine' of which the nameless one speaks. We were its first victims."

"You and I weren't even born when that happened."

"It's worse in our time. I'm sure in their time your mothers and fathers thought the milk of our land would be enough to sustain them forever. Now they know, it is *never* enough."

Evie doesn't know what to say to that.

"Don't pay 'er too much mind," Lariat warns. "The B'ors like their stories about the past, and only half of 'em are made-up."

"And the other half?" Evie asks.

Lariat snorts into his mustache. "Lies."

She's certain believing that is soothing to most Crachians, even a man like Lariat, but Evie has doubts.

"Reminiscing won't ford this muck, nor change it back to solid ground," Mother Manai reminds them all.

Evie nods. "Mother's right!" she announces to the whole band. "We'll have to go around. There's no other choice. So let's get moving."

The subject is left there, but being forced to skirt the edge of the rolling abyss is a constant reminder to Evie of the haunting words they've exchanged.

The Savages hike along the hillcrest for what must be three miles. Evie spends most of that trek worrying after Brio, for whom every step seems to cause more and more pain. He refuses to give his increasing agony voice, however. Brio simply hobbles along in silence with sweat pouring from his brow in thicker sheets than any of them. Whenever Evie offers him support he refuses.

"That leg isn't getting any better," she finally says.

It's not a question.

"To be fair," he manages through steadily grinding teeth, "I haven't exactly had a chance to rest it."

"It's getting worse," Evie states flatly. "You're just learning to ignore it."

"And a harder lesson I cannot recall."

It's Brio making an attempt at his usual humor in the face of dire straits, but it feels even more forced than it did before the camp massacre.

"I'm sorry, Brio. I'm sorry I didn't find you sooner."

"That you found me at all is more grace than I expected in what remained of my increasingly shortened life. Never apologize for that."

"But that leg—"

"There's nothing to be done about it now. We have to keep moving, and I intend to do so until I can't anymore. Hopefully it will be enough to take us all somewhere useful without you having to carry me."

There's little else to be said about the matter that will make any difference.

It's another mile before the tar pit gives way once more to solid ground. An incline of gritty dust and yellow blades that are more thorn than grass slopes several hundred yards into a broad, open valley. Beyond that valley a line of dead trees is visible in the distance.

"What're the chances of coming across a town out there?" Evie asks Mother Manai.

She laughs, grimly. "If this was ever a place for livin' it's only fit for killin' and dyin' now, my dear. It'll be a hundred miles before we start seeing settlements outside the Tenth City."

"Manai!" Lariat hisses at them. "Riders at our backs!"

Before she can spare a glance over her shoulder, Evie is being pulled down the hill and pressed flat just below the crest by Lariat's powerful hands.

"Hit the dirt, the rest of you!" she hears Mother Manai order the rest of the Savages.

Evie looks to her right to see that the B'ors are already pressed flat below the hillcrest, silently and stealthily surveying what's coming from the other side while the rest of them are still hunkering down in confusion.

She follows suit, carefully peering over the top of the hill. Evie counts twenty riders galloping two abreast, keeping a tight formation as the hooves of their mounts pummel the salted earth. The two columns are little more than slender lines in the distance, but they're growing larger with every passing moment.

They're obviously soldiers, but they aren't wearing the same plate scale armor as the Sicclunan ground-pounders Evie faced in her first battle with the Savages. These riders are clad in lighter leather armor and splattered muddy shades of brown, green, and yellow, as if it has been painted to blend in to the wasteland itself. Instead of steel helms they wear cloth hoods and half-masks dyed the same smattering of colors. Each rider carries a long sword and a short sword sheathed from opposite hips, and Evie can make out larger skirmish weapons strapped to their saddles.

Their leader rides alone and out front of the two single-file columns. A wide-brimmed hat hides their face, and they've forgone the armor worn by the soldiers in favor of a thick leather tunic and trousers dyed a deep crimson. Evie spies no sword carried by the leader, long or short.

"They're not outfitted like Sicclunan soldiers," she observes.

"Oh, they're Sicclunans, all right," Lariat assures her. "They just ain't infantry."

"Outriders," Mother Manai says. "Special Selection. We've heard about 'em, hadn't run up against any on the battlefield. They're special trained. Guerilla fighters. It was probably them that hit the camp in the night."

Lariat grunts. "Sicclunans are tired'a losin', it seems."

"Took 'em long enough," Manai adds.

"What are they looking for?" Evie asks.

"Us, no doubt," Brio says. "Or any of the Skrain who survived the night raids and are trying to make it back to wherever the line has moved."

Mother Manai nods. "Yer fancy Gen man there is right."

"That seems like a lot of effort and risk just to kill a few strays."

Manai shrugs. "Mayhap they're lookin' to take prisoners fer interrogation. Who knows, really? We've more pressing matters here. They'll be at the foothills in no time."

Evie nods. She pushes herself away from the ground and peers across their backs at where Brio is sprawled.

"No matter what happens, you stay planted in that spot. With that leg you'll only get yourself killed."

"Yes, Captain."

Evie slinks back down the hill and crawling below their collective feet until she reaches the tight row of B'ors warriors. She creeps up beside Yacatek, returning her gaze to the approaching columns of horses.

"Sicclunan riders," Evie tells her. "It's a war party."

Yacatek only nods.

"I count twenty. We have the numbers, but we don't have the soldiers to match them in an open battle. We can't flee and we can't fight. Not to mention they're on horseback—"

"Why are you wasting words on what we can all see with our eyes?" Yacatek asks irritably.

Evie almost grins. "Fine. What do we do?"

Instead of answering, Yacatek's eyes flash at one of the B'ors warriors, then another. With the slightest gesture of her chin she seems to convey an entire plan of action to them, as they both nod and spring immediately into action, rising and sprinting over the hillcrest, weapons in hand.

Evie can feel the Elder Company watching the B'ors break cover and then looking to her in desperate rage, but she has no answers for them. Instead she watches the B'ors warriors charge down the other side of the hill in opposite directions, waving their handmade weapons and letting out loud and challenging hoots and hollers. By the time they reach the bottom of the hill they're spaced yards apart, almost perfectly spanning one end of the hiding Savages to the other.

The Sicclunan party's captain raises their left arm. The column of riders on that side of the leader's mount quickly break formation and begin galloping toward the foot of the hill. They split into teams of five, each group riding to bear down both of the taunting B'ors warriors. When each team of horses has closed half the distance between their riders and the Savages, the B'ors warriors turn and begin charging back up the hill.

It's at that moment Evie is struck by the stratagem unfolding. She spares a quick glance in Yacatek's direction, surprised and appreciative, before turning to the Elder Company and the row of Savages beyond.

"Get ready!" she shouts across their sprawled bodies, drawing her pilfered short sword. "Take down the riders! Save the mounts if you can! We need those horses!"

"You heard her, you dogs!" Lariat growls at the largely timid untested assemblage of conscripts. "You don't fight, you don't eat!"

The first of the B'ors to draw the Sicclunan riders crests the hill and leaps over the waiting bodies of his fellow warriors. Before his feet have touched down, the rest of the B'ors are already springing from where they lie in wait with the speed and ferocity of mountain cats breaking cover to take down prey. The first rider to reach the top of the hill has an ax blade buried in their shoulder before they can even know what's happening. The B'ors warriors are on the backs of the mounted riders that follow before they can draw their weapons.

To Evie's left, Bam swings his mallet into the chest of an encroaching rider and knocks them clear of the saddle, their mount floundering and tripping over its own legs. The horse falls past her, raising six-foot clouds of dust as it tumbles down the hill.

Evie practically skips to catch up with the beast. She grabs the reins of the toppled mount and wrangles the horse back atop its hooves. Peering over its back as she attempts to quiet and calm the animal, Evie is shocked to see dozens of dirty, spindly hands dragging Sicclunan riders from their saddles with a shocking fury and precision; the Savages are not only rising to the occasion, they're acting almost as one violent organism, overwhelming the more experienced soldiers with sheer force of will. Even as Evie sees hands and arms lopped off by Sicclunan blades, more hands reach over to replace them, clawing and climbing and engulfing the riders.

Frantically, she searches their numbers for Brio, finding him cradling his leg down the hill. He looks as though he attempted to join the rush, but the injured, infected limb finally gave out on him.

Evie's mind only registers that he's safe for the moment.

"Bam!" she calls to the mallet-wielding giant. "With me!"

He strides toward her, the mallet's haft held in both of his hands. It's the only weapon carried by their band with enough reach to be effective from a mounted position, and wielded by Bam it recommends him to lead their forthcoming impromptu charge more than strongly enough to Evie's thinking.

She turns over the reins to him, and Bam swings up onto the saddle with little more than a single step. Evie leaps up and settles behind him, hanging on to his cloak with one hand. She looks around, shocked again. All the B'ors warriors have claimed mounts, Yacatek riding double with a club-wielding tribesman. The rest of the Elder Company is mounted beside Evie and Bam, two of the more battle-hardened Savages behind them.

Evie slaps Bam on the shoulder. "To the hillcrest!" she urges him.

Bam steers their mount to the summit. Evie expected the rest of the Sicclunan outriders to rush up the hill as soon as they saw the ambush begin. Instead, their leader has held them back and formed them into a line several dozen yards from the foot of the hill. They wait there, swords at the ready. Evie has to admire their discipline. They couldn't know what numbers were waiting for them on the other side of the hill, and rather than charge headlong into that potentially lethal unknown, they've gathered their remaining force and prepared for an attack, even at the expense of coming to their fellow soldiers' aid.

The rest of the mounted Savages have joined Bam and Evie along the hilltop. On Evie's left, Mother Manai grins and holds up a cleaver dripping with Sicclunan blood. On Evie's right, Yacatek and the warrior riding behind her silently and intensely await the charge to come.

"Thirty-two battles and I've never sat a horse!" Lariat calls to her, sounding as though they're preparing to ride to a feast. "I feel like the Lord Commander of the Skrain!"

"Give the order, little Sparrow," Mother Manai says to Evie.

Evie blinks at her, uncertain.

"You brought us here, together," Mother reminds her. "That makes it your command as much as any. Give the order!"

And they truly are awaiting her command, even the Elder Company. Evie looks to her right and sees Yacatek waiting as well, though even in that moment something tells her it's more courtesy than anything else.

Evie nods. She stares down the hill at the waiting enemy line, raising her short sword.

"At them!" she cries.

Bam kicks and reins their horse into motion and Evie feels the rush of descending the hill at high speed. The Sicclunan captain orders their riders forward at the same time. Seconds later the mounted warriors clash like two waves made of horseflesh and steel, the mounts whinnying and the Savages howling their unrestrained cries of battle and the desperate bloodlust left to warriors with nothing else. Bam immediately knocks the head of the center rider between the man's shoulder blades.

Evie leaps from behind Bam at the rider on his opposite flank, taking advantage of the soldier's attention being focused on the mallet-wielding Savage. She hooks him around the throat and drags him from his saddle, managing to hang on to the bridle as she bears the soldier to the ground. Evie centers herself in the saddle. Below her, the soldier recovers to their feet, though they've lost grip of their sword.

Evie launches a kick into the outrider's face, feeling bones shatter beneath meat. The soldier falls to the ground.

As the remaining Sicclunan riders contend with Evie, the Elder Company, the B'ors, and the remaining Savages swarm them on foot. Desperate and hungry hands again claw armed and armored soldiers from their saddles.

They're slowly overtaking the remaining half of the Sicclunan war party. Evie rears her mount back from the battle and scans the ongoing wreckage for the party's leader, but neither they nor their white mount are anywhere to be seen. Looking from the small battle to the flat lands across which they all came, Evie spots that oversize hat and a large white rump shrinking in the distance.

Without thinking, she turns her commandeered mount and charges after the Sicclunan captain.

By the time Evie realizes she's left the battle, and her fellow Savages, behind she's already closed a large portion of the gap between her horse and crimson outrider. A voice she's begun to forget, her true voice, Ashana's voice, warns her that she's acting in haste and without any of the resources needed to cover her flank if things go wrong.

Evie the Savage doesn't listen.

A large formation of dry, dust-laden boulders rises from the wasteland in front of them. Evie spurs her mount forward, galloping alongside the Sicclunan outrider captain. When she's close enough, Evie jerks the reins to the right as hard as she possibly can, forcing her mount to collide with the other horse. Their front legs entwine and they're both born to the ground, throwing Evie overhead and into the dirt between the beginnings of the rocks. The wind can't seem to escape her body fast enough, and everything between her pelvis and neck goes numb.

Evie ignores the pain and the constriction choking her body and mind, scrambling to locate her short sword. The tsuka practically leaped from her hand when she went over her horse's head. She spots the blade partially wedged inside the crack of a boulder. Evie crawls up the narrow pass into which they've toppled and retrieves the weapon. Thrusting its blade into the hard ground, she uses it as leverage to pull herself to her feet, though she has to half lean on the rocks just to turn herself around and maintain her footing.

The Sicclunan captain is sitting against another boulder on the other side of the pass, looking almost casual in their fine crimson leather and ridiculous hat. They might be reclining at an afternoon picnic. The only indication they've just been through a near-fatal fall is the steady rise and fall of their chest accompanying every shallow breath.

"You're still alive, then?" Evie asks.

That moon-brimmed hat rises and she spots a flash of the queerest purple eyes beneath.

Evie can recall only one time in her life when she stared into eyes that color. They belonged to the Sicclunan agent disguised as a serving woman who attempted to poison the wine at Evie's first and only Revel as a Savage. She was the only one besides Spud-Bar to realize Evie didn't belong among the Legion.

Sirach smiles up at her. "Well, hello," she says, jovial and effortless despite her labored breath. "We seem to keep meeting under the most dire of circumstances, don't we?"

THE GOD RUNG

THERE IS NO RULE AGAINST ANY MEMBER OF THE PLANNING Cadre, be they a planner or a lowly floor sweeper, leaving the keep and roaming the island outside. The sole reason Dyeawan has yet to explore the island is access. It's no easy trek from the main hall of the Cadre to the nearest level ground. There are no real paths to speak of; the Planning Cadre uses ropes and pulleys to take in supplies and large equipment.

Edger has told her the impassibility is no accident. He's also apologized to her for it.

Despite the number of surprises that have filled her hours of late, Dyeawan finds there's still a wellspring of bewilderment inside her when Edger asks her to "walk" along the beach with him one morning. She's even more surprised to find ramps of smooth wood have been laid from the doors of the main hall over the rough incline of rocks and tall grass that separate the Cadre from the forest line.

"Were these built just for me?" she asks Edger as she steadies the tender rolling down the ramps.

"These should have been built long ago," he says, following her. "You're hardly the only one here with difficulties. And you've taught me that I've taken that for granted. In many ways."

It's just the two of them. Dyeawan wheels herself down the beach with Edger trailing behind. The wind in her hair feels so different from the breeze that blows through the window of her tiny beloved room in the Cadre. It feels freer and wilder.

She realizes she does, too.

"How have you recovered from your ordeal?" Edger asks her.

"I want to swim in the bay more often," Dyeawan replies without a trace of irony.

"I see. Then you aren't angry with me?"

"No. I chose to take the test. I know I could have refused."

"You could have, yes."

"You knew I wouldn't, though."

"Of course I did."

After a mile or two they reach a rise in the sand. From the top of it a long finger composed of piled stones shaped smooth and flat by centuries of waves extends a hundred yards out into the water.

"I want to show you something," Edger tells her. "This is very special."

He helps her navigate the tender up the incline in the sand. Once they're abreast, Edger doesn't so much push Dyeawan as stabilize her tender as she rows its wheels carefully over the uneven terrain of the rocks.

"Do you know or remember anything of your parents, Slider?" he asks her. "Where you came from?"

She shakes her head. "I only remember the other children, when I was even smaller and my legs still listened to me. There was a whole pack of us, like wild dogs, living in the street in the Bottoms."

"Nothing before that?"

"No."

"Does that seem . . . odd to you? With a mind and a memory like yours?"

"Yes," Dyeawan answers honestly. "I had a lot of long days to think about it, to really . . . *concentrate* on it, but there's nothing there, not even little pieces. There should be something. I know that. But it's like whatever happened then was dug out of the ground and there's only a dark hole left. All I can see is the hole."

"Interesting."

Dyeawan grins. "Now that I know so many more words, I'm not sure that is the one I would choose."

"I'm sorry, that was callous of me," Edger says, sounding sincere. "I only meant . . ."

"I understand, Edger. I know what you meant. It's okay."

They've reached the end of the stony bank. A solid granite monolith rises from it, perhaps ten feet high and as big around as a centuries-old cypress tree. Dyeawan moves her gaze up its length. What appears to be an iron plate has been forged and set into the side of the monolith facing the shore. A single large rung hangs from the center of the plate. It's wide enough for Dyeawan to crawl through, and thicker than one of her arms.

She's immediately taken by the fact that she can't discern its purpose, or what it could possibly have been built to do.

"What is this?" she asks Edger.

"A relic from another time," he says, staring just as intently at the monolith. "It has stood here for thousands of years. It was here before the Planning Cadre was built, before Crache existed. We call it the God Rung."

"I thought mythology was dangerous," Dyeawan echoes his words without a trace of sarcasm.

If Edger could, he would grin, but he hasn't even brought any of his masks. Dyeawan didn't notice at first, but she is suddenly aware of his lack of expression. She finds herself wondering if that means he's more comfortable around her than others.

"This isn't mythology, it's history, and one known only to the planners. Our studies of it and this island lead us to conclude it was used as a form of punishment, or more precisely, judgment."

That sheds no light on the monolith for Dyeawan. "How?"

"At high tide the waves crash over this stone bank with ferocity. Were we to remain here for another few hours, we would be easily swept out to sea. In another age, the accused were brought here to the end of the bank before high tide. They would hold on to the God Rung with their bare hands. If they were able to resist the waves, they would be set free. If not, the sea or the gods, or whatever the so-called 'nobility' of that time pretended to believe in, judged the accused."

Dyeawan wonders why she was unable to figure that out for herself. Now that Edger has explained it, the purpose of the God Rung seems obvious.

"You're quiet," Edger observes. "You want to know why the answer eluded you."

"Yes."

"Don't worry, Slider, this wasn't another test."

"Then what is it? Why have you brought me here?"

"It's a lesson. You couldn't see the God Rung's purpose because your mind isn't capable of working like those of the people who built this. You're not cruel, punitive, cowardly, or conniving."

"I've seen cruelty before."

"Not like this, not used by those who rule."

"Maybe they believed in what they were doing. Maybe they had faith, like you have in me and in what the Planning Cadre does."

"Faith does not relieve one of obligation or action. True faith isn't in an imagined deity or some mystical force that solves all one's problems. True faith is a reason to act, or it has no useful function. The men and women who built this rung used faith to excuse themselves from acting, from responsibility. They were cowards, and their cowardice bred cruelty. These were petty people who attained their station and status through lies about the sanctity of bloodlines, of extraction. Their entire lives were built, not around function or purpose, but around lies and self-interest."

"Not like now, like us," Dyeawan says, almost as if repeating words from a poem or a song.

"No. Crache was founded on a very simple doctrine: on the belief that the best person for a job should do that job, regardless of their parentage or how the flesh between their thighs was formed. Their beliefs even excluded women from performing many tasks simply based on the fact they were women, viewed as weaker and inferior to men in all ways. *Our* belief is that people, not gold or steel or wood or stone, are our finest resource. Finding their purpose, their function is everything . . . even in the condemned. That's why we allow citizens to form Gens, to pool resources and talent and offer their skills and services. The best are rewarded as we are rewarded with the benefit of their function."

"I've read about nobility. Being noble is supposed to be a fine quality in a person—"

"So is faith, and it is until it's twisted and misused for personal gain. That's what nobility was. If gods were the greatest lie ever told, nobility was the second. And their lies gave life to monstrosities like this thing in front of us. Nobles did not seek function in people, only submission and fear. The God Rung was only one such means. There was also a thing called 'ritual combat,' the idea that an accused person, regardless of their supposed crime, was innocent if they could win a physical fight, or if their chosen champion could win such a fight against their accusers."

"I don't understand. . . ."

"Of course you don't. You didn't understand the God Rung, either, and for the same reason. It's a cruel fallacy. It was another way to twist the idea of faith and gods into a means of petty, wasteful control, and to absolve one's self of responsibility or consequence for a cruel action. Inaction is often the harshest cruelty. Remember that."

Edger falls silent then, allowing her to digest all he has told her.

"I can see the truth in what you're saying. I don't know if it's . . . what's the word . . . *absolute*. I don't know if anything is absolute."

"The nature of people is, I promise you. You can predict it like the coming and going of the seasons. Fortunately, unlike the weather, that nature can be controlled and harnessed, molded."

"Is that what you think the Planning Cadre is?"

"That is part of it, a large part. The rest is simply keeping things running smoothly and making the lives of our people as rich and long and full as we can."

"But no God Rungs," Dyeawan says, more to herself than to Edger.

"That's the difference," he confirms. "Remember that, too."

"Is this lesson the only reason we're out here?" she asks, sensing more.

"That's my girl. The God Rung may have puzzled you, but you still see through me."

"So there is something else?"

"Yes. There's a question. It's one every candidate must answer before they're welcomed into the fold as a planner."

"I thought you said my last test was the last test."

"It was. Think of this more as an initiation rite."

"I've read about those. Most of them sound very much like the God Rung without the dying part."

Edger laughs. "That is customarily astute of you, but I promise this is nothing like that. As I said, it's a question. Nothing more. Almost a riddle, but it's about Crache, and the Cadre, and earning the right to be the keepers of all that's lost or unknown to most people."

"What's the question?"

"You know the Spectrum?"

"*That's* the question?"

"No, I'm explaining what the question is to you."

"I've never been inside, but I lived in the shadow of the Spectrum all my life."

"Do you know how it was constructed?"

"No one does. No one knows how to make things like that anymore, not for longer than . . . I don't know, but a long, long time."

"Thousands of years, before even the God Rung here. It's a craft lost to even Crache's master and mistress artisans. And that's the question."

"How was the Spectrum built?"

"Yes."

Dyeawan tilts her head back to look up at him. "The planners know?"

Edger nods. "We are the last ones with the knowledge of it."

She asks the obvious question. "Then why don't you use it to build things?"

"Because there is a vast difference between knowing how a thing was done and doing it yourself."

"So I have to figure out how the Spectrum was built?"

"Yes, and present your theory to me and the rest of the planners."

"What if I can't?"

"I promise all you've gone through will not have been a waste. You'll still be invited to join any other part of the Cadre. They're practically frothing to have you. Word has spread."

"But I won't be able to become a planner, like you."

"No, I'm afraid not."

Dyeawan stares out across the water. She can't see the shore of the Capitol through the mist obscuring even the horizon.

"You figured it out?" she asks.

"I did."

"When you said the Cadre hadn't seen test results like mine in forty-three years, you were talking about yourself, weren't you?"

"I was, yes. You're very much like me, I suspect. In many ways."

"Then I can figure it out too," Dyeawan says resolutely.

"That's what I wanted to hear. Shall we head back?"

"Yes, thank you."

Edger begins maneuvering the tender around to point it in the opposite direction of the bank.

As Dyeawan shifts the paddles to aid him, she leans over the side and looks down at the rocks beneath her wheels. Acting on an impulse she doesn't fully understand, Dyeawan reaches down and seizes one of the round, flat stones. She allows Edger to push her up the bank as she cradles the stone in her palm while her other hand runs over its unnaturally smooth surface.

Still unsure of why, she slides the stone inside her tunic before returning her arms to the paddles and urging them forward.

KNIVES SPEAK LOUDEST
IN THE DARK

DAIAN DOESN'T LIKE THE SEA. HE WAS BORN IN THE TENTH
City, about as far inland as a Crachian can be extracted before changing
nationalities. He didn't come to the Capitol until well into manhood.
The air that permeates the Bottoms never sat right in his nostrils, and
always seems to cause his stomach to perform unpleasant acrobatics. The
sea itself looks untrustworthy to Daian's eye. It's too vast, too silent, and
yet always moving. That perpetual motion disturbs him the most. It's
not something to which he feels safe turning his back.

The Bottoms isn't composed of the docks exclusively, but they are
the center of its microcosmic world. The constant commerce and trans-
port and construction draw those who belong to no Gen and accept no
other place in Crachian society, those who choose to live outside the aus-
pices of the state, but can either ill afford to leave the Capitol or refuse
to do so. They come to feed off the scraps left by the massive machinery
of the shipping trade and hide in the monolithic shadow cast by such
towering enterprise.

Daian salutes the Aegins stationed there by grasping the hilt of his
dagger in its scabbard with one hand and raising his other. They respond
by holding their weapons aloft. Seafront Aegins carry daggers only
as last-resort weapons, very few if any of them devoting the time and
energy to the discipline of the short blade that city Aegins do. Not confined by the narrow streets of the Capitol, the seafront Aegin is issued a

gleaming silver trident with a four-foot haft. They're useful for crowd control, and as lifelines on the oft occasion a drunkard goes plunging off a dock.

For close-quarters combat, they carry short breaching axes that can also be used as tools to cut through line, mast, or hull in the much more likely event of an emergency onboard one of the ships docked in the bay.

Daian breathes through his mouth in a concerted effort to mitigate the smells carried on the sea air. The colossal trading ships crowding the bay are a city of wood writhing atop the low tide. He watches dozens of vagrants tethered to one another by thick wrist and ankle chains being led away from the docks by fellow Aegins. The triple prongs of their tridents prod the reluctant and the stragglers along.

Daian heard there'd been a recent sweep of the shipbuilding yards. Apparently dozens, if not hundreds of such vagrants had long taken up residence in the excess hulls stored there. He stops to watch the procession of new prisoners, the sight giving him pause. He thinks about those numbers, *hundreds* of vagrants, and the limited space in the Capitol's cells.

It didn't take Daian long to realize that most Aegins are concerned with precisely two mandates from the Spectrum and two mandates only: aesthetics and statistics.

Aesthetics refers to the appearance of the city, and then strictly its veneer. No one in the Spectrum seems to care what goes on behind closed doors, as long as it never under any circumstance spills into the clean, conflict-free streets of the Capitol. Daian can count on one hand the number of raids he's experienced in his tenure as an Aegin. He's often reflected on the notion that the brilliance of the sky carriages isn't making travel within the city faster and more efficient, it's in clearing the streets. Keeping people moving keeps them from quarreling or robbing or killing, and bottlenecking them in elevated sky carriage stations makes them easy to watch and control.

Statistics refers to the number of "undesirables" arrested and incarcerated by every Aegin. Officially, there is no number Aegins are required to meet. Unofficially, that number is handed down to them from their superiors on a weekly basis. Likewise, there is no official punishment or reprimand for not meeting one's non-existent quota. In truth, going several weeks with low numbers of arrests is the same as an Aegin requesting a posting at some stinking stable in a satellite hamlet outside the cities.

In a society that demands constant proof of one's value, that demands pure function in exchange for food, shelter, clothing, and above all, status, forcing a street Aegin to live by a number alone is enough to make that number lethal for others.

Daian isn't naive; he understands the necessity of appearance in all things Crachian. If anyone, in fact, understands the importance of keeping up appearances, it's him. Be it the picturesque street or an Aegin's arrest record, image is the veneer that maintains order, far more than any number of men and women in green tunics carrying short blades. He doesn't believe in arresting the innocent or even targeting harmless vagrants, however. In his mind it's counterproductive. Crache worries too much about the aesthetic of every street and alley. What difference does it make what these people do down here? The only goal is not to be one of them.

His relationship with Chew is the perfect example. Any other Aegin in the Capitol would've clapped manacles around Chew's wrist the second they witnessed him practicing his chosen form of grift.

Daian, on the other hand, recognized an opportunity presenting itself.

He finds Chew where Daian always finds Chew, plying the trade of an everyday fishmonger in the market. He's a pudgy man approaching the twilight of his life, although most of his gray hair has already expired. His eyes have remained sharp and his arms strong, and the latter is hardly the result of tossing freshly caught fish across the market, something Daian doubts the man has ever done.

Most of Chew's fish is several days old, some of it approaching a week or more. The smell alone is enough to keep most regular citizens from patronizing the stand, but Chew travels that extra mile by having his minions pound the fish into battered, unappealing roadkill.

"How's today's catch, Chew?" Daian asks him as he approaches the stand, pinching his nose between two knuckles.

"Couldn't tell you," Chew answers blandly, never particularly happy to see the Aegin. "You should've asked me four days ago, when it was the day's catch."

"That's a shame. Uni sounded mighty good for supper tonight."

Chew grunts. "Plenty other fish stands, if you had not noticed."

Daian nods sincerely. "True, but none so informative as yours."

The older man sighs. "What you want now?"

"I just have a little something that I need you to take a look at, perhaps offer your rarified expertise on."

"I don't suppose this is work for which I'll see compensation," Chew says drearily.

"Isn't breathing free air the best compensation one can receive?"

"I've grown weary of that line, Daian. I am even wearier of being forced into your personal servitude. I am a humble businessman. Why torment me?"

Daian smiles. He closes his fist around the hilt of his dagger and draws it smoothly from its scabbard. Without looking down, he stabs the blade into a pathetically small, sickly green-skinned and eyeless tuna that's been slit and gutted for sale. The tip pierces its rotting flesh easily, but stops short as it strikes what sounds and feels like steel.

Chew frowns, averting his eyes as the guilty do.

"Now, what did this little fellow swallow, I wonder?" Daian asks.

He removes the tip of the blade and uses it to lift one of the slit folds of the tuna's body. A small, intricately forged piece of metal now occupies the space where the tuna's guts once rested. It's a decorative pendant folded and hammered into the crest of Gen Feng, who breed the insects that power the city's streetlamps and oversee their maintenance and construction. Their allotment from the state is immense.

In Crachian cities a Gen pendant is more valuable than any hard currency. Each pendant allows one access to the cooperative bazaars, to food and even temporary shelter from inns and eating-houses that service Gen members exclusively and are supported by the state. Pendants bearing the right Gen's symbol on its rim can grant the wearer a fortune's worth of allotments from all those merchants. Falsely posing as a member of a Gen is a crime punishable by death.

Forging Gen pendants carries no less a penalty.

"This tuna has gone bad, Chew," Daian informs the fishmonger.

He scoops up the body of the fish, fake pendant still concealed within, and cradles it on the flat of his dagger's blade. Daian turns and flings the tuna across the wharf. It disappears over the break line and hits the water somewhere unseen.

Chew curses violently under his breath.

Daian turns back to the forger. "Shall I inspect the rest of your stock for you? You can't be too careful with seafood, you know."

"Just show me whatever it is you have to show," Chew demands.

"Thank you so much," Daian says pleasantly. "That's very kind of you."

Daian removes the coins he discovered among the charnel house ash and offers them to Chew. He's cleaned them up enough to make the shaggy, hollow-eyed face gracing one side of each of the coins more visible.

Chew picks one up and holds it between two calloused fingers, examining it.

Daian watches the old forger's face closely as Chew reacts to the image on the coin. What he sees written in the fine wrinkles and sharp eyes of the man's face are uncertainty and something that might be alarm.

"This is not a coin I would take in trade," he informs Daian. "It is not one I have seen before, either."

"I'm not hearing you say you don't know anything about it, Chew."

"I may have heard some stories."

"Stories of what?"

Chew hesitates, and whether it's the nature of the knowledge or being forced to share it with Daian, it's obvious he wishes to say no more.

Rather than press him further, Daian decides to simply wait.

In the end, Chew takes a deep labored breath and places the coin back in Daian's hand.

"Blood coins," he relents.

"What does that mean?" Daian asks, turning the small burned pieces of metal over and over in his palm.

"I am not certain. I have heard stories about coins as markers. Against the return of runaways."

"Runaways? Like escaped prisoners?"

Chew shakes his head. "Military conscripts."

Daian's eyes refocus on the forger with a new intensity. "Soldiers?"

Chew shrugs. "Recruits for the Skrain are never compelled. This would be something . . . different."

"The Bottoms' pleader, Brio Alania, do you know if he ever came down here asking about anything like these coins, or military conscripts?"

Again, Chew shakes his head. "I never had dealings with the pleader. Our interests were usually contrary."

"Do you know of anyone in the Bottoms he did speak with about such things? A confidant or a source of information? Anyone he trusted among the people?"

"No. I would make it my business to know about such a person, and steer clear of them."

Daian searches Chew's face for any glimmer of insincerity. He finds none.

"Good luck washing away the smell," Daian says to the forger as a form of parting.

"I have learned to live with it."

Daian grins. "I was talking to myself."

He leaves the forger to the rotting façade of his fish stand and retraces his path back to the port archway. Daian turns over in his mind every word he extracted from Chew, examining them for any hidden truth or unintended information. It's clear the assassins who went after Lexi were some of the "military conscripts" of whom Chew spoke. They could not, however, have been on the run. The attack on Lexi and Taru was not random, nor was it a simple robbery. They were sent.

Though he'd already suspected as much, this confirmed it.

None of that helps him locate Brio or whatever evidence Brio had collected. He needs to know whom Brio trusted outside of his Gen. His only thought is to return to the Spectrum. Records are kept of everyone pleaders call to testify before the Arbitration Council. Daian can cultivate a list of residents from the Bottoms who aided in Brio's pleadings. If he can locate them, perhaps one of them will prove to be the person he's seeking.

Daian puts the sea to his back and heads for the nearest sky carriage platform that will take him back to the Spectrum. He's preparing to ascend the stairs when he sees the signaling fire lighting the sky above an alley several buildings from the corner on which he stands. The fire was created by powder, lit in a small mortar with a base the size and shape of a dinner plate designed to be placed on the ground.

Daian knows this because he wears a similar mortar and carries that powder in a pouch, both lashed to his belt.

It's a signal from an Aegin in distress.

He breaks into a run, charging toward the source of the signal fire. He doesn't spot any other Aegins answering the call; in fact, the area seems to be unusually bereft of green tunics. Daian ducks into the alley directly under the waning amber light of the signal fire, dagger upended in his knife hand.

He stops, chest heaving from the long sprint.

The alley is deserted.

Daian sees the mortar resting on the alley floor. Smoke is still spiraling in ghostly wisps from the tip of the barrel. He does not, however, see the Aegin who lit the powder.

"Your response was swift, Aegin," Grath congratulates him.

Daian spins around to find his fellow acolyte instructor leaning casually in a back doorway, dagger sheathed in his baldric.

"Grath? What's happening? Did you light the sky?"

Grath shakes his head.

"You did," he informs Daian. "But I'm afraid we got here too late to save you."

Daian stares back at him quizzically, opening his mouth to question Grath further. The words are literally choked from him as a strong arm appears around his neck, quickly cinching against his throat. At the same time, the blade of a dagger enters his back just above his right kidney. Daian arches his spine with his head thrown back and mouth agape in surprise. He raises his own dagger and the arm around his neck relents, a gloved hand taking hold of his wrist to restrain it.

Kamala's Cyclops face appears in the corner of his eye, grinning in sadistic satisfaction.

"You chose the wrong friends," she whispers in his ear. "And you ask too many questions. The Protectorate Ministry doesn't like that."

Kamala forces another half inch of steel into his back, and Daian groans through painfully clenched teeth. He tries to wrest his upended dagger free, but Kamala's grip is too unyielding and the blade piercing his body seems to be draining all his strength. Trembling, Daian tilts his head forward and opens his mouth wide, biting down around the pommel of his dagger's handle.

He doesn't see Kamala's expression change or her eyes slit in confusion. Daian jerks his head and the pommel snaps free of the rest of the dagger's handle. The pommel is revealed to be a tiny dagger of its own, its short triangular blade concealed inside the handle of Daian's larger knife. He clenches his jaw tight around the pommel, the blade attached to it extending from his lips like a steel tongue. Kamala's hands remain occupied restraining him and keeping Daian's knife hand at bay. He twists his neck and cranes his head back as far as their struggle will allow. Kamala's eyes widen in realization a second before Daian drives his head forward and pushes the blade clenched between his teeth through her throat.

Her eyes stretch even wider as a single ribbon of blood escapes around the stubby blade. Daian unclenches his jaw, releasing the pommel. Kamala lets loose his restrained wrist without thinking and presses her gauntleted hand against her throat and around the small dagger embedded there. Blood begins to pour between her fingers in thick, deep crimson spurts.

Daian shrugs himself free of her. Kamala's grip loosens around the handle of her dagger, its blade remaining in Daian's back as he collapses forward onto his knees. She looks past him at Grath, whose perfectly shaped eyes are wide in abject shock. Kamala tries to speak as she staggers back several steps, but she loses consciousness before she can force out the words. She collapses onto her back, the blood continuing to drain from the deep gash through her neck and throat.

Daian, sweat pouring over his brow and his entire body either numb as stone or screaming in pain, forces himself to one knee. He reaches behind himself, every small movement causing him agony. He closes a shaking hand around the handle of Kamala's knife and pulls the blade free from his back. There's a brief, resplendent relief followed by an entirely new pain.

Grath leaps from the doorway, unsheathing his dagger and holding it at the ready. He charges forward toward Daian, but halts before he's closed the gap between them even halfway.

Daian is now standing, both feet securely planted on the alley floor and spaced apart in a fighting stance. He's brandishing both his and Kamala's daggers in each hand, ready for what comes.

Grath hesitates, eyes flicking between the edges of those two blades and Daian's face.

"If you think you're going to wait until I bleed out," Daian says in a trembling voice that's nonetheless filled with menace, "I'm afraid I'm going to disappoint you."

"I don't know," Grath says, carefully, forcing a version of that winning smile onto his handsome face. "I'd give myself fair odds."

"Bad bet," Daian insists, and takes a long stride toward him.

Grath drops his knife arm. He turns and runs down the alley.

Daian flips Kamala's dagger in his hand, grasping it by the flat of the blade. He rears back and, screaming through the immense pain it causes him, hurls the weapon after Grath.

The dagger sails through the air with a perfect arc, the blade embedding itself between the man's shoulder blades. The impact alone is enough to knock him off-balance and cause Grath to fall forward in midrun, his body skidding several yards over the alley floor before stopping.

He does not get up.

Daian tries to walk forward, but his legs feel as though they've disappeared. He careens to the left, stumbling and reaching for the alley wall to keep him from falling to the ground. He leans his body there, his torso impossibly warm while his legs feel cold and numb.

He looks down at the signaling mortar attached to his belt. Daian could light the sky, but he has no way of knowing who would answer the distress fire. There's just as much chance they'll finish what Grath and Kamala started as there is that they'll help him. Even if the responding Aegins are among the uncorrupted, he also has no idea how to even begin explaining what's happened here. Daian isn't sure himself what just happened.

Instead of signaling for aid, he drags himself along the alley wall, streaks of blood trailing him in the polished stone of the building. Daian doesn't know where he's going. He only knows he can't be here.

THE INTEREST PAID IN BLOOD

EVIE HAS TO LAUGH. SHE FINDS SHE CAN'T HELP HERSELF. IT bubbles up within her and comes spilling out like water over a broken dam. The sword she's gripping in preparation for a battle to the death falls to her side. She laughs until her eyes well with tears and her breath is all but gone. Evie's aching back slowly slides down the boulder that's been partially supporting her. She stabs the blade of her short sword into the hard ground and holds on to the tsuka for support as she lowers herself to sit.

Sirach watches her all the while, silent, staring at Evie as if she's a particularly amusing curio in a cabinet.

"You are the oddest duck, aren't you?" the Sicclunan agent asks, though it is clear she's already formed an opinion.

"It's strange, isn't it?" Evie muses, ignoring the non-question. "People you meet in your life, and then meet again? I mean . . . with all the people there *are* in this world, chance must have been so against you meeting any one person to begin with, let alone running across them again?"

"I imagine that's so. Though we are in the same business, even if only as competitors."

"I don't even know whether that's true or not anymore. I didn't think so in that wine cellar. Now . . . I can't honestly recall who I am anymore. I have a purpose, a mission, and that's all. Everything else has become very . . . fuzzy around the edges."

It is clear Sirach has no idea what Evie means. "I suppose I should thank you for sparing my life."

"For all the good it did. You found another way to kill off all those Savages."

"It was a much costlier way for my people, but yes."

"Do you think it'll make a difference?" Evie asks her, earnestly. "I mean, really. You surprised them, yes, but you know they've only fallen back to regroup. They'll come again, with more Skrain and more Savages. As many as it takes."

Sirach shrugs. "What else are we to do? The only other option is to give up."

"There's nothing else? Nothing to be negotiated? Or—"

It is Sirach's turn to laugh. "You really have no idea who your people are or what Crache is, do you? None of you do. Though I suppose it's not your fault. They go to great lengths to make it that way, raise all of you that way, at least the ones they need."

"Battle is one thing," Evie says. "Slaughter is another."

"Say that to me when you've fought on my side and seen what I've seen."

"Fair enough. Siccluna has been under siege for decades. I know you've been pushed to this."

Sirach watches her with the oddest smile on her lips. "You really don't know, do you? None of you do."

"What don't I know?"

Sirach leans forward. "What is Siccluna?"

Evie only blinks at her at first, the question finding no purchase among the peaks of her mind.

"It's . . . your nation. This country we're in now, what's left of it."

Sirach shakes her head. "Siccluna isn't a place, my dear. It's a word in a language scarcely spoken anymore, because those who spoke it scarcely exist anymore. The word 'siccluna' means 'last home.'"

"I don't understand."

Sirach laughs. "I know you don't. That's the point. My dear . . . every city in Crache was once its own kingdom, its own realm, its own lands with its own people and language and customs. One by one, they all fell. It began with your Capitol."

"The Renewal," Evie whispers.

Sirach nods. "I don't know how it began or who was usurped or how it happened. No one outside the Capitol does anymore, I imagine. But it started there. Then it spread. They consumed everything they conquered to build their well-fed, well-kept paradise of marvels and wonders. It was never enough, and it still isn't. They just kept taking and taking and taking."

Her words spark a recent memory for Evie, something Mother Manai said to her about the Sicclunan war not being a war at all. Mother Manai told Evie that Crache was expanding, something even more dangerous than war, and now, hearing what Sirach has said, Evie finally understands what that means. Crache isn't growing, it's eating, consuming everything it touches to grow fat. The fatter it grows, the more Crache must consume to sustain itself.

That's what this entire bloody campaign is about. That's what it has always been about.

"Why didn't any of these kingdoms fight them?" Evie asks almost helplessly, although she suspects she already knows the answer.

Sirach shrugs. "They did, once the siege began, but before that they all thought they wouldn't be next, that Crache would be satisfied. They made treaties, drew up new maps, new borders. Crache burned all of it. My people built what you call the Tenth City. They all had eyes like mine. Crache conquered them and worked them to death in the mines. I haven't seen another person with these eyes since I was a little girl."

Evie says nothing. Her head almost refuses to hold the truth in Sirach's words.

"Siccluna is what we call the remnants of all those realms, those people. We banded together and retreated to wilds of the east. We have no cities, no castles, just villages of sticks lashed together in trees, mostly."

"But . . . your armies . . . armored soldiers—"

"Every resource we've mustered is poured into the war effort. Every scrap of steel, every crop we grow, every scrawny piece of game we hunt, every arm experienced with a hammer. Siccluna *is* the army we field. We have nothing else. The people beyond the line to the east wear rags and sleep on mats. They eat rice with a swig of milk to keep their strength, twice on a good day. All we fight for is existence. Nothing more."

Evie suddenly feels as weak as the people Sirach is describing. The strength seems to be flooding from her knees. Nothing Sirach is saying describes the world Evie knows.

"I . . . I can't believe it."

Sirach shrugs again. "I have no reason to deceive you. Especially since it seems I'll have to kill you in a moment. But you're not Crache, even if you're Crachian-born. I can see that. I can at least offer you the truth."

The greatest threat in Crache's history, nothing more than a rabble of desperate people hunted to the edge of extinction. The lies every good citizen of Crache has been told. Though Evie knows now the true breadth of Crache's madness, and the goal of their war-waging, this knowledge, that their opposition isn't another nation, it's a collection of the sole survivors of entire peoples Crache has decimated and destroyed, is the most harrowing revelation of all. So many kingdoms, so much history lost, and so many innocent people having everything taken from them.

It's monstrous.

It's evil.

All of it.

Evie realizes there are tears in her eyes. She tries to blink them away, but like the knowledge Sirach has just shared, they won't stop plaguing her.

She's nearly breathless when she speaks again. "If it is as you say . . . you can't possibly win."

Sirach chuckles, wryly. "The only reason we've held this long is because of how wide and thin Crache has spread itself. If they had more Skrain and Savages to commit to this front, we'd have been annihilated long ago. But there's unrest in their many cities, no matter what they tell you or how clean they keep their streets. For all I know, they're fighting wars across the sea, too. It wouldn't surprise me."

"I . . . I don't know . . . I am truly sorry, Sirach," Evie says. "I'm sorry for your people and all the others. My only cause was to protect those I hold close and dear."

"I believe that. Did you find whatever or whoever it was you were looking for, by the way?" Sirach asks.

Evie nods. "For whatever's that's worth now."

"I do apologize if I've had a hand in upsetting your mission."

Evie swallows what feels like broken glass. "Likewise."

"Well, then . . ."

Sirach doffs her wide-brimmed hat and twirls it down the narrow, rocky path. With several different aching groans in succession, she rises to her feet.

Evie follows suit, almost without thinking, again grasping the tsuka of her short sword and using it to pull herself up. Once she's on her feet, she plucks the sword from the ground and shakes the dirt from the tip of the blade.

"So now we'll try to kill each other, then?" Evie asks.

"I imagine you might contend that I owe you, that I should allow you to walk away as you allowed me to do."

"You don't owe me anything. After what you've just told me . . . I almost feel I owe you."

"We shall call it even, then."

Evie manages a nod.

"Well, then. This time, yes," Sirach pronounces. "I'm afraid one of us dies."

Sirach reaches behind both hips and draws forth a pair of matched daggers, their blades long and thin and so sharply curved they're almost half circles.

"Delicate," Evie remarks.

Sirach grins cattishly. "Aren't we all?"

They square off, standing just several strides apart, both women bending their knees slightly and leveling their feet with their shoulders.

Evie grips the tsuka of her sword in both hands and holds it at the ready.

Sirach holds her matched blades at different angles, her arms sweeping in hypnotic arcs as she executes a few practice form movements to loosen herself up.

The bolt strikes Sirach dead center of her chest. Upon impact her body folds inward before being flung back against the rocks. She collapses in the dirt in almost the precise spot she was sitting before.

This time, however, there's no visible sign she's breathing.

Evie turns toward the direction of the sudden crossbow bolt, raising her sword just in time to intercept a squat figure that leaps at her from atop the larger boulders, blotting out the sun in the process. The switch from burning bright to pitch dark temporarily blinds Evie as the impact knocks her off her feet. She feels something bite into the blade of her short sword. She instinctually tightens her grip on the tsuka and pushes back against that weapon or sudden force, even as her back hits the unyielding ground.

Once she blinks the world back into focus, she finds herself staring at her blade entangled in a field of spikes. Those spikes are embedded in the half-face of a man Evie remembers as Namrok, the blood coin hunter. There is no mistaking him with a dominant feature such as that. His right arm is occupied with the crossbow it still supports, but his left hand has gripped her wrist and is attempting to wrest her hand from the tsuka. Evie responds by dragging the blade horizontally through the spikes, its bottom slicing across Namrok's ear, drawing blood.

The blood coin hunter growls until spittle dangles from his scarred half-mouth. He jerks his head viciously to one side, the spikes embedded in his cheek snapping the blade of Evie's short sword cleanly at its center.

Evie seizes the opportunity to smash the hardest part of her skull into the fleshy side of the blood coin hunter's face. Namrok's head snaps back awkwardly, and he freezes atop her, stunned. Evie pulls her knees toward her chest, wriggling her legs between their bodies, and shoves him back into the rocks with her feet. She nips back up to her feet quickly, readying herself for him.

Leaping away from the boulder, Namrok tosses aside his empty crossbow and draws a dull wide blade with a tanto tip and jaggedly serrated edge that's more machete than short sword.

Evie has no idea how she'll defend against that wicked-looking thing with three inches of broken blade, but she clings to the tsuka all the same. Her mind races for a strategy, a method of attack, but her body and brain are weary.

Fortunately and unfortunately for Evie, her mind is relieved of that responsibility when an unseen force crashes into her side and sends her careening against the nearest boulder. The broken short sword flies from her hand and her body bounces against the surface of the stone in a wholly unnatural and remarkably painful fashion. She rolls across the bottom of the narrow path in a daze, the world continuing to spin around her even after she's stopped moving.

Evie stares up from the gritty earth at armored legs and an equally armored torso that seem to rise all the way to the sun. The armor is composed of huge animal bones, ending in a bear's skull helm with jaws full of teeth as large and jagged as stone arrowheads. Evie remembers Tomoe, the giantess, as the other hunter Laython introduced her batch of Savage recruits to before blood coins were forced down their gullets.

The bone-armored warrior is still cradling the poleax that's as tall as she is; its foot-long wedged pommel must be what struck Evie to the ground.

In the next moment the slanted tip of Namrok's dull blade is at her throat and the ugly lump of a man is laughing through the side of his mouth that remains intact.

"I'd'a had her," he gleefully insists.

"I was becoming bored," Tomoe says, tapping the edge of her boot's sole against the pommel gently as if she's concerned that Evie's broken body damaged it somehow.

The slanted tip of Namrok's machete flits down to Evie's belly.

"She sliced up my good ear," he says. "I want her coin while she's still alive."

"She fought like a warrior," Tomoe reminds him. "She will receive a warrior's death."

"Damn your codes!" Namrok growls.

"There will be plenty of runners and beggars left among the others, I am certain. You will save your butcher's wrath for them."

Namrok grumbles unintelligibly, but his blade continues to hover harmlessly above her.

The bone-armored giantess steps forward, looming directly above Evie as tall as a centuries-old tree. Tomoe twirls the haft of her poleax with practiced ease as she raises it above her head. Evie watches the sunlight blink through the revolutions of that massive blade, catching in the steel and burning even brighter for a sliver of a moment each time.

Dying in the sun, Evie thinks. *That's not so bad, is it?*

At the very least, she will finally be allowed to rest.

Evie closes her eyes just after that poleax ceases to twirl, as Tomoe steadies her grip on the haft in preparation to strike. She hears Namrok laugh; an ugly, gravelly noise that she deeply wishes wasn't the last sound she'll hear.

The impending strike doesn't come, and Namrok's laughing is abruptly replaced by the sound of Tomoe screaming.

Evie opens her eyes. Sirach has ripped the bolt from of her chest and leaped onto Tomoe's back. The Sicclunan agent hooks both curved blades deep beneath Tomoe's armor, sinking them through the meat and sinew just below her shoulders.

Namrok's attention turns to his distressed companion. Evie doesn't hesitate, first batting her forearm against the flat of his blade to remove its threat from her neck and then burying the sole of her foot deep into the blood coin hunter's groin. The kick doubles him over where Evie meets the whole side of his face with a sharp elbow strike. She rolls from beneath him and retrieves her broken sword from the dirt, springing to her feet.

Behind her Tomoe is screaming her rage and pain unbidden, thrashing from side-to-side in an effort to unseat Sirach despite the agony every movement causes her. Sirach answers by sliding another half inch of blade beneath each of Tomoe's shoulders, her legs wrapped around the waist of the giantess with her ankles and feet locked together. Tomoe finally ceases thrashing and instead backpedals toward the rocks, her long strides quickly building up a lethal momentum. Sirach has no choice, she rips her blades from the blood coin hunter's back as roughly as possible and lets her body fall to the ground, where she quickly rolls between Tomoe's legs.

Despite being half blinded by the intense pain in her back, the giantess has enough facility to bring the thick haft of her poleax down atop the Sicclunan. Sirach raises both her daggers from one knee, the deep curves of their blades catching and holding the poleax haft. She stands, hooking the weapon with her daggers and twisting her body into Tomoe's, leveraging more than brute force disarming the larger woman and flinging her poleax into the opposite wall of rock.

As Sirach turns to face the hunter and deliver as many killing blows as it takes, Tomoe draws her pair of matched daggers from the scabbards tooled into her forearm gauntlets. Seeing the flash of steel clearing leather causes Sirach to quickly back up several steps rather than advance.

Only feet away, Namrok swings his machete wildly at Evie. She ducks each feral strike, steeling her nerves, waiting for an opening to present itself. In his frustration the blood coin hunter puts too much power behind his next swing. When the slash misses its mark, Namrok is overextended and thrown off-balance. Evie quickly slips behind him and drives the broken end of her blade into his back, piercing his right kidney.

That side of Namrok's body shrinks in upon itself, and he drops to one knee. His sword arm is held aloft and momentarily forgotten. Evie reaches out and takes that arm by the wrist, delivering a blow into Namrok's elbow that breaks it cleanly. The new source of pain causes him to growl like an animal caught in a trap, and the machete falls from his suddenly limp fingers.

Evie half kneels and snatches up the bone handle of the weapon almost before it hits the dirt. Namrok has just enough time to twist his neck and bring his one remaining eye angrily to bear on her before Evie swings the wide, heavy blade in both hands and separates his neck from his shoulders completely with one slash. The force of that swing carries the blade through and strikes the nearest boulder, the crooked serrations in the blade's edge catching in several cracks zigzagging the rock face.

As Evie wrestles with Namrok's machete, Tomoe and Sirach duel their matched daggers. The towering blood coin hunter swings her long arms heavily and mechanically, relying on size and strength to intimidate and overwhelm her opponent. Sirach is the exact opposite, using speed and finesse and the curved blades of her daggers to deflect and parry and slash. She manages to slip through the falling-tree blows of Tomoe's arms and lacerate her armor several times, finally drawing blood from her side. It only serves to further enrage the giantess, who answers the slash by growling ferociously and launching a straight kick into Sirach's chest.

It's like a hammer hitting an anvil made of mud. Sirach flies backward several feet until her back collides with the rocks, her entire torso seizing under waves of intense pain. As she stumbles away from the boulders, Tomoe sweeps Sirach's feet out from under her with another powerful swipe of the hunter's leg. Tomoe quickly reverses her grip on both daggers, but before she can raise them to stab down at Sirach, her arms seize, along with the rest of her body.

Sirach looks up to see the woman's eyes have gone wide and glazed. She doesn't understand until the hunter topples forward. Sirach has to roll from the path of the falling giantess to avoid being crushed.

Evie has swung Namrok's severed head into the back of Tomoe's skull, shattering her bone helm and planting most of those face spikes through her brain. Blood is still spilling down her neck and over the white bones of her armor's back plates.

Evie offers Sirach a hand caked in dirt and blood from three different bodies. The Sicclunan agent takes it and stifles a shriek as her body's every fiber lights in pain at being forced to stand.

The two women stand above the elongated form of the slain blood coin hunter, less than an arm's length apart. Their shoulders rise and fall with each labored breath almost in perfect time with each other. Eventually they both look up from their shared enemy.

Their eyes meet, and Sirach's grip tightens around the handles of her curved daggers.

Evie holds no weapon, but her hands begin to rise.

Neither woman strikes, however.

"Now," Sirach says, "*now* I owe you."

Evie shakes her head. "I'd say we're even."

Sirach doesn't answer her right away, and Evie can see the heavy clouds of thought swelling in her eyes.

"Then perhaps I just don't want to kill you anymore."

Evie grins. "Perhaps I feel the same way."

"Where does that leave us?"

"Well . . . if we aren't enemies, that *does* narrow our remaining options, doesn't it?"

"I suppose it does."

Evie slowly relaxes her posture, allowing her tired body to fold forward just enough to give relief to the frayed muscles of her upper body. She braces her hands against her knees and lowers her head, sighing deeply.

Sirach watches her, again with that quietly marveling gaze, but she's also lowered her weapons to her sides.

"I think I have an idea," Evie says a few moments later.

Sirach continues staring at Evie in silence, then looks between the crescent blades of her daggers. With a sigh of her own, she sheathes them both behind her hips in their scabbards.

The cattish grin returns to her lips.

"I'm listening," she says.

RIDDLES SHAPED IN STONE

RIKO HANGS SUSPENDED FROM THE CEILING ABOVE THE massive scale model of the Capitol on the maps level. She blows a dark tanto-tipped bang from her face as she concentrates on affixing the experimental sundial over the great stone awning that crowns the entrance to the Spectrum.

Dyeawan is lying on her stomach in the street outside the Spectrum, chin propped on her small balled fists as she scrutinizes every inch of the building's perfectly replicated-in-miniature form. She takes a break from her staring to look up at Riko.

"Are you mad at me?" she asks Riko. "Because Edger wants me to be a planner?"

The fine young features of Riko's face twist up as if she's just swallowed something sour. "'Course not. I'm really happy for you. And I *know* you've got the brain. I've never seen anyone pick things up as fast as you do."

A cool and genuine relief rushes through Dyeawan's torso. "I'm glad for that, Riko. I don't think Tahei feels the same way."

"Tahei *worships* Edger, and he's Edger's favorite builder. Tahei is amazing with his hands. But Tahei isn't a planner and he knows it. Deep down. That has nothing to do with you."

"What about you?"

"Me? I just like tinkering with things. I'm lucky to be here at all."

There are several tiny mirrors resting atop crooked pole arms that extend from the sundial's outer rim. The face of each mirror is partially obscured by intricately painted lines as black as night. It is Riko's hope that her sundial will be able to measure time in smaller, more exact increments. She's not certain it will work, but she believes deeply in the idea, and she's often found that when she refuses to relent on an idea, she finds the path to its realization.

"Why do you think we need more time?" Dyeawan asks.

Riko laughs. "It's the same amount of time, yeah? It will just be measured more precisely."

"Then why do you think we need that?"

"You can never create too much precision. That's why it's called precision. That's what Edger says, anyway. Besides, you can't tell me *you* can't think of a million ways this will be useful."

"Of course I can. I asked why *you* think we need it."

"Oh."

Riko's hands pause in what they're doing. The only sound for the next few moments is her body swaying just so in the leather harness cradling it.

"I suppose that is a different question, isn't it?" she says.

Dyeawan squints up at her friend. "You don't just 'tinker' with things, you know. You have as keen a mind as anyone I've met in the Cadre. I just think you don't know you do. You're more clever than Tahei. You're probably more clever than Edger."

"*No one* is more clever than Edger," Riko insists.

"I'm not sure that's true," Dyeawan says quietly. "I think you not knowing how smart you are holds you back. In the same way Edger is convinced he is smarter than everyone. That can be even more dangerous, I think."

Riko's eyes on the models below her turn dark. "Slider, I know you're just saying what you see, but you should know it can sound . . . bad, the way it comes out."

Dyeawan frowns. "I'm sorry. I didn't mean anything. I just think . . . the things you make are so beautiful, and so . . ."

She can't think of the word, despite all the new ones she's learned in her time here.

"You've been staring at that thing for hours, you know," Riko observes, changing the subject.

Dyeawan looks back at the Spectrum, frowning for a different reason now.

She finally says aloud what she's been thinking for the last hour. "It could've been cut and chiseled, just like any stone. Why couldn't it have been shaped and smoothed like any stone?"

"There isn't a single grain on the stone's surface, outside or inside the entire Spectrum. There isn't a mason in Crache who can polish stone like that. Besides which, there *is* no other stone like that."

"It was probably a mountain," Dyeawan muses. "No one could have moved one solid piece of rock that big from somewhere else."

Riko nods. "That makes sense, but you know it won't satisfy the planners, yeah? It's not enough to know what it was before. You have to know how they turned it into what it is now."

Dyeawan nods. Nothing she's seen or read since coming to the Planning Cadre provides an answer to that question, and she remembers all of it, all she sees and all she reads, in every exacting detail.

Concentrating so intensely on a single problem is making her head ache. Dyeawan returns her attention to Riko, more for relief than anything.

"How did you come to be here at the Planning Cadre?" she asks.

Riko's tongue is occupied between her teeth, its tip just barely visible at the corner of her mouth as she finishes securing the sundial to the model of the Spectrum.

"Aha!" she proclaims triumphantly.

Dyeawan hangs her head, grinning. Riko's seemingly inexhaustible excitement and enthusiasm are the qualities she admires most in the older girl.

"I, uh, what?" Riko asks, distracted.

"I asked how you came to be here."

"Oh! Right. Sorry. Well . . ."

She reaches down and takes up a lengthy wooden pole lying in the street ahead of Dyeawan. Jerking her body to the right, Riko's harness pivots easily, turning her around. There's a lamp hanging from the ceiling several feet above her. It's not an ordinary lamp, however. Instead of a flame or even a luminescent insect encased in glass, it's a series of mirrors bolted together, harnessing the rays of the sun pouring into the maps level from an open skylight.

Riko extends the wooden pole toward the lamp. There's a short hook on the end.

"I was, uh, born in the Fourth City, which is where most of Crache's mining is done, yeah?" she explains as she jiggers with the mirrors. "My kith-kin was part of Gen Fan. They were responsible for maintaining most of the mining equipment. So, they were very successful, yeah?"

Dyeawan nods, hearing something rueful in Riko's voice.

"When I was very little," she continues, "the city Arbiters gave our mining equipment concession to another Gen. I never understood why, or how those things work. But one day we lived in a big, fancy keep tower in a big, fancy cooperative in the Circus, and the next day Gen Fan lost its franchise and was dissolved."

Dyeawan frowns. "I'm so sorry, Riko."

She shrugs, more concerned with angling the hanging mirrors just right.

"It's nothing next to what you've been through, yeah? Anyway. My father opened a small shop in the tinker's quarter. Only he drank too much to fix anything most days. So . . . I started doing it. And I found out I was really good at it, fixing things. Didn't matter what someone brought in, I could take it apart and put it back together better than when it was new."

Dyeawan grins. "That doesn't surprise me."

"I tried to keep it a secret. I didn't want anyone to know it wasn't my father doing the work. But somehow . . . Edger knew. A woman dressed like that horrible Oisin who skulks around the levels of the keep, all in black, came and took me from the shop. She brought me here. Edger showed me what the Cadre does and asked if I wanted to stay and be part of it. It was hard to leave my father behind, but . . . he wasn't himself anymore. He hadn't been for a long time."

Riko takes a deep breath, and Dyeawan senses that's all she wishes to say about that.

"But you're happy here," Dyeawan says.

The smile returns to Riko's face, and she nods. "I am. I love it here. I love every day that I get to make something or test something. And now you're here!"

The implication is so genuine that Dyeawan feels a lump rising in her throat, though she doesn't say anything.

Riko curses under her breath.

"What is it?" Dyeawan asks.

She doesn't answer at first. Riko is busy studying the shadows cast by the light hitting her sundial. Instead of one darkened sliver moving over its face, there are several.

"It's not working," Riko says. "Maybe the mirrors are calibrated wrong . . . or maybe it just isn't possible to measure time so precisely using the position of the sun."

"Can I help?"

Riko grunts. "You've got enough problems to solve. I don't know. Maybe a sundial is too simple. Maybe . . . I don't know . . . maybe the solution is metallurgic. Something with gears? I'll keep working on it."

"You'll figure it out," Dyeawan assures her.

Riko smiles down at her. "And what about you? Is staring at this thing getting you any closer to the answer?"

Dyeawan sighs. "No. Not at all."

She presses her hands against the street and pushes her torso up, arching her back to peer across the model. Dyeawan looks to the edge of the Capitol, to the Bottoms beside the ocean. There's a giant stone pool beneath the surface of the model there that's filled with real seawater. Miniature ships bob atop it, most anchored at the docks, although some have been left to drift out in the open water.

Riko watches her oddly. "You don't miss it, do you?"

"No."

"Then why are you looking at it?"

Dyeawan's straining shoulders give the scantest shrug.

"Things were always easy for me to figure out there," she says.

"Oh." Riko nods, sagely. "I get it."

As she moves her gaze over every minutely captured detail of the docks, the absence of something familiar gives Dyeawan pause.

"Where are all the hulls of the ships?" she asks.

Riko doesn't understand. "Huh?"

Dyeawan points. "Near the ship yards, there. They store rows and rows of ship hulls there, upside-down. They have since I was born. They were on the model before. They're almost all gone now."

"Well, the surveyors are responsible for changing the models when new things are built in the Capitol or old things are torn down. They must have taken away the hulls."

"But . . . there were people . . . people live under those hulls. What did they do with them?"

"Um . . . I don't know about the people, but maybe they finally used the hulls to build new ships? That's what they're for, yeah?"

"They couldn't have finished building that many ships that fast."

"I'm really sorry, Slider, I don't know what happened. Did friends of yours live in them?"

"Not friends, just . . . people like me, a lot of them. And I . . ."

Dyeawan remembers telling Edger about the stockpile of unused hulls in the Bottoms, and about those who used them as shelter and to hide from Aegins. She'd thought nothing of it at the time; they were just talking, and the subject of their discussion wasn't even aimed at the Bottoms or its homeless residents. He hadn't asked her about either, in fact. She certainly didn't feel as though she was being interrogated.

"Maybe you could ask Edger," Riko suggests.

"Edger can be funny with answers," Dyeawan says without really thinking.

"What do you mean?"

Dyeawan looks from the miniature world of the Bottoms to Riko still hanging above her head.

"I think . . . sometimes there's a lot more truth in what Edger doesn't tell us than what he does tell us."

Riko shrugs. "Talking in riddles is another way of testing us, yeah?"

"Maybe. Unless . . . unless we have to figure out what the riddle is for ourselves first. Does that make sense?"

Riko shakes her head. "I'm not sure what you mean."

Dyeawan reaches inside her tunic and removes the stone she picked up beside the God Rung. She lies back down on the model street and holds it in front of her face, turning the stone over and over with both hands and examining its smooth, flat surface.

Eventually her hands stop, and her eyes begin to glaze, no longer seeing the stone.

"What is it, Slider?" Riko asks her.

Dyeawan should feel elated, especially after everything she's put herself through to reach this moment, but she can't stop thinking about all the years those ship hulls took up space, untouched and forgotten, until suddenly, immediately after she spoke to Edger about them, they were neither.

She learned the word "coincidence" several weeks ago, and she knows this isn't one.

Dyeawan looks up at Riko, still holding the stone in her small hands.

"I think it's the riddle *and* the answer," she says.

THE CALLING HOUR

LEXI REALIZES, SETTING TWO CUPS IN FRONT OF HERSELF AND Taru, that this is as close to being truly happy as she's felt since Brio's disappearance.

She pours Taru and herself rice wine from a jug and spikes each with just a few drops of Voxic's sting from a separate, smaller bottle.

Taru raises a single brow with the oddest of half smiles. "Te-Gen?"

"Small victories, small celebrations," Lexi insists. "They are even more important in times like these."

They're sitting in her father's old study at the bottom of the Xia tower. Since the old man passed, not long after Lexi's mother did from the same illness, it's been left largely untouched. That includes the collection of spirits long cultivated there, from the finest fermented wine to the rare nectar contained in a bottle shaped like the meat-eating Voxic plant from which it's extracted.

Lexi takes up her cup and raises it in a toast, smiling at her retainer triumphantly.

Taru shakes their head, but reaches for the other cup and holds it against Lexi's just the same.

"Small victories," Lexi repeats.

Taru nods, adding, "May enough of them win the war."

Lexi's eyes come alight and her smile only widens. "Well said, my friend."

They touch cups and drink, Lexi more deeply than is at all customary for a Gen hostess, while Taru sips. The spike of Voxic's sting sets its hooks in their tongues at the same time, and judging from their expressions they both might have just had swords lanced through their bellies.

"Why do people enjoy this?" Taru asks with equal parts confusion and contempt.

Lexi is shaking her head as if to expel the burning sensation in her skull. "I thought all warriors were drinkers."

Taru coughs. "I remain the exception in all things, it seems."

"It is the first quality required in being exceptional, I'm afraid."

"Thank you, Te-Gen."

The deep thrum of the giant steel rung rapping against the main hall's doors reverberates through the tower. Taru immediately sets down the cup and takes up their sword belt with its two low-hanging scabbards. The retainer stands, strapping on the belt with practiced ease.

Lexi watches, her smile turning to a frown. "I'm sure it's nothing worthy of a blade's answer."

"It is also not an hour for callers, Te-Gen," Taru reminds her darkly.

"I dislike it when you're right. Why is that?"

"Possibly because I have a tendency to only point out dire things," Taru answers matter-of-factly.

Lexi nods. "That's it."

The retainer leaves the study and crosses the main hall, keeping one hand closed around the hilt of their short sword. Taru throws back the latch and pulls open one of the heavy double doors.

An older Aegin with a sour face is waiting on the other side.

"Te-Gen Xia has a caller," he informs Taru.

Taru's hand tightens around the hilt of the short sword suspiciously.

"Who is it?" Lexi asks, walking to the middle of the main hall.

"One of . . ." The Aegin hesitates, looking up at Taru's face. "It's one of *them*. Says they're an armorist, delivering an order."

"'Them'?" Lexi asks.

Taru's fiery eyes remain fixed on the Aegin. "He means Undeclared."

Lexi frowns.

"Did you place an order with an armorist, Te-Gen?" Taru asks.

Lexi hesitates. Images wreathed in the blood of their last unexpected guests scream through her mind in brief flashes. Fear almost compels her to admit the truth, but something stops her, a feeling she can't quite explain, even to herself.

"Allow our guest entry," she says.

Taru gestures stiffly to the Aegin, who appears more than happy to silently stomp away from their door.

A few moments later Taru is standing aside to allow Lexi's "delivery" passage (after thoroughly inspecting it to assure that delivery is unarmed). There is no parcel, just a person. In fact, the armorist is the first person Lexi has seen in the Capitol who is as tall and broad through the shoulders as Taru. They also share the same plain, angular features that could easily belong to either man or woman. Also like Taru, the armorist prefers to wear their hair in a topknot with both sides of their head shaved bare.

"Welcome," Lexi greets their guest.

"I'm called Spud-Bar." The armorist quickly adds: "Te-Gen."

It is clear Spud-Bar is unaccustomed to addressing Gen members. The armorist also smells heavily of long miles on a hard road far outside the cities.

Lexi bows formally. "I am Lexi Xia of Gen Stalbraid, and this is my friend and retainer, Taru."

Spud-Bar becomes very aware of not bowing, shifting uncomfortably from foot to foot.

"Thank you for seeing me."

"Of course. Although I am afraid, Spud-Bar, I did not place an order with any armorist."

"I know, Te-Gen. The . . . order . . . was placed by a young girl I've known as Evie. It concerns your husband, whose name is Brio."

Lexi is forced to reach out and grip Taru's forearm in order to steady herself. Hearing Brio's name, spoken as if he is still alive, causes her knees to buckle.

Taru may be equally as shocked, but it's quickly replaced by suspicion.

"What do you know of Evie?"

"She's also called Ashana," Spud-Bar answers, recognizing the test in that question. "She willingly gave herself over to . . . to the Legion to find Brio. Do you know of the Legion I speak?"

Even Taru's guard softens at that.

"I do. My husband was investigating such a Legion when he disappeared. You're saying Brio . . . he's . . . he's alive?" Lexi asks.

"Yes, Te-Gen. Worse for the wear, but alive, and with Evie when last I left them."

Lexi closes her eyes for just a moment, every hope and every fear she locked away lest either of them overcome her springing forth and saturating her being.

Taru channels relief into more practical concerns. "And where was that?"

"The Sicclunan front. At least, it was when I left. The Skrain is making a big push into what's left of Sicclunan land. The front has probably moved another ten leagues by now."

"I am grateful to you for bringing us this news," Lexi begins, ever the formal hostess. "However, can you tell us why you are here instead of Ashana and my husband? Her mission was not only to find him, but to bring him back to me."

"For all I know, Te-Gen, they've already made their escape. It's not that easy for Savages. Most of 'em are plucked from their lives against their will and for no true crime. The Legion, and most especially who exactly makes up the Legion, isn't meant to be known among you folk in the cities. I'm only allowed to return here to draw weapons and materials and help with new recruits. They mark Savages with a special coin that stains their blood and their skin in case any of 'em run. A Savage caught out of camp by blood hunters usually returns with their guts ripped out. Pardon me."

Taru frowns heavily, looking to Lexi, whose expression says she's having the same thoughts: The men who tried to murder her were Savages, and Spud-Bar has just confirmed that Savages couldn't have reached the Gen Circus unless they were sent by those in power.

However, Lexi has moved beyond shock and shaking knees on the subject. Now that she knows that Brio's alive and Ashana has accomplished half her mission, her mind is spinning with how to see the rest through. She also knows how much she owes Ashana for what the woman has apparently been through and what she has accomplished on Gen Stalbraid's behalf, even if, Lexi suspects, Ashana accepted the mission for her own reasons. Lexi had been far too desperate and frantic when she first went to Ashana to consider emotions like jealousy or hesitation, or think about the consequences of reuniting Ashana with Brio, and she's determined not to waste time on those feelings or speculations now.

Still, for all those reasons, Lexi wishes in that moment that she'd taken the time to know Ashana better, just as Lexi regrets only finally coming to know Taru over the past few months. She regrets ever allowing herself to feel disconnected from what Brio did as a pleader. Lexi had always thought of the foundlings their parents took in as wards of Brio's father, being groomed and trained to attend to the Gen's pleaders in the course of their duties. It created a distance for her that didn't need to exist.

Like most things Lexi thought before Brio's disappearance, her perspective is vastly changed.

"What can we do?" she asks Spud-Bar. "Ashana must have had some message beyond letting us know Brio is alive. How can we help bring them home?"

"Evie said nothing about aiding them in escape, Te-Gen," Spud-Bar assures her. "But she did give me a message. It's about something Brio left behind. It's supposed to prove what the Legion really is, if that's of any use to anyone. She seemed to think it was more important than the both of them."

Before Lexi can respond to that, a crash from up the spiraling stone steps of the tower draws all their gazes.

Lexi looks up at Taru. "The Ministry agents?"

"They would have seen Spud-Bar come to the door," Taru confirms, drawing both short sword and cooperative-forged hook-end blade.

"What's happening?" Spud-Bar asks.

Lexi holds up a hand to silence the armorist as Taru steps between them both and the staircase, stance widening and weapons expertly raised.

A tall shadow falls down the steps, cast by the lit sconces along the tower wall. They all tense, especially Taru, until that shadow is replaced by the red, green, and brown blur of a body tumbling fast and uncontrolled down the staircase. Taru leaps back, arms spreading wide to shield Lexi and Spud-Bar, as that body rolls free of the bottom step and lands at their feet.

"Daian!" Lexi calls from behind Taru, fortunately not loud enough to alert the agents posted outside.

The right side of his tunic is almost completely soaked through with blood. It gloves his right hand and streaks his face and neck. Sweat pours from his brows, pasting his hair to his scalp, and virtually all trace of color has drained from his face. His eyes are dilated and glassy, barely conscious of their surroundings.

Taru immediately sheathes both blades and kneels beside him. Lexi gathers the hem of her wrap and runs around them both, dropping to her knees on the other side of Daian's body.

Taru quickly assesses his condition. "His heartbeat is dangerously slow, and all this blood appears to be his. The wound may be mortal."

"Are we under attack?" Spud-Bar asks in alarm.

"No," Lexi assures the armorist impatiently. "He's not a guard, he . . . he must've climbed the tower and come through a window. Though I can't imagine how, you utter madman! What were you thinking?"

The demand only thinly masks Lexi's obvious concern and anguish at seeing Daian in such a state. There are tears welling in her eyes as she looks down on him.

Daian's words come slowly and on trembling breath. "You said . . . Ministry . . . was watching you . . ."

"Don't talk," Taru orders him.

Lexi's hands hover over him, wanting to fix him without knowing how.

"Te-Gen, please," Taru bids her urgently, "I will attend to him. Give me leave to do that."

Lexi nods, removing her hands and rising to her feet. She swallows hard and wipes away the tears, stepping away from them to allow Taru to tend to Daian's wound.

Lexi looks over at Spud-Bar, teary eyes turning hard and resolute. "Are you willing to testify to what you know, all that you've seen, before the Arbitration Council? We can keep you safe."

"Begging Te-Gen's pardon," Spud-Bar says, glancing down at Daian, "but this doesn't seem the safest of places. In truth if I'd known you're being watched I wouldn't have come here, promise or no. My life may be forfeit as it is."

"I'm sorry for that, but what's done is done. Stay with us. Help us. There is change coming."

Spud-Bar can't meet Lexi's eyes. "That's an easy thing to say from a tower, Te-Gen."

The expression on Lexi's face hardens to match her eyes. "Very well. Then just tell me . . . what did Brio want me to have, and where can I find it?"

WE BURIED OUR STORIES
IN THE EARTH

"I SAY WE CUT 'ER FUCKIN' HEAD OFF AND GIVE 'ER BODY TO that black foulness over the hill."

"Thank you for offering your wise counsel on the matter, Lariat," Evie says. "We will take it under advisement."

Mother Manai laughs, and even Bam snorts a half chuckle through his cavernous nostrils.

Lariat is not amused.

Neither are the rest of the remaining Savages.

Six of Sirach's outriders survived the battle, although two of them are badly wounded. Evie's side lost six Savages, including the former mine worker who told Evie his name didn't matter. More than anything else at this moment she wishes now she'd insisted on hearing it. None of the B'ors warriors suffered so much as a scratch in the battle.

Sirach and her remaining Special Selection soldiers sit upon the ground in a tight grouping. They've been disarmed, but Evie insisted they not be bound or restrained in any way; that was part of the bargain she struck with Sirach back in the outcropping of rocks before Brio and the Elder Company came back for Evie. They had no notion of what to think when they found their Savage sister and the Sicclunan agent sitting casually among the boulders, chatting over the maimed corpses of the two most feared blood coin hunters in Crache.

Lariat spits on the ground in front of the Sicclunans. "Not sayin' I know all that many numbers, but she's killed more'n I can count of our kind."

"And how many times that number of her kind have we killed?" Evie asks. "It's a war none of us here started or chose. She understands that."

"You claim a lot on 'er part," Lariat says. "Were you back in those rocks longer'n we think somehow."

"She saved my life and I saved hers. We understand each other."

"All I understand of Sicclunans is cuttin' 'em down before they do the same to me an' mine."

Evie places a gentle hand against the leathery skin of his chest. When she speaks it's as if to a child or a much older parent or grandparent.

"You are a marvelous bear of a man who genuinely cares for his compatriots, and I admire you greatly. But you're also an old grouch who solves all his problems by punching them. Where we are now requires thinking and compromise, and I submit to you, respectfully, this is not a place your leadership is best tested."

"She's right, old man," Mother Manai says. "She has a better head on those tiny shoulders of hers than any Savage I've ever met. Just listen to her."

Lariat blows air through his mustache in exasperation, looking helplessly between the two of them.

"Fine!" he declares, and then, to Manai, *"Old woman."*

Evie pats him on the chest gratefully and turns away, bowing briefly to Manai, who returns the gesture with a smile.

All the while, Brio has sat silently apart from the debate, his injured leg stretched out across the ground. It seems to be occupying most of his attention.

Evie kneels in front of him, gently prying apart the dressings she applied that are now both seeped through and filthy from their cross-country hike. Brio hisses in pain as she does. What Evie sees beneath the bandages looks less like flesh of any condition and more like a swamp.

340

"This leg is going to have to come off," she informs him quietly, her expression as grim as it has ever been.

Brio tries to smile, but even that effort seems to cause him pain. "I didn't know you'd become a surgeon in the last hour. That's impressive."

"Brio," she whispers, almost pleading. "Your leg will poison you if it stays on much longer. It's already started. You're running a fever. That's why you're sweating so much. And you can barely stay awake."

"What's to be done out here?" he asks, looking at her with eyes that have abandoned hope.

Evie glances to where the B'ors have chosen to rest and await the decision of their Crachian counterparts concerning the Sicclunan, having offered no counsel in either direction.

"I'm working on it, all right? I promise. I just need you to hold on a while longer. Please. Can you do that?"

"I can try," he says.

"Then try."

Yacatek sits against the hill with her legs folded beneath her. She's unsheathed her stone neck knife and is using a small, jagged sliver of rock to carve upon the blade. Two of the B'ors warriors stand like sentries at the foot of the hill below her, weapons in hand and eyes surveying both the cold camp and the surrounding wasteland.

Evie leaves Brio and walks between them.

"May I sit with you?" she asks Yacatek.

"I do not own the ground," Yacatek answers without looking up from her etching. "That is a belief held by your people, not mine."

Evie chooses not to respond to that. Instead she trudges painfully up the hill and lowers herself beside the B'ors woman, groaning as she does. It feels as though every part of her body is angry at every other part.

"What's the meaning of the marks on that blade?" Evie asks.

"History."

"Of your people?"

"Of my band, before I was taken, and now the history of this new band we have formed."

A new thought strikes Evie.

"Is this why the others follow you?" She motions to the two B'ors sentries. "Because you record their history?"

Yacatek nods. "I am a Storyteller. There is no more sacred calling among my people. It is given to Storytellers to keep the words and names and deeds of our bands. We preserve them in stone because it will outlast us all."

"What do you do when there's no more room left on the dagger?"

"Begin another."

"And what happens to that one?"

"I bury it."

"Where?"

"In the earth. It does not matter where. There will be those who come later, who will uncover it. Everything in the earth is revealed in time. People feed off the earth so ravenously it cannot be helped. There will always be those who come later, and they will uncover our stories, and that is how we will remain. Our time of living is short now. Only a small band of Storytellers still mark the stone. Your people will finish what they began."

"You're not gone yet."

"No. That is why I sit here carving this knife."

"Why a knife?"

Yacatek shrugs. "Knives are useful things. People will keep a knife."

Evie would laugh if the implications behind what she's watching weren't so dire and horrific.

"We are, all of us here, dying in the same way. You know that? It doesn't matter whether we're Crachian or Sicclunan or B'ors, not to those hunting us."

"That is true," Yacatek concedes.

"So . . . we can die or we can fight."

"Fighting and dying walk hand in hand."

"True enough. So you'll keep fighting?"

"My band are warriors," the Storyteller says simply.

"Would more of you fight with us? Do you know where the other bands are?"

For the first time, Yacatek looks up from her recording to regard Evie.

Evie expects to find suspicion in the Storyteller's eyes, but the aspect there is more akin to surprise.

"You say 'with us' and not 'for us.' "

Evie nods. "You're not mine to command. But we have common enemies, common goals. Your warriors are the best fighters I've ever seen. Savages have proved to be a powerful weapon when they're aimed correctly. The Sicclunans have taught themselves to be brutal stealth assassins. The death knell for all of us is numbers. The Skrain and their forces overwhelm us. If we formed . . . a new band, all of us together, and fought together . . . they wouldn't be ready."

"You speak beyond the few warriors here and now."

"Far beyond," Evie confirms. "I'm speaking of whatever's left of the Sicclunan armies, every band of B'ors we can find, and turning every damn Savage they've conscripted against them if we can."

Yacatek's eyes bore into her intensely. "Who are you to bridge these worlds and make such a fight?"

Evie looks down at her hands. She remembers the first morning she awoke to find runes staining their flesh. Twice as many runes cover her fingers and palms now, and she can feel them upon her face and the rest of her body. She finds she has trouble recalling what her flesh looked like before she swallowed the blood coin.

Evie stares back at the Storyteller without wavering. "My name is Savage. That's what they've made me, and I plan to use it."

She can't be certain what's occurring inside Yacatek's head in the silence that follows, but Evie has given it her best.

Finally, the B'ors woman nods her chin, just once, and returns to her carving.

"It will be a good fight" is all she says in the end.

Evie accepts that gratefully, standing with even more agony than it caused when she sat. She carefully trots back down the hill, pausing after a few steps.

"Am I mentioned on that blade?" she asks.

Yacatek again nods her chin a single time.

"What does it say?"

"That you too often say what is there to be seen, but that you are a warrior to be contended with."

Evie nods. "I can live with that."

She walks between Yacatek's sentries and leaves the B'ors to their hillside retreat for the moment, returning to the other Savages and their Sicclunan wards/prisoners.

"What's it be, Sparrow?" Mother Manai asks her.

"It comes to this. Whether we can reach the Tenth City or not, we can't go back. We can't return to the Legion, not now. We're runaways, plainly and simply. And even if we find a way to remove these coins and the runes fade from our flesh, we can't go back. There's no place for any of us in any of the cities. There will always be Aegins and Skrain and blood coin hunters. There's no life outside the cities, either. The land between isn't fairing much better than this stripped earth around us."

"Where do we go, then, if not back to the Legion?" Lariat demands. "Is yer new Sicclunan friend offerin' us sanctuary with 'er people?"

"There is *no* sanctuary," Evie assures them all. "I promised Brio I'd return him home, and I promised you could return to your families. But that can't happen with Crache as it is."

"What are you saying, love?" Mother Manai asks. "What do you want us to do?"

"I want to do what we were *all* going to die doing, no matter which side of the line we find ourselves on, no matter how much we lied to ourselves. I want to fight. I want us to stop being a Skrain weapon and become the worst enemy they've ever faced. I want to make Crache a place we can return to and live."

"I don't mind cuttin' down Skrain," Lariat says. "You're askin' us ta kill Savages? For Sicclunans?"

Evie shakes her head. "No. I want to turn the Savages against them. ALL the Savages."

She expects another spar with Lariat and is already readying her counterargument when he delivers the last response Evie expects.

He bursts out laughing.

"Now *that's* a notion!" he bellows gleefully. "Why didn't ye say so in the first place?"

Lariat claps a hand on Evie's shoulder and shakes her hard enough to send lances of pain through every aching muscle in her body. However, the rest of the Savages have taken their lead from the elder states-man of their ranks and they join in on the sudden merriment, all of them ready to follow along wherever Evie's plan of action leads.

In the wake of the laughter, Sirach delicately stands and brushes the ground from the crimson-dyed leather of her trousers and tunic.

"So pleased we've worked this all out," she announces.

Lariat quiets, and the other Savages fall silent with him.

"Look 'ere, girlie," he says, fisting a katar and pointing the tip of its triangle blade at Sirach. "This doesn't mean I like you."

"And I find you to be just a hair above a pig rolling in muck," Sirach says. "It's the perfect place for us to start."

With that, Lariat begins laughing anew, deeply and genuinely.

"Pig rolling in muck!" he echoes her, giving rise to a new wave of guffaws from the Savages.

Evie watches them figuring one another out, hoping it's enough. She looks from the strange scene to where Brio is leaning over his necrotic leg, summoning all his strength just to stay conscious.

"The easy part's over, then," she whispers quietly to herself.

PART THREE

REVELATIONS
OF THE THROAT

FORMLESS, SHAPELESS,
IT CAN FLOW OR IT CAN CRASH

"WATER."

Dyeawan lets that single word hang heavy in the air above them all, as if it might become a banner flown between two charging warhorses.

The planners are convened in another room she's never seen before. Dyeawan is beginning to understand that in many ways, the façade of the Planning Cadre is only that, and there's far more beneath the surface she's yet to see or know. The chamber is a microcosm of the keep itself. There are twelve planners including Edger, six men and six women, all of them clad in the same simple gray tunic as him and wearing the same pendant of concentric circles. They're seated within a table that's actually a thin stone slab winding inward several times to a central point. The planners sit along its path like children hiding poorly inside a hedge maze.

Edger sits at the winding stone snake's center point, an array of masks arranged facedown on the surface in front of him.

They are the only ones in the chamber save for Oisin, forever draped in his black cape. The Protectorate Ministry agent is lurking against the wall in the back of the room, surveying them with his usual obvious contempt.

Dyeawan's spoken only one word, but she can clearly see it has affected all of them deeply. No one responds at first, but the subtle expressions and glances that pass between several of the planners speak volumes.

Edger is the first of them to address her directly. "Pardon me, Slider, but might I ask you to elaborate?"

"That's how the Spectrum was built," she says. "Or . . . formed . . . would be the right word. Water."

Now several of the planners actually turn to whisper to one another heatedly. Some of them seem excited to Dyeawan, while others seem suspicious, even hostile.

It is, as always, impossible to read Edger, though as in the bay when she emerged from the test in the drowned room, Dyeawan can't help but picture him smiling.

"How did water form the Spectrum?" he asks.

Her slight shoulders shrug. "The same way water shapes all stone, I imagine."

Dyeawan takes out the flattened rock from the stone bank upon which the God Rung sits. She gently wings it across the nearest curve of their snakelike table. It skips several inches before rattling to a halt like a flipped coin.

"Time," she says.

This statement elicits murmurs among the planners, to which Edger raises his arms, signaling for their silence.

"If you're asking me how the builders created such specific forms, I don't know," Dyeawan explains. "I don't think you do, either. If you did, you would be using the process to create more palaces and keeps in the Spectrum's likeness. I think you know how they did it, but you also do not know how they did it."

Edger takes up a jovial, smiling mask and holds it over his expressionless face. He turns his head to regard each fellow planner with the painted expression.

"I believe, comrades, this demonstrates with finality that my faith in our little Slider here was not misplaced," he says.

"She's magnificent," one of the other planners says.

She's a young woman who can't be much older than Riko. She also has more purple in her eyes than anyone Dyeawan has ever met.

"She is . . . undeniably adequate," another among them says, begrudgingly, and Dyeawan is not at all surprised to see it's a much older man.

In fact, their opinion of her, read on their faces, seems to be divided strictly by age. The younger planners are all smiling at her, while their elders either appear dubious or scowl outright at her.

No one else speaks. The majority opinions on Dyeawan seem to have been expressed.

"What happens now?" she asks them. "Do you vote?"

"I don't believe that's necessary, no," Edger says, raising his arm and motioning behind her.

Dyeawan turns her head and peers over her shoulder. She did not notice Quan standing there before, waiting attentively just inside the chamber doors. He strides forward, smiling and cradling a length of cloth in his long arms.

It's a gray tunic, like the rest of them wear. Dyeawan can see the concentric circle pendant already pinned to the garment.

Quan kneels beside her and bows his head, presenting the tunic ceremonially.

"Please don't do that," she says, quietly. "Not for me. Please."

Quan lifts his head in surprise. The smile on his lips remains, but it's changed somehow. His eyes regard her oddly, as if he's seeing something in her he had not before.

He nods, but extends his arms and continues to offer her the tunic.

Dyeawan takes it, gratefully, bowing in return as best she can. She turns back toward the planners, instinctively cradling the tunic against her chest.

"We are thirteen now," Edger informs the rest of them.

Again, Dyeawan sees that elation and excitement in the faces of the younger planner contingent, and what she can't deny is resentment and even anger carved into the expressions of the older members. She doesn't understand why. Neither does she understand the significance of the number thirteen among them.

"Welcome, Slider," Edger bids her. "Please take your place at our table. There's a space open beside me, if it suits you."

More seemingly benign words, and yet every time Edger speaks Dyeawan feels silent cords of discontent stretching between every planner being plucked by steel fingers.

She stares back at Edger, her own expression turning hard.

"My name is Dyeawan," she says, for the first time since she awoke in this place.

Until this moment she'd kept that name to herself, because it was all she had that was hers. None of them knowing it somehow made it more valuable. If they didn't know her name then they couldn't take it away from her. Growing up and barely thriving in a place where everything could be taken from her at any time made any possession dear. She'd had her sheet of greased metal and that was enough. When she'd awakened here without it, totally vulnerable to these people, her name was all that was left.

Dyeawan realizes now that she no longer dwells in that place of no possessions and no privacy. She's no longer Slider from the streets of the Bottoms. Here she can have whatever she wants, and be whatever she wants.

"That's my real name," she continues. "I'd like to be called by my real name, please."

Even Edger falls silent at that, and in that moment she feels something pass between them akin to what she's just experienced with Quan, that sense of Edger waking to new qualities within her of which he was previously unaware.

"Of course," he finally says. "And our welcome to you . . . Dyeawan the planner."

THE SPARROW GENERAL

SHE SHOULD BE FIRMLY MIRED IN THE NERVY DEPTHS OF FEAR and anticipation that precede a battle, but all Evie can think about is how she's going to squat in this thing if the need arises.

The armor is constantly trying to drag her down. The extraneous weight isn't quite as unbearable as how it limits her movement, however. Each step feels as though her feet are shackled together at the ankles. Evie was trained as warrior, not a soldier. She knows how to fight with and defend herself and others against hands and feet and weapons. She knows how to assess danger and plan accordingly. She's never worn steel armor before, let alone a full suit of scaly plates complete with helm.

The armor doesn't seem to bother Mother Manai. She's removed the blades from the stump of her right wrist to more easily conceal the severed appendage. A steel glove with no hand inside it has been flame-melted to the gauntlet covering her forearm. The fingers of that gauntlet have also been flame-melted into a perpetual fist that hangs ready at her side.

The two of them march in tandem through the sprawling Skrain encampment, past pages and servants and other soldiers in matching armor who pay them no heed. They slipped in easily enough, blending with the dozens of sentries surrounding the camp being relieved by fresh bodies.

"Try not to be so stiff as you walk, love," Mother Manai quietly urges her.

"How are you doing this so easily?" Evie asks through gritted teeth. "Were you Skrain before you were a Savage and you just didn't tell me?"

Manai laughs. "No, but I *was* once accustomed to carrying half a dozen babes in one arm while I fended off the riffraff tryin' to steal their food with the other. A few dozen pounds of armor is nothin' to me."

The Skrain encampment is massive. It's at least four times the size of the one Evie was carted past alongside the other Savages en route to the meager tents and burned logs that passed for a Legion camp. There must be five hundred Skrain marching, feasting, sparring, and grooming themselves all around Evie and Mother Manai. They can't even spot the edge of the adjoining collection of sticks and cloth that house half as many Savages.

Combined, the encampment is far too big to attempt the kind of silent overtaking Sirach and her night force inflicted on the Skrain attached to Evie's former collection of Savages. There are too many soldiers and too much area to cover by sneaking tent to tent. Evie, with Sirach and Yacatek and the Elder Company's input, has devised a different strategy for this assault.

"There it is," Evie says.

The alarm is erected on a wheeled pedestal in the center of the Skrain camp, surrounded by several large barracks tents. It's a horn of pure white bone that almost glows in the moonlight. The mouthpiece is little more than the size of a reed flute, but it spirals out into a six-foot cone large enough for Evie to crawl inside. With the proper application of breath, the horn's bellow will resound throughout the entire base of operations.

Sentries posted around the camp's perimeter carry smaller horns that are also meant to alert the others and signal to blow the main alarm, but the Sicclunan night warriors should be seeing to them one by one at this very moment.

A lone Skrain soldier has been stationed beside the encampment's main alarm. He totes a javelin and is currently occupied with spectating a game of dragon tiles being played on the ground in the distance.

"We'll plant ourselves here," Mother Manai says. "Wait for it to start. It shouldn't be long now. No reason to tax the young man premature-like."

"You spoke of grandchildren," Evie says to her. "How many do you have?"

"I'm not really sure anymore. A fair score more than I did when I swallowed my coin, I imagine. Damn kids don't seem to know what else to do with their time besides breed."

Mother Manai tries to sound lighthearted, but Evie can hear that wavering sadness and longing underneath.

"I'm sorry if my asking about it causes you pain. I didn't mean—"

"I like thinking about 'em, remembering 'em," Mother Manai insists. "It's one of my favorite things."

"What are your other favorite things?"

Manai shrugs. "Drinking, supple young men who appreciate an older woman's experience. I'm not more'n a simple peasant with simple tastes."

"You're a great warrior," Evie reminds her, and she means it.

"I'm a survivor, love. That's all. Fightin' just comes with the territory."

"Can I ask . . . why you're here? Why you agreed to follow me into all this?"

"I like you. You remind me of one of my daughters. And you remind me of me when I was young and fresh and new."

"That's it?"

"What more is there for a Savage?" Mother Manai asks, sounding almost surprised.

Evie doesn't press the issue further. In the silence that follows, the truth of what's about to happen begins edging between her temples, touching the previously occupied parts of her mind. The inescapable notion that a plan she's made is moments away from causing the deaths of hundreds of people, possibly on all sides of this conflict, takes center stage for Evie. In that moment she asks herself dozens of questions all at once, with no answer for any of them. She also knows the answers don't matter; the course it set.

The first firelights appear in the sky overhead just as the moon reaches its zenith. Evie never saw them like that when the Sicclunan night force attacked her camp; by the time she was aware of them, tents were already ablaze. Hanging in the air as they appear to be, the volley of flaming arrows look as gentle and graceful and harmless as a flock of birds in flight. It isn't until they begin their descent and she hears the flames crackle and whip in the wind that their violent intent takes form.

The first of the arrows strike a random tent on the other side of the camp, quickly spreading waves of flame across the brittle cloth in hungry streaks. Half a dozen more tents are on fire only moments later, and a second volley of arrows is already falling from the sky.

Evie steps forward, but Mother Manai raises an arm across Evie's midsection, halting her.

"Wait," Manai bids her. "Wait until all of 'em that're near to us are fixed on the fire and runnin' about, else we'll have 'em on us as soon as we touch the horn."

"But he'll raise the alarm!" Evie insists.

"He's starin' at the pretty lights like the rest. His brain won't catch up for a while yet, I promise. Just wait!"

Evie's feet ache to rush ahead, but she halts them, trusting to the older woman's instincts. The Skrain are all beginning to buzz around them, some standing and watching the falling fire while others run around in confusion and panic.

While Evie watches the genesis of chaos, Mother Manai keeps her eyes affixed to the soldier stationed at the warning alarm. She's right, his first move isn't to send a warning bellow through the horn; he's watching the arrows descend like the rest.

Finally, some captain or another yells from a distance: "Sound the alarm! Blow the damn horn and sound the alarm!"

Mother Manai calmly approaches the Skrain soldier attending the horn as he turns to the massive spiral of polished bone. She's more than a head shorter than him and slighter in frame by half, but from the way she carries herself you would have to explain the difference and its implications to her.

"Good evening, son!" she brightly bids him.

It's enough to puzzle the soldier and give him pause for a just a moment. That span of time is more than enough for Mother Manai to extend the empty steel-fisted gauntlet attached to her right wrist up against the edge of his helm and tilt it back just slightly. Her other hand, already having deftly palmed a dagger, thrusts the blade into his throat. The soldier is dead before his feet even know it, and he continues to stand there, leaning slightly into Manai as his knees begin to buckle and his body wriggles beneath its armor.

Evie is on Mother Manai's heels, drawing her sword and rushing past the death dance. She grips the tsuka with both hands and raises the sword, slashing down expertly and chopping through the horn's mouthpiece with one swipe. In almost the same motion she gives her shoulder to the blossoming spiral of bone and pushes the entire thing, horn and pedestal both, until they tip over.

Mother Manai removes her blooded blade from the soldier's throat and does her best to ease his body to the ground quickly and quietly. She leaves him lying there, sheathing her dagger as she steps away to join Evie. No one appears to have yet noticed what they've done, but the certain remedy for that is to remain beside the body and the disabled alarm.

"Move," Mother hisses at Evie. "Don't run, just move!"

Evie nods, lowering her sword and keeping it unsheathed at her side as they both walk away from the scene.

They begin to hear the battle cries of Savages rising above the fiery tent peaks on the far side of the camp. Evie's heart feels as though it's rising through her throat. The sound either means the Savages have turned on the emissaries sent to infiltrate their camp and enlist their aid, or it means they've raided the armory wagon and are attacking the Skrain, led by Lariat and Bam. They couldn't risk trying to send signals back and forth between the Skrain-guarded lines before the attack. Evie trusted to the Elder Company's reputation and influence over the rest of the dominant Savages attached to these companies of Skrain.

The soldiers stationed in the center of the encampment have begun mustering together en masse, most of them fleeing burning tents and flaming arrows. Small groups have gathered water in buckets and troughs and are attempting to extinguish as many tents as possible. The attention of the rest is being collectively pulled toward the commotion originating in the Savage Legion quarters. Evie and Mother Manai remain in the background, far enough removed from the others to flee, yet close enough to blend in with the rest of the Crachian helms and scaled armor.

"What happened to the alarm?" an angry, authoritative voice demands. "Where're our sentries, our scouts?"

Almost as if in answer to him, a shrieking voice pierces the scattered and confused chatter among the rest of the Skrain. A lone soldier is bolting between the tents, running away from the direction of the Savage quarter. Evie glimpses him through the mass of other armored bodies. The man has lost his helm, and his face and breastplate are streaked and splattered with blood.

"The Savages are attacking the camp!" he's screaming, frantic and obviously in shock. "They're killing everyone! There was no warning! We had no warning!"

He continues his raving, but the same voice of authority from before shouts over him, barking orders at the mustered Skrain to form ranks. In moments they're advancing from the center of the encampment toward the fighting outside the Savage quarter.

Evie looks to Mother Manai, who nods her head. The adrenaline is causing a deafening rush inside Evie's ears, as if someone is banging stones together inside her head. The Savages appear to be doing what they do best, creating chaos and drawing the enemy into false skirmishes designed to whittle their numbers, weaken their position, and scatter their forces. Even if small pockets of the Skrain have managed to ascertain the situation and form limited ranks, they'll still find themselves in the middle of a disorganized battle, outnumbered and surrounded by a world on fire.

The Savage Legion is bred to thrive in the center of chaos.

If the rest of her plan is unfolding as expected, the Sicclunan shadow warriors should be attacking the camp from the southeast while the B'ors fighters attack from the north, their ultimate goal to drive whatever number of Skrain they don't take by complete surprise toward the center of camp, where they will be trapped between the three separate forces.

Evie and Mother Manai find a blind spot between two large tents that have remained untouched by the fires. The volleys of flaming arrows, meanwhile, have stopped falling above the encampment; now that the full assault has begun the collective forces of the Sicclunans, Savages, and B'ors don't want arrows striking their own warriors. The two women aren't immediately visible from either end of the small pass, and though it's a good spot to remain unnoticed until the final phase of the battle, they have no intention of hiding.

Instead, they wait, weapons at the ready. Soon enough a trio of Skrain soldiers comes trotting between the tents, the scales of their armor bouncing and jostling loudly as they move. Evie and Mother Manai press themselves into the tents on either side of the pass, waiting. When the three soldiers move between them they strike, Evie slicing through the backs of the nearest pair of knees with her sword while Mother Manai rams the blade of her dagger between plates of armor around the first torso within reach.

The third soldier isn't even given time to realize they've been attacked by what appears to be their own comrades. Evie removes a large portion of his throat with a powerful swing of her sword.

Behind her, Mother Manai has knelt over the soldier whose legs Evie disabled and is delivering the death blow with her dagger.

Evie finds she's breathing laboriously despite the minimal exertion of the last few moments. It's not fear. Evie finds she's left fear somewhere far behind without realizing it. Perhaps it's the knowledge, banished somewhere in the dungeons of her mind, that she's given herself over fully to what was only meant to be a role she'd play until locating Brio. Ashana the retainer and bodyguard is now Evie, a Savage Legionnaire who ambushes men and women under cover, and slaughters them before they know what's happening.

And perhaps it wouldn't affect her so if a large part of Evie didn't find satisfaction in this killing.

With no way to quickly and efficiently conceal the heavily armored bodies, Evie and Mother Manai leave them where they lie and calmly walk from between the two tents. The center of the camp is largely deserted, and what soldiers and pages are there are to be seen running through the space en route to join one battle or another. Evie and Mother Manai can hear fighting in every direction now, steel clashing with steel and the screams of the fighting and the dying a familiar symphony to them both.

The two of them find another spot with enough cover to shade their next ambush from the sight of any passersby. The pounding in Evie's ears only grows louder, entire mountain ranges being pulverized to dust between her temples. They waylay half a dozen more soldiers, picking most of them off one at a time as they scatter from one fracas or another in confusion. Evie ceases to hear the voices of the dying, or focus on their eyes as the slash or thrust of her blade darkens them eternally.

It seems to her as though much more time has passed than actually has when Evie feels Mother Manai rapping the empty fist of her gauntlet against the back scales of Evie's armor. She turns to see the older woman's lips moving, but somehow it is several moments before she hears her words.

"Look here, love! They're bein' pushed back! It's just like you said it would be!"

Mother Manai guides her to the edge of their concealment to peer out at what looks like stragglers joining the end of a heavy retreat.

The Skrain, composed largely of the soldiers Evie and Mother Manai watched form ranks and strike off to battle the Legion, are soon falling back to the center of their camp. Evie watches as they quickly arrange themselves in a skirmish line two columns deep. They still believe they're fighting only rogue Legionnaires from the Savage quarter, and they've chosen to take up a position facing that side of the encampment. Evie watches several soldiers fleeing the battles raging in the north and southwest quarters of the base try to inform the others forming the line, but their warnings either aren't being understood or heeded, or they aren't spreading through the ranks fast enough.

Ahead of the line, trampling and pulling down the flaming and smoking remnants of several tents, Savages a hundred strong are slowly approaching the center of the camp. Most are wielding their rusted, secondhand melee weapons, but others have appropriated the finely forged blades of fallen soldiers. Even in the sparsely firelit dark of night, even amidst the mass and chaos of bodies, Evie can see Lariat striding ahead of the Savage pack. Beside the walrus-mustached fist fighter, Bam's mallet is held high above his head, almost like a standard for an army that carries no banners.

With half a hundred yards separating the two forces, Lariat spreads his leather-strapped arms, blooded katars held in both fists, and the Savage Legion halts.

Other than the scattered shout or order given, the Skrain line is silent. They've never faced a horde of Savages across a field of battle before. They've never seen what the face of chaos fueled by bloody desperation looks like, let alone stared into its maw as that maw opened to swallow them all whole.

On the Legionnaire side, Lariat begins to laugh. It echoes throughout the center of the camp, an ugly sound like the gleeful braying of some animal in heat. The other Savages soon join in, filling the burning encampment with noxious, twisted laughter.

Evie can almost feel the tension and fear radiating off the Skrain soldiers. They don't know what to make of anything that's happening. They've had their whole world torn asunder in a matter of moments, very much like every Legionnaire when they were plucked from a dungeon cell or directly off the street and flung through rotted doors onto a dying field of grass to be told that their new name is Savage.

Evie, on the other hand, knows exactly why and at what the Legionnaires are laughing, and why they're holding their position.

In the next moment black-masked Sicclunan soldiers are swarming into the middle of the camp from every path and opening between tents. The long, curved blades of their swords seem on fire as the steel traps the light of the burning landscape. Among them are B'ors warriors issuing their whooping, taunting, and challenging battle cries as they brandish their axes and war clubs and long knives.

"It's time," Evie says, and Mother Manai nods in both agreement and assent.

Evie and Mother Manai quickly divest themselves of their Skrain armor, lest they be mistaken for the enemy as the tri-force converges on what's left of the Crachian soldiers. Beneath the steel scales they're both wearing light leather breastplates over thick woolen tunics woven to slow a blade's penetration or deflect its slash. Evie briefly recalls thinking that begetting an impossible revolution was a fair price to pay for burning her filthy, torn Savage rags.

The two women join the surge of Sicclunans and B'ors warriors. By now the rogue Legionnaires have also begun their charge. The Skrain don't know which way to turn, and their remaining commanders begin issuing conflicting orders as each beholds a different attack from a completely different angle than the others. When the combined forces converge on the Crachian soldiers it is less a skirmish and more a massacre. It is their own Savage Legion strategy evolved. Rather than using human artillery to precede the main attack, they have become the main attack.

Evie fights until eventually she can no longer find a Skrain soldier to face down. She turns wildly in every direction, certain more are coming, certain they can't have suppressed the entire base camp. What she sees is her own forces standing over the armored bodies of the fallen, only the occasional death blow upsetting the blood-soaked calm that's draping across the field of battle.

Evie looks down at her sword. She can't see a single glint of steel for the blood bathing the blade.

One of the black-masked Sicclunans approaches, peeling away their hood. Sirach smiles at Evie, her dark violet eyes making a black reflection of the flames all around them.

"I believe the day is ours," she says.

"The *night*," Evie reminds her. "The night is ours."

Sirach laughs, sheathing her sword. "I guess you just turn day and night upside down for me, my dear."

Evie looks down, flushing slightly at those words, the red hidden beneath her Savage runes.

Several dozen black-masked warriors have gathered behind Sirach. She turns to them without missing a beat.

"Search every tent for survivors!" she commands.

Evie grunts. "What about the Skrain that have no doubt fled?"

"We have archers surrounding the perimeters, night-trained just like us. They'll pick them off to a soldier."

Evie hears Lariat approaching before she ever lays eyes on him, as loud and brash and exulting as ever. She's barely turned around before he scoops her up in a bear's hug, squeezing the life out of her. She can feel the blade-encumbered leather straps encircling his body threatening her flesh.

"I 'aven't felt this since I knocked my first man cold in the prize ring!" Lariat announces directly into her ear. "Ya surely were sent by the God Stars themselves, little Sparrow!"

"Put her down before you crush our godsend, Lariat," Mother Manai bids him.

He does, laughing all the while.

"She's tougher'n she looks by miles," he says, gripping her shoulder and shaking her in that way he does.

Evie is too tired to protest, and in a strange way his levity makes the killing normal and tolerable for her.

Lariat is joined by Bam, who has already replaced his deep hood, and is flicking bits of entrails from the face of his mallet, and another Savage Evie has never seen before. He may be even older than Lariat, but his physique is that of a much younger, fitter man. He's more slender than Lariat, right down to his graying mustache, which is thinner by half, and almost a head taller. He's swinging the haft of a lengthy mace in one hand, its head a fist-size knot of hard, polished wood.

"Sparrow!" Lariat announces, grandly. "I want ya ta meet a foundin' member of the Elder Company! This is Diggs! He's markin' thirty-one battles, countin' this'n here."

"*This* is the little girl Lariat speaks of like she could topple the Spectrum with her bare hands?" Diggs marvels, scrutinizing Evie up and down.

"This is the young *woman* whose plan just made you a free man," Mother Manai corrects him.

Diggs bows, deeply. "Meaning no offense."

"Thank you for joining us," Evie says gratefully, the rest mattering little to her.

Diggs laughs, reaching up and grasping the back of Lariat's neck as if collecting the scruff of a misbehaving pup.

"I had little choice! It was that or I would've had to kill this crude old gasbag. And I've never cared for the killing of friends."

Lariat laughs and presses his forehead against Diggs', the two of them growling nose-to-nose like feral boys.

"Pay 'em no mind, love," Mother Manai says. "It's my belief they were parted at birth. Diggs just learnt to talk prettier, that's all."

Lariat turns back toward Evie. "You make one helluva general, little Sparrow," he declares. "This is a night fer celebratin'!"

"This is only the beginning," Sirach interjects. "And this is the *last* time we'll surprise them, I promise you."

Lariat stares down at the Sicclunan captain distastefully, lips tightening beneath his mustache.

"She's right," Evie insists. Then, gazing at the expectant and bloodied faces all around her, her voice lightens, "But you did well this night! And this night is ours!"

Scattered cheers arise from the battle's survivors.

Mother Manai turns to the hodgepodge of warriors, soldiers, and Savages gathered around them.

She raises the fist of her empty gauntlet, her words like thunder. "Let's hear it for the Sparrow General!"

Now the cheers are unified and deafening, arms and fists and blooded weapons rising to the sky as they begin chanting the title of Evie's abrupt battlefield promotion.

Again she moves her gaze across their faces, dirty faces and bloody faces and masked faces, some marked with runes and others painted with battle decoration. She listens to her name on their hungry lips. It's the first sound to drown out the pounding in her ears. She feels herself smiling despite everything that's happened and is continuing to happen around her.

The smile lasts only until Evie glances once more at the blade of her sword. It's still sheathed in Crachian blood, blood no amount of chanting, no matter how loud or resplendent or devoted, will ever wash away.

THOUGH IT BE HARSH,
COME BACK TO THE LIGHT

———————————

"ARE THEY STILL OUT THERE?" LEXI ASKS.

Taru latches closed the tower doors, turning to face the Te of Gen Stalbraid waiting at the top of the first flight of steps.

"The small round one left for a goodly while, but I believe it was simply to use the facilities. One of them always remains."

Lexi frowns. "I suppose we should simply be thankful neither of them followed Spud-Bar."

Taru nods. The retainer is carrying a basket filled with goods retrieved from the Gen Circus's bazaar.

"You've been busy," Lexi observes.

"I have, Te-Gen. I took the sky carriage to the Spectrum. Copies of all ship manifests and schedules are required to be submitted for their records daily."

Lexi descends several steps. "And so?"

"*The Black Turtle* is scheduled to arrive one week from today."

Lexi nods, that steely resolve falling over her expression like a curtain. "Then you will meet them one week from today and retrieve whatever Brio left with its captain."

"Are you certain, Te-Gen? I do not like leaving you unattended."

"I am never unattended. The Protectorate Ministry is erecting a colony on my doorstep."

"That is the reason I do not like leaving you unattended."

"It cannot be helped," Lexi insists. "I can't leave Daian in his condition. Speaking of which, how went the other half of your task?"

Taru raises the basket. "We will find out momentarily."

The retainer begins stalking the steps to join Lexi.

"You might wish to wait in the parlor, Te-Gen."

Lexi shakes her head, following the retainer up the spiraling steps. "You may need help."

They have installed Daian in one of Xia Tower's disused servant's quarters, just up the steps from the entrance hall. Lexi and Taru stripped him of his uniform, baldric, and other tools. Lexi did her best to wash and stitch Daian's tunic, hoping he'll eventually need it again. It was too dangerous to summon a surgeon, so Taru did their best to field treat the Aegin's wound, cleaning and sewing and wrapping his torso in fresh bandages that both Lexi and the retainer have taken turns changing twice a day.

He hasn't opened his eyes since the night he scaled the tower and toppled down its steps with half the blood drained from his body. Taru still insists it was only by the grace of a force beyond the retainer's reckoning that they were able to keep his heart beating. Taru also insists that if he remains unconscious any longer they risk him never opening his eyes again.

"What are you going to do?" Lexi asks.

"As little as possible."

"I don't find that particularly comforting, Taru."

"Forgive me, Te-Gen, but I very seriously doubt anything that is about to happen in this room will be comforting. That is why I invited you—"

"I'm fine. I simply want to know what to expect."

"As do I," Taru mutters almost inaudibly.

"What was that?"

The retainer shakes their head. "Nothing, Te-Gen."

Lexi frowns as Taru sits on the edge of Daian's sickbed, placing the basket between his motionless ankles. Taru removes a small stone well the size of their palm. It is tamped with a balled-up bit of cloth. The moment Taru removes that piece of cloth Lexi finds herself backing away toward the wall. She throws a hand over her mouth and nose to prevent her retching.

"What is that?" she demands.

"Many different substances that together have no single name."

"Why is it that I can both smell *and* taste it from here?"

"Execution," Taru answers simply.

The retainer passes the well under Daian's nose. The nostrils of the unconscious Aegin flare and quiver, driven by his body's natural senses. Taru continues waving the foulness back and forth, and a moment later Daian's head turns to one side to avoid the unbearable smell.

Lexi steps forward excitedly. "Is he—"

"Not yet, Te-Gen. A moment, please."

Taru chases the well after Daian's nostrils, continuing the smell's assault on them. His head spasms again, and his closed eyelids begin trembling. Daian's lips part, and his breathing intensifies. It appears as though his eyes are trying to flutter open, but it is as though his eyelids are straining against a great weight they cannot overcome.

Eventually Taru relents with a sigh, taking away the well.

Lexi deflates. "I thought you had him."

"That was only the initial volley," Taru explains. "The attack has yet to commence."

The retainer tamps the well and returns it to the basket. Taru's hand reemerges holding dozens of slender strands of vegetation wrapped in a swath of rice straw mat to bind them together. Taru stands and turns to the nearest wall, touching the end of the bouquet to the flame of the torch there, igniting it. All the strands burning together create a large flame from which tendrils of white, acrid smoke drift.

Taru turns back to the bed, hovering over Daian's comatose form.

"What is that?" Lexi asks. "Is the smoke strong enough to rouse him?"

"I'm afraid not," Taru says. "In point of fact, the smoke has nothing to do with anything."

Without further warning, the retainer shoves the burning end of the bouquet into Daian's side, above his bandages. Taru grinds the flaming stems into his skin, letting the fire eat and smolder his flesh.

Lexi claws at her neck in horror, opening her mouth to order Taru to stop.

Daian awakes with an agonized scream, arching his back and balling his fists. His eyes are wide open without yet seeing.

Taru pulls the fire away and drops the bouquet to floor, stamping it out with a booted foot. The retainer reaches for a cloth on the bedside table and dunks it in a basin of water there before pressing the cloth to Daian's sudden scorch wound.

Daian blinks, his head snapping from side to side as he wildly scans his surrounding. He begins attempting to rise from the bed in earnest.

Lexi rushes forward, taking him by the shoulders and easing him back down on the bed. Fortunately, he hasn't the strength to fight her.

"You are just fine," she promises him with a perturbed sidelong glance at Taru. "You are in Xia Tower in the Gen Circus. You came here after you were attacked. We've been tending to you."

Daian gradually eases, his wordless protests quieting and his shallow breathing returning to normal. He continues blinking the world around him back into focus, finally looking up at Lexi and Taru and actually seeing them.

He nods, attempting to speak and finding it only sparks a fit of painful coughs.

Lexi quickly fetches him water, permitting him only small sips until the wave of hacking passes.

"Go slow," she bids him. "Go gently."

Daian nods once more, sipping the water eagerly and relaxing against the soft sheets.

When he's regained his breath and soothed his throat, he again attempts to speak, whispering something inaudible.

Lexi leans her ear close to his lips. "Again, please."

"What's he saying?" Taru asks.

A moment later Lexi grins inexplicably. She leans away from Daian's weary lips, looking at Taru.

"He asked if you tried shaking him awake first."

Taru is visibly not amused.

"Well," the retainer says, "at least his tenuous grasp of humor is intact."

THE NEW DEVOURING THE OLD

DYEAWAN'S FIRST MEETING AS A PLANNER IS SURPRISINGLY ILL attended. In fact, almost half of the other planners she met during her initiation into their ranks are absent. Edger is seated at the center point of the table that mimics the concentric circles of their pendants. There are five other planners spread throughout the interior of winding stone slab, all whom greet her with bright eyes and welcoming smiles. Dyeawan can't help noticing they are all among the youngest members of the planners.

"We welcome the freshest fowl to our brace," Edger announces. "It seems a perfect time for a new planner, as we appear to be shorthanded today."

The rest of them giggle or snicker or guffaw while Dyeawan stares about in confusion. She doesn't understand the comedy of the moment.

Dyeawan falls into silence as Edger commences the meeting. He sparks a lively discussion concerning the Gens involved in various operations of Crachian docks and seaports, and how their practice and philosophy differs from other Gens nationwide. Corruption and misuse prevail heavily among Gens invested in seafaring trades and port functions, far more than levels deemed "acceptable" among other Gens.

It is strange for Dyeawan to hear these things spoken about so openly and honestly, without pretense or concealment. What Aegins spend their every day attempting to hide from the goodly citizens of the Capitol, these people treat as just another feature of the city.

"Perhaps the problem is that people who live and work in places like the Bottoms are taught to see themselves as existing outside Crache," Dyeawan finds herself chiming in. "Perhaps this would not be a problem if the people allowed to live and starve in those streets were better tended to."

Dyeawan expects her words to be met with reprimand and scorn, perhaps even attack. Instead the faces surrounding her are alight with curiosity.

"Please continue, Dyeawan," Edger bids her.

"Gens, from what I've seen, feel no loyalty to any people outside their own kith-kins. Feeling loyal to Crache and loyal to its people are not the same thing. When it comes to people, Gens are loyal to the people inside that Gen. But at least, outside the Bottoms, Gens see citizens protected and cared for by Crache. In the Bottoms people do not matter. It teaches the Gens entrusted with running things there that they can do whatever they like without consequence. If they saw Crache invested in those people, they might think differently."

"What if we lack the resources to feed and house so many, especially those too weak or old or infirm to provide function for that care?"

"The attempt would be enough," Dyeawan insists, bitterness creeping unchecked into her voice. "Ignoring a problem you can't solve is not itself a solution. It only allows the problem to grow."

Her hypothesis ignites an excited volley of mixed chatter among the half dozen young planners. They spend the next two hours debating and discussing methods of practical implementation for Dyeawan's theory. Every disagreement is used as springboard to new ideas rather than as the foundation for an argument. Dyeawan isn't certain what she is witnessing here, but the interactions of these people are like nothing she has experienced.

By the time Edger adjourns the afternoon session, Dyeawan feels almost drunk. She isn't sure any of them truly understood her points, or that she was speaking of real people and very real pain. They seemed to treat even the direst description of the Bottoms as an exercise for the mind. Dyeawan wonders if Edger doesn't cultivate that kind of detachment among them, separating them from the reality of Crache so that they may plan its life and future without emotion.

The others rise, and navigate the simple maze of the table before filing out of the chamber. They all pause to offer a few kind words of parting to Dyeawan, several of them enthusiastically suggesting she join them for activities later in the evening. Dyeawan smiles and bows her head, responding in kind to each fellow planner. She is aware of how much she should be enjoying this, their display of the kind of acceptance and camaraderie she's spent her entire life dreaming about. Yet she feels only emptiness and despair.

She and Edger remain behind when the rest of them have departed.

Edger raises his broadest, most jovially smiling mask to his face. "I believe that went exceedingly well for your first session."

Dyeawan has only raw honesty left in her after hours of forced pleasantry. "When we first met I thought those masks were for you, to allow you to express yourself in a world that denied you that ability. But they're not, are they? Those masks. They're to put other people off. They might pity you or be repulsed by you when they first see your face, but in either case they are in control and see you as inferior. Those masks disturb and unsettle them in a way that puts *you* in control. It forces them to take you seriously, because we always take things that frighten us seriously."

She doesn't know why she's telling him this now. It's one of many observations she's hidden in the back of her mind so no one would become aware of how much she sees. Perhaps she no longer cares what Edger knows about her.

Edger continues holding the mask in front of his face for several silent moments. He finally lowers it to the table.

"You continue to surprise and impress me," he says.

"Do I belong here?" she asks him plainly.

"You belong here perhaps more than any of us, Dyeawan."

"But is that the only reason I'm here? Is that the only reason you made me a planner?"

Edger hesitates, rolling the handle of his disused mask in one hand. "No."

"Why twelve people at this table?"

"Because it has always been so."

"That sounds dangerously close to mythologizing, Edger."

"I fear we crossed that threshold long ago."

"But now you are thirteen."

"*We* are thirteen. Yes."

Dyeawan looks down at herself, fingertips involuntarily plucking at the material of her tunic. They lightly touch the smooth, polished surface of the concentric circles pinned below her shoulder.

"I saw the looks on their faces when you gave me this. The planners closer to my age, the ones who attended this meeting today, they looked like they were being given a gift. The planners who are closer in age to you looked like something was being taken away from them."

"Your insight has clearly grown to match your powers of observation."

Dyeawan ignores the compliment. "Was something being taken away from them, Edger?"

"Yes. The teat was taken away from their mouths. And it was long overdue."

"I don't understand."

The air moves swiftly from Edger's neck through Ku the wind dragon's mouth and backbones. It may be a sound of exasperation, or perhaps anger, Dyeawan can't be certain.

"Becoming older affects us in many different ways, Dyeawan, some of them beneficial and some of them detrimental. Many of my elder colleagues amidst this table have suffered mainly ill effects, I'm afraid. They become set in their ways. They become convinced the ideas they conceived and implemented decades ago, which were admittedly brilliant for the time, need not be changed or further innovated. They resist new methods and new discoveries. Observing this, I've strived to fill this table with fresh young minds imbued with fresh young ideas. My elder colleagues have been particularly resistant to that."

"But before today there was a balance," Dyeawan says almost without thought, as if the words were a muscle reacting to being prodded.

"Correct. There was division, but it was equal because we were twelve. Six of the new guard and six of the old."

"Now we are thirteen," she repeats, this time with understanding.

"Your presence tips the scales toward the future and makes them feel even more like part of the past. Their voluntary absence today is a form of protest, not unlike a mass tantrum. It's funny, really. The older we get, the more we become children again. It's a futile gesture, however. Whether they are here or not, there will no longer be a stalemate over every petty issue."

Dyeawan frowns. "You used me to give you a majority over them, for control."

"I elevated you to this position because I believe you to be an instrument for creating the future of Crache. It is that simple. Much of that will come from the ideas created in that remarkable mind of yours. Another part of that function is clearing away old ideas that are of no use to Crache any longer."

"Why didn't you explain any of this to me before I wheeled myself into this chamber?"

"I didn't want to cloud your mind or your judgment with unnecessary details, particularly not during your tests and trials."

"That is a lie."

It is the first time Dyeawan has openly exposed one of his falsities, and the first time she has ever openly revealed her ability to discern truth from fiction in people and their words. She immediately regrets it, but doesn't let it show through her hardened expression.

"It was a half truth," Edger says carefully a moment later. "That was a reason, simply not the entire reason."

377

"A half truth is a whole lie, Edger."

"Do you wish to return your tunic and pendant?" he asks quickly and impatiently. "Do you wish to return to sweeping floors and ferrying messages?"

"No."

"Then this discussion is moot, is it not?"

Dyeawan's fingers curl into fists above the paddles of her tender, but her mind refuses to delude her on the matter.

"Yes, it is."

Edger seems appeased by her admission. His words come slower and with less emphasis.

"You deserve to be here, Dyeawan. I apologize for not apprising you fully of the situation you were entering, but your knowledge of it would have changed nothing."

"Will any of them return to the table?"

"Of course not. Even if their pride would allow them to make that overture, I won't allow it. They tipped their hand, foolishly, and in doing so only further prove why they must be swept away. Their obstinence was creating a constant stalemate among the planners, and that threatens all Crache."

"That seems . . . excessive. I mean, they just skipped one meeting—"

"Should we wait for an open rebellion before we act, little Slider? Allowing them more time to plot and scheme and fester won't solve the problem, it will only exacerbate it. This little protest, if unchallenged, will only embolden them."

"Are you sure it's not just you?" Dyeawan asks carefully. "Are you sure you don't just want them gone?"

"Perhaps I do. They weary me. The mind ages, but that doesn't necessitate it growing old. They've all grown old on me. Rigid. Incapable of learning new things. Perhaps I do resent them for that. It doesn't change the issue, however."

"What will happen to them?"

Edgar shrugs.

"They remain brilliant people. They will be reassigned to oversee other areas, the builders or the architects and so forth. They will find purpose in those roles if they embrace them."

"Then we are actually eight now."

"It is a number, Dyeawan, and a completely arbitrary one. It holds no power or influence over anything. I am eager to see what my fresh young minds may achieve unbidden, and today's meeting did not disappoint."

Dyeawan rows the paddles of her tender, wheeling herself away from the curve of the snaking slab in front of her. She turns the tender away from the stone hedge maze of a table and begins rolling across the chamber, her back to Edger.

"I look forward to tomorrow," he calls after her.

The wheels of her tender keep spinning, and Dyeawan does not look back.

A PLOT OF CORPSES

EVIE WRINGS OUT THE CLOTH OVER A LOPSIDED WOODEN basin and carefully folds the dampened rag into a rectangle before laying it across Brio's forehead. His fever has dissipated drastically, but his skin is not yet cool. Brio clung to life tenuously for several nights. At its worst his entire body burned as bright as a red-hot coal in the dark and even his sweat seared to the touch. He was delirious beyond reason, experiencing funerals for people who were not yet dead, mourning Lexi who was murdered in his mind a hundred different ways. He was struck down over and over again by a half-mad giant named Taru whose betrayal he bemoaned more than his own death at their hands.

Brio was still in the throes of it when Evie was forced to leave him in preparation for their assault on the Skrain encampment. She'd forced herself to banish thoughts of him from her mind, certain she'd return to find a corpse if she returned at all. Evie is still uncertain whose survival surprised her more, Brio's or her own.

The Sicclunan surgeon took his leg just below the knee. She proved to be a skilled cutter and healer. Though the Sicclunans may lack every resource that isn't funneled into their war efforts, they do seem to possess knowledge in abundance. What's left of Brio below that kneecap has been burned and sealed with oils and carefully wrapped with clean silk. Every few hours the surgeon returns to unravel the seeping bandages and replace them with clean wraps.

Brio is still incredibly weak, but he's conscious, staring up at Evie with glassy, weary eyes like a man watching his own dreams. They've shaved his filthy, ratted beard and most of his hair. He looks very much like the boy Evie remembers, apart from the blue runes staining his skin and covering his face.

"The Sparrow General?" he asks churlishly in a voice that's barely a whisper.

"Stow it, will you?" she fires back at him. "It's hardly a name I chose. And I'm no general. It was agreed among the three parties we'd share tactical command equally, and I'm not even senior among the Savages."

"Yet it was your plan they followed, and your name they chanted after the battle," Brio points out.

"Are you just riding me, or are you making a point?"

Brio closes his eyes. "A smidge of both, I suppose."

She removes the cloth from his forehead, using one corner to dab at his temples before returning it to the basin.

"I wasn't looking for any of this," she insists. "But I couldn't ignore what was there in front of us. We never would've made it to the Tenth City, not even with the Sicclunan horses. You were dying. And even if I'd been able to heal you, even if we did make it through the Skrain vanguard, the both of us would still be fugitives, with these fucking runes on our skin and because of what you know. An opportunity presented itself."

"So you started a revolution," Brio concludes mildly.

"I seized the opportunity. You're alive. We have a chance, slender though it may be."

"We have a war. That's what we have. And it will no doubt be a short and bloody one."

"What would you have me do, Brio?" she demands. "What did *you* want to do, if not this? You wanted to change things in Crache, didn't you? You wanted to stop the lies and the oppression and things like the

Savage Legion. Wars, revolutions, what else brings about that kind of change?"

"I wanted to expose the truth," Brio says, and now the bitterness has crept into his voice. "I wanted to bring the crimes of Crache into the light, where the people could see. They are *not* all tools of oppression, they simply believe what they're told, what they're presented with every day of their lives. The truth would have changed things, without bloodshed."

Evie stares at the ground, unable to meet his eyes in that moment. She isn't ashamed of herself or her actions, she simply doesn't wish to see him in the throes of such naivety.

She shakes her head. "Someone always bleeds, Brio. Your father never understood that, and neither do you. You plead for the people in the Bottoms, but you've never lived their lives. You may know one truth, but Crache and its Gens have still blinded you."

He sighs. "There is nothing to be done now, I suppose."

"You've done all you can. If Spud-Bar delivered your message then it's given to Lexi to bring light to your truth. Maybe she can, and maybe it will be enough. I hope so, because if my 'revolution' as you call it fails here, no one in the cities will ever know. Your truth will be the only weapon that's left."

"I never wanted to put Lexi in this position," he whispers, no longer speaking to Evie.

"How are you feeling?" she asks him, certainly to change the subject, but also because she's still worried about his condition.

"Alive. Although the smell of this place isn't helping."

Evie tries to laugh, but there's nothing real fueling its fire.

The Sicclunan base camp from which they launched their assault on the Skrain vanguard is deep in a swampy marsh of foul, poison sludge. Evie thought the cursed earth over which they hiked before meeting Sirach was a wasteland, but that ground was fertile compared to the muck here. Sirach explained that's one of the ways they keep their mobile camps hidden from Skrain patrol; no Crachian would think to venture this deep into the swamp, despite the fact Crachian mining and harvesting efforts created these sunken wastes.

A large head draped in a leather hood and stringy tendrils of brown hair poke through the tent flap, along with the double-sided hammer of a gargantuan mallet.

"What is it, Bam?" Evie asks.

"Sunset-eyed girl," he mutters, the words sounding flattened by his thick lips.

"That's fine, Bam, you can let her inside."

His head and war hammer retreat, and a moment later Sirach enters the tent, an irritated expression on her face. She's traded in her masked night warrior garb for another expansive hat whose crown is decorated with brightly dyed horsehair and leather armor, the breastplate of which has a magnificent phoenix painted on it, the fiery bird's wings extending down her arms. Sirach has several parchment scrolls rolled up tightly and clenched inside her right fist.

"Did you order that great ape to guard your tent and deny me entry?" she asks Evie.

"No. He just sort of . . . stationed himself there. He's been following me wherever I go."

The irritated twist to Sirach's lips relaxes into a grin. "He's taken a shine to you, dearest. I think I'm jealous."

"Lariat or Mother Manai probably told him to keep a watchful eye," Evie says, although she doesn't really believe it.

"It's probably for the best. I'm sure you're already becoming a figure of some lore amongst the Skrain and the Savage Legion."

"We picked off all their soldiers. How would they know?"

"There are eyes everywhere, even out here. Everyone employs their own spies, scouts, and informants. Information is the most highly prized Crachian currency, dearest, or rather *control* of that information. They may not know where we went, but they'll find out who led the charge. Soon the Protectorate Ministry itself will know the name 'Sparrow General.' And they'll kill to ensure not one citizen ever hears it."

"You're the bird they should be worried about," Evie says, eager to dismiss what Sirach is telling her.

Sirach spreads her arms and glances down at the phoenix blazing from its own ashes on her breastplate.

"Being hunted and exploited to the brink of extinction should not deter one from displaying a personal flair when allowable. If anything, it makes one's individuality more important, I should think."

"I see how all this came to pass now," Brio remarks wearily. "You two are exactly alike."

Both Evie and Sirach laugh, but Evie is already shaking her head.

"Hardly," she says.

"We've had the good fortune to share common goals."

"How is everyone getting on out there?" Evie asks Sirach.

"Much better since we raided the Skrain larders. It's miraculous how full bellies sate even the most contrary of companions."

"How long will the supplies last?" Brio asks.

"Long enough to see us to our next battle, which will in all likelihood be our final battle. In either case, the matter will be resolved."

Evie's expression turns grim. "Does it look that dire?"

Sirach unfurls the parchment scrolls in her hand and lays them out before Evie on the part of Brio's sickbed not occupied by his missing limb.

"Confiscated dispatches," she explains. "If they read true, there would've been another thousand Skrain and five hundred more Savage Legionnaires arriving at the encampment we razed by tonight."

"Then you struck at the right time," Brio says, trying to focus on a positive.

Sirach nods. "We did. Now, however, those forces will be recalled to the border. They'll be combined with the garrisoned army there and that's where they'll wait."

"What's our strength?" Evie asks.

"I can field eight hundred soldiers, regular infantry and my Special Selection outriders. We have around two hundred of your Savages, and with the B'ors bands that arrived tonight we add another hundred of their warriors to that."

Evie nods. She has no idea how the B'ors communicate over such a long distance, but Yacatek has been gathering bands from every direction, and each band seems to find the Sicclunan's very secret base camp with little effort.

"You'll be outnumbered almost three to one," Brio says to both of them.

"That's only counting the Skrain," Sirach agrees. "If they still trust their Savages, they'll send every one they have at our front line before we ever see a scale of armor. And the next battle will be fought on open ground. We won't catch them unawares again. We'll have to march in force right up to that border."

"We could hold the line here, gather our own strength," Evie suggests. "I began this for my own reasons. I won't push all of you into suicide for my purpose."

"It's no longer your purpose. And they won't simply allow us to sit here. We've tried that before. I promise you they're already mustering more troops from the cities and every garrison in between. They'll gather the largest force we've ever seen and come for us. They have to. It's not about some upstart rebellion to your people. You've seen the wastelands here. They need the land beyond. That's always been their purpose."

Evie looks down at Brio. He meets her eyes with the same silent, reluctant acceptance. They both know Sirach is right.

"We've begun something here," Sirach continues, "like moving the wheel of a great machine. There's no reversing it. The longer we wait, the worse it'll be. We have to strike now. It's our only hope."

"Is 'hope' the right word?" Brio asks dryly.

Sirach laughs, and it even sounds genuine. "I won't pretend to understand why you went through all this just for him," she says to Evie, "but for a man he isn't entirely uninteresting."

Brio does his best to bow his head. "Thank you so very much."

Listening to the two of them, Evie can almost bring herself to smile, although it never quite reaches her lips.

"We may very well all die, and quite soon," Evie says, "but at least between now and then . . . we won't be bored."

Sirach laughs again, and she's still laughing when she turns and ducks out of the tent, leaving the two of them alone once more.

Brio's expression and tone turn serious. "Is she right?" he asks. "Did you go through all this just for me?"

Whatever mirth Evie felt leaves her. She sighs, not wanting to confront this now, just as she didn't before the Sicclunan's night raid on the Savage camp.

"I allowed myself to become a Savage for you," she admits. "But I didn't know what that meant at the time. I do now."

Brio cocks his head, curiously. "Do you regret it?"

"No," Evie answers without hesitation, surprising even herself. "No, I don't. But not because you're worth it."

Brio nods slowly, lowering his eyes. If that wounded him, it was only a glancing blow, judging by his reaction.

"I loved the boy you were, Brio," she continues. "I respect the man you've become. But I'm not doing this for you. These people trusted me when they had no reason to trust anyone. They're following me. I owe them a chance at reclaiming their lives, however small that chance is. I want to do everything I can to give it to them. As I said, this has all moved far beyond you and me."

"Then you've moved beyond you and me, as well?"

"I think so."

Brio nods. "I love my wife," he says. "That has never and will never change. But . . . seeing you again was enough to confuse me for a time, I will admit."

Evie grins ruefully. "Good. I was confused for years. It took a war to clear things up for me. You deserve a little of that, at least."

Brio grins back, but there's a sadness in his. "I know you said the past and our feelings about it don't matter now, but I'm still sorry. You risked your life to help me. I'll do whatever I can to help you."

Evie takes a deep, cleansing breath.

"Let's just hope we live long enough to need your particular skills," she says.

THE BLACK TURTLE

THERE IS A PART OF TARU THAT BELIEVES THAT IF THEY
return to the Bottoms alone they won't be allowed to leave again. In fact,
if Taru has one recurring nightmare, it is that. The retainer never minded
revisiting the streets and docks that bore them when accompanying Brio
in his capacity as pleader for the Bottoms. It was Brio's father who had
pulled Taru up from these same streets and the docks and oversaw their
training as Gen Stalbraid's retainer, who tasked Taru with protecting
him and his son and their kith-kin. That mission, and Taru's singular
focus upon it always overrode any fear entering the minor nether realm
of the Bottoms would otherwise inspire.

It is much different on their own, Taru finds.

Taru presents arms for the inspection of the Aegins with their
steel tridents stationed at the arch. They take far too long scrutinizing the proofs on each blade that signifies its lawful carry within the
city limits. Taru listens disinterestedly and silently to their grumbled
diatribe about how the law allowing Gens to keep armed retainers
should finally be repealed, and how it is an affront and danger to
every Aegin brave enough to strap on a baldric and dagger. Taru
flatly ignores their predictable suspicions concerning the retainer's
race and the Aegins' thinly veiled disgust toward Taru's obvious
Undeclared status.

The smell of the water and the perpetual odor of fishmonger's fare churns Taru's stomach, but only for the memories those olfactory assaults recall. The retainer marches past the grand row of Crachian merchant and military vessels, all of them as tall as keep walls. The wood of their hulls is polished as finely as steel and flashes in the sun in almost the same way.

The Black Turtle is an ugly wedge of wood that doesn't appear to bob atop the water as much as it appears to be sinking with imperceptible sloth. The sails are the color of mud and the rust sheen over its anchor chains are like a muted rainbow. The masthead is a turtle carved from solid blackwood that appears to be diving from the vessel's bow, its stubby limbs spread as wide as their limited reach will allow. A pattern of stars is painted on its belly, an entire constellation that itself forms the vague shape of a turtle.

At the top of the gangplank Taru spies a boatswain calling out orders to the deck crew. The man is stumpy and ugly and he's made even uglier by sucking the juice from a piece of dragonfruit.

"Permission to come aboard!" Taru calls up the gangplank.

The boatswain turns and stares down at the retainer, tossing the deflated piece of fruit into the bay. He squints against the sun, scrutinizing Taru closely for long moments before answering.

"You one of them Undeclared?"

Taru draws in a deep, calming breath and exhales. "I am."

"Never seen one of you up close before."

"I hope you are sufficiently impressed."

The boatswain shrugs. "I've stuck it in plenty of worse lookin' women. Men, too."

Taru white-knuckles the tsuka of the short sword sheathed at their hip, teeth grinding murderously.

"May I come aboard?"

"Crachians ain't allowed on Rok vessels unless they're conducting state business."

"I'm a member of Gen Stalbraid here in an official capacity."

The boatswain licks the excess juice from his lips, seeming to ponder those words.

"Yeah, okay, why not. Come on up."

Taru carefully stalks up the flimsy gangplank, the boatswain magnanimously stepping aside and bowing to the retainer with a smile on his face. Taru notices both his upper and lower teeth have been filed perfectly flat and straight.

"I need to speak with your captain."

"I kinda expected you'd say that."

The deck is filled with salty hands, all whom are at least two heads shorter than Taru. The retainer is unfamiliar with the island of Rok or its people. Like the boatswain, every set of teeth Taru can see has been filed down.

The man leads them across the deck to a shaded arch, under which a small puffy figure is reclining.

"Captain, you have a guest. Here on official business, they say."

Staz, the Rok merchant vessel captain, looks like a human lounge chair. She's one of the smallest women Taru has ever seen, and she's utterly engulfed in a full-length wool coat that might've been stung by a thousand bees, so swollen are its folds. Captain Staz's tiny wrinkled face and her head, covered in a cloud of dark, gray-threaded hair, barely rise from the top of the coat, like the turtle the ship is named for recoiling into its shell. Her equally tiny hands are folded in front of her. There are darkened rounds of glass guarding both of her eyes from the light of day.

"You don't look Crachian," the Captain observes.

Taru stiffens. "So I've been told."

"I imagine they confuse you for one of us, don't they?"

"It has been implied a time or two."

Staz grunts. "You don't look like one of us. But your everyday Crachian can't tell the difference between an Islander and a B'ors outrider anyway."

"My name is Taru. I serve Gen Stalbraid as retainer. I am here on behalf of Brio Alania. He left certain articles in your charge. I must claim them."

Staz cocks her head. "Where is Brio?"

Taru expected her voice to match her stature; perhaps high and squeaking like a creature from a folktale. Instead Staz sounds like a sage speaking from atop a mountain.

"He was . . . taken. We do not know where. We only know he is alive, or at least he was several weeks ago."

The Rok captain's lips purse tightly, though she doesn't seem entirely surprised by this news.

"I don't know you," Captain Staz says, less an accusation and more a puzzled observation.

"Brio always chose to visit you alone," Taru explains. "To keep your confidence as well as his own. I often accompanied him as his protector when he came to the Bottoms."

"Brio is a good boy. His father brought him here many times when he was a child. I enjoyed watching him run around the deck, playing pirate. I never had any children of my blood. The sea gets jealous, you know."

"I am afraid I do not. I have never been one for boats or the water."

The Black Turtle's crew laughs, though its captain remains quiet.

"Brio told me nothing of you," Staz said. "What did he tell you of me?"

"The same."

Staz nods. "A good boy. His father also saved my life, a long time ago. I was a guest in your dungeons during the Fifth Invasion of Rok, the last invasion, as it turned out. When the war ended, Brio's father negotiated the release of all Rok's children from Crachian custody. No small feat, I assure you. Your Protectorate Ministry wanted to murder us out of spite."

"I . . . have never heard of this conflict before. This invasion you speak of."

Again, the crew laughs at Taru's ignorance.

Staz does not. She only smiles thinly, staring at Taru's knees through her blackened shades.

"Of course you haven't," she patiently explains. "Those who rule over you without name don't tell your people about the wars they win, let alone the ones they lose. Crache tried for generations to conquer our mother island and her children. They even succeeded briefly a time or two. But no matter how many ships and Skrain they sent, Rok's children always repelled them in the end. We refused to be conquered. It must have frustrated your nameless rulers to no end, that the great machine they've built that feasts on many kingdoms and realms and nations could not eat one tiny island. In the end, they chose to do the one thing Crache never does. They compromised. Rok possesses qualities whose grace they require, you see. So, now we trade instead of fight. We are permitted to dock and offload pieces of Rok, as long as we do not 'taint' the citizenry by leaving the ship."

It makes sense to Taru, with what they know about the Savage Legion; that Crache could wage such silent war, although Taru can't believe Crache could not defeat a small island nation.

"I tell you all this so that you know who I am, and what I owe Brio and his Gen."

"I can appreciate that."

"I know Crache has no love for what they call the 'Undeclared.' So I doubt very much you're a spy for them. I would offer to take you back to Rok. We have no such prejudices against the twin-spirited there. But this also is part of our bargain with your people. We do not mix among you and none of you are allowed to travel to Rok."

"Again, I appreciate your words. Does that mean you will give me the articles Brio entrusted to your care?"

"No."

Taru stares down at the small plush pile.

"No?"

"Brio left me no such instructions, though the ones he did leave

393

were very clear. I am to relinquish what you seek to no one save him. Perhaps he did not wish to endanger anyone else. Perhaps he simply did not think to provide a contingency. He seemed hurried. In either case, I can only follow the instructions I have."

"Captain Staz," Taru begins carefully, "I cannot leave this ship without those dispatches."

The old bundled-up woman shrugs. "Then you cannot leave this ship."

In scarcely the blink of an eye Taru's hands are filled with both short sword and hook-end.

The jovial mood pervading the deck is snuffed out in that hiss of steel against leather. Every member of the crew not standing leaps to his or her feet. Taru watches half a dozen weapons drawn, hears twice that many being drawn and picked up. Rok blades are strangely curved, turning forward toward the end, almost as if each sailor is holding their dagger backward. Taru can imagine the chopping power of such blades.

The retainer slowly kneels and places both their weapons upon the deck, relinquishing them there and standing.

"I hold no man in this world more dear than Brio Alania," they announce to the deck. "He held fewer dear than Captain Staz. You are her crew. I will not disrespect Brio by taking the life of any hand on this deck. But I *am* leaving here with Brio's possessions."

Staz smiles her thin smile. "You intend to defeat us all with your bare hands, do you?"

Taru nods. "I intend to try."

Many of the deckhands tense at those words, choking the handles of their weapons a little tighter. Several edge just a few spare inches closer toward the patch of deck supporting Taru. The collection of hardened sailors is like one animal with many limbs, all of them preparing to strike.

The Rok captain laughs. It's the sound of a file dragging against soft steel. She claps her tiny, barely visible hands together in appreciation of Taru.

"Little Brio chose his people well," Staz says. "Very well, I should say."

Taru feels the mood of the deck shift once again. Bodies relax and several of the sailors add to their captain's laughter.

The retainer feels a modicum of relief, but quickly tamps it down. Nothing has been resolved yet, and a fight may still come.

"I have a question I need ask you," Captain Staz says to Taru.

The retainer nods.

"You know you cannot win. My crew will cut you to pieces, many of them, seeing as you are a big one. Even if you take two or three of them with you, there's no hope of victory here. You cannot retrieve the thing you want. Why fight knowing for certain you will die?"

"I don't fear death," Taru says without hesitation.

"That is half an answer. What is the rest?"

Taru is caught only for a moment, and then, "I fear failing the ones who've put their trust in me. The ones . . . the ones I love."

"This is worse than death?" Staz asks as if she's surprised by the notion, though it's clear she's only baiting Taru.

The retainer nods. "It is to me."

"I wish we could take you back to Rok with us. I believe you would thrive there. You are very much like one of her children. I would have enjoyed having a child of my blood like you."

Taru recognizes the scope of such a compliment, but is ill equipped to respond. Luckily, Captain Staz isn't awaiting an answer. She summons a deckhand and whispers something in the young girl's ear before sending her scurrying away. After several moments the girl returns with her hands clasped around a worn binder fashioned from thick horsehide. It's enclosed by a flap and toggle bound together with a cord of catgut. The binder is large enough to hold a stack of parchment.

Staz takes it from the girl and extends the binder toward Taru. "Go with whatever gods watch over you. And tell Brio he owes his old Aunty Staz a visit . . . when he returns to us."

Taru quickly bends down and snatches up the short sword and

hook-end from the deck, sheathing both weapons expertly. The retainer reaches out and takes the binder from the small, bundled woman.

"I thank you. I give you my word I will use this as Brio intended."

Captain Staz refolds her hands and nods.

Taru carefully fits the binder beneath their leather breastplate and bows deeply to the Rok vessel's mistress. The retainer turns and tromps across the wooden deck. Taru halts just short of the gangplank, uncertain, but in the end the retainer turns back to address Staz.

"I think I should like to visit Rok one day. I would hope to see you there."

Captain Staz bows her head. "I wish for a world in which this would be possible."

Taru raps gloved knuckles against their leather breastplate, feeling the binder beneath shift subtly.

"It is coming."

MARCHING TO A
HEADLESS DRUM

THE WASTELANDS ARE TURNING LUSH AND GREEN BENEATH their marching feet.

"Clearest sign we're nearin' the Crachian border," Mother Manai remarks, reaching down to pluck several blades as rich as jade from the ground and rub them between her fingers. She lets the wind take the remnants and inhales against her stained fingertips gratefully.

Evie is marching alongside the Elder Company at the head of a Savage snake composed of blue-runed faces. Their B'ors counterparts follow, silent and stoic and never losing pace. The Sicclunans, on foot and on horseback, round out the column in front of the rogue Legionnaires. A company of Sirach's outriders and the best of the B'ors scouts have been sent ahead, while more of her stealth warriors flank them from cover to guard against any trace of an ambush.

"The border doesn't move, does it?" Evie asks, although it's clear she's already discerned the answer.

Mother Manai smiles ruefully, shaking her head. "Not since before I was born, I imagine."

A stallion whinnies and Evie turns her head to see Sirach astride her mount, falling back to join them.

"Continuing to unravel that shiny Crachian tapestry, are we, General?" the Sicclunan captain asks Evie, invoking her unofficial title with relish and a grin.

"They keep taking land and territory, but they've stopped extending the border."

Sirach nods, the expansive brim of her hat nodding along with her. "They've pushed as far as they can while continuing to sustain the divine paradise they've built for their citizens."

"And they sustain it by stripping everything beyond the border, right down to the bones of the world, and feeding it all to the cities."

"You can't argue with the results," Sirach says, only a drop of bitterness poisoning her jovial tone.

"I didn't notice any of this when they were carting us to the front," Evie marvels.

"You're seeing a lot you never saw before," Sirach reminds her.

With that, the Sicclunan warrior puts heels to her mount and takes off at a gallop, riding up the column and eliciting a barreling wave of cheers from her soldiers.

"That girl is something," Mother Manai says.

Evie nods. "Of all the things she could be, yes, she is indeed something."

"I think in spite of all that brash, she's soft on you."

"Maybe she is."

"And you?" Mother Manai asks.

"My love life is complicated enough as it is," Evie dryly laments.

It was strange enough for her to part with Brio after making finding and protecting him the center of her life for so long. It was agreed between everyone, except him, that Brio belonged back at the Sicclunan's hidden camp to await the outcome of the border battle. Evie had to remind him that even if he still possessed both legs, he was no warrior to begin with, and in the high likelihood the rest of them were killed, the Sicclunan leadership would need someone like Brio who knows the Crachian mind and bureaucracy from the inside.

Evie admires the man he's become. She once truly loved the boy, and she's found it difficult separating the two.

Bam continues his new habit of perpetually flanking her protectively as they march toward their fate.

"Why do you keep that hood pulled so low all the time, Bam?" she asks.

Nothing at first, and then his deep hound dog voice murmurs, "They said my face scares the children."

Evie's brow furrows. "Who said? What children?"

Bam motions with the hammerhead of his mallet at Lariat and Diggs who've been keeping their own Council on the march, laughing at war stories and foul jokes.

"I fought with Lariat in the alleys before the Aegins took us. That's why m'face looks like this. The man who ran the fights told me to keep my face covered because it could scare children in the street."

Evie frowns. "He sounds like a man who needs his ass kicked, and he was just teasing you, cruelly. I like your face. It reminds me of a sock puppet I had when I was a girl. I always smiled when I looked at it."

Bam tilts his head toward her. He doesn't raise his hood, but Evie glimpses a fleeting smile on his thick, scarred lips.

They march an hour past dusk and then make a cold camp. No tents are erected or wagons unloaded; the Sicclunans have only a few wagons, and they're all reserved for pilfered Crachian supplies, and their armorists and surgeons. Fires are built and everyone is watered and fed with the barest amount of dry rations, save for the B'ors, who refuse without explanation (Evie has learned no member of the B'ors is fond of explaining themselves or their actions, at least to outsiders) to eat or drink anything offered to them by the Sicclunans. They draw their own rations and water from pouches and skins carried by each warrior, their food consisting mainly of roots and dried berries, and the occasional piece of jerked animal flesh.

The three forces naturally group with their own kind, keeping to their own fires and eating and commiserating among themselves without breaking ranks.

Sirach is the only exception. Evie has settled around a small campfire with the rest of the Elder Company, reclining on the cool, thriving grass and reveling in the feel of it. She lets her eyelids rest for only a moment, and when she pulls them back her Sicclunan counterpart is sitting cross-legged beside her, sharpening one of her crescent-bladed daggers with a worn whetstone.

"Shunned by your own?" Evie asks.

Sirach grins, eyes transfixed on the edge of the blade she's refining. "I've put all my children to bed and tucked them in. I thought I'd make certain your rough and tumble brood were enjoying the accommodations."

Evie inhales deeply. "I'm certainly enjoying the air."

"Yes, it does lack the acrid undercurrents of our rolling wastes."

"You spoke of building your 'last home' in the treetops. Is it still lush there?"

"Oh yes. Everything is green and alive. It's near the water. And it has yet to suffer a single Crachian boot print. We could really make something of it if we weren't constantly defending it from the likes of you."

There's no malice in that final accusation, just one of her usual jibes.

"You deserve that chance," Evie says.

"We deserve a lot more than that, but I'd take it, gladly."

They hear voices rising only a few yards away, and then see legs rushing past them toward the source of those voices. What begins as excited chatter soon escalates into a mangled chorus of angry shouting.

Sirach sighs. "Well. I wondered when this would begin. I almost thought we'd make it to the real battle first."

"What?" Evie asks, not understanding. "What's going on?"

Sirach is already on her feet and turning toward the commotion. Evie quickly springs up and joins her. The two of them soon have to push their way through a crowd of packed shoulders, all of them facing the same direction.

One of the Sicclunan infantry soldiers and a B'ors warrior are circling each other while a larger circle of their peers goad them on toward clashing. The Sicclunan has drawn a short sword, while the B'ors brandishes a long stone knife with a jagged blade.

"What's the meaning of this?" Evie demands.

The B'ors warrior is practically frothing. "She killed my sister!"

"It wasn't me!" the soldier insists.

"I remember your face! It was the Fight for the Fruit of the Last Trees! My sister was fleeing with a wound and you cut her down from behind!"

"I wasn't even part of that battle! I never touched her!"

"Then you wear the armor of the one who did!"

"Empty your hand!" Sirach orders the soldier.

The infantrywoman looks to her silently, obviously unwilling to directly disobey Sirach, but also hesitant to stand defenseless in front of an angry B'ors.

Evie searches out Yacatek with her eyes, finding the woman standing silently only a few feet away at the edge of the spectating crowd, watching without expression.

"Yacatek! Order this warrior to sheath their knife!"

"Why?" the Storyteller asks, genuinely incredulous.

Evie sighs. "Because we have a bigger war to fight. Together."

Yacatek shrugs. "This fight is theirs. Let them have it. We will know who is right when one of them is left standing."

"I have no fight with your people who bear the blue marks!" the B'ors warrior shouts at Evie, his eyes never leaving the Sicclunan soldier. "We have banded with them and suffered the same whip at their side! But *this* one is no different from the Skrain, than all the steel serpents who hunt my people!"

"We have never hunted your people!" Sirach fires back at him. "We've fought over the scraps we've been left by Crache and their Skrain, and you've killed as many of us as we've killed of you!"

Evie steps between the two opposing fighters. "We're marching to kill Skrain, and we can't spare either of you. If you live through *that* battle, you can turn your blades on each other and whomever else you like. But not here and not now!"

She holds the eyes of the B'ors warrior as she speaks that last, knowing any sign of weakness will render those words hollow.

The warrior looks from Evie to Yacatek, who offers him nothing.

Behind Evie, the Sicclunan infantrywoman slowly lowers her sword and relaxes her fighting posture.

Watching her over Evie's shoulder visibly takes some of the fight out of the B'ors warrior. He stares into Evie's eyes, his own still burning with the pain of great loss, although beneath that there's an even greater sadness. He takes a step back and slowly sheathes his stone knife.

Evie bows to him respectfully to show her gratitude. After he's walked away, she turns to the infantrywoman and nods to her gratefully as well.

The crowd begins to disperse, some relieved and others loudly disappointed. Evie looks for Sirach.

One of her Special Selection soldiers is whispering something privately in her ear. She listens without a change in expression, then nods to the soldier, who quickly turns and jogs away.

"What is it?" Evie asks.

Sirach sounds genuinely intrigued. "We have a visitor, it seems."

"Should I be worried?"

Sirach arches a brow. "Was there any particular reason for you to *stop* worrying?"

Before Evie can press her further, a fresh commotion arises as bodies part to permit a trio through the camp.

Two of Sirach's black-masked warriors, stationed to guard the perimeter from the shadows, bear a Savage between them clad in ratty furs. The coin poisoning his blood has raised blue runes only on one-half of his face. The Savage needs both hands to support the twisted-up end of a bulging and dampened-dark sack held in front of his body. It looks like a rat catcher's sack, viscous-soaked and rancid and drawing flies even as he moves.

The Sicclunans march him before Evie and then stop. Their charge doesn't appear frightened, just weary and confused.

"He says he's a messenger," Sirach explains. "He was sent here from the border garrison, by an old friend of yours."

Evie's eyes are full of questions, but she keeps them to herself as she watches the Elder Company forming around her, staring at their visitor suspiciously.

"Who sent you here?" Mother Manai asks the man directly.

"Laython," he says in a shrill voice. "I've a message for the . . . the uh . . . Sparrow General."

Evie shoots a glance at Sirach, who shrugs with that devilish grin of hers as if to say, *I tried to warn you.*

"I was kind of hoping you'd killed him," Evie all but grumbles under her breath.

Mother Manai laughs. "He wouldn't die that easily. I've no doubt he chased after the Skrain who fled."

"Why would he send a Savage to us?" Evie asks.

Diggs shrugs. "Why would the Skrain waste a trained soldier or page? Savages are disposable. If we keep the boy it's just one more piece of fodder they'll have to sweep away."

"I want to join you!" the messenger quickly yelps. "I want to stay! Please don't send me back."

"What's the message, boy?" Lariat demands. "Let's have that first."

The Savage swallows. As he speaks it's obvious he's not reciting a speech he memorized as much as remembering the important facts he was issued.

"Laython says the price on all yer coins is doubled. He says don't expect no more Savages after me to join your side. He says I'm the last one you'll get."

"He sent you all the way here just to tell us that?" Biggs asks, dubious.

"The sack," Lariat says. "What's in the sack, boy?"

Evie looks up at the broom-mustached elder Savage. The expression on his face is unusually serious.

The man glances between the black-masked warriors holding him.

"Let him go!" Lariat barks.

The warriors stare at him through the thin eye slits in their hoods with obvious contempt, then they both look to Sirach.

She nods, and they release their hold on the Savage.

Laython's messenger steps forward, cautiously. Without another word he untwists the top of the sack and upends the putrid bulging burlap.

Instead of dead rats, the severed heads of half a dozen men and women tumble from within. They've already begun to rot and several of them crack like eggs when they hit the soft ground. The smell that's unleashed in their wake is enough to gag spectators several dozen yards away. Everyone gathered around the messenger can make out the faded runes on what's left of their faces.

Savages, all.

"Who are they?" Evie asks with a hand clamped over her mouth and nose.

"Us," Mother Manai answers her in the coldest tone Evie has heard the woman invoke.

"They're the rest of the Elder Company," Diggs explains calmly, though it's clear from the way his handsome features have dropped he's as shocked and repulsed as the rest of them.

Lariat approaches the messenger slowly, almost tentatively. Evie has yet to witness such somber and delayed behavior in the perpetually raucous man.

"You knew what was in the sack?" he asks the messenger in a quiet voice that might belong to someone else entirely.

The Savage nods.

Lariat launches his right fist with an awesome speed and power that defies both his advanced age and rotund frame. When that fist collides with the messenger's jaw he collapses onto the ground as if the hand of a God Star itself pressed him to the earth. Lariat takes one step over the messenger's crumpled form and drops to his knees, mounting the already dazed Savage on the ground.

"Lariat—" Evie begins, striding forward only to have Mother Manai roughly grab her by the shoulder.

She looks back at Manai and sees the many lines of the older woman's face hardened into a warning expression. Mother Manai shakes her head, slow and definite.

Evie watches helplessly as Lariat begins pummeling the messenger's face. The Elder Company's champion pugilist isn't wearing the barbed leather straps over his knuckles, so he uses the points of his elbows, alternating between them like pistons. No one speaks and no one intercedes. There is total silence as Lariat brutalizes the man beneath him, chopping away with bone at the man's rune-stained features until blood and gore overtake them all.

No one stops Lariat, he simply runs out of momentum on his own, like a machine wound to perform a specific task. When his elbows stop falling there's no distinguishing the messenger's blood from Lariat's own juices up and down his arms. His face is passive, almost calm, except for the heavy exertion of his breathing. What's left of the messenger's face is no longer recognizable as human, Savage or otherwise.

Lariat slowly rises, his knees creaking loudly in the abject silence of the camp.

The first pair of eyes his meet belong to Evie, who is still watching him with that needless expression.

"Was *he* the one who deserved that?" she asks him seriously.

When Lariat speaks, again so contrarily soft in tone, he sounds far more sad than angry. "He rode near a hundred miles with that sack in tow. He coulda buried 'em. He coulda told us what happened in private, like. What he didn't need to do was dump 'em infronta everyone like this. He wanted to join us, but he was no Savage. He was a Skrain with a coin in his guts, whether he knew it or not, no better'n a trained dog."

"This was an attack," Yacatek adds, and it's clear she's seconding Lariat's position. "This man made himself culpable in our enemy's attack. We cannot bear such betrayal among our own band."

"Not all traitors carry knives in the dark," Sirach says to Evie.

Evie looks back at Mother Manai, whose expression remains unchanged. Evie realizes why the older woman stopped her. Gazing around at their three separate forces, she sees them all galvanized in that moment, each one, whether they be Sicclunan or Savage or B'ors seeing themselves in Lariat's actions, and their enemy in the mangled face of the corpse at his feet. Rather than becoming demoralized by the sight of Savage heads rolling across the healthy green grass of the Crachian plains, their rebel army is hardening like a quenched blade forged from several different billets of steel.

Lariat bends down with a quiet groan and retrieves one of the heads from the ground. He holds it aloft by the hair, turning so all three forces can see its face.

"Take a good look!" he commands them. "Remember this well, 'cause every shittin' ass in this camp owes me ten Skrain heads fer erry one they sent us tonight! Do you hear me? I want ye to dump 'em at my feet when we hit that border! Ten Skrain heads fer erry one of ours!"

A thousand voices answer him in unison, crying out their promise to deliver those enemy skulls.

Evie keeps her breath steady and even, attempting to steel herself and maintain a composure that matches Lariat's angry resolve. Staring at those heads, however, is forcing her to confront the end result of her choices. Evie knows she can't afford to question those choices now. They have all come too far and are risking too much. There is no going back. That doesn't stop her from feeling a twisting in her guts as she witnesses what her decisions have wrought.

She thinks of Brio in that moment. She remembers questioning her own motivations in leaving her life behind a second time because of him. Looking back from where she now stands, Evie considers the possibility she chose her mission to rescue Brio precisely because it was hers to choose. She wasn't given a choice when Gen Stalbraid turned her away as a girl. Evie wonders if that lingering part of her came here to show Brio she was stronger than that now, to exercise some power she felt she'd lost. Perhaps it was her way of trying to take back control of her life all these years later, as absurd as that seemed to her.

Whatever brought her to this point, Evie knows she has to take control of this situation, if she can. There is only one way she can see to do that without getting them all killed.

Evie slips beside Sirach, whispering in the woman's ear. "There's one head they didn't think to take, and it may be a head that can help us."

Sirach looks at her with the same curious expression she wore as they stared at each other from the ground after Evie unseated Sirach from her horse.

"Whatever's churning in those eyes of yours frightens and thrills me," she says.

"Wait until you hear my plan," Evie warns.

"Is that what you have? A plan?"

"I have an idea that may sprout a plan."

"Is it dangerous?"

"It is, but don't worry, I'm the only one it'll kill. Unless it succeeds, of course."

Evie's expression in that moment is unreadable, and though she can see Sirach has several questions already springing to mind, Evie can only hope Sirach believes her.

SEEK NOT THE EAVES
AT MIDNIGHT

DYEAWAN AND SLEEP HAVE BECOME DISTANT RELATIONS OVER the past several weeks. She still loves her small room, and Dyeawan could never bring herself to resent the first soft bed she's ever called her own. She simply cannot find that place where one's eyes separate from their mind and truly rest. Instead she lies awake, staring at the darkness beyond her window and listening to the island sounds of midnight surf and nocturnal birds. Dyeawan recalls sleeping inside empty barrels and behind garbage bins in alleys for so many years. She marvels at how well she slept then, day or night, despite the cold and the constant fear and the harshness of her surroundings.

Eventually she declares defeat for the evening, pulling herself from the bed and onto the litter of her rebuilt tender. Dyeawan decides to row through the keep until her body tires enough to overcome her mind.

The corridors of the Planning Cadre become a tomb in the dead of night. There are no armed guards stalking about, and there's no enforced curfew keeping the many residents in their quarters. In fact, Dyeawan knows people on every level of the Cadre who work through the night often, finding they do their best work then. However, everyone seems confined to his or her little corner of the keep at this time. It's rare to find anyone traipsing through the corridors.

Dyeawan finds herself paddling toward Edger's quarters before she is truly aware of the action being undertaken by her arms. She's begun to feel she may have treated Edger too harshly. If Dyeawan is going to be a planner and coexist with the others she must learn to set aside her suspicions and distrust.

A seam of warm amber light slices across the corridor. Its source is the door to Edger's private rooms, opened just the scantest inch. Dyeawan can hear voices rising inside, the timbre of the words growing fast and heated. She rolls as quietly as possible up to the door's edge, careful not to place herself in the path of that light where her shadow will be noticeably cast. Dyeawan leans forward from the litter of her tender and creeps a single eye past the edge of the door's frame.

Edger is reclining in a salon chair. His vacant eyes stare at the ceiling as Quan deftly stripes Edger's cheek with a razor, expertly shaving his face.

"I understand it is a requisite of your trade to overreact to virtually everything," Edger says to someone unseen. "However, in this particular instance I do wish you would tamp the weed, as it were."

"I am hardly overreacting."

That voice Dyeawan has come to know well, especially its reprimanding tone. It belongs to Oisin, the Protectorate Ministry agent who seems to act as both roving sentry within the Planning Cadre and liaison between Edger and the Ministry itself. Straining the edge of her viewpoint, Dyeawan is able to glimpse the flourish of a black cape, confirming her suspicion.

"We have consistently advanced the Sicclunan front for more years than I've counted wearing this eagle's eye on my chest," Oisin continues. "In the past few months we have *lost* more ground than at any time on record since the Sicclunan campaign began."

"Considering all that time during which we consistently advanced the front, if we'd lost an inch it would've been a shattering record loss, would it not?"

"We've lost far more than an inch," Oisin counters impatiently.

"Perspective, my friend."

"If I can't make you take this revolt seriously, at least consider the practical implications. If we do not regain that ground within a fortnight it *will* begin to affect both production and sustainability within the eastern cities. Lumber, steel, fruit, fertile soil, *everything* will begin to reach dangerously low reserves. If it continues we will have no choice but to reroute supplies from the northern and southern cities. Soon after that we'll have the Gens and the citizenry questioning the source of the shortage."

"If Mister Quan accidentally nicks me with his razor I can extrapolate that tiny wound until it becomes the end of the world as we know it if I take it far enough."

"This is happening *now*, Edger!"

"And it will *cease* happening when the rabble reaches the border. This is an aberration, nothing more, and the system we have built will correct it as a body corrects a minor illness. You must calm down."

"I am perfectly calm."

"Yes, I'm watching it drip from your body as we speak."

"At least recall the Savage Legion," Oisin pleads. "Bring them back from the front until this thing is put down."

"Would you take the swords out of the Skrains' hands, as well? You want to deprive our forces of their greatest weapon before the first serious opposition they've faced, as you say, since before you pinned that eagle eye to your chest?"

"The Savages have proven themselves unreliable on several occasions—"

"They're Savages! They're *meant* to be unreliable. Their strength lies in that unpredictability. What has occurred is a matter of discipline and readiness, that's all. These are easily solved in the field. I've seen to it with the taskers."

"You will forgive me, but I must question your perspective on the Savage Legion as of late, particularly when we consider that conscripting a dissident Gen member is no doubt what spawned this rebellion in the first place!"

There is a brief silence. Dyeawan shifts her focus through the thin crack from Oisin's cape to Edger reclining in his chair. He's not bothering with any of his painted facemasks.

"I fail to see the correlation," he says a moment later.

"Conscripting mindless dregs is one thing. Conscripting those with intelligence and leadership ability and scorn for the Crachian government is quite another."

"They are all the same when they are stripped bare. You are reaching, Oisin."

"I don't think so."

"Really? Were you thinking when you took it upon yourself to send Savages into the Gen Circus? Explain to me how your perspective is beyond scrutiny in the face of actions such as that."

Oisin grits his teeth. "They were disposable and less recognizable to the average Crachian eye than Ministry agents or Aegins in the event they failed. And I maintain they would've been remembered as no more than two tattooed dregs if the woman hadn't survived to press the matter."

"Hypotheticals serve no purpose to us."

"I recognized my error and saw to the disposal of those bodies before anyone could confirm their identities. I took responsibility and *learned* from my error."

"And yet the Xia woman does persist, does she not? Is that not why we needed to eliminate her in the first place? Her inability to simply accept the loss of her husband and her Gen and go quietly into obscurity. She would not let the matter rest. And she still won't. If anything, she has become emboldened and even more vocal in public about the situation. Her persistence, and our problem, has only been exacerbated."

"She is being *allowed* to persist at this point because she is too visible to make disappear. If a woman who is raving that her husband was abducted is suddenly abducted herself, they no longer sound like ravings."

"That is my very point, Oisin. Any situation is all in how you frame it."

A massive shape abruptly eclipses the world beyond the crack. Dyeawan's breath catches in her throat and she throws her head back as the door is pulled open.

Mister Quan looms above her, staring down at Dyeawan quizzically. She's completely obscured from view by his oversize frame.

She shakes her head, mouth opening to offer some apology or excuse.

Quan quickly brings a long, slender digit to his lips, silently instructing her to remain quiet.

Dyeawan closes her mouth and nods.

"Is there a problem, Quan?" Edger asks.

"I have forgotten what I was stepping out to do."

"It must not have been so terribly important, then."

Quan points down the corridor, his face wearing a sincere and urgent expression.

Again, Dyeawan nods. She quickly and gratefully reverses her tender and wheels herself away from the door.

By the time she hears it close and a steel lock snap home, she's halfway down the corridor.

Dyeawan finds she is suddenly exhausted, and sleep cannot come fast enough.

REUNION

EVIE HAD JUST BEGUN TO ENJOY FEELING CLEAN. WHILE IT'S true her last real bath was perhaps months ago at this point, aligning herself with Sirach and her Sicclunans had granted Evie release from her Savage rags and the filth of everyday life that came with them. She'd gratefully taken a damp cloth to her face and body and meticulously removed every smudge of dirt and every sheen of her own collected and unsavory juices. Evie had reveled in the feel of unsoiled clothes against her skin, as well. She'd even brushed out her hair, which has gained an inch since she was conscripted.

She's traded those fresh pieces of clothing for the tattered and tainted garments of half a dozen rogue Savages who were more than happy to swap with her. That's torture enough, but Sirach insisted she still appeared far too clean and kempt. Evie's face and hands are once again covered in muck, and she's not even certain all of it is mud. Her hair has also been tangled and snared and splattered with filth.

Convincing Sirach of the potential and necessity of her plan was easy enough, no doubt because Sirach has learned to live with the specter of death haunting her every waking action. Convincing the Elder Company to let her make the attempt was another beast to tame entirely. Mother Manai was ready to weep like the grandmother she is over one of her own squandering their life, while Lariat flatly forbade Evie from the course she purposed.

Bam, on the other hand, only insisted on accompanying her, but Evie knew if she was to have any hope of penetrating the Skrain garrison she had to be on her own. He actually pushed back his hood to plead his case, and Evie found she was touched beyond reason, but she stood her ground on the matter. She did ask Bam to look after Sirach and Brio should she fail to return, emphasizing the sanctity of the task to her and his importance in fulfilling its duties. It seemed to placate him as much as anything could.

Evie dons the black head and body veil of a Sicclunan night warrior over her rags, and two of Sirach's best stealth fighters guide her over the border and through the Skrain patrols without incident. It's Evie's first up-close experience with watching the shadow warriors operate, and if she didn't fully appreciate the Sicclunan's discipline and training before, she's now in awe of both. The black-masked warriors move without a single sound, their hands and feet seeming to touch the ground without disturbing it. They can both see perfectly in the almost total darkness, and for a mile ahead. They become every shadow they enter, and surveying the landscape ahead, seem to possess the ability to instantly discern a route, however circuitous, that will conceal them from even the most direct gaze.

They instructed her to stay close and do what they do, and those are orders Evie follows to the letter, doing her best to match them step-for-step, crawl-for-crawl, always keeping pace on their heels. It becomes more arduous with each passing hour, but Evie is determined. She compels her mind to remain sharp and attentive and her limbs to never slacken.

The night warriors lead her through a grove of dying trees, and at the edge of the grove, concealed in the brush, they silently bid her to join them shoulder to shoulder to peer out across the valley beyond.

The garrison is an ominous keep of black stone guarding the main road through the western border of Crache. The towers on either side are filled with the Skrain's best archers and artillery weapons. The keep walls extend around an expansive ward of rice paddies and fish hatcheries that feed the tall bamboo barracks rising from its center. Anyone traveling the main road attempting to enter or leave Crache has no choice but to pass through the keep. On any normal day the garrison would hold five hundred soldiers, but across the border the days have become anything but normal.

Circumventing the keep walls is no easy task, but it pales beside the larger challenge; the garrison is completely overrun by Skrain and Savage Legionnaires. The barracks and ward have overflowed beyond the walls, and a huge encampment has been erected along the main road leading to and from the keep gates. It adds several further layers to her approach, and Evie knows she'll have to go on alone; the Sicclunan stealth fighters will only increase her risk of discovery beyond this point.

She feels a sudden rush of hesitation as they leave her to the meat of her mission, a few moments in which Evie actually considers abandoning her plan entirely and returning to the fleeting safety of her cold rebel base camp. She actually feels herself shaking, from her toes all the way through the ends of her ratted hair. It's enough to convince her that not only shouldn't she do this, she's obviously incapable of it.

Fortunately, that sudden bout of panic is only the feverish precursor to a moment of clarity. Staring at the lights of the roadside camp, Evie realizes the situation isn't more difficult, it's actually providing her with the perfect cover and concealment. She's dressed as a Savage Legionnaire and wears the blue runes. If the garrison was locked down, she'd have to scale the walls and risk being found outside and alone with no explanation.

As it stands, there's an overwhelming mass of people who look just like her wandering freely and fervently inside and outside the keep without suspicion from the Skrain.

Evie waits until the perimeter patrols have passed. She sheds her night colors and creeps swiftly across the valley to the nearest uninhabited edge of the camp she can navigate. The familiar clamor of many voices colliding over the crackling of a hundred firelights fills her ears and moments later she's stepped into the flow of the camp itself, seemingly unnoticed. She pilfers a horn of rice wine from an inattentive Legionnaire and adds a drunken sway to her walk. It carries her all the way through the outlying encampment and through the open gates of the keep.

The Legion fills the ward inside the walls; the Skrain not sleeping in tents must be enjoying the seclusion and shelter of the barracks. Evie has never seen so many Savages gathered in one place. There must be hundreds if not thousands of them, conscripts from every city in the Crachian nation. It's easy enough to move among their numbers, particularly the ones drawn from the back alleys and wharfs and disused nooks of places like the Bottoms, the simple out-of-doors folk who've never held a weapon and don't belong on a battlefield. They huddle together in silent, dead-eyed groups, keeping close to the nearest fire or gnawing on some tasteless strip of meat that was dried for a sliver of a moment before it turned rancid.

The truly deserving of this fate, the condemned, murderers and rapists and thieves who prey on the weak and defenseless, they move in raucous packs howling in anticipation of battle, and are also easy to avoid. This many Savage Legionnaires also means there are four times as many taskers as Evie is accustomed to seeing in camp. They stalk between the tents and around the fires, clubs and whips in hand, their hard leathery faces unstained by blue runes surveying every coin-tainted Savage with suspicion and perpetual disdain. Their presence seems enough to enforce the Legion's rules against brawling and raping. It helps that they disarm the Legion between battles; the only weapons in camp are flagons of rice wine, carried by most of the criminal rabble.

Evie can only assume they've discontinued the Revel until the rebellion is put down, although whether it's intended as a punishment or mandated out of necessity she can't know.

Evie notices many of the battle-ready Legionnaires are enthusiastically slathering their faces with a deep blue grease. They then smooth it out until precisely half their face is completely covered with a thick sheen of the foul-smelling muck, as if their flesh runes have spread to overtake the flesh there completely. Evie reasons that this must be how they intend to distinguish conscripted Legionnaires from rogue Savages on the battlefield tomorrow.

She enters a clearing free of tents, necessitated by crops roped off in the middle of the ward. The smell of rice paddies is unappetizing, but the scent of these crops is beyond foul. In fact, they smell like death. Evie quickly realizes it's not the paddies assaulting her nostrils, however. It's a new decoration that's been added to the ward recently, after the arrival of the Savage Legion. Evie's gaze is drawn high into the air above the paddies, and what it beholds curdles every drop of blood in her veins.

The decapitated bodies of those Elder Company members Laython slaughtered and whose heads he sent to the upstart rebellion have been impaled on towering wooden spikes. The spikes are planted in the middle of the Savage Legion camp inside the keep walls. They're arranged in a perfect row, the headless corpses elevated high enough to be seen from every edge of the ward. As the heads were intended to be seen by Evie and her forces, the bodies are a message to the remaining Legionnaires who might be tempted by their fellow Savages' betrayal.

Her eyes drift down from the atrocity to the base of the spikes. She sees him for the first time since the day of her inaugural battle as a Savage. Laython is reclining in a bamboo chair draped with thick and perfectly tanned furs, stripped to the waist and enjoying the thickly redolent smoke of a long bone pipe. His massive, doughy torso is a mess of strange scars at whose origins Evie can't even guess, but she refuses to let them evoke even the scantest wraith of sympathy within her.

Laython is staring up at the grotesque remains of his victims like a grandfather enjoying the warmth of the evening's hearth on his weary bones. A scrawny Savage little more than a boy of thirteen or fourteen kneels beside his chair, carefully oiling Laython's night-black leather armor pieces. In one moment the boy's hand slips, and he compresses the oilskin too hard, drenching one of Laython's pauldrons.

As Evie looks on, the chief tasker of the Savage Legion kicks the boy in the face with his bare foot. There's no outrage in the strike, no emotion, there is only detached impulse. The boy falls onto his back, and Laython uses the same foot to press the side of his face into the grass.

"I'm sorry," the boy squeaks. "I'm so sorry!"

Evie's hand seems to move on its own, delving inside a special patch of fabric sewn into her blouse. Its purpose is concealing the cloth scabbard there and the small dagger it cradles. Her hand closes around the dagger's smooth, worn, welcoming handle, and an inch of steel clears the sheath before Evie realizes what she's doing and stays her hand.

You could do it, a voice very much like Sirach's whispers inside her head. *You could kill him. Right here and now. You know how to do it.*

She does. Evie has certainly killed, but she has never murdered anyone in cold blood. She's no assassin. But she was trained in the knife. She knows how to creep up silently from behind and clear his chin with her defending hand, knows where and how to apply pressure with the dagger's edge, and how to slash so the blade opens his throat wide. He wouldn't make any sound. He would simply wriggle like a fish for a few moments until the cold hand left in the wake of his fleeing life's blood claimed him.

Laython lifts his foot away from the boy's cheek and returns to smoking his pipe and gazing fondly at his macabre artistry. The boy pushes himself up from the grass, wiping the crushed green blades and rich black earth from his face with one hand.

Watching, Evie's brief and murderous reverie is broken. She slips the exposed steel of the dagger's blade back inside its sheath and lets go of the handle, removing her hand from the secret pocket.

This is not what she came here to do.

She leaves him there, walking in a direction just out of Laython's periphery until she can duck behind a tent.

He never even looks away from those headless corpses.

It takes Evie another few minutes of searching the camp before she finally reaches the true objective of her mission. The sight of the armory wagon overburdened with its hundreds of rusted and jagged steel and iron limbs transports Evie back in her mind to the first time she met Spud-Bar. She remembers sorting through the junk pile of second-hand weapons remaindered for the Legion, just hoping to find one solid instrument that might see her through her first battle.

That day seems like a lifetime ago from where she stands now.

Spud-Bar squats on a stubby tree stump in front of one of the wagon's wheels, sharpening swords against a small grinding wheel the armorist has placed in front of the stump. There's an array of mostly shoddy, poorly forged blades splayed out across the grass around the wheel.

Evie approaches the armory wagon as silently as possibly without appearing as though she's trying to be stealthy. Before Spud-Bar takes notice of her presence, Evie has slid onto the grass beside the armorist, sitting halfway under the wagon to conceal her face and most of her body from sight.

"What do you need, Savage?" Spud-Bar asks disinterestedly.

"The same thing I always seem to need from you," Evie says, "a favor I have no right to ask."

The moccasin-covered foot of Spud-Bar's powering the grinding wheel stops, but only for a few moments. Nothing else about the armorist's outward demeanor seems to change, and soon that foot is working the wheel twice as fast as it was before.

"You can't be here," Spud-Bar whispers, each word as cold as a winter burial plot.

"I have to be," Evie insists.

"They will tear you apart if you're discovered here. Laython knows *exactly* who you are, Sparrow General. You tend to leave an impression. If they find you here he will give you to the worst scum in this camp as supper. Do you know that?"

"Then I advise you to keep doing precisely what you're doing and not draw attention to us. As I said, I have to be here. There was no other choice. I have a lot of people ready to die tomorrow when this battle begins who are looking to me for a way to survive. And I can only think of one."

Spud-Bar places the newly sharpened sword aside and takes up another place, putting its edge to the revolutions of the stone.

"I'm not involved in that."

"You *have* to be if we're to succeed."

Spud-Bar's emotions finally threaten to froth over. "I delivered your damn message!"

"Quietly, please," Evie calmly reminds the armorist.

"I delivered it," Spud-Bar reiterates, wrangling their self under control. "You said it would be a simple thing. It didn't feel simple."

"You returned unharmed and without any further incident, didn't you?"

Spud-Bar sighs. "Yes."

"And I thank you. I trusted you because you're worthy of trust, and strong enough to act in its service. I need those qualities now more than ever."

"Why?"

"We can't defeat the Legion *and* the Skrain on the open field."

"You'll turn no more Savages to your cause, I tell you. Executing the Elders would've been warning enough. Laython is offering gold now, and battles taken away from the required hundred for every rogue Savage ear or nose claimed by a Legionnaire before the Skrain take the field tomorrow. He's convinced the whole camp that they can win their freedom and walk away from the Legion rich at the end of a single battle."

"There *have* to be Savages here who are smarter than that," Evie insists. "You are. I am. I know there are others."

"And if there are? What would you have me do, Evie? Or whatever your true name is? Are you and your new friends going to raze the whole garrison? Do you even have any siege weapons between you?"

"No," Evie admits. "We can't attack the garrison. We have to face the Skrain on the open field tomorrow."

"The whisper from the Skrain scouts is you've less than a thousand fighters. Is that true?"

Evie hesitates, then slowly nods. "Close enough to only be slightly untrue."

Spud-Bar's every muscle seems to tense at once. It's clear the armorist wants to scream their frustration and anger in Evie's face, but the dire circumstance surrounding Evie's presence precludes Spud-Bar drawing any attention to them.

"You're mad," the armorist hisses at her. "If you were ever in possession of your senses, they've abandoned you altogether!"

Evie's expression hardens. "Lariat, Mother Manai, and the others saw fit to join me. They believed in my plans, and they believe in what we're doing."

"They're mad, too!" Spud-Bar maintains. "And their madness got the rest of their ilk killed!"

"Laython and the Skrain did that, *not* us!"

Spud-Bar turns away from her, frantically moving their gaze around the wagon, searching for any eyes aimed at them and finding none.

"I'm not asking you to lead an uprising here, Spud-Bar. I'm not asking you to risk instigating a slaughter within these walls."

"Then what are you asking of me? What *now*?"

"You're as known and respected among the Legion as any member of the Elder Company. You know the Legion, you know the experienced warriors remaining among them. Most importantly, you know whom you can trust and whom can influence others on our behalf."

"I tell you that knowledge is useless now," Spud-Bar maintains.

"And I tell you that knowledge is worth more than every blade and every soldier who'll take that field tomorrow, if you'll just *help* me."

"Why did you have to do this?" Spud-Bar demands, miserably. "Any of this? *Why?* Why couldn't you just let . . . let . . ."

Their words sputter and die pitifully, and their foot ceases to work the grinder pedal.

Evie leans away from the shadows, seeking Spud-Bar's eyes with her own. She holds the armorist's gaze with as hard and as serious a shine in her eyes as she's ever offered anyone.

"If you can't finish that thought," she says, "then you know exactly why I've done everything I've done. I'm sorry if you feel this isn't fair to you, but I don't care. Do you understand? You're either going to let us all die tomorrow knowing you could've prevented it, or you'll risk your life to help us win. Choose. Now."

Evie can see the hateful words of refusal brewing behind the armorist's eyes. She can see the angels and devils wrestling in her mind. A desperate voice implores her to say more, to convince Spud-Bar, but Evie remains silent. She's put the armorist to the final test, and any more words would only muddy the waters she's attempted to purify.

In the end, Spud-Bar's entire being seems to deflate like a punctured bellows. The armorist stares back at Evie with tragic, defeated eyes.

"What do you want me to do?" Spud-Bar asks.

SLEEP, AND HIS BROTHER DEATH

LEXI GENTLY STRUMS THE THREE STRINGS OF BRIO'S OLD reed-of-the-stone-lake, making every effort to focus on the tune she's attempting to elicit from the classical instrument and not the memory of smashing her own childhood reed on the skull of a blue-veined assassin sent to murder her in her home. It's the first time she's played since Brio's disappearance, or rather the first time she's been able to contemplate such an action without the pangs of loss and fear crippling her.

Daian watches her play from his sickbed, the sight inspiring a tired smile. His wound has closed and appears to be healing. The color has returned to his skin, and he's remained conscious since he first woke, but he still can't stand under his own power. In fact, beyond turning his head and raising his arms, both of which seem to require immense effort, Daian hasn't been able to move much at all. He claims he can still feel his legs all the way down to the tip of his toes and his strength will return in time, but with each passing hour Lexi's concern rises.

She finishes the song with a subtle flourish, her fingertips dancing briefly against the trio of taut strings and for a moment it sounds like rain falling on rose petals.

Daian claps his hands together, able to produce only the barest applause.

"You were right," he says, still sounding impossibly weak. "You really are terrible at that."

Lexi laughs, and it's the flavor of the spontaneous laughter that surprises her with its unabashed volume and intensity. She raises a hand to her mouth, almost embarrassed by the outburst.

"Does laughter violate your formal training?" Daian asks.

Lexi nods. "Entirely."

"We could do with less formality in this nation."

"I agree."

Lexi removes her hand, a silent smile left in the wake of the unrestrained burst of laughter.

"Can I bring you anything?" she asks.

"You've done more than enough for me."

She frowns. "That might be true if we ignored the fact that I caused your current condition. I have to believe those other Aegins attacked you because you took up Brio's investigation."

Daian shakes his head. "This wasn't your fault. You only asked for my help. You couldn't know how deep and how vile the corruption among my own people was."

"But I've cost you so much—"

"You only asked me to do my duty. You reminded me what that duty is. I'm grateful to you for that."

Lexi doesn't know what to say to that. Her hand travels across the bed sheets and lays over his, almost hovering rather than touching.

Daian turns his palm up and clasps his fingers around hers. His grip surprises Lexi with its strength, but she's more taken with the direction of the moment. She deftly slips her hand from his and sets her reed aside.

"When you've fully healed," she says quickly, "I promise you we'll make certain you're able to return to—"

The loud and unexpected echo of a heavy wooden creak rising from the bottom of the tower interrupts her next words. They can both hear heavy footfalls clacking against the stone floor in the silence that follows.

"That must be Taru," Lexi reasons.

"It's too soon," Daian says. "Far too soon."

Lexi stands. "I will go see to it."

"No," Daian insists.

He tries to lean forward, to rise from his sickbed, but the first inch of movement sees him grimacing in pain and falling back against the sheets.

"Stop that!" Lexi commands. "You are in no condition. This is my house. Just rest."

"Go carefully" is the best he can manage through the haze of pain and exhaustion.

Lexi nods. Leaving the room, she gathers the hem of her wrap and descends the tower steps quickly.

The first thing she sees is a mass of black boots awaiting her. She takes the last flight of stairs at an even faster pace. The lamps of the entrance hall make their uniforms look like oil slicks. The three Protectorate Ministry agents with their gaping eagle eye pendants have shut the doors behind them.

Their leader is the bone-white woman with the close-cropped hair to match who interrogated Lexi.

Ginnix bows formally. "Good evening, Te-Gen."

"What are you doing in my home?" she demands. "No one granted you permission to enter here as you please."

The two absurdly contrasting agents who've been surveying Lexi's every move since after the attempt on her life are flanking the pale woman.

"You are by now familiar with my colleagues, Agents Jindo and Nils."

Ginnix waves a black-gloved hand at each man as she says his name. The bald scarecrow is Jindo and the one as round as a wheel of cheese is Nils, it seems. Jindo remains a skeletal monument during the brief introduction, but Nils bows to her, his slick of dark hair flopping forward like a fish on a dry dock.

"Stalking my door doesn't give them the right to enter it unwelcome, either," Lexi maintains.

"I'm afraid we've finally reached the end of civil pretense in this . . . situation."

"I do not take your meaning."

"Of course you do," Ginnix casually insists. "Your Undeclared retainer left your side for the first time since the disappearance of your husband. I can only imagine that the reason must be dire. We know you are colluding with an Aegin and that he was asking a great many questions in the Bottoms about your husband's activities. That same Aegin murdered two of his comrades in an alley shortly thereafter. We discovered their bodies, but of him we found only a great deal of blood. He's here now, isn't he? Did he survive? Perhaps long enough to inform you of the location of certain articles?"

"I have not the slightest notion about anything to which you are referring."

Ginnix waves a hand dismissively. "It's of no consequence," she says. "We will soon have your retainer and whatever they've unearthed in our custody."

Lexi feels the acid edge of panic rising from her guts. She subtly balls her fists and forces a quenching calm over it.

We are not flowers. We do not wilt.

She sidles slowly to her left, taking care to appear to be the exact opposite of a person who is running away.

She bows to them. "I must apologize. However inappropriate, you are in my home. May I invite you into the parlor for refreshment? We can discuss these matters further in comfort there."

She backs through the archway leading into the parlor, then turns and walks slowly past the receiving sofas and chairs to the buffet upon which many bottles of wine and spirits are kept.

Ginnix follows her, the other two agents keeping a respectful distance from her heels.

"I appreciate the offer of hospitality, but I'm afraid there's nothing left to discuss. You'll be coming with us now."

Lexi, her back to them, caresses the long neck of a large bottle with fingers that are beginning to tremble.

"Am I under arrest?" she asks in an even tone.

"Again, we've reached the end of civil pretense," Ginnix reiterates. "You are coming with us. We will utilize you as needed. It's that simple."

"I am not a thing," Lexi says, barely above a whisper.

Her hand closes tightly around the bottle's neck.

"You are a national resource. And this is how that resource serves your nation at this time."

Ginnix steps forward, leaving Jindo and Nils in the archway. She strides past the ornate and lavish furniture, black-gloved hand coiled around the handle of her dagger in its scabbard.

Lexi listens to the approaching footfalls, steeling herself to swing the bottle.

Ginnix has closed half the gap between them when a sudden, awful gargling sound stays her feet and snaps her attention back to the parlor arch.

Nils's shoulders are flung back and his stubby arms splayed awkwardly. His eyes have gone wide and have rolled far back to expose the spidery red veins of their underbelly.

The agent's body twitches to one side and a head of dark hair and two burning eyes rise above Nils's stumpy height.

It's Daian. He's left his sickbed, and not only managed to replace his trousers and boots and make it down the winding tower stairs, he's somehow summoned the strength to creep up behind the agent and end him.

By now Lexi has turned around as well, and the sight of him causes her to forget all about the bottle and using it as a weapon.

The blade of Daian's dagger has impaled Nils at the base of the agent's skull, piercing his brain and scrambling it like the contents of an egg in a frying pan. With nothing left to control his limbs, the only thing keeping his rotund body aloft is Daian's grip on the dagger.

"Three black eagles, all in a tree," Daian intones in the cadence of a child's nursery rhyme. "Count them down and see how they bleed. . . ."

He quickly kisses Nils on the man's chubby, sweaty cheek and pulls his blade free of his skull, allowing Nils's body to collapse in a heap at Daian's feet.

Jindo's dagger is suddenly in the agent's bony hand. His knees bend until they appear bowlegged as the agent crouches down to seek Daian's level for a proper frontal knife attack.

Daian casually, even gracefully steps over Nils, flipping the dagger in his hand as he does and catching it by the handle with ease.

Lexi feels as if she's entered a dream state, especially when her eyes report that Daian is grinning.

Jindo lunges at him. The two trade a series of feints and blocks with their blades, hands, and wrists, each movement faster than a cat's paw. The exchange lasts less than three full seconds, and ends with Daian trapping the wrist of Jindo's knife hand and yanking it downward as the blade of Daian's dagger slices through the skeletal man's throat, opening it wide.

He's already turning away from the dying man by the time the blood sprays half Daian's face.

Ginnix has remained calmly in the middle of the parlor the whole time, gloved fingers encircling her sheathed dagger's handle. She draws and releases a loud, weary breath, the only visible sign of her exasperation with the performance of her agents. Now she skins her blade and takes a step forward, her posture shifting to that of a practiced duelist.

Daian again flips his bloodstained dagger as he enters the parlor.

"Daian—" Lexi begins to call to him.

"Just stay back, Lexi," he orders her in an eerily calm voice she doesn't recognize.

Lexi quickly reaches behind her body and retrieves a pointed stirring stick from the buffet top, enveloping it in the folds of her wrap skirt to hide it from sight.

"For whom are you working, really?" Ginnix demands.

"I am merely a humble servant of Crache," Daian insists, though his grin belies that sentiment.

The Ministry agent's smile is as joyless as a funeral march. "Aren't we all?"

She strikes first, rushing forward and slashing at him from one angle after another, each time in a perfectly centered and straight line. Daian backs away, staying out of her attack range and avoiding her initial volley. When Ginnix loses her initial momentum he swipes at her head, causing the woman to duck down to where he meets her face with his knee. The blow stuns Ginnix and throws her off-balance. She slashes blindly as she blinks and shakes her head to recover her faculties.

Daian seizes the opportunity to ensnare her knife-wielding arm with his own, trapping it. He reverses his grip on his dagger and stabs Ginnix just above her collarbone, piercing the artery there and spraying the parlor ceiling with her blood. An animal sound of surprise and rage escapes her throat as she falls to the plush carpet.

Daian places the sole of his right boot on the agent's chest and jostles her tentatively.

"No black eagles sitting in a tree," he whispers.

"Daian . . . ?"

He looks back at Lexi, almost as if he's forgotten she's standing there.

"Oh, don't be afraid anymore," he softly bids her. "They can't hurt you now. I promise, the Protectorate Ministry will never hurt you again."

Somehow Lexi is anything but soothed by his words.

"You seem . . . very different than you did just a relatively short while ago."

Daian only blinks at her vacantly at first, then a light of realization seems to ignite behind his eyes.

"Oh well." He shrugs, smiling pleasantly. "I'm afraid I wasn't quite as incapacitated as I let on."

"Obviously," Lexi says, glancing at the carved-up corpses that have once again turned her parlor into a charnel house.

Daian's expression turns grave. "I do apologize for deceiving you. That was wrong. You have been nothing but an exceptional hostess, and I thank you."

"It's more than your injuries," she persists. "You appear to be acting . . . quite differently than you did upstairs."

Daian sighs, his demeanor quickly becoming annoyed and impatient. "Yes, well, we're downstairs now, aren't we? And the situation has changed, as you said, from what it was a short time ago."

"How is it different?"

Daian uses the tip of his dagger to very lightly scratch his right temple, smearing a mixture of the three Ministry agents' blood above his eye there.

"Well, I *was* waiting for Taru to return with this mountain of evidence your husband is supposed to have uncovered. I had originally hoped to find it on my own, just as I had hoped to find Brio himself if he was still alive. You see, I really *was* on your side this entire time, Lexi. We sought the same things. We simply have different motivations. But my investigation was cut short, if you'll pardon the choice of words."

"Taru was right," Lexi says. "It was no accident you answered the call and came to the tower the night I was attacked."

Daian shakes his head. "I've been keeping a close eye on your Gen for a very long time. I simply seized an opportunity."

"Is spying on my Gen part of your Aegin duties?"

"Of course not. But being an Aegin makes it much easier. That's why I chose it. It gives me just enough power to perform my true duties while rendering me obscure enough to go unnoticed by our enemies in the Ministry."

" 'Our' enemies? Who do you truly serve, Daian?"

"You'll meet them soon."

"And what do you . . . what do *they* want with Brio, whoever they are?"

"The same thing I want with you, now. You see, plans have changed. My friends have decided you'll serve our purpose well enough."

Daian laughs then. It's a joyless, disturbing sound.

"I'll tell you," he muses. "The Ministry and the Planning Cadre truly won't know what's hit them until the blood fills their beady little eyes."

"The Planning Cadre?" Lexi asks, lost in his words. "What is that? And who are your . . . friends?"

"You'll meet them soon," he repeats brightly, as if it's delightful news.

"Are they coming here?"

"No. This place isn't safe anymore. We'll have to go to them."

"I don't want to leave my home, Daian. Besides, Taru—"

"By now they have Taru." He shrugs. "There's nothing to be done about that now. Plans will have to be altered."

"Perhaps, but I still do not wish to leave my home, Daian," Lexi repeats slowly and carefully.

He walks toward her then, and if he wasn't holding a bloody dagger and half covered in the same spatter Daian might not appear threatening at all.

"I hear you," he says, "but then the day doesn't seem to be working out as *any* of us planned."

The pointed drink stirrer is still hidden from sight among the ripples of her skirt. Lexi deftly and carefully upends it, reversing her grip on the handle without drawing attention to the movement. She's never perforated anyone before, and although it might make more sense to thrust with the spike, stabbing down feels more natural to her. Being so inexperienced in combat, she decides the latter quality is more important.

"What were you going to do when Taru returned, Daian?" she asks. "If the Ministry hadn't come here, for me. What were you going to do?"

He stares at her strangely. "You sound afraid, Lexi. I told you, you don't have to be afraid anymore."

"What were you going to do when Taru returned?" she asks again.

Daian spreads his arms helplessly. "I like Taru! I respect Taru, very much. I respect both of you, but your plan was very misguided, Lexi."

"What plan?"

"Exposing the Savage Legion. Presenting proof of their existence and the crimes of the Ministry to the Arbiters and the people. Counting on the public to provoke change is . . . well, let's just say naive, Lexi. Perhaps even foolish, if you'll pardon me."

"And these . . . friends of yours? They have a different plan?"

Daian nods soulfully. "They do. They really do."

"You haven't answered my first question, Daian. What were you going to do when Taru returned with Brio's proof?"

He sighs, spreading his arms out in front of her in a helpless gesture.

"Precisely what I did to these poor ghouls," he relents.

"And what were you going to do to me?"

"As I said, you're going to serve our purpose. If I was going to harm you, you'd already be harmed."

Moving as swiftly as she can command her limbs, Lexi raises her arm and brings the makeshift weapon down toward his chest.

Daian reaches up and easily captures her wrist before the strike completes half its arc. He twists her arm to one side, painfully, causing the dagger's handle to slip from her fingers and wringing a short yelp from her. He presses the tip of his blade beneath her chin, lightly, not hard enough to pierce her flesh yet firmly enough to give her pause.

"Lexi, please," he chastises her, like a child. "You keep your steel on the inside. That's the steel that's dangerous under your command. You're a different kind of warrior, not one made for the battlefield. Violence does not become—"

The rest of his words are mangled by growls as Lexi leans away from his blade and rams the hardest portion of her skull into his nose. Bones break beneath the blow and blood pours over his lips. The tears that involuntarily well up in his eyes sting and blind him. Lexi tears her wrist from his grip and takes off running across the parlor, knowing that if she can make it through the front doors and out into the cooperative he won't be able to touch her. She doesn't look back to see if he's on her heels, she only runs, dashing over the bodies of Nils and Jindo and practically leaping from the parlor into the tower's entrance hall.

The front doors are only a few yards in front of her, and Lexi sprints faster to reach them, extending an arm toward the nearest rung. She's ready to close her fist around it and tear the doors open when they seem to be physically pulled away from her. The doors become a distant sight sinking farther and farther away in her field of vision and Lexi realizes she's no longer running; she's falling. Whatever just slammed into the back of her head has also turned the world upside-down and caused Lexi's entire body to go numb.

A moment before she loses consciousness, Lexi sees Daian's dagger lying where it landed after he threw the weapon at her, on the floor in front of her face. The pommel that struck the soft back of her skull is now decorated with a smear of her blood to which several strands of her hair have stuck.

Lexi wonders, briefly, if he truly meant to hit her with that end of the dagger, but the only answer to her question that presents itself is darkness.

MISSIO INTERRUPTUS

TARU HAS NEVER BEEN ONE TO EMBRACE THE IDEA OF "SHORT-cuts," be they metaphorical or literal; to their way of thinking anything worth the effort, be it practicing with a blade or trekking over mountains as part of a long cross-country journey, must be earned without leniency from others or one's self. It was Brio who impressed upon Taru the importance of taking shortcuts, especially when engaging in clandestine affairs, and particularly when the errands he undertook before his disappearance began to endanger them both.

The alleys Taru is circumnavigating were also introduced to them by Brio, providing the quickest path from the Bottoms to the Gen Circus without making use of the sky carriages. The retainer moves swiftly, accepting the necessity of slinking through narrow, poorly seen spaces even as they resent having to do so.

Taru's booted feet abruptly stop short, halting almost instinctively.

There's an Aegin waiting at the head of the current alley, and he's not alone. Three other Aegins flank him.

"You are Taru, Gen Stalbraid's lawful retainer?" their spokesman asks.

He's shorter than Taru, but appears in fair shape for a man of his middle years.

"I am."

"I have to ask you to come with us."

"You're arresting me?"

"I'm detaining you."

"What is the difference?"

"Manacles and the absence of my asking you beforehand."

Taru grunts something like a laugh. "I refuse your request."

"If you refuse then we'll *have* to arrest you."

Taru becomes aware of more Aegins swarming up from the back of the alley. Without looking, Taru judges there to be four of them, from the sound of their footfalls.

"You've brought along an excessive number of helpers, if you don't mind me saying."

"We were informed you're a warrior who demands to be taken seriously."

"May I know your name?" Taru asks.

The Aegin stares for a moment, suspicious, and then says, "Kamen. Kamen Lim, Aegin second-class. Why?"

Taru holds Aegin Lim's eyes with a hard stare. "I was recently forced to kill two men whose names I'll never know. That felt wrong to me somehow. I told myself I'd never again take a life without knowing the name of that person first."

With that, Taru unsheathes both short sword and hook-end in one greased motion that is a blur to the eye. The retainer's feet spread, knees bending, the blade of the short sword held across one shoulder while the retainer extends the hook-end defensively.

The Aegins surrounding Taru immediately draw the daggers from their baldric scabbards and shift into defensive postures of their own.

Aegin Lim instinctively takes a step back, his hand going to the handle of his dagger. However, he doesn't unsheathe the weapon.

"This doesn't have to be," Lim pleads with Taru. "Our orders are only to detain you, not to harm you in any way. I give you my word. If you surrender your weapons now, no retaliation will be taken against you."

Taru senses truth behind his words and even sees it in his eyes, whether the retainer wants to or not. It's possible they've sent an honest Aegin to carry out a dirty deed, and if so Taru doesn't want Kamen Lim's blood on their hands.

He cannot, however, possibly vouch for every other Aegin surrounding Taru in the alley. Any one of the tunic-wearing stooges could be tasked with sticking their dagger in Taru's back while the retainer is down on the ground.

Taru probably cannot win this fight, but they will not be gutted on the filthy alley floor while lying there helpless. The retainer refuses to relinquish their duties under such conditions.

"I thank you for your offer and accept the spirit in which it is intended."

Taru lowers the short sword and hook-end.

Kamen Lim visibly relaxes his posture, breathing a subtle sigh of relief.

"I only wish I could find it in myself to place that kind of faith in your comrades here," the retainer adds.

The sole of Taru's boot smashes into Lim's face, flattening his nose and cracking his chin in one blow. The Aegin's head is snapped back and the rest of his body attempts to follow it, causing him to curl awkwardly over the street until his feet give out.

The rest of the Aegins immediately close in, rushing forward to slash Taru to ribbons. The retainer swings both blades in a single wide, complete arc, driving them all back. Taru takes a long stride toward the nearest Aegin and slashes at her, trapping her wrist as the woman blocks the strike, and driving her against the wall with one shoulder. Another Aegin comes at Taru and the retainer deflects his blade while kicking his feet out from beneath him.

Taru tries to fend the rest off, but there are too many to keep track. The retainer defends strikes as they come, feeling the bite of Crachian blades against their leather armor. Finally, Taru feels a blade slice through their left leg just above the back of the knee. The cut is deep and the impact jarring, causing that leg to buckle. Taru collapses to the left, landing hard on one hip. They all seem to fall atop the retainer at once, pinning Taru to the street and seizing both short sword and hook-end.

Taru is only able to peer up from the corner of one eye. The retainer sees Kamen Lim breathing laboriously and with obvious pain. There's blood streaming over his lips and down his bruised chin and neck. His dagger is still secured in the scabbard tooled to his baldric. He stares down at the constrained retainer with what appears to Taru to be frustration rather than the anger or rage one might expect.

Lim crouches down in front of the mass of bodies and digs inside Taru's breastplate. The retainer makes a vain attempt at struggling further, but the dozen hands and arms and bodies crushing Taru to the street only constrict like an angry python. One of the Aegins kicks Taru with numbing force in the kidney.

"There's no call for that!" Kamen Lim barks in a compressed voice at the unseen Aegin who delivered the blow. "It's over!"

If nothing else, Taru is satisfied with the decision not to kill the man.

Lim fishes the thick hide binder from within Taru's armor and removes it. He stands, groaning and spitting blood onto the street. Lim untwines the binder's cord and peels back the flap, peering inside.

This time his sigh is heavy and accompanied by the faint sound of gargling.

Kamen Lim upends the binder and pulls its edges apart, shaking it above Taru. Sheafs of parchment begin flitting out between the leather folds.

Taru begins thrashing anew, seemingly still intent on stopping him despite the retainer's untenable predicament. The pile of Aegins only press the combined weight of half a dozen bodies down harder on Taru.

Kamen Lim begins laughing. It's not a mocking or contemptuous sound. His laugh is rueful, almost admiring.

"I swear, I wish you were on our side," he reluctantly admits, shaking his head.

"Undeclared aren't allowed to become Aegins," Taru reminds him.

"Yes, well." Kamen Lim closes the binder and tucks it under one arm. "The world is an imperfect place full of imperfect people."

"I am inclined to agree."

"Help our stubborn friend to their feet and secure manacles around their wrists," Lim orders the other Aegins.

The swarm of hands roughly pulls Taru from the grit of the street. This time the retainer doesn't fight them.

"You seem like a fair man," Taru says to Lim as the Aegins shackle the retainer's wrists together. "I'm afraid you take orders from corrupt people."

"I'm sure you're right, but neither am I a complicated man. I'm good at what I do and my family also eats and is sheltered in winter. That's where it begins and ends for me."

With that, Kamen Lim drives an elbow into Taru's nose. The force isn't enough to break bones, but it does rim the retainer's nostrils with blood and draw tears from their eyes.

"That makes us even," he says.

Taru sniffs and blinks away the salty discharge, staring down at Lim passively.

"As I said, you're a fair man."

BORN ON THE BATTLEFIELD

THE VEST IS THICKLY ARMORED, ITS LEATHER THE DUSKY YEL-
lowed russet color of blood drying in sand. Emblazoned on the chest in
a deep, bloody crimson is a sparrow in flight. The sparrow has a single
white eye, and lines the same color trace its plump body and capelike
wingspan. Sirach presents it to her inside the armorist's wagon.

"I had it made for you," she says to Evie. "It was high time to make
it official, Sparrow General."

Evie is dubious. "You don't think this a little wasteful under our
current circumstances?"

"I think it wholly necessary, and for the same reason. We're going
into battle against a superior enemy. There's conquering the body and then
there's conquering the mind. They know your name because you inspired
this rebellion. They need to see that you're quite real, and leading that
rebellion to their doorstep. And it's not only the enemy's mind that needs
conquering. This will help you win the minds of those men and women
out there who need a Sparrow General behind whom they can rally."

"Fair enough," Evie relents, more than a little exasperated. "You're
as dangerous with words as you are with blades, you know that?"

Sirach bows as if she's been thoroughly complimented. "Siccluna
teaches you to use every weapon at your disposal."

Evie pulls the armored vest around her thick, woolen battle tunic,
securing its strap at her right shoulder with a gloved hand. She's already

wearing her sword in its scabbard, and a matching dagger, both of them Sicclunan weapons.

Sirach is clad in light leather armor designed for the most amount of maneuverability. The leather has been dyed the same wilted violet color of her eyes. She also wears a curved Sicclunan saber, but her half-moon daggers are sheathed beneath each arm in scabbards hung from her shoulders.

"Are you ready, General?" she asks Evie.

"Please, I'll wear the sparrow, but stop calling me that."

Sirach doesn't try to stifle her grin. "Whatever you say."

The two of them emerge from the armorist's wagon to waiting war columns of Sicclunan soldiers, B'ors warriors, and rogue Savages. They've struck camp and are mounted, armored, and armed for battle.

The Elder Company approaches the duo. Mother Manai smiles brilliantly at Evie and presents the stump of her right wrist. A finely honed single spike designed for lethal thrusting has replaced her usual makeshift finger blades. It is fastened to her wrist and shoulder by leather straps, equally well tooled.

"What do you think?" Mother Manai asks Evie. "I think the master armorist took a likin' to li'l ol' me."

"I think you're ready to take on the Skrain all by yourself," Evie says.

"Ya've got a bird on ya," Lariat chides her.

She looks up the gruff old man, dozens of knuckle-size blades strapped to his every joint effectively turning his entire body into one lethal fist. The razor-edged triangle blades of his katars are casually shoved through his belt and other than the leather strops crisscrossing his chest his torso is bare and exposed.

Evie shakes her head. "You will never make a soldier, old man," she launches right back at him, "and I'm eternally grateful for that."

Lariat laughs, his mustache dancing above his upper lip.

"It's very becoming for a General," Diggs assures her.

"Thank you."

Evie looks from them to Bam, ever expressionless and still hiding beneath his hood. He does, however, reach out and tap a finger against her chest and the sparrow's eye there.

"I like your bird," he says quietly.

"Thank you, Bam."

"It's time," Sirach informs them all.

"Then let's not be late!" Lariat hollers loud enough to be heard by the ranks.

The de facto commanders jog to the head of their columns and lead the army out.

They don't have far to travel. The Skrain have drawn their battle line a mile from the eastern road and five miles from the garrison keep and the Crachian border. They seem determined to keep the Sparrow General's Savage Rebellion from ever touching Crachian soil.

Evie and her combined forces mass a hundred yards across the valley from the enemy line. Their rogue Savages serve in their usual capacity as vanguard. Everyone knew that this battle would hinge one way or another on Savages fighting Savages.

In fact, they can't even see any columns of Skrain for all the Legionnaires gathered in front of the Crachian line in their usual jumbled, frothing, chaotic formation, as if they are a single organism undulating in heat. Many of the Legionnaires with their half-faces painted blue are also wearing bright red bands of cloth around their neck.

"Is that what we look like from this side?" Lariat asks Sirach.

"Uglier when you were over there, but essentially, yes," she informs him.

Lariat guffaws through his nose. "Well, yer first mistake was always waitin' for us ta come ta you."

He coils his gnarled, scarred pugilist's fists around the horizontal handles of his matched katars, drawing them both, and holding his arms aloft with those deadly triangular bladed extensions of his hands effectively turning his arms into swords.

"Savages!" he growls fiercely and loudly with every bit of breath from his lungs. "I want my heads!"

The rogue Legionnaires raise whatever weapon they've been issued, be it sword or ax or mace, and cry their bloody intentions across the field at their former brothers and sisters.

Mother Manai grips Evie's shoulder briefly with her remaining hand, then draws a large, gleaming, finely forged rendition of her favored meat cleaver fashioned for her by the same Sicclunan armorist who made her spike.

"I think that armorist does fancy you," Evie says to her.

Mother Manai winks at her, and the old woman says no more. This is not a time for good-byes.

Evie looks from her face to Lariat's, then Bam's.

"Die well," she bids the three of them.

Lariat laughs. "What else do we do, little Sparrow?"

By now the Skrain and Savage Legion taskers know what's coming, and they've ordered their Legionnaires to advance, hoping to make as much ground as possible before the field is cut off.

"Bring me their fuckin' heads!" Lariat yells down the line, and hundreds of howling blue-rune-covered faces surge across the valley.

The rebel Savages aren't marching, they're charging, and their Legionnaire counterparts soon pick up their pace to match that ferocious speed. The Skrain are visible up and down their battle line now, armored scales blazing in the sun. Their Savages should be able to wrap around the smaller force of rogue Legionnaires like a snake once they meet, but the sheer animal energy of Evie's Savages makes the odds appear slightly more even despite the disparity in number.

After the two armies of Savages clash there's no telling them apart, not if you're watching from either side's battle line. There's no stoic holding of the ranks to counterpoint the feral attack of the Legion. This is war without technique or pretension or mechanical unity. This is the chaos of human nature given form, and it is an ugly, horrific thing to witness. Bodies are being shredded and torn apart everywhere there is to look. Savages don't retreat, they don't regroup, and neither side is going to be recalled from this fight. They're battling to the last of them and they know, and the brutality of their fight is a reflection of that.

Evie doesn't want to watch, but neither can she justify looking away. She is responsible for this. She committed to this course of action, and if she's not there in the midst of it she must at least see it through.

In truth, the battle of the Savages lasts no more than fifteen minutes. Such unrestrained combat easily breaks bodies not packed in armor, but the sheer violence of the encounter makes it feel like what they're witnessing goes much longer.

Neither side wins, not really. The Skrain's Legionnaires do not overwhelm the smaller force. They are two wildfires lit to meet and snuff each other out, and that's precisely what happens. The fighting is soon reduced to small pockets of groups, then single combat here and there. Even those are only the final, weak throes of a dying giant.

When the fighting ceases, the field is littered with bodies covered in as many splatters of blood as blue runes. Only a few stragglers, most of whom appear gravely injured, are still stirring among the carnage.

She looks to Sirach, whose expression is as grim and serious as Evie could've ever imagined it.

Neither of them says a word.

Across the valley, the Skrain march forward, spears and swords and shields and armor all gleaming brilliant and majestic. They are three thousand strong and four columns deep, waves of well-trained, well-armed cogs forming a perfect killing machine, aimed at the heart of Evie's depleted rebellion.

Her forces do not advance, however. They simply hold their position, waiting, despite the fact that much of their line is exposed and vulnerable to frontal assault.

The Skrain enter the killing field of bodies, stepping over dead Legionnaires with long-practiced indifference and efficiency.

Then, above the crunching chorus of steel joints on the march, a lone scream rings out from within the Skrain ranks.

It doesn't halt or even slow the march, and there's no visible disturbance from where Evie and Sirach stand. Then a second scream rings out, and perhaps it is Skrain soldiers delivering death blows as they move. A flash of steel armor, however, accompanies the next scream, as one of those Skrain soldiers appears to be sucked down by the earth itself. Then a scream that must belong to Lariat rings out like thunder as he and the rest of the Elder Company spring from the ground and begin hacking and slashing into Skrain legs by the half dozen.

The dead rise, or so it appears to those observing the battle from a distance. Half the fallen Savages awaken and sit and stand up, some attacking the Skrain with blades and bludgeons while others drag them down to the ground as though their arms are reaching up from a lonely grave. It's as if the Skrain have marched into a field of living weeds hungry to coil around their legs and feed them to the soil.

Soon the Skrain advance has halted almost completely, and the portion of the columns that continue are suddenly caught between the rebel line and their own soldiers skirmishing with what they thought were dead men and women. It's not only the Savages under Evie's command; many of the Legionnaires who fought for the Skrain have risen to attack them, all those Savages wearing bright red cloth around their necks.

Many of the Legionnaires have truly fallen, and given to the earth they remain. Spud-Bar quietly gathered and converted as many small groups as the span of one night allowed, and those groups absorbed others before the dawn, but their numbers only totaled slightly more than a third of the Savage ranks belonging to the Skrain. Their battle would be pantomime, pretending to hack and maul each other to death, and a grand show they did stage for the Skrain. The rest of the Legionnaires knew nothing of Evie's plan, and there was no sparing them from it, or Evie's Savages from their weapons.

What's left, however, is more than enough to do what Savages are conscripted and trained by the whip to do; rise like chaos itself in the ranks of the enemy and scatter them to the winds before the real strike closes its fist.

Sirach draws her sword. "The Sparrow General!" she calls down the line, and every Sicclunan on horseback and on foot surges forward.

The B'ors warriors act as vanguard, rushing ahead of the Sicclunan infantry and Special Selection soldiers, though Sirach's forces are right on their tribal companions' heels. They fall on the exposed Skrain still forming ranks.

Evie and Sirach, joined by several dozen reinforcements, rush past that skirmish to aid the Savages fighting in the heavy midst of Skrain. They begin slashing their way through soldier after soldier, doing their best to alleviate the pressure on the Savages risking the most by attacking from within the Skrain's own closed ranks, giving the surviving Savages a chance to regroup. Those ranks are soon thinned out and displaced across the battlefield, the Skrain's march all but obliterated. They find themselves being attacked from all sides, the chaotic shock of the situation disintegrating the unity that make the Skrain such an effective force on the field, reducing them to fighting soldier-to-soldier.

Evie meets a Skrain sword with her own, quickly enveloping its blade in hers and crushing her body against the soldier's breastplate. With their swords trapped between them, Evie unsheathes her dagger and rams it under the soldier's raised right arm. As the soldier reels from the puncture wound, Evie steps back, pulling her blade free and thrusting it through the Skrain's throat. Retracting the blade just as quickly, Evie lowers her head against the spray of blood that stains her hair to the roots. By the time she's raised her chin the soldier has fallen to their knees, clawing at their neck as they collapse to one side.

The moment Evie turns from the fallen foe, what feels like a tree trunk smashes into her blade, nearly knocking the sword from her hands, and Evie off her feet. She quickly regains her balance and chokes against the sword's handle, raising the blade defensively only to watch as the thick end of Laython's blackwood mace snaps the blade cleanly in two.

He towers above her like a demon made of shadow, almost every inch of his body covered in black leather armor as thick as rhinoceros hide. His helm is molded to the features of his face, and two crooked horns rise at asymmetrical angles to complete the awful visage. The eyes beneath that helm smolder at her.

"I didn't like you the moment I laid eyes on your worthless, skinny ass!" he spits at Evie.

"The feeling was mutual," she assures him before rearing back and winging her dagger at the singularly exposed flesh of his neck.

Laython swings his mace with a growl and bats the blade away in midair, but Evie is already charging headlong into him. She lets loose a feral war cry and rams what's left of her broken blade into his guts, aiming for the large portal vein she knows lies beneath.

Unfortunately for her, barely half an inch of steel penetrates his armor.

Laughing, Laython jams the butt of his mace against Evie's forehead. The blow raises a giant knot there. Its impact causes a flash of light to fill Evie's gaze. The next thing she's aware of is lying on the ground.

Evie blinks the world back into focus just in time to see the end of Laython's mace blot out the sun. She rolls to her right and is showered in the shredded earth the mace raises when it hits the patch of land she was occupying a sliver of a moment before. She springs to her feet, never before so agonizingly aware of how empty her hands are. Her entire head is reeling, and angry hornets seem to fill the space between her temples.

Laython swings his mace again, and Evie ducks underneath its arc, the wind current raised by the weapon and the power behind it enough to sting her ears. She sidesteps and ducks several more swings, backpedaling after each feint, not quite running away, yet at a loss as to how to engage the giant tasker. She finally runs out of road as half a dozen Skrain and Sicclunans clash inches from her back.

Evie has no choices left. Laython raises the mace high and brings it down in an overhead swing. She quickly steps forward and ducks under his arms, avoiding the mace and closing the distance between their bodies. Pressed against his armor, she reaches up and digs her fingers into his throat, clawing at his neck with the overgrown edges of her nails.

She's able to draw blood before Laython takes the mace at both ends and brings its haft against the small of her back, crushing her between the weapon and his armor. The air is forced from her lungs, and her spine and ribs feel as though they're about to shatter. Her grip on his neck goes slack as her feet are lifted from the ground. Evie's eyes close and she gasps for breath, wriggling in vain. Laython's grip is like steel jaws being wound closed by sky carriage pullers.

His laughter is the sound of many hells reaching up to swallow her whole. "You made an adorable little plan, but it's not enough. You'll never cross the border. You die here, *all* of you."

Evie can't wriggle herself free, but she can snake a hand between their tightly clenched bodies. Despite a numbness spreading through her lower half, Evie forces her knee to bend, raising her right boot. Her trembling fingers close around a familiar handle there.

"You're no general," Laython whispers, hot spittle hitting her cheek. "You're not even a Savage."

"You're half right," Evie manages through painfully clenched teeth.

The blade of her push dagger, that first reluctant gift ever given to her by Sirach, pierces the flesh of his chin beneath the leather helm. It lances Laython's soft palate and tongue before entering the roof of his mouth. For one terrible moment his body tenses against her, squeezing the breath out of Evie with even more intensity, then his grip on her begins to loosen. With his head tilted back by the force of the push dagger, Evie leans in and sinks her teeth into his neck, ignoring the alien sensation of that flesh filling her mouth as she clamps her jaws together, and ripping out a large chunk of his throat and painting her face with his blood.

Evie spits in disgust, feeling her feet touch the ground as Laython's body begins slouching toward the earth. She yanks her push dagger free of his skull and thrusts her hip against the mace still pulled across her back, knocking it free of Laython's hands, and allowing her to back away from him.

The fire in his eyes that burned as bright as volcanic tears just moments ago have turned to cold stone. Blood continues to bathe the finely oiled pieces of his leather armor, spilling down his torso until it begins falling in thick hot drops upon the grass. Finally, he slumps forward, remaining on his knees as his face hits the soft ground. It's a wholly undignified death pose.

Evie couldn't approve any more than she does.

Her breath comes in staccato gasps and her mouth is slathered with blood inside and out. The red spatter fills in the empty spaces between her blue runes, and the knot in the center of her forehead adds a purple hue to complete the frightening composition of Evie's battle-torn face. She stands over the fallen taskmaster of the Savage Legion and feels the rush of elation and victory overwhelming the pain wracking her body.

Evie moves her gaze over the field. The fighting that was so fierce and heated and thick what seems like only moments ago has largely ceased. The ground between the dead Savage Legionnaires is now littered with more bodies, and most of them are wearing Skrain armor. Evie sees Sicclunans and B'ors warriors and Savages with faces both painted and unpainted tending to the wounded, either helping their injured compatriots from the field or dealing mercy to mortally wounded enemies.

She turns and peers into the distance, at what began this day as the Crachian battle line. It no longer exists. Evie sees Skrain soldiers and Savage Legionnaires fleeing the field, running for the safety of the garrison. They're met by several scattered Skrain officers on horseback, their pages, and a few flag soldiers. Eventually all the remaining Skrain turn tail and flee.

Let them run back to the safety of the keep, Evie thinks to herself.

She's seen the inside of the garrison. She knows they hurled every soldier and Savage they had at her little rebellion. There will be virtually no one left behind to defend the keep. It will fall to them before the day is over.

Evie's weary eyes search the battlefield, past B'ors warriors separating the few worthy fallen among their enemies for honorable burial; Yacatek is among them, leading the way, already etching in the blade of her stone story dagger. Evie's gaze finally locates Lariat, punching a katar blade down into the chest of still-moving Skrain soldier. Not far from him, Mother Manai is pulling a dagger from between Bam's shoulders. Evie's self-appointed bodyguard is standing under his own power, and he barely seems to take notice of the blade leaving his back, so she has to believe he'll live.

Evie begins to feel a creeping sensation along her battered spine. It's not a physical malady plaguing her; it's the cold tingle of fear. She can't seem to spot Sirach among those still standing on the field, and she's not a woman who is difficult to pick out of a crowd. Evie realizes she hadn't considered an outcome in which she would live and Sirach would not. She also hadn't considered how much that outcome might affect her.

"You know, you are quite simply a good planner." The voice is familiar and as inappropriately delighted as always. "You do, in fact, plan good things."

Evie drops her head, her broad smile concealed there until she's forced the expression into something more restrained.

When she turns around, Sirach is grinning through a face that's been pummeled and sliced down the cheek by a close encounter with a Skrain sword.

"You look just awful," Sirach says.

Evie nods. "I think we both forgot to duck."

"Oh, I didn't forget. Ducking is just so . . . expected."

"I promise you," Evie says, a new warmth replacing the chill that was threatening her spine, "you are never expected."

"That is quite a compliment, General. And don't tell me not to call you that."

"I'm wearing the vest, aren't I?"

"And you won the day."

"*We* won the day," Evie corrects her.

Sirach bows to her, grandly. "Fair enough."

They seem to run out of words then. They stare at each other across a dozen slain bodies, and yet the blood and shit and carrion birds circling overhead aren't enough to reclaim this moment from them.

Sirach's expression turns unusually dour. "General, I must now ask you a very serious question."

Evie is taken aback by the sudden change in mood. "What's that?" she asks, tentative.

The grin returns to Sirach's swollen lips. "Do you feel like laying siege to a Crachian keep?"

Evie sighs, somehow relieved despite the very real weight of the question. She sheathes the push dagger still clenched between her knuckles, returning it to the inside of her boot.

Evie stands tall, staring back confidently at Sirach.

"I'll need a new sword," she says.

IN THE HOUSE OF THE IGNOBLE

IT'S A FINER PRISON CELL THAN LEXI WOULD HAVE EXPECTED, to be sure.

She wakes with a dull and occasionally throbbing pain in what feels like the very pulpy back of her head. The bed beneath her is feather-soft, and large enough for Lexi to spread her arms akimbo without touching its edges. Four ornately carved posts supporting a silken canopy rise to the ceiling above her, and the sheets and pillows are even softer than the canopy appears to be.

Lexi is wearing the same clothes in which Daian took her. She doesn't appear to have been molested in any way, beyond the fact she was bludgeoned with a knife pommel and kidnapped.

She rises from the luxurious bed and takes in her surroundings. The walls and the floor of the bedroom are heavy stone blocks draped with tapestry and rugs to hide their drab and rustic appearance. There's a porcelain basin and chamber pot. A towering archway leads to another room beyond. It looks like a room from a castle ruin, before modern stone masons began striving for the smooth, angular perfection of the Spectrum's construction.

The drawing room outside the bedchamber is like an ancient wood-block rendering of a scene from a historic castle. The stone floors, walls, ceiling, and even the large hearth have the same antiquated construction as the bedchamber. A large oak wood slab serves as a table in the center of the room, a large vase of orchids and a silver bell arranged atop it.

Lexi begins to realize these rooms and this castle are from another time and another world, one far more primitive yet striving for an aesthetic sense of civility, even high culture. She hasn't seen an interior like this fully intact in any building in the nation.

Two heavy doors are closed off to her right. Lexi moves to them quickly and pulls on the rungs, finding herself locked in.

Light is filling the space. It's the afternoon sun pouring in through the panes of large picture window on the other side of the room. Lexi gathers her skirt and jogs across the cold stone floor. Unlike the door, the windows are unlocked. She pulls them open and steps to the edge, peering several hundred feet down at an expansive and beautiful garden. Manicured hedges extend over a hundred yards to a wall separating the courtyard from the treeline beyond.

Lexi doesn't see anyone moving among the foliage, and it's far too great a distance to jump, even if she landed on the softest patch of the garden. There are no ledges of crags in the walls outside her window, either.

Her mind reels with rough drafts of plans that range from improbable to impractical to utterly absurd. They all seem to end in failure when played out inside her head.

The sound of footsteps on stone echoes loudly beyond the locked doors of her apartment cell. Lexi turns from the tall picture window and walks quickly across the drawing room. She pauses when she sees the shadowy outline of feet through the crack beneath the doors. Lexi hears the outside latch spring free, and watches as both halves fling open.

Daian enters the drawing room. He's no longer wearing his Aegin's uniform. He appears to have traded its green tunic and baldric for a pitch-black tunic and vest. His dagger is sheathed from his right hip, slung low so the handle rises just above the heel of his palm when his arm is at rest at his side. He winks at her silently as he moves inside the room.

"You've given up your costume, I see," Lexi says to him, hoping she sounds unafraid and in control.

Daian wags a finger at her, a chastising gesture. "Hardly a costume. I was a very good Aegin. I served the common folk. I resisted the corruption of my fellows. Some of them even tried to kill me for it. I simply have a higher calling, that's all."

"You're corrupt in a much deeper way, from what I've seen."

"Was it corrupt to save your life?"

Lexi ignores that, not even wanting to entertain the possibility that there's truth in those words.

Instead, she asks, "Why this masquerade, Daian?"

"We were both looking for the same thing, at least at first. We share a common enemy. The Protectorate Ministry. We both wanted leverage to use against them, to expose them. I suspected they sent Savages to kill you, but I couldn't be sure. We don't know much about the Savages, you see. Aegins simply round up candidates and pack them off to . . . wherever. Aegins aren't privy to the Ministry's machinations. We're simply their occasional lapdogs. I hoped to be able to turn up some evidence, even if it was just a body, some solid proof of who the assassins were and who sent them. It would have helped us to help you shine a light on them in open session at the Spectrum, in front of all your new dreg friends. Not to mention if we could turn up Brio or his evidence that would have been an equal boon. Unfortunately I fear news of my poking around on the matter made it back to them. I'm certain they tasked the Aegins you met in the dojo with eliminating me."

"Then I suppose I saved your life, too," Lexi says, the irony dripping from every word.

"You sheltered and healed me, and I thank you."

"And I'm sorry your investigation failed."

Daian shrugs. "It's moot now. We're moving on."

"Who is moving on? To *what*? Who are these mysterious benefactors of yours who seem to have such a deep-seated issue with the Crachian governance?"

A smaller figure emerges behind him, one draped in brightly shining colored robes of the purest silk. Its embellishments appear to Lexi to be real gold and silver. Such opulence almost stops her from immediately recognizing Councilwoman Burr. Even the woman's mousey hair, usually brushed and bound straight back, has been made-up elaborately in multiple braids. Her face is painted in tones of bone white, night blue, and crimson red. Her styling is much like the room around them; it is from a time that no longer exists.

Burr smiles welcomingly at Lexi, seeming far warmer than she ever did at the top of those steps in the Gen Franchise Council chambers.

"Welcome to my ancestral home, Lady Xia of House Stalbraid."

Even the form of greeting and the title she invokes is archaic, recalling a long-forgotten time of "lords" and "ladies" who presided over noble "houses."

"I wish to apologize for the brutal circumstances under which you have come to be our guest here," Burr continues. "I had hoped to speak with you in my own time about pressing matters of state, and apply the . . . appropriate context to the situation. And while the Ministry moving against you as they did accelerated our timeline, Daian here could have been more . . . discreet. I fear he has given you a false impression of us."

Burr looks up at Daian briefly, a flash of genuine annoyance revealed in her gaze.

Or a perfectly accurate impression? Lexi wonders.

"What timeline?" she asks instead. "What are you talking about? Where are we? We cannot be in the Capitol."

"Oh no, we're quite a ways southeast, well-hidden in the lowlands. My family spent centuries cultivating the vegetation that conceals this keep from prying eyes. There are a few others like it, but not half as many as there should be."

"If this is the land and keep that belonged to your family before the Renewal, when they were a noble house, it was to have been remitted to the nation for repurposing."

"Oh yes," Burr admits bitterly. "So the newly born nation of Crache could fill it with lowly rabble, or turn it into a fish hatchery or some such abomination. My family turned over their holdings, just not all of them. They knew a base of operations would be needed for the fight to come, regardless of how long it might take to rebuild ourselves in preparation for that fight."

"That was hundreds of years ago," Lexi marvels.

Burr smiles haughtily. "Nobility has a long memory, My Lady."

"Obviously. What am I doing here?"

"Long ago, a great crime was committed, Lady Xia, and a great many lies were told to conceal that crime."

"You are speaking of the Renewal."

"I'm speaking of the truth behind the Renewal. You are here to help those of us descendants of noble houses finally, at long last, put things right. You're here to help restore this nation to its rightful wards."

Lexi stares at her as if the woman is speaking gibberish. "Nobility is an absurd and arcane notion," she insists. "The idea you're fit to rule simply because of your blood is insane."

"Blood, the right blood, built empires. It dragged people from caves and rallied them to construct a society, taught them how to live their lives within that society."

"Taught them to know their place, you mean."

"I do. Have Gens done any better? Are they any less corrupt? They merely allowed peasants to connive and scheme and plot to amass wealth and power."

Lexi's eyes narrow. "That is *not* my Gen."

"You are a rare exception, and I congratulate you. I'm afraid you're in poor company."

"What do you want?" Lexi demands.

Burr's eyelids narrow and fire flashes beneath them. "I want what my ancestors relinquished. I want what I have been denied. It is the most tragic misfortune imaginable to be born in the wrong age, My Lady, as I was. I am meant for a time when the greatness and destiny of lineage was not only recognized, it was revered. I am meant to rule. Yet here I dwell, as a bureaucrat in drab robes navigating a paltry political arena, subject to having my every decision and action voted upon and submitted to half a dozen committees before being sent back amended and annotated and vomited over with every tiny civil servant's opinions and demands. In my ancestor's age, their will alone was law. So it will be again, for me. I cannot go back to a time that has past, but I can change the times in which I find myself."

"I meant, what do you want from me?" Lexi clarifies, speaking slowly.

"What you know, what you are, and what you and your husband have uncovered, they are all weapons. They are leverage that can be used against the Planning Cadre and the Protectorate Ministry, not to topple them, but to gain an advantage. Where you would have used that knowledge as a bludgeon to blindly hammer at Crache, we will use it as a blade, with precision and delicacy, to rouse the right people at the right time in the right way."

Lexi looks up at Daian, who stares back at her serenely. He almost appears friendly, and it's the inappropriateness of that demeanor in this situation that makes it so disturbing. She wonders if any piece of the man she came to know actually exists within him.

"And what of you, Daian?" she asks. "Why are you helping her? Do you share some secret bloodline with ancient nobility?"

He shakes his head. "I'm nothing but a country boy, Lexi."

"Then what's in this for you?"

"Daian is as dissatisfied as we *both* are with the current state of Crache," Burr answers for him. "That is what unifies us, what should unify us *all* in this room. Crache lied to you your entire life, and took your husband away when he asked too many questions. When you tried to save him, Crache attempted to murder you. This nation is a disease that either infects your mind and alters your thinking, or destroys you."

"*People* did the things you're talking about," Lexi fires back at her.

"Crache is a place, and any place is nothing more than an idea. It's left to people how that idea is executed. The idea of Crache has been corrupted by the self-interested and indifferent. *They* are the ones we must unseat. You want to split the foundation of our society in two. I will not raze fertile ground to kill a few weeds, especially to seed it with an antiquated notion like the purity and entitlement of blood."

Lexi's breathing is shallow and labored as she finishes speaking; such is the fire in her own blood. She stares back at Burr defiantly, even challenging the Ignoble with her gaze.

Daian bursts out laughing, shattering the tension of the moment. He begins applauding Lexi, loudly clapping his hands together.

Burr flashes eyes filled with reprimand at him and he quickly falls silent.

Daian clears his throat. "Sorry," he placates her. "But it was a good speech!"

The Ignoble moves her focus to Lexi once more. "I truly hoped you would understand and accept my position. Perhaps even see some value in it. A futile hope, I suppose. This would have been much easier and much more effective with your full cooperation."

"Why?" Lexi demands. "Why do you need me? I don't have the evidence Brio collected. If Taru was able to retrieve it, the Protectorate Ministry has them both by now. I can't prove anything. What good am I to you or your cause?"

"All is not as it may seem," Burr says cryptically.

Lexi glances at Daian. "Nothing is, as of late."

"You have far more value than you may be aware," Burr reiterates, again without further explanation. "However, the usefulness of your Gen, to Crache and to my cause, has expired. I'm afraid you won't be attending the academy or becoming a pleader after all. You and your retainer have murdered several agents of the Protectorate Ministry and disappeared. No doubt you're hiding amongst the rabble in the Bottoms you love so much."

The implication lashes Lexi like the chain of a flail. Winter fills her veins and she takes a wild, angry step toward Burr.

Daian deftly steps between them, raising a hand to halt her. "Now, now, tread softly. Your eyes don't hold murder well, Lexi. They're too innocent."

"I'm learning," she all but spits up at him.

"The Council will most certainly revoke the Stalbraid franchise by week's end," Burr assures Lexi.

"What value can I possibly have to you, then?" Lexi demands. "Why hold me here like this?"

"It's actually quite simple, my dear," Burr patiently explains. "For our plans to bear fruit, we will first need a revolution. You're going to give us one."

Lexi can't even begin to find meaning in those words. "What are you talking about? I'm not a revolutionary. I'm not any kind of military leader."

"No, of course not. But you will make a *fantastic* symbol. Better than your husband would've, I'm beginning to believe. We were quite distraught when he disappeared, you see."

"I don't understand."

"Well, originally we were going to use him. Daian would've approached him at the proper time to confirm all his suspicions about what the Protectorate Ministry was up to. We waited too long, sadly. Then Daian was presented with an opportunity to get close to you. At first we hoped it might lead us back to Brio, or at least to whatever leverage he had over the Ministry, but now I see we don't need him. We have you. It's fascinating how these things work out sometimes."

"What did you want Brio for? What do you want me for now?"

Burr seems genuinely delighted. "Because you've exceeded all our expectations. Oh, you should have seen yourself on the pleading floor of the Spectrum. You were a shining light for every dreg and vagabond in the Capitol. I never would have expected it from you, but the filthy peasants in those galleries were thoroughly unhinged. They would have named you their empress then and there. They loved your husband, and they now *adore* you. It's absolutely perfect!"

The pieces revealed in Burr's words begin to form a clear picture in Lexi's mind.

"The Bottoms," she says. "You want the people in the Bottoms to rise up and attack the Capitol."

"I told you, we need a rebellion. The oppressed are traditionally the ones who rebel, are they not? And the Bottoms is filled with them. They're angry and abused and gnashing their rotten teeth, ready to lash out. They simply need a flag under which to form."

"Why would you want that?" Lexi asks, more aghast than outraged.

"Disorder," Burr answers simply. "Chaos. Social breakdown. These are the things that create the greatness of opportunity. Opportunity we shall seize when the disorder reaches a healthy crescendo of blood and madness and destruction."

"To what end?" Lexi demands. "What will you gain from sending the entire Capitol . . . the entire *nation* spiraling into chaos?"

"We will fill the void, my dear," Burr explains patiently. "We will bring what's left in the wake of that chaos under the yoke of nobility once more. The Crachian philosophy of submission through illusion is a fallacy. You do not gain control over a people by convincing them they are the ones in control. You do it by making them accept that they are your inferiors. They must all at once fear and revere the purity and power of your bloodline. They must know they can *never* be your equal. Then they submit. Then they live to serve."

"The people of Crache will never yield to nobility."

"Of course they will. Because I intend to see to it that we are the only choice left to them. When I'm done, they will beg for a return to the old ways."

"If the people of the Bottoms rise up they will be slaughtered by Aegins before the Skrain is even called."

Burr shrugs. "That's simply a matter of organization and the proper, albeit clandestine support. Logistics are a matter for another day, however. You're going to be a guest of my house for a goodly while. I want to give you time to reconsider. As I said, this will proceed much better with your full cooperation. I strongly suggest you use the time I'm gifting you to find common ground with our position."

Lexi's eyes again flash defiantly. "And if I simply cannot locate that common ground?"

"Then I will be forced to turn these negotiations over to Daian, my house's very skilled master of persuasion."

"He promised no harm would come to me."

Daian shrugs, a thoroughly pleased smile on his face. "I'm afraid I lie quite often."

"He's very skilled at that, as well," Burr seconds. "Trust me, Lady Xia, you have no wish to experience his other specialty. I will leave you to ponder that. And please remember, for our purposes a martyr will serve just as well as a symbol. Decide which you'd prefer. And should you require anything in the interim, please do not hesitate to ring your bell. We shall speak again soon."

Burr gathers her gleaming skirts and exits the room without waiting for a response.

Daian lingers, watching Lexi with that same smile edged with madness.

"You know, I'm happy you're here with us," he says. "I find your presence . . . comforting."

Lexi forces a mocking smile to her lips. "That's very kind. My only wish is to live long enough to watch Taru rip your manhood from your body so that you may gaze upon it from a previously unseen angle before you die."

"Now that will be a *fight* worth waking up in the morning for," Daian says with a wicked grin. "Let's just hope your retainer is in battle-ready shape when next we meet."

He leaves her with that, closing the doors behind him and latching them both from the outside.

Lexi suppresses the urge to take up the nearest vase and hurl it at those doors. She turns and walks back to the open picture windows, staring down at the magnificent gardens far below. The serenity and beauty and seeming openness completely belies her predicament, and Lexi can't help bitterly reflecting on her fate.

If it comes to that, I will *jump*, she promises herself.

The true absurdity of this situation is that Burr and Daian are in essence offering Lexi exactly what she and Taru have needed since Brio disappeared: allies with the power to help them. It would be a blessing if not for the obvious truth that Burr is a megalomaniac and Daian is a madman. In Lexi's eyes, the Ignobles are the same as the Protectorate Ministry they are opposing. The only difference between the Ignobles and the Ministry seems to be that the Ignobles want to openly oppress the people while the Ministry is content to rule from the shadows and fool the people into thinking their lives are free from subjugation and control.

There has to be a third option for Crache, though Lexi cannot see it from where she stands now.

Lexi finds she can't command her heart or mind to stop racing. Her only goal since Ashana took on her role of Evie and departed has been to hold Stalbraid together, by any means necessary, first to preserve Brio's position, and then because Lexi found that not only did she have the ability to lead the Gen herself, she wanted to lead. More than that, Lexi wanted to best their enemies on the only battlefield available to her.

The thought of having that small victory snatched away, and watching the home built by their mothers and fathers be ripped apart and buried is almost too much for Lexi to bear.

When this all began she was a woman driven solely by loyalty, to her husband, to her Gen and its legacy. Now she finds the fire burning in the pit of her stomach is fed by principle, by that which Gen Stalbraid represents and its duty to the people for whom they've spent generations advocating. She won't betray that, whether the Council razes the Stalbraid franchise or not. She won't see harm come to those people who have no one else to speak for them, either.

Her thoughts turn to Brio and Taru and Ashana, wherever they may be in that moment. Perhaps they're all dead by now, and in the end Lexi's best efforts for them have amounted to ash. Perhaps they're all still alive, and even if constrained are plotting their own means of escape. She wants to believe that above all else.

One thing holds true in either case: Lexi cannot depend on anyone else to come for her. There will be no rescue, no saving grace forged from the bravery and risk of others to aid her in her darkest hour.

It's up to her to save herself.

It's up to her to protect the Bottoms and all its children.

It's up to her to stop Burr and Daian.

It's up to her to be Gen Stalbraid.

We are not flowers. We do wilt.

Even in winter, the strongest flower may find a way to thrive.

And Lexi remains her mother's daughter.

THE ONES WE KEEP CLOSE

A STORM IS BREWING IN THE EAST.

Dyeawan can see swollen clouds, as large as godheads and gray as cold steel, rolling in over the steadily agitated waters of the bay. It's the peak of afternoon, yet the sun is a thing poorly remembered by a pale and sickly sky that might have known nothing but gloom since it first spread over the Earth. The wind has teeth and a hunger to match, its appetite seeming to grow and bite more fiercely with every passing moment. Barely rising above the crashing of angry waves, thunder is a whispered warning on the horizon.

Dyeawan paddles her tender up the beach herself, politely declining Edger's offer to push her. The tender is aided through the wet sand by a new set of hollow wheels around the exterior of which a series of three-inch spikes protrude. A bellows affixed to Dyeawan's right-hand paddle operates the spikes. Compressing the bellows fills the hollow body of the wheels with air, deploying them, while decompressing the bellows' lung sucks the spikes back inside the wheels.

Edger walks beside her, silent and pointing his corpse's face toward the advancing storm clouds.

"You've chosen a strange afternoon for a walk along the beach," Dyeawan observes, mostly speaking because Edger is not.

"The weather seems appropriate for this discussion," he says, the muscles of his throat straining to pipe the words through Ku's body with enough volume to be heard above the excited climate.

"What do you mean? What discussion?"

Edger hesitates a moment longer, and then, "I feel as though something has changed between us. There's a division I didn't anticipate, and I fear it's growing."

"Do you regret elevating me to planner?"

Ku pipes the sputtering hiss of wind that serves as Edger's laughter.

"I might as well regret the expansion of your vocabulary. No, you *are* a planner, Dyeawan."

"Then what is it?"

"I foresaw you upsetting the balance among the rest of the twelve, but I never expected you to begin pulling away from me, as well."

"Is that what you think I'm doing?"

"I may not be quite as observant as you, but I do possess some facilities. I can't help but feel as though the closer I bring you, the less you seem to trust me."

"You choose to share your truth with me in slices," Dyeawan states plainly. "Every time you bring me closer it only raises more questions about the Planning Cadre that you choose not to answer."

"And there it is, the rancid core of the problem. Thank you for being honest with me. You are absolutely correct, Dyeawan."

They reach the finger of piled stone that extends out into the bay. It was one of those stones, flattened and smoothed by centuries of waves, which aided Dyeawan in solving the riddle of the Spectrum's construction that clinched her place at the planner's table.

It is clear Edger intends to traverse the stones.

"Why are we returning here?" Dyeawan asks.

"Indulge me" is his only answer.

With a sigh, Dyeawan lifts the handle of the bellows, filling its bladder with air from the tender's wheels and causing their many spikes to retract. She has no choice but to allow Edger to push her and the tender up onto the uneven surface of the stone bank, but at least once they're astride the rocks Dyeawan can steer and paddle the tender on her own once more. They make their way across the stone bank in silence, Edger leading the way.

The God Rung hangs from its hand-carved monolith rising at the end of the rocky terrain. The wind is causing the heavy steel circle to creak and clank loudly against its rusted base.

Dyeawan finds she dislikes the sight of it even more now that she knows its history.

"The weather is *not*, I'm afraid, conducive to what I must ask you to do next," Edger tells her. "Fortunately, I know you are more than strong enough to adapt."

"What do you need me to do?"

"Go for a swim. More precisely, a dive."

Dyeawan stares up at him without surprise, but with a clear amount of resentment.

"I thought I was done taking tests."

"You are," he assures her. "This isn't a test. There's something at the bottom of the bay I need you to investigate. I need to know your understanding of it."

He's telling the truth, though what that truth means to Edger is always open to debate.

He reaches inside his tunic and removes a pair of glass rounds bound together by a thick hide cord. The rounds of glass are set inside what appear to be covers fashioned from some form of shell. Longer lengths of cord are attached to either cover. The article looks as though it's meant to be worn around the head, over one's eyes.

"These will allow you to see beneath the bay. The glass is specially treated so it will neither fog nor streak, thus obscuring your vision. I refined the process myself."

"Of course you did," Dyeawan says, and Edger can't discern whether she's in awe or mocking him.

He offers her the eye covers. "Will you do this thing? Will you trust me this one final time, with the provision that I will never have to ask you again?"

Intrigued, Dyeawan accepts the pair of covers. She ties the hide straps together around her head, carefully fitting each viewing piece over her eyes.

"Where am I going? And how will I know I've reached whatever it is you want me to inspect?"

"Simply swim straight down. I know you're a strong swimmer. And you'll know what you're looking for when you see it."

Dyeawan sets the brake of her tender and begins pulling herself over the edge of the litter.

"May I assist you?" Edger asks.

Dyeawan ignores him, climbing down onto the rocks with the fluid ease of one accustomed to navigating the world by their hands while pulling the lower half of their body behind them. She crawls across the rocks, and slinks down the incline toward the bay, reaching the final boulder rising above the water. Dyeawan glances back at Edger briefly through the lenses he's fashioned for her, then pulls her body over the boulder and lets its own momentum propel her through the surface.

The water is cold and dark, and though the lenses over her eyes are clear Dyeawan isn't certain how she's meant to see anything down here. The bottom of the bay appears black when she first enters the water, though it can't be more than a few dozen yards deep this far from the shore. She strokes her arms and swims straight down, the natural buoyancy of her legs pulling them toward the surface and keeping her body level.

An object rises from the darkness below, very nearly colliding with Dyeawan's face. She reaches out simply to deflect whatever it is, finding her hands grabbing at the material of a garment. It is a simple dress, thin and not well made. She yanks it aside, turning the body of a young woman. Dyeawan stares through her lenses into the eternally closed eyes of her shrunken face.

The girl is missing her arms and legs. Even in the grip of shock and panic and fear, Dyeawan's mind can't help examining the stumps left of her limbs. It's clear they have not been severed, either in life or death. The girl was born that way. Her arms and legs grew only a few inches and then ceased growing forever.

Dyeawan allows the girl's body to drift back toward the shadowy depths. She is ready to swim back up to the surface then, but something in her gut even colder than the water surrounding her compels Dyeawan to remain there. A moment later she begins stroking her arms anew, driving herself deeper into the shadows, following the path of the limbless girl's corpse. Dyeawan watches her sink back to the shallow ocean bed, her descent abruptly halted. As Dyeawan swims closer, shapes beneath the girl begin to reveal themselves to her adjusting eyes.

The warning comes from the back of her mind, that place which knows before the rest of her truly sees. That warning is rooted in a horror Dyeawan cannot fully comprehend until she blinks, and the focal point of that warning is brought into focus.

There are more bodies beneath the limbless girl, and not just a few or even a few dozen. The bottom of the bay is one ceaseless mass grave. There are men, women, children, young and old. There must be hundreds, perhaps thousands of them interred beneath the water here. All of them were either born with some disability, or, like Dyeawan, injured later in their lives. She sees open eyes overwrought with milky cataracts. She sees withered limbs and empty spaces where most possess sturdy flesh.

Dyeawan's blood freezes even as the space between her temples is lit aflame. She can't stop looking at their faces, one after another, all of them carved by death's hand into masks of torment and longing and pain and terror. None of them died naturally, and none of them wanted to experience eternity here in a watery grave off the coast of a hidden island.

She turns from the sight of the bodies, feeling her lungs begin to burn and her cheeks straining painfully. Dyeawan swims for the tenuous light above. Her veins are ready to unravel from both the lack of air and the rush of repulsion and confusion emanating from her mind. She explodes through the surface of the bay. She clings to the nearest boulder, wrapping her arms around it like a small child seeking solace against the leg of a parent. She sputters and coughs up seawater, tearing away the cord binding the lenses to her face. She casts them away violently.

Dyeawan feels Edger's hands closing around her forearms before she actually sees him attempting to lift her from the water.

"Don't touch me!" she shrieks, the outburst shocking even her.

Edger releases her. It is ten times more difficult to pull herself back up onto the rocks than it was to dive from their edge, but Dyeawan claws and scrapes until her legs are free of the tainted water. Edger remains silent, blending into the background as he watches her drag her body to the foot of her tender.

"I could not tell you," Edger says, almost as though he's reassuring himself. "I could not simply *tell* you. You had to see it. You had to see them. It was the only way. I am so very sorry, Dyeawan."

"What have you done?" Dyeawan demands in between ragged breaths. "Why would you . . . who are . . . why did they . . ."

She climbs up onto the litter of her tender, lying upon it like a funeral cairn.

"They are no one," Edger explains. "Like you were. Like I was. The difference is they had nothing to offer Crache beyond the burdens with which they were born. Not like us. Their fate was simple. They were intended for liquidation. The rest of the planners would have seen their bodies burned or buried or experimented upon until we could discern a way to use them to feed crops or the like, but I wouldn't have it. I had them placed here to keep them close, to remind me of what must be done, and because of the kinship I feel toward them. They are family, in a way. Wouldn't you agree? This is, in its way, our familial burial plot."

Dyeawan cannot stay the tears that overwhelm her eyes. Her mind races to find any reasonable way to not accept what she's just seen and what she's hearing, and at every turn her mind is met with a closed door.

"They did not suffer," he assures her, sounding almost offended, as if she'd already made the accusation. "They were ferried here in small groups after being plucked from the streets or dungeons. They were given a hot meal and mulled drink. The herbs secreted in that drink are a perfection of nature. They drew them into a deep, all-consuming sleep. Each slumbering body was then gently and respectfully lowered into the waters of the bay. None of them ever felt a thing, I promise you. I insisted on that."

He waits for Dyeawan to speak, even if only to allow her to vent her initial shock and anger, but words continue to fail her.

"I have spent a great deal of time explaining the inner workings of Crache to you. Most of those lessons have consisted of telling you what Crache is *not*. Now you have to understand what Crache is. Crache is balance, Dyeawan. It is a perfect, harmonious balance of people and purpose and resources. That is what is essential. That is what feeds the fire burning in the forge of Crache. There simply is no place in our society for those people below. They can serve no useful purpose. Regular citizens will never accept them. They live only to drain precious resources. I give shelter and purpose to the few I can justify having here in the Planning Cadre as helpers and staff, Makai and the others, even you when you first came. However, that space is very limited."

"How did you know I was capable of more when you first met me?" Dyeawan asks.

"I didn't. I hadn't an inkling of how remarkable your mind is. It was sheer luck. You were like a bird with a broken wing, even for . . . our kind. I have a severe weakness for broken birds. That's all."

Dyeawan has spent her entire life starving in the streets alone. She had nothing to begin with and then had her legs taken from her. Until this moment, however, she's never truly felt defeated.

"Why would you show me this?" she asks miserably. "Do you expect me to be grateful?"

"I've told you, Crache has no rulers of name, only a bureaucracy composed of endless councils and committees. That is, of course, wholly on purpose."

In that moment, hearing those words, Dyeawan understands why.

"People usurp rulers," she says with certainty. "But they cannot rebel against a ruler who does not exist."

"Correct. A ruler is a target. A bureaucracy, on the other hand, is an endless forest in which the discontent lose both their way and their will to rebel, with nowhere and no one to focus their ire upon. We give them no direction, no bull's-eye for any anger or frustration or malice they may harbor against the state. However, no nation can function without strong leadership. If our fate was left to a Crachian committee, the Capitol would topple within a week. There must be a ruler, even if their name is never spoken and no monuments are ever erected in their likeness."

"I understand," she bitterly affirms.

"Dyeawan . . . would it surprise you to learn I am that ruler? Would it surprise you to learn the final word on this nation's fate falls to me? That I administer the Protectorate Ministry at my will?"

Dyeawan doesn't answer right away. It should surprise her, of course. The fact that this afflicted little man of advancing years, living in a ruin on a tiny island, is the master and commander of a nation such as Crache should be shattering news. Yet somehow she'd silently accepted that Edger was in control of all this. Perhaps it is because he became her mentor, her teacher, her sole source of knowledge, direction, and approval. He has been the master of her ultimate fate.

It's easy enough to believe those that control you must control everything.

Slowly, she shakes her head.

"Of course," Edger says. "Of course it wouldn't surprise you. Very little does. But do you appreciate the scope of that? Do you appreciate the responsibility, the singular weight I bear?"

Dyeawan turns over on the litter and pushes her torso up, carefully folding her legs beneath her and settling atop the tender in her usual position.

"You still haven't explained why you would allow me to see such a thing as this."

"It is exceedingly simple. I would choose you to succeed me. I would choose you, not only to lead the planners after I'm gone, but to truly rule all Crache."

His words aren't any more believable than the reality of what she just witnessed at the bottom of the bay, yet Dyeawan cannot deny the truth of both.

Her next question is obvious. "Why?"

"The others, they possess keen minds and a breadth of vision for invention and innovation, but they are planners, not rulers. They do not inspire people. They barely see people. They certainly do not empathize with them. I see in you the potential to be both. That is a rare thing, as rare as you are. I believe you will one day exceed anything I have managed to accomplish, perhaps anything my predecessors did. Your mind is that unique, and your temperament that suited."

"And to you being a ruler means exterminating anyone whose purpose isn't obvious to you?"

"If you are to be Crache's future, you have to know how Crache functions. You have to see and know every single cog and wheel. What lies at the bottom of this bay is an atrocity, but it is a necessary one. You must be able to reconcile that fact and truly accept it if you are to ascend to my position one day. Do you see?"

Dyeawan nods. "I believe I finally do see through your eyes, Edger."

"But can you accept what you see?"

"I have no choice, do I?"

"You have more choices than most, Dyeawan. You are one of a very few people to truly know all sides of Crache. Now I'm offering you the opportunity to shape its future. So I ask you again, do you accept?"

In answer, Dyeawan extends a hand toward him.

Though his face remains ever unreadable, Edger's body seems to visibly relax.

He steps close to her tender, taking Dyeawan's hand in his.

Edger hasn't noticed her other hand reaching beneath the litter of her tender for the object concealed there. Dyeawan raises like a knife the small bellows with its hollow needle. She does not stab Edger, however. Instead, Dyeawan brings the point of the needle down into the neck of Ku, the wind dragon, piercing the creature's flesh and squeezing the bellows tightly.

Edger, acting on instinct more than anything else, quickly slaps the bellows from Dyeawan's hand, loosing the needle from Ku's neck. The bellows flies over the edge of the piled boulders and disappears into the waters of the bay.

"What have you done?" he demands.

"I've just killed you," Dyeawan calmly informs him. "I'm very sorry."

The bony pipes rising from Ku's back begin issuing an eerie chorus of crackling wind. It's not a sound being filtered from Edger's throat; this is the result of an event occurring inside the wind dragon's small body. Ku, perfectly docile a moment before, begins writhing in a frenzy against Edger's flesh.

Edger's hands fly to his neck as he realizes that Ku is becoming feral. Dyeawan imagines what the expression on Edger's face would look like were his features capable of forming any expression at all. His fingers attempt to pry Ku from his throat. The hollow protrusions on the creature's back begin whistling like a boiling teakettle. The rest of Edger's body seizes as the wind dragon closes its jaws, biting through the patch of flesh its mouth would otherwise harmlessly occupy.

Edger would scream if his throat were still sending sounds through the wind dragon's body. In his panicked agony he tears Ku from his neck, the wind dragon's mouth taking a large chunk of the man's throat with him. Thick red blood begins regurgitating down the front of his tunic. Edger squeezes Ku in one hand until those long backbones pierce Edger's palm and he crushes the wind dragon's tiny body, very nearly popping the creature's yellow and black eyes from his skull.

Dyeawan watches him stumble backward, the strength fleeing Edger's legs even as his command over them wanes. He falls against the God Rung, sitting awkwardly at the base of the monolith as his life's blood continues to gush from his torn asunder throat.

Dyeawan paddles a few feet closer to him.

"I learned well the lesson of Greenfire, my little duck," she explains. "I've been studying other animals since that test, reading everything I could find and examining live specimens when I could. I was particularly interested in wind dragons. I took a portion of Ku's blood while he was last off your neck, in the highest heat of his mating cycle. I tried injecting it into different creatures. It sent all of them into a killing frenzy. They weren't easy experiments, but I knew it would be worth the effort. I'd like to think that, at the time, it was just simple curiosity. But the truth is I always knew this could happen. I knew one way or another I might have to make your death look like an accident, as though Ku had entered his mating cycle prematurely while on your neck and killed you."

Edger is attempting in vain to staunch the flow of blood from his neck with one hand, pressing his palm into his throat and in fact only making matters worse.

"I am truly sorry, Edger. I owe you so much. And I have learned so much from you. I hoped . . . I hoped *so hard* for you to be different from the Aegins in the Bottoms, from the men who led packs of other men like feral dogs. But you're not. You are what happens when those people are smart enough to see a world beyond themselves and the little place where they're born and raised and live their lives. You are the world they make when they are given the chance to make a whole world. There's no room for people in your world unless they serve your purpose, and I've lived under the yoke of such men long enough."

Dyeawan's gaze sinks from Edger's face, ever as much the monument as the monolith rising above him, to the hand still clutching the crushed body of his beloved wind dragon.

"I'm sorry to you, too, Ku," she says. "You didn't do anything to deserve this. But perhaps it's better this way. You're free now."

Edger removes the bloody, tremor-wracked hand from his throat and extends it toward her, fingertips straining in his final few moments of life.

Dyeawan only shakes her head, wiping the tears from her eyes with the sleeve of her planner's tunic.

"Thank you for everything you've done for me," she says. "I hope at least a part of you understands. I hope you can forgive me."

Edger's arm gradually falls until it rests at his side. His head lolls forward, and in the next moment the rest of his body finally matches the slackened death mask of his face.

When she is certain he's gone, Dyeawan looks up at the God Rung hanging above Edger's head. She wonders if the people who built it deceived themselves about what they'd created the way they deceived those whom they subjected to its judgment.

That is the lie I won't tell, she promises herself. *That I'm somehow better than my actions, no matter how dark they are. That is the lie that turns you into the people who made the God Rung, and people like Edger.*

High above them, the rain finally begins to fall.

DAWN IS THE MOMENT YOU WAKE

THE LIGHTS OF THE TENTH CITY ARE A SWARM OF FIREFLIES IN the darkness somewhere very far away.

From a high window on the nation's border, Evie watches the farthest bastion of Crachian civilization and her patchwork rebel army's next destination. The Tenth City seems quiet at such a distance, peaceful, but Evie knows the entire city must be bustling, even at this late hour. Skrain and Aegins will be fortifying the walls and the approach to the gates.

Have they told the people, Evie wonders? Have they told them anything? Have they even bothered to feed them a string of lies to conceal the fact that an invading force has seized control of the western border and has its sights set on their city?

Invaders, Evie thinks to herself. *We're invaders now.*

Behind her, Sirach stirs beneath the silken sheets of the bed they've shared since taking the garrison. Their temporary quarters once belonged to a Skrain captain and the steady string of pleasure girls and boys who kept them entertained at night. They've uncovered evidence in the form of perfumes and oils and several toys hidden beneath the bed, none of which belong in a military barracks.

Evie isn't certain even now how she and Sirach ended up together; everything immediately following the Battle for the Border, as the Legionnaires are calling it, felt unreal to her, like a dream. Nothing ever feels wrong in a dream. There's no hesitation and no inhibition.

Enjoying each other's body has undeniably brought her repeated bliss. However, Evie can't deny that taking her first bath in months was even better.

Evie listens to the rustling of Sirach gathering the sheets around her naked body and slipping from the bed. Her bare feet padding across the room make even less sound, and in the next moment Sirach envelopes Evie in the sheet, pressing against her bare back and embracing her gently.

"Can't you sleep?" she asks.

Evie lightly grips Sirach's arms and leans against her gratefully. "I barely remember what sleep feels like."

"Then I feel I've failed utterly at my task."

Evie smiles. "Not at all."

She rests her chin on Evie's shoulder. Sirach's gaze fixes on the lights in the distance.

"It's like one big, bright jewel with a thousand eyes that sparkle in the dark," she says. "And we're going to pluck it from the bedrock."

"You make it sound quite lovely. You have a gift for that. A siege, however, and sacking a city isn't lovely. It will be wading knee-deep through streets filled with blood and shit and screams of pain and fear and death. It won't look like a jewel then."

Sirach grins, kissing along the outline of Evie's collarbone. "You know what I *really* like about you?" she whispers.

Evie tenses, feeling the prickling of flesh that should be wholly unrelated to her shoulder.

"You've seemed to develop a lengthy list over the past few nights," she says.

"Besides those things," Sirach amends.

"What's that?"

"You utterly refuse to become what you quite clearly have become."

Evie shakes her head. "I don't know what that means."

Rather than explain, Sirach poses a new question: "Are you saying we shouldn't attack the city?"

Evie takes a deep, resolute breath. "No, we have to. Right now Crache can still control what's happened here, or at least the knowledge of it. As long as they have that they'll do everything they can to quietly wipe us out before the people learn about what we've done. There'll be no bargaining with them until we hold something real."

"One of their cities," Sirach says.

"One of their cities."

"And you truly think they'll bargain with us?"

"I have to hope. Taking the Tenth City will be a miracle, even with more of your people and every band of B'ors within two hundred miles. Holding it will be impossible."

"We've defied the odds thus far," Sirach muses. "Largely thanks to that beautiful mind of yours, of course."

"Then let's hope I don't run dry of ideas."

Sirach glances over her shoulder at the closed door to their quarters, more precisely at the shadow of two large boots eclipsing much of the torchlight streaming under the bottom of that door.

"Do you think Bam is jealous?" she asks Evie quietly. "Or do you think he's enjoyed the sounds escaping this room as of late?"

"I didn't ask him to stand guard," Evie reminds her. "I never do. I hope it hasn't hurt him. He has a good heart. Simple. There's not enough simple in our world."

Sirach ponders that silently for a moment before saying, "Well then . . . should we invite him to join us?"

Evie's head turns toward her, both her brows raised high and tight.

"Is that something you'd enjoy?"

Sirach shrugs. "I suppose I think about it the way I thought when you first proposed, after a life spent killing every Savage I see, that I ally myself with them to attack the largest nation in the known history of the world."

"And what did you think?" Evie asks.

Sirach's grin is an animal flash of teeth in the dark.

"It sounds like a good time," she says.

THE GRAY AFTER THE STORM

THE PLANNER'S HIDDEN CHAMBER WITHIN THE CADRE IS unusually empty. Dyeawan's tender is parked in the spot formerly reserved for Edger's seat at the concentric stone circles that serve as the planner's meeting table. She is the winding slab's sole occupant. Quan serves her hot tea in a small cup. The attendant is forced to double his body over to pour the steaming, camellia-scented concoction. He still wears the black band of mourning around the right sleeve of his brown tunic.

"Thank you," Dyeawan says. "You really needn't fuss over me so, Mister Quan."

"It is what he would have wanted," Quan insists. "You were as a daughter to him."

Those words sink hooks into her heart and drag the organ in opposite directions, but Dyeawan doesn't allow the sensation to reshape her expression. She sips her tea silently, bowing her head in thanks to the kindly attendant.

Riko enters the chamber, her gaze clearly overwhelmed by its features and its mere existence. The lithe builder's tanto-edged bangs are bound up in a topknot, and there are fresh grease stains streaking her tool-encumbered vest.

"This room is impossible," she observes, her eyes soaking in every feature like a thirsty sponge. "I mean . . . like, truly impossible. Architecturally, I don't understand how it exists."

"This room is only the beginning of the impossible," Dyeawan assures her.

Riko cocks her head, regarding the winding stone snake with Dyeawan as its head.

"This table doesn't make much sense," she says. "It's not impossible, it's just . . . stupid."

Dyeawan grins. "I think it's meant to be symbolic."

The bridge of Riko's small nose becomes a mass of wrinkles. "I *detest* form over function."

Dyeawan shakes her head, never ceasing to enjoy the bluntness and honesty in Riko's perception of the world and the people in it.

"Will you come to sit with me? Please?"

Riko leaps up onto the outermost circle of the stone slab, gleefully skipping across each interior circle with a smile untouched by the judgment of others until she reaches the center point beside which Dyeawan's tender rests. Riko hunkers down with a giggle and sits atop the table, folding her legs comfortably. She uncoils the toggles of her overburdened vest, its dozens upon dozens of tools jostling and jangling as she slips it from her slight shoulders and lays it next to her.

Riko leans back, resting on the heels of her palm. "I feel like we're getting away with something being here, yeah?"

Dyeawan nods. "I know precisely what you mean."

Riko's impish smile fades, the clouds of dark memory sweeping across her eyes.

"I'm sorry about Edger," she says. "I know he meant a lot to you."

"He will always mean a lot to me," Dyeawan admits, and that much is true.

More than the act itself, Dyeawan regrets not being able to tell Riko the truth about Edger's death. Riko is her truest friend, perhaps the first one she's ever known, but she wouldn't understand. She can't understand, not yet, not without having seen inside Edger's head the way Dyeawan did and having witnessed the results. Perhaps one day, when Riko knows the whole truth about Crache, Dyeawan will be able to reveal everything to her.

Riko leans forward and whispers almost conspiratorially. "Are they really going to let you lead the planners? I mean . . ."

"You don't have to whisper, Riko. And no one is going to 'let' me do anything, not anymore. I'm going to do what needs to be done, regardless of what they want. They need us. Really, there is no 'they' anymore. They are gone. We are the new 'they.' Do you understand?"

Riko stares at her in awe, and with something skittish underlying that awe, fear for her friend, perhaps.

"I need to ask you something," Dyeawan says.

"Of course."

Dyeawan turns and raises her hand, looking like a tentative child in the back of a classroom requesting permission to speak.

Quan strides forward, his usual broad and warm smile on his face as he bears forth the same gray tunic he once presented to Dyeawan.

Riko watches him approach, her mouth agape and her eyes wide and rapidly blinking.

"What . . . what's this?"

"I need someone I absolutely trust to sit here as a planner," Dyeawan explains. "You deserve to be here, anyway. You have the best mind and the most capable hands in the entire Cadre."

"What about . . . I mean, what about Tahei? He—"

"I still like Tahei. I believe he has a good heart, but he lets what he doesn't have and others do poison him. He acts on his emotions too often."

Riko clearly doesn't understand the implications of that statement, but she's more overcome by Dyeawan's request.

"I'm not sure this is a good idea," Riko protests. "Everything is happening so fast."

"This is overdue," Dyeawan reminds her.

"I just don't think—"

"If this isn't something you want, I won't force it on you. I wouldn't do that to a friend. But I think you *do* want this. You just thought it could never happen, so you let yourself believe it shouldn't happen."

Riko's eyes soften on her, the doubt and shock beginning to melt from her features.

"Tell me if I'm wrong," Dyeawan bids her.

Riko shakes her head. "You're not wrong. You're never wrong, it seems like."

"Then please accept, Riko. You're my best friend. I need you."

Riko hesitates a moment longer, then she nods several times in quick succession, a genuine smile spreading across her lips.

Dyeawan smiles. "Thank you."

Riko slides down from the tabletop and throws her arms around Dyeawan's shoulders, rocking her from side to side atop the litter. "Thank *you*!"

Dyeawan can't help laughing as she gratefully returns the embrace. "I told you, it's overdue."

Riko releases her and turns to Quan, staring at the tunic with hands cupped against her chest as if she is afraid to touch it, lest the back of her palms be rebuked by a switch.

Quan bows to her, deeply, extending the tunic between his arms.

"Go try it on," Dyeawan bids her. "It's a little stiff and it takes some getting used to, but I think the color will suit you better than it does me."

Riko accepts the tunic, grinning unabashedly.

"Can I . . . I mean, is it all right to still call you 'Slider'?"

Dyeawan nods, the question inspiring a warm sensation in her chest.

"I still like the name," she says. "Especially when a friend uses it. I suppose I just . . . I didn't want to *need* the name anymore. Does that make sense?"

"I think I get it. Can I . . . try this on now?"

Dyeawan smiles. "Please."

Riko practically skitters away, clasping the tunic against her.

They watch her go with shared pleasure, Quan smiling down at Dyeawan without comment.

A repeated echoing from the shadows filling the far side of the chamber draws their attention. It is the sound of two gloved hands clapping, slowly, with monotonous insincerity.

A moment later Oisin, still mocking Dyeawan with praise, steps from the shadows. The Protectorate Ministry agent is also smiling, but his is an expression filled with malice.

"And to think," Oisin muses ruefully, "when I first saw you winding the corridors on that contraption I thought you the most pathetic of Edger's pet rats."

"Please leave us," Dyeawan gently bids Quan.

The impossibly tall attendant immediately bows to her, though he does cast a sidelong glance of disdain in Oisin's direction. Quan strides from the room in the same direction Riko left it.

"Are you here to kill me?" Dyeawan asks Oisin a moment later without a trace of fear or anticipation in her voice.

The agent laughs, empty and hollow and forced. "What a question."

Dyeawan frowns. "If you aren't going to kill me, what do you want?"

"How did you do it?" Oisin asks. "How did you cause Edger's death? I know somehow you did, but I cannot for the life of me imagine how you arranged it."

Dyeawan remains perfectly calm. "Edger spent his life with a wild creature's teeth at his throat. It allowed him to speak, but he knew it came with great risk."

Oisin waves a hand dismissively. "Fine. It doesn't matter. His time was passing with or without you."

"It matters very much," Dyeawan disagrees.

"You cannot really believe you'll sit in his place at that table, can you? You've been privy to enough Cadre information to know what we're facing. There's a full-blown rebellion in the east that must be dealt with. There's an army marching on our border. You're a child, however clever. You're not equipped—"

"Stop speaking to me," Dyeawan orders the sour-faced agent, and surprise more than anything else momentarily silences him. "Maybe Edger enjoyed dueling you with words, but I don't. I find you very unpleasant, and I refuse to endure unpleasant, malicious men any longer. I don't want to hear your complaints or your opinions or your accusations. Edger created you as a tool. You will *act* as one, and you will speak only as much as one of Riko's vise grips from this moment forward."

Oisin stares incredulously down at her.

"You impudent little—"

"There is *nothing* you can do to me. Nothing. Unless you are willing to take out your dagger and kill me here and now, you will do *exactly* as I say. You will do it because I am the only one left who knows what Edger knew and truly understands his methods. No one else has seen the whole of the picture. They only have pieces. No one else can replace him."

"You think my only option is to murder you? Do you realize who I am? Do you comprehend the resources at my disposal?"

"You are a specter created by a dead man to frighten the ignorant, and nothing more. What will you do, Oisin? Rally the Protectorate Ministry to overthrow the Planning Cadre? What do you imagine occurs in the wake of such an act? Crache would fall apart. You know how to protect secrets and make people disappear. You haven't the slightest idea how to maintain the machinery of Crache, whether this rebellion in the east you refer to succeeds or not. Not to mention you would have to rule openly. The people would rise against you before your first year saw its end. The Protectorate Ministry only functions in the shadows. Standing in the light of day you are powerless, and you know it."

Oisin's eyes are smoldering, but there is a tight-lipped recognition of the truth in her words, even if he isn't ready to consciously accept it.

"You forget you are not the only planner in this keep. You are not even the—"

"Yes. The old men and women who wear this pendant would certainly side with you. Perhaps they hold enough sway in the Cadre to cast me and the other young planners out. What will you be left with when they are the only ones seated at this table? Every worthwhile idea they've had has been realized. They are equally worthless to you. Edger knew this, that's one of the reasons he gave me this tunic, to drive them out. Planners, Oisin, don't rule Crache. Leaders rule it. You have no leaders. You have *no one* to comprehend the shape of things, let alone reshape them as needed."

"Is that what you are, little girl? Are you a leader?"

"I will learn," she says, her resolve brooking no dissent. "I am *very* good at that, Oisin."

The Protectorate Ministry agent swallows imperceptibly, the battle all but drained from his expression.

"I should say you're off to a fair start," he admits, however reluctant. "We shall see how you finish."

"Say my name," she instructs him.

Oisin blinks at her in surprise. "What? What do you—"

"I wish to hear you say my name. I wish to hear you say it with respect and recognition rather than disdain. If you cannot say my name without those qualities imbued in it then you and I obviously remain at odds. I do not wish to be at odds with you. I must know if I will be forced to resolve the matter another way."

Oisin no longer seems to recognize her. The look on his face is surprised, even astonished. Dyeawan imagines he isn't used to being bested, let alone by someone he thought of as a defenseless child confined to a chair with wheels, a little girl who should be vulnerable and frightened and grateful for the smallest kindness.

"As you wish, Dyeawan," he says, and though it is quiet, the only emotion contained in his voice is repressed fear.

Dyeawan nods, her expression satisfied.

"You may go now."

Oisin turns, sweeping his cape over his shoulder and pacing back into the shadows of the chamber.

Dyeawan waits for the report of his footfalls to become very far away before she commands him to halt.

"Oisin," she calls to him.

The sounds of his footfalls cease.

"Gather as many agents as you need. I want you to remove every body from the bottom of the bay. You will have them properly wrapped. You will build pyres for each. They will be burned and you will show them all the deference and respect they deserve. I want it done immediately, in secret. I know you can manage that."

No immediate answer is forthcoming. Dyeawan imagines Oisin stroking or perhaps gripping the handle of his dagger there in the dark, reconsidering the notion of slitting her throat and seizing the power he'd no doubt been dreaming of since Edger's body was carried back to the Cadre.

Dyeawan knows the next moment will either solidify her new position or destroy it.

She finds to her surprise that her heart isn't beating any faster than it would otherwise.

"As you wish," Oisin repeats mechanically.

Dyeawan feels muscles she wasn't even aware were tensed suddenly relax. The rest of her, most importantly her expression and voice, remain unchanged.

"Thank you," she says. "There is one other matter with which I require your assistance. It is a service you and the Ministry are in a unique position to provide, being the authority on unearthing secret knowledge."

She can practically hear his teeth grinding as Oisin asks, "And what is that?"

"I want to know where I come from," she says. "I want to know who my parents were."

"Why does that matter?"

Oisin sounds genuinely confused.

It takes a moment for Dyeawan to respond. Her mind is momentarily preoccupied with all those memories she can't quite bring into focus, and an image of Edger, telling her again and again how special and unique she is and asking her about her origins.

"It may not matter at all," Dyeawan admits. "It may also be very important. In either case, I want to know."

"Even if I could find out what you want to know, aren't you concerned I'd use such information against you?"

Dyeawan has weighed that very concern against her need to learn the answer, just as she's sized up Oisin as an adversary.

"You don't concern me, Oisin," she says with finality. "*Now* you may go."

For a moment she thinks he has a retort in him, but it never comes.

Dyeawan listens to the final chorus of his fading footfalls, and when she's certain that he's left the chamber her body involuntarily slumps against the litter of her tender. Rationally she knew that their conversation would proceed and end precisely as it unfolded, but the part of her that will never truly leave the alleys of the Bottoms remained terrified that this entire illusion would shatter.

Just don't lie to yourself, Dyeawan entreats like a silent mantra. *You're pretending you know what's going to happen next, but you don't.*

She doesn't. Dyeawan has no idea what will happen next. She has no plan beyond the actions she's taken thus far. She only knows there must be change. There must be a way to make room in this world for all people, especially the weakest among them. She cannot accept that people like her are a burden at their worst, and a cheap and expendable resource at their best.

FINAL SELECTION

DOORS OF ROTTED WOOD ARE FLUNG OPEN AND TARU AND the rest are prodded from inside the darkened tunnel out into the harsh light of day. Taru limps across an expansive field of dead grass surrounded by tall walls beginning to crumble from age and neglect. The retainer has been divested of armor and short sword and hook-end, left in the simple street tunic and trousers they've always worn beneath. Taru has never felt so naked and vulnerable as an adult. The retainer's hands physically ache to cradle the well-worn handle of a weapon.

There are perhaps fifty of them, gathered from three separate cities, including the Capitol. Taru has only been able to surmise this by interrogating several of them in the tunnels. It's whispered that there are a few hardened murderers and criminals among them, but most of these people seem to be petty thieves or simply vagrants. The only quality they all seem to share is that no one in Crache who matters will miss them.

"Form a line!" a mush-mouthed voice hollers at the collection of minor lawbreakers and out-of-doors folk. "Facing me! Spread out an arm apart from each other, and stand straight! I don't give a stallion's steaming load whether you're drunk, sick, or half dead! *Stand!* Now!"

The voice belongs to stocky man with the shoulders of a bull. His small head is shaved completely bald, making his thin mustache stand out far more than it should. He wears a tunic that is quite obviously too long for him, almost reaching his knees. He's at least had enough sense to tear away the sleeves. Over the tunic, he's strapped an armored leather vest decorated with the polished skulls of small animals, including a fanged monkey's maw on his chest.

"I'm your wrangler!" he announces in a voice that sounds as though he's speaking through a mouth full of wet seaweed. "My name is Erazo. You call me 'Tasker' or 'Freemaster,' and nothing else! *You* don't have a name anymore. D'you hear? From right now until you die bloody fighting the enemies of Crache, your name . . . is Savage."

Erazo emphasizes that final statement by pointing the butt of the short club in his hand at Taru and then sweeping it back and forth across the line.

The full impact of what's happening bats the retainer upside their head in that moment.

Savage.

Taru has been conscripted into the Savage Legion. Did Brio stand in this very spot, listening to this man strip away his identity? Did Ashana experience the same thing in her drunkard persona of Evie?

"Look to the spires of this field . . ."

Erazo continues his cruel welcome speech, but Taru ceases to listen to the man's garbled voice. The space between the retainer's temples is burning. Taru's only thought for the past several days has been escape, returning to Lexi's side to guard her from their enemies. Every moment that thought has become more dire and desperate and painful within the retainer's mind.

Now, however, Taru knows there will be no escape. Taru has the chance to follow the path of those they've lost, Brio and Ashana, and bolstered by the message Spud-Bar delivered, Taru has to believe they are still out there somewhere, awaiting their opportunity for freedom while fighting to stay alive. Taru must find them and aid them in both of those things.

Taru is no less concerned for Lexi, but that concern cannot magically change the world. The retainer is here and Lexi is back in the Capitol.

Besides, there's Daian. If the Aegin recovers he can protect Lexi, and Taru knows he will. It's obvious that affection has grown between them. Taru saw that immediate connection the first time they met. While the retainer doesn't believe Lexi would ever betray Brio's heart or his trust, that affection could save her life in Taru's absence.

"There's rebellion brewing in the east!" Erazo announces, and those words bring Taru's attention back to bear on the tasker. "A small band of renegade B'ors and a few runaway Savages have joined with the Sicclunan scum to seize a keep along the border.

"We'll be moving you out sooner than we would otherwise, and chances are you'll be fighting mutts just like you. You might even know some of them from the rat holes you've called home. Remember what you are and the nation you serve! As a reward, when this rebellion is put down, and it will be put down, you'll all be given your freedom! And a big bag of gold to live a proper life when you return to the cities!"

Taru wants to laugh at that, but banishes the very idea.

There's rebellion in the east? That's an intriguing notion, and one that gives Taru even more reason and motivation to seek out Brio and Ashana among the Legionnaire ranks. If they're still alive and conscripted, this rebellion could provide a safe haven for them far more easily reachable than attempting to return to the cities. If they've already joined the rebellion, then they will need Taru even more.

The retainer sets a hard stare upon Erazo, and up at the few disinterested Skrain idly stalking the walls around them.

They don't know Savagery, Taru silently promises them. *They've never seen what a true Savage looks like. But I'm going to show them. I'm going to show this whole damn nation what they've made.*

ACKNOWLEDGMENTS

THE BOOK YOU'RE HOLDING IN YOUR HANDS OR READING upon your chosen screen represents the end of a very, very long road. It has been, in fact, the longest journey any finished work of mine has ever taken. I doubt I will ever publicly admit to the exact number of years it took me to finish the first draft, but saying those years were plural is enough. I never would have reached the end of this road without a *lot* of help, and I am grateful beyond my insufficient command of words to every one of those folks. The first and ever the foremost is my wife, Nikki. This book would not exist without her. In point of fact, *I* would not exist without her. My agent, DongWon Song, believed in this story when it was nothing more than a badly composed pitch in a hotel bar, on the strength of which he also signed me as a client. My mother, Barbara, remains my most tireless advocate and the best unpaid publicist in the business. Helljack has been my longtime friend and webmaster. Nicolette Barischoff was an immense help to me in preparing to write this book, and I'm grateful. Thank you to the brilliant and impossibly kind Sarah Gailey for their support. Kameron Hurley also provided pivotal counsel (whether or not she will admit it was pivotal) that helped me reshape important aspects of this entire thing. My editor, Navah Wolfe, is a taskmaster worthy of the Savage Legion who is tempered by a compassion no Savage tasker could ever fathom. Her insights and ruthless campaign against plot holes, faulty world building, and clunky prose made this book and this story infinitely better. My copyeditors, Jeannie Ng, Lauren Forte, and Alexandre Su, chiefly aided her in that. My marketer/publicist, LJ Jackson, kicked down doors to make people aware of this book. Joe Monti, editorial director of Saga Press, has been a longtime supporter of mine who also taught me about the shrimp in New York City's water supply. There are several other folks under the Saga Press banner who also deserve shine, including Kaitlyn Snowden, Kathryn Barrett, Jennifer Bergstrom, Jennifer Long, Sara Quaranta, Caitlin McCreary, Caroline Pallotta, Allison Green, Rosa Burgos, and Madison Penico. It takes a village that's more like a pirate ship that crashed into a circus to raise a novel, much less put it on your shelf/screen.

And if you're reading this now, thank *you*.

Now go tell a friend.

Matt Wallace
Los Angeles
June 28, 2019

Turn the page for
an exciting sneak peek of

SAVAGE

BOUNTY

BOOK TWO OF THE SAVAGE
REBELLION TRILOGY

THE SMALL ATOLL RISES A MILE OFFSHORE, LITTLE MORE than a halo of sharp rocks anointing the slate-gray waters. From a distance one would scarcely take notice, and upon closer inspection their perception wouldn't be much altered. Yet this nothing of a stone formation has been, since the Planning Cadre took up residence on the island, the closest thing to a sacred site observed by the brilliant and unknown conspiracy of men and women who secretly control the destiny of Crache.

Mister Quan dutifully crews the tiny rowboat, ever the pleasant stoic as he guides the oars smoothly through the lapping tide. Dyeawan sits at the bow, her back to the atoll. She isn't entirely ready to take in the scene that awaits them there.

She studies Quan's face, its broad and congenial features. Dyeawan has always possessed the ability to read people. She never knows their thoughts, but she sees their nature and intentions revealed in the smallest ticks in the flesh of their face, or the way they move their body, or the quiver in their voice, no matter how slight.

Mister Quan does not speak, and Dyeawan has yet to witness a single crack in his veneer, not even when he discovered her spying on Edger and Oisin's private conversation and displayed sympathy by not exposing her. He is perhaps the only person she has ever met who appears to act purely and selflessly in aid of those around him.

It has been weeks since Dyeawan ascended to the center of the planners (for there is no "head" of their winding circular table), replacing Edger, Crache's modern architect and unnamed ruler. What everyone save Dyeawan knows is that Edger's death was an accident. The wind dragon ever affixed to his neck, which enabled him to speak, prematurely entered its frenzied mating cycle and tore out Edger's throat.

What no one but Dyeawan knows, at least not for certain, is that Dyeawan triggered Ku the wind dragon's violent mating cycle in order to kill Edger. It wasn't something Dyeawan planned, not exactly, but it was something for which she'd prepared. She knew what kind of person Edger truly was, even if Dyeawan hadn't wanted to believe it when she first came to the Cadre. She also couldn't have known the depth of his cold, passionless view of people, or the ultimately genocidal impact of it.

Killing Edger was necessary.

Maintaining the Cadre's perception of his death as an accident is also necessary.

Dyeawan sees no dishonesty in Quan, and certainly no malice, but neither can she be certain what he knows or suspects. Quan served Edger with unwavering dedication for more years than Dyeawan has drawn breath. He obviously cared for the old man, yet Quan seems to care for everyone he encounters.

She wonders if inwardly he suspects, as Oisin clearly does, that Dyeawan played a part in Edger's demise. She further speculates whether or not those suspicions, should Quan harbor them, place her in jeopardy.

Dyeawan hopes the stoic attendant will continue to keep those thoughts unspoken. She has come to like him very much, and has even begun to depend on him.

Their rowboat approaches the rocky shore of the atoll as dusk dims the light of the world. Other skiffs are anchored there, harmlessly knocking against one another as the current sweeps them back and forth. Mister Quan ceases his slow, steady rowing and draws the oars into the boat. Dyeawan watches as he delicately rolls back the wide sleeves of his robe, and then takes up a bell-shaped anchor tethered to a chain. Quan leans over the side of the rowboat and gently lets it slip below the surface the water, carefully feeding the chain to the end of its length.

Dyeawan finds there is something calming about watching Quan's silent, precise, and unobtrusive movements. She wishes she could feel the inner peace he seems to represent.

The other members of the Planning Cadre are already lining the tops of the stony barrier. They stand shoulder to shoulder with their fellows, each of them denoted by their disparately colored tunics, each color representing their divisions with the Cadre.

The Divisions—builders, architects, and so on—are grouped in their own rows, separate from one another. The planners are different. All of them wear their gray tunics, but the planners are represented by two separate rows opposing each other across the atoll. One of the groups is composed of elder planners, while the other is significantly and consistently younger in age.

One of the reasons Edger elevated Dyeawan to planner was to tip the balance between the younger, forward-thinking members of the planners and the older guard, whom he labeled as too set in their ways and accomplishments. Before her ascension, the planners numbered twelve. With Edger gone, the unspoken ruling body of Crache would have been evenly divided once more.

Dyeawan has already remedied that by inviting Riko to join her amongst the planners. It was Dyeawan's first act as their leader, and not strictly a calculated maneuver. She genuinely trusts and respects Riko, who is one of the Cadre's most gifted minds and able inventors.

The fact her presence allowed the younger members of the planners to maintain that newly won superiority is simply an added boon.

Riko spots the rowboat docking tenuously beside the atoll and quickly separates her slight figure from the rest of the younger planners. She darts across the tops of the rocks with the speed and nimbleness of a cat to meet Dyeawan and Mister Quan.

"I should have built a ramp for you," Riko says breathlessly. "I'm such a taro head sometimes."

"Don't say that about yourself," Dyeawan replies, mildly chastising her friend.

"They've been having funerals here for a thousand years or something. You'd think someone would've thought to construct a dock at least, yeah?"

"People whose legs obey their commands rarely think of those of us whose legs do not."

Mister Quan rises carefully. He bows to Dyeawan, awaiting her permission to aid her out of the boat. It has become a common gesture between them, and one that always creates a warm, syrupy sensation deep inside her chest.

Dyeawan nods with a gentle smile. She's spent so much of her relatively short life being treated as part of the landscape, both as a girl, and even more so as an urchin seen by most as wholly immobile and incapable. Too many have viewed her as an obstacle they are allowed to move or adjust at their whim. Of all the indignities and hardships of scraping her existence literally from the floor of the Bottoms, that feeling was often one of the absolute worst.

Being given that courtesy by Quan and exercising control over her body is healing in a way Dyeawan could not have anticipated or identified before coming to the Cadre.

Mister Quan carefully and respectfully gathers her up in his arms and lifts Dyeawan from the boat. He steps onto the rocky shore and, despite his long, billowy robes and Dyeawan's weight, easily negotiates the way up the uneven terrain to the summit where the rest of the Cadre is gathered.

Riko follows closely, though Dyeawan can see she's already deeply lost in thought as she examines the spot from which they just departed.

"Maybe a rope and pulley system that moves a pallet up from the shore to the top of the rocks."

"Perhaps now is not the time, Riko," Dyeawan suggests, not unkindly.

"No, yeah, you're right. Sorry. You know how I am."

Dyeawan stifles an amused grin. "I do."

They reach the summit of the atoll's rim, the spot where the younger members of the planners are gathered.

There is a sturdy chair awaiting Dyeawan, its thick wooden legs standing on a flat, level rock. Quan eases her onto the cushioned seat and steps away quickly to allow Dyeawan to adjust herself as needed. She grips the arms of the chair and settles her hips and spine comfortably against its back. Her own arms have lost some of the strength they'd developed in their years of pulling her body along alleys on a pig-greased sheet of tin, but they've remain as hard as sprung steel, and adept at compensating for her lack of control over her other limbs.

Dyeawan stares down into the middle of the atoll. The interior rocks and the waters between them are awash in light, a dozen shimmering colors folding into one another like the reflection of some invisible aurora. The true source of the light is a scattered fleet of paper lanterns floating atop the water. The flame of the candle cradled within each lantern is specially treated to produce different colors and shades, from bloody red to emerald green to sun-fire yellow.

The lanterns swim around a pyre bobbing gently in the center of the calm water. The pyre is draped in white silk to conceal the eternally still form beneath.

Edger's body is merely an outline, barely a silhouette, suggesting a shape rather than defining one.

At first it helps Dyeawan that she cannot see him, and then it's all somehow worse *because* she can't.

She distracts her mind from the matter at hand by scanning the assemblage surrounding the small funereal lake. Dyeawan spots Tahei amongst the builders. He's standing behind a large wrought-iron wheel encumbered with heavy links of chain. The pudgy young man has his head bowed respectfully, his hands clasped in front of his body. Dyeawan can't see his face. She wishes she could read his expression, and perhaps take comfort in his smile.

The two of them haven't spoken since she put on the gray tunic of a planner. He and Riko were Dyeawan's first true friends at the Cadre, and Riko insists to her that Tahei wanted more than Dyeawan's friendship. All of that seems to have changed. Riko says he's jealous of Dyeawan's unexpected rise through the ranks. Dyeawan knows Riko is right, but she still wants to believe Tahei is capable of dismissing such petty impulses.

Dyeawan's gaze leaves him, continuing to sweep over the summit of the rocky halo. After a few moments her eyes single out another figure among the rest, before Dyeawan is even consciously aware of the person's identity.

One of the other planners is standing apart from both factions. She is, in fact, the only member of the Cadre occupying her own space there on the atoll. Dyeawan remembers her, like most everything she sees, but she realizes she never truly *noticed* the woman before.

She stands a head taller than Dyeawan or Riko, and appears to be several years older than either of them. She is thickly and powerfully built, with long hair the color of dying embers. The features of her face are large and strong. She has painted her cheeks with violet rouge, and her eyelids with a powder that sparkles in the last light of the setting sun.

Dyeawan studies that face, looking past superficial observations. The woman's expression is solemn, as suits the occasion, but there is more beneath that. Her eyes and her posture project something like defiance. It's reserved, dignified, but it is definitely there.

"Who is that?" Dyeawan quietly asks Riko. "The planner standing alone?"

"Her? Oh, that's Nia. She was kind of like Edger's pet planner. Before—"

Riko stops short of finishing the observation.

"Before what?" Dyeawan presses.

"Nothing."

Dyeawan studies her briefly. "You were going to say, 'Before you came along.'"

Riko frowns, looking down at her with regret. "Yeah, but I didn't mean it like that."

"I know what you meant," Dyeawan replies without judgment or reproach.

Riko seems to realize how intensely Dyeawan is studying Nia, and her friend looks with new eyes at the woman across the atoll.

"Why *is* she standing by herself?" Riko wonders aloud.

"She's making a statement," Dyeawan says.

It is clear Riko doesn't follow her line of thinking. "What do you mean?"

"By joining neither us or what Edger called the 'old guard,' she's protesting the division that exists among the planners."

"Maybe she just made it out here late, yeah?"

Dyeawan shakes her head. "It's symbolic. It's also smart. A bolder gesture than using words, but less . . . antagonistic. You can argue with words. You can't argue with a silent gesture. She's placing herself above our petty squabbling. Setting an example."

Dyeawan looks up at her friend to find Riko wearing a strange, delighted smile.

"Why are you grinning? This isn't a festive occasion."

"I was just thinking about when you first came to the Cadre. You never would've noticed something like that."

"I would've noticed, I just wouldn't have understood what it meant."

"That's life, yeah? Trying to understand what it all means."

Dyeawan says nothing to that. She's studying the other planners now. The rest of them have also taken notice of Nia's gesture. The younger planners on either side of Dyeawan and Riko are staring across the atoll with what appears to be open admiration. It's clear they look up to Nia, which makes sense. If she were a protégée of Edger, whom both sides revered, Nia would be the natural object of envy and aspiration.

Even the old guard seems compelled by Nia's stance. Many of them look confused, some even appear slightly embarrassed or ashamed by the mirror Nia is aiming at them all, but none of them are wearing expressions of anger or resentment. And that surprises Dyeawan the most.

She is left contemplating why, if Nia is such a galvanizing figure, did Edger pass over his "pet," and name Dyeawan as his successor.

Mister Quan now respectfully presents Dyeawan with the narrow end of a large paper cone that will amplify her voice so that she may be heard throughout the atoll.

Dyeawan blinks up at him, unprepared for the cue to speak about Edger to the entire Cadre. As their new leader, it is appropriate, of course. She supposes she should have expected this, but perhaps she didn't want to think about her role in his funeral.

Dyeawan reaches up and takes the cone. Uncertainty clouds her mind. There is so much the rest of the people gathered around the atoll can't know about Edger's life. There is so much they can never know about his death. How can she speak about the man without giving any of that away?

In the end, Dyeawan decides to simply tell the truth.

She speaks into the mouth of the cone: "Edger raised me up from nothing. He was the first person to truly see what not even I perceived; that I am worth more than scraping out a meager existence along the broken cobbles in the shadow of the Capitol. He also showed me how to become more. I imagine many of you have a similar story, and similar thoughts about him.

"I am *not* Edger. He taught me much. He prepared me as well as he could in the time he had. But I am not him. I will use his lessons to guide the Planning Cadre as best I can, in the direction I believe is best for the people we serve. Whether that is enough . . . we will all see in time."

Dyeawan pauses, aware she's revealing too much of her interior thoughts about what is left in Edger's wake. These words are meant to commemorate and eulogize the dead.

"Edger believed in function, not legacy. He didn't want his name known, or his story told. He knew the power of such stories; stories that become legends, and legends that become myth. I will not mythologize him or his life or his impact now. He served his function, and he served it perhaps better than even he could have hoped. Now that function has come to an end. And so has he. I like to think . . . he would find it fitting."

Dyeawan returns the cone to Mister Quan. No one speaks, but the mood of the crowd seems to her to be one of satisfaction, at least with her eulogy.

She stares across the atoll, at Nia in particular. The lone planner meets her gaze. More than anything else, and instead of the suspicion or even resentment Dyeawan might have expected, she reads curiosity in the woman's expression.

Mister Quan hikes the hem of his robes and carefully files down to the edge of the interior rocks. He kneels above the water and removes a small pouch from his belt. He loosens the strings of the pouch and empties its contents, a pale and grainy powder, into the nearest floating lantern.

The reaction is energetic. The lantern's color darkens and the light it casts swells until the small vessel bursts. The paper is incinerated and colorful flame spits forth in every direction. The lanterns closest to it catch fire and quickly combust.

That single lantern coming aflame creates a domino effect spreading across the water inside the atoll. Tendrils of rainbow fire reach out from each affected lantern and touch all those within a few feet. The chain reaction continues until the lanterns swaying at the edges of the funeral pyre are touched.

As they explode, so too is the pyre lit ablaze. The silken white sheet covering Edger's body is quickly consumed.

Stationed at his wheel, Tahei begins turning it by its dimpled iron spokes. There are heavy chains running through the rock and beneath the waves linking to the bottom of the pyre. As those chains retract, the fiery heap is slowly drawn underwater.

Dyeawan feels her hands begin to tremble. Watching Edger's body being lowered beneath the surface of the water sparks her recall, and images of the horrors she saw before her last conversation with Edger at the God Rung fill her head.

Since that day, her thoughts have stayed with the bodies that formerly occupied the bottom of the bay; bodies belonging to the disabled people of Crache liquidated on Edger's orders. Dyeawan sees them every night. She's barely been able to sleep since Edger showed her what lay beneath the God Rung, hoping she would understand the necessity of his actions and be willing to carry them forward in his stead.

Edger believed there was no meaningful or useful place in Crachian society for those people. He believed they were a drain on Crachian resources the state could ill afford. The few of them he took into the Cadre to perform menial tasks, like Dyeawan, were his paltry way of assuaging what conscience he had left. Dyeawan knows that now.

On her orders, Oisin and the Protectorate Ministry have moved, in secret, all the remains to the deepest part of the island forest. The remains were separated and each soul was put to rest in the ground, in their own grave. The graves cannot be marked, and the names of the dead were not recorded, but Dyeawan instructed Oisin to bury each person with a Planning Cadre medallion.

It doesn't mean much, she supposes, but Dyeawan feels that at the very least, the Cadre should claim those bodies in some way.

The *click* of that large iron wheel on the other side of the atoll breaks Dyeawan from her dark reveries.

As the pyre is finally sucked under, the blaze is extinguished, until all that's left of Edger is a phantom made of black smoke, dancing eerily atop the water.

MATT WALLACE is the Hugo nominated author of *Rencor: Life in Grudge City* and the Sin du Jour series, and he won a Hugo Award alongside Mur Lafferty for the fancast *Ditch Diggers*. He's also penned more than a hundred short stories in addition to writing for film and television. In his youth, he traveled the world as a professional wrestler and unarmed combat and self-defense instructor before retiring to write full-time. He currently resides in Los Angeles with his wife, Nikki.